HURRICANE
Days

Renée J. Lukas

Bella
BOOKS

2015

Bella Books, Inc.
P.O. Box 10543
Tallahassee, FL 32302

Printed in the United States of America on acid-free paper.

First Bella Books Edition 2015

Editor: Medora MacDougall
Cover Designer: Sandy Knowles

ISBN: 9-781-59493-467-4

Other Bella Books by Renée J. Lukas

The Comfortable Shoe Diaries

For my parents
Richard and Marita
and
for everyone who has struggled
and fought to live an authentic life

About the Author

Renée J. Lukas is a humorist and cartoonist, as well as a screenwriter and novelist. Her work can be found in all four corners of the United States and points in between. When she's not teaching screenwriting, she loves to overanalyze films. Originally from Tennessee, she now calls Massachusetts home.

CHAPTER ONE

"Governor Sanders, I have some news." Peter Fordham was a sweaty mess who seemed to be choking on his tie.

"I'm sure you do," she responded in a syrupy drawl. Governor Robin Sanders, the pride of the South, appraised her stressed-out political advisor, then handed him a flute of champagne. "Enjoy a sip or two first, Peter. You work too hard." That was her way of telling him he was a sweaty mess.

He loosened his tie, eyes darting around the crowded living room of the governor's mansion. She couldn't tell how important his news was because he treated everything as if it was the apocalypse.

Surrounded by supporters, Robin Sanders had the easy smile of someone hosting a dinner party, not the surprise leader in a hotly contested Republican presidential primary. Of course it was too soon to celebrate. But she instinctively knew to give the impression of a winner anyway. Never show them a moment of doubt. She once did an entire television interview, calm and poised, with a beetle squirming in her shoe. Anyone who knew of her freakish bug phobia would have been impressed to know that.

Tonight she was throwing one of her famous galas at the mansion. She'd become well known for these events. She'd always had a flair for throwing parties and impressing people. As she always told her staff: "This isn't politics, it's show business."

Robin was a commanding presence everywhere she went, a late-forties Scarlett O'Hara, with thick, dark hair, medium-length—styled conservatively, of course—and stunning ice-blue eyes that always seemed to throw others off balance. She had that charisma up-and-comers like Peter could only wish for—the kind where the air actually seemed to change color the moment she entered a room. People *listened* to her. She could convince anyone of anything no matter how misguided. As a child, she convinced her brother Kenneth to put his G.I. Joe doll down the garbage disposal, assuring him that the doll was tough enough to climb out. Needless to say, Kenneth cried for days after the machine chewed G.I. Joe's legs off. She was a natural at the art of persuasion, had been ever since she was in diapers. This skill ran deep in the Sanders gene pool.

"You don't understand," Peter persisted. "Something bad has…" His words faded into the party banter, and he was immediately tuned out. Peter was her long-suffering right-hand man, the seventh person to occupy the position since she had been elected to the Georgia state senate. Each of the other six had been chewed up and spit out their first day on the job.

"Give that boy a stiffer drink," bellowed Jimmy Sanders, slapping Peter on the back. A distinguished Southern gentleman and a former Georgia state legislator himself, Robin's father had had no higher ambition but to return to his beloved farm when he retired. In truth, he related better to horses, cows and chickens than to people. He always said they were easier to understand. Tonight his tux-covered chest was puffed out in pride as he basked in the acknowledgment of his daughter's grand achievements and national prominence. It mattered so much to her that he was here tonight. She held his opinion in such high regard that she sometimes couldn't tell the difference between what he wanted for her and what she wanted for herself. Jimmy winked at his second wife, Abigail, who poured herself another martini—her only salvation at functions like these—though she claimed it was Jesus.

"To the latest poll numbers," Robin exclaimed to the roaring, puckered-up crowd. As everyone raised their glasses, Robin didn't notice Peter zipping into the library. She wouldn't have cared, though. The air at the party was electric tonight—because Robin was getting closer than any woman had been to the highest office in the country.

According to everyone present tonight, these were critical times. For too long liberals had been let loose in the nation's capital, breeding like bugs and being allowed to spread their sinful, diseased messages and pass unnatural laws granting equal rights to homosexuals—all evil deeds sure to make God cry.

Even more dangerously, liberalism had been catching on with the younger generation to such an extent that conservatives were wetting their collective pants, trying hard to come up with ways to make their Grand Old Party relevant to the youth. A new movement had begun in the South, sparked by a resurgence of Civil War pride. More reenactments were taking place. There were more protests in the streets and more "No Adam and Steve" signs at events, even those that had nothing to do with homosexuals, like ribbon-cutting ceremonies for hospitals and cancer fundraisers. It had gotten a little strange at times. Southern states were pushing for an amendment to the Constitution, "The Marriage Purity Act," insisting that unless a marriage was between a man and a woman, it wasn't a true, *pure* marriage and shouldn't be recognized. They wanted to push it a step further, taking those who had entered into civil unions, or "illegal marriages," as they called them, and slapping them with huge fines. The time was ripe for a conservative star to emerge, and the environment in the South had become so weird, so charged, that it was the obvious place from which that star should appear. As it turned out, all five of the top contenders hailed from south of the Mason-Dixon line. Only one of them was female though.

Robin Sanders' political star had risen quite accidentally, although with her ambition she would have found some way to get noticed eventually. It began when Robin, already an outspoken leader in the Georgia senate, was asked to fill in for an ill colleague who was going to be interviewed on CNN. When she stepped in, she surprised everyone with her charisma and unrehearsed candor. Simply put, the camera loved her. Unlike her male counterparts, who tended to rattle off the same, uninspired talking points, she spoke off the cuff, winning admirers among people of both parties—and earning repeated invitations for future commentary.

Asked during a later appearance to comment on a female senator's low-cut dress in what became known as "Dressgate," she shocked Jay Savage, a popular CNN anchor, and the rest of America, with her response. He'd expected harsh criticism from her, especially because the woman was a Democrat. What he'd received instead was a stern rebuke.

"Mr. Savage," she said coolly in her tough Southern accent. "I don't care if her dress was cut down to her belly button. What I *do* care to talk about is what she has to say and why I don't agree with her."

"Well, certainly…"

"Furthermore, given the looks of your tie, I'm surprised we don't have a new scandal on our hands."

Conservative women labeled her a "new kind of feminist." She wasn't sure that fit, but she was willing to wear whatever label helped her to gain more recognition. She graced the covers of *Time*, *Newsweek* and even *Rolling Stone*, which featured her in a piece about the new crop of powerful women.

Even for those who despised her, Robin was fascinating to see in action. Her success was partly her own ability as a first-rate orator, as well as the current state of candidates of both parties; they made many Americans snooze at a time when they most needed to be awake.

For the past four years, the incumbent President Mark Ellis, a Democrat, had been a good, but uninspiring leader. He looked like most US leaders who had come before him—a straight, white male with a plastic smile. He'd been coached and briefed on what to say, how to be politely vague and how to make a nondecision seem like a decision. He was exactly what everyone was tired of, someone who seemed like a talking wax figure.

Enter the charismatic Robin Sanders, as compelling as watching a movie star. It was no wonder people who didn't even agree with her rhetoric found themselves watching her anyway. She livened up the news channels in a way no one else had before.

When asked about gridlock in Congress, she'd say, "There were four of us in my family. We couldn't all agree on what to have for dinner. Why should we expect five hundred thirty-five members of Congress to agree on anything?"

When Robin was later elected governor of Georgia, she made even more frequent appearances on the Atlanta-based CNN, where she became very popular, embracing the new wave of conservatism, but with enough attitude to make some liberals take notice. Before long, she was on track to become the first female president of the United States.

There was much good she intended to do if given a greater platform. Among her biggest concerns was the US dependence on foreign oil and lack of stronger laws about domestic and sexual violence against women. It wouldn't be easy, but from her time in the Georgia senate and as governor, she knew how to get the laws she cared about passed. Many of those supporting her campaign were "family values," antigay protesters, however, so she had to do that dance as well. She didn't agree with fining gay couples for entering into civil unions, but for now, she was keeping that to herself.

Only one more debate remained. Florida was the last frontier—the state that would determine who would be the Republican candidate in the presidential election. The final debate would take place in Tampa in three weeks.

"To the final debate!" a voice thundered. Tom Rutherford, Robin's husband, was making his way down the grand staircase. He was the last person anyone expected to see tonight. The rumor mill was always churning about their marriage. He'd been making fewer public appearances lately, so there was speculation that he was either staying in the shadows to keep the focus on her, or he was a blithering drunk whom she had to keep locked upstairs during social events. The crowd parted in front of him, everyone eager to see his condition for themselves.

Tom smiled genuinely. He was handsome, late forties, with sandy hair and wings of gray on the sides of his head. His retiring, quiet demeanor was the perfect complement to that of his wife. It also didn't hurt that he was a prominent Atlanta attorney. "My dear." Tom kissed Robin's hand as if he were Ashley Wilkes, returning home from the war.

"Governor Sanders, you certainly snagged the last of the Southern gentlemen." Minnie Douglas, a popular gossip columnist, fanned herself with her own hand for dramatic effect.

Robin was pleased to have Minnie in the crowd tonight. Her column would surely be buzzing tomorrow with her personal knowledge of Robin's perfect marriage. Minnie was an absurd little blue-haired woman whose phony laugh echoed all the way to the chandeliers. But anyone who was anyone, or who was trying to be someone, invited Minnie to their gatherings—for the sole purpose of being featured in her column.

"I heard Joe's bowing out," Tom announced. He smiled and took a sip of his whiskey. "It's true," he told the crowd. "We're down to the final four. Wait, is this basketball season?" The place filled with polite laughter. Nothing Tom said was really that funny, and Robin didn't have the heart to tell him.

Robin knew it wasn't easy for him. She also knew she had a chance to be important, to make history—not only by virtue of her gender but through the changes she thought she could bring to the world. Her ideas might have been grandiose, but her methods were extremely practical. Too often idealists took straightforward approaches and were defeated. To succeed in politics, she knew, you had to play the game. There was no other way. She knew too that in an age of technology, where a lie could spread so quickly on Twitter that it became perceived as the truth, everything about her life had to be perfect. From paparazzi to a wayward drone, there were always forces out there conspiring to catch her in a lie—or a pair of discount jeans. She couldn't let that happen. If she was to reach her goals everything had to be planned down to the last detail and well rehearsed.

Tom had been taking antidepressants for some time and shouldn't be drinking. Robin didn't mind as long as he didn't embarrass her. Tonight he simply needed to play the part of the doting husband. Good ole Jack Daniels would hopefully make it all much easier. In moments of solitude, feelings of guilt over what this might be doing to Tom would creep in. But she quickly let them go. Otherwise they would destroy her. She couldn't let that happen.

"Joe Henderson is bowing out? Are you sure?" It was easy for Robin to pretend not to hear potentially bad news, but surprisingly hard for her to trust good news either. She looked around for her political advisor, seeking his confirmation. "Peter?"

Where was he? How odd. He'd been tugging on her sleeve most of the night, and now he was gone.

"Excuse me a minute," she told Tom. She flitted through the crowd, searching, until she noticed the library door was closed.

"Governor Sanders," Peter exclaimed as she entered. He muted the TV.

She closed the door behind her, heels clicking across the marble floors.

"What is it?" she demanded.

Staring into the ice-blue eyes so close to him, Peter stumbled.

"Well?" she repeated.

He aimed the remote at the TV, turning the volume back on. Ann DeMarco, a popular journalist, was posing a question: "Will this scandal destroy Governor Sanders' political career? Does her road to the White House end here?"

Robin faced the screen. "*Scandal?* What scandal?"

Then she saw the photograph. It was larger than life, a picture of a young, college-age Robin with her arm around another girl.

Peter changed the channel.

"A lesbian affair in college?" Benny Rhodes, the most obnoxious of all the conservative pundits, was shouting. He was very afraid of women intruding in the old boys' club of politics and frequently ranted for hours about female politicians' weights and hairstyles— both subjects that seemed to keep him up at night. He would be the first to skewer her. "How can you run a campaign based on Leviticus and be caught with your hand up another woman's skirt?" He chuckled to himself. "I think she's ruined."

Robin grabbed the remote from Peter and flipped the station again. Lindsay Vaughan was the next pundit to dissect the situation. Her commentary was usually a bit more balanced, but this was a pundit's Christmas come early. "The higher your moral high ground, the farther you have to fall when a skeleton like this comes crashing out of your closet."

"Governor," Peter sighed.

She raised her hand. "Please."

Again the photograph was splashed across the screen. It looked as though the two girls were outside in front of a fire. Robin stood frozen, staring at it. The girls' smiles were saved for posterity, both of them looking so happy, as if their futures were limitless. Robin caught her breath. She'd never forgotten Adrienne. She could only vaguely remember the other girl—the girl she used to be.

CHAPTER TWO

"The problems of two people don't amount to a hill of beans…" Humphrey Bogart gazed into the eyes of Ingrid Bergman while the propeller of a nearby plane whirred in the background.

On the day I left for college, I watched *Casablanca* in the beige, velvet easy chair that was usually reserved for my father.

Mom rushed in. "Robin! Marc's on the phone."

I bristled at the sound of his name. "Could you tell him I already left?"

"All right, but he's called once today already."

"Please?"

Mom nodded reluctantly, then glanced at the TV. "I never understood this movie," she said. "How could he let her go with that other man? That isn't what he really wants."

The truth was, I would have rather been standing in a trench coat with rain pelting my face inside an old black and white movie than dealing with my high school boyfriend, even by phone.

Marc Tolland was a handsome drama major who was under the impression that he and I had been going together for the past year. He was a kind, good-hearted guy, someone who held open doors for me at the movies and probably carried groceries for old people, though

I hadn't actually seen him do that. But he was a good Christian boy. Mom and Dad approved of his family, and he went to our church. So as far as they were concerned, I could marry him right after I got out of college.

He never did more than hold my hand or give me a quick goodnight kiss at the end of our dates. One night when we were sharing a slushy at the local *Cheese 'n Freeze*, he got this look in his eye. It was a look I knew but didn't want to know.

"Uh, Robin?" His voice quivered.

I watched the Adam's apple in his throat bob up and down. "Yes?"

"You wanna still see each other after high school?" He knew I was planning to go to an out-of-state school, while he desperately wanted to be a University of Georgia bulldog.

"Sure," I said. "I guess." I hadn't really given it that much thought.

He squeezed my hand. I liked the softness of his skin. He wasn't one of those super hairy boys who had developed early and had full beards as seniors. Or one of those who were held back so many years they now looked like their fathers sitting at small high school desks. No, Marc was smooth all over; I'd once seen him without his shirt in the summer, swimming at a lake. He had a cleft in his chin and light brown hair and the kindest eyes I'd ever seen. Everything about him was something I liked. I imagined this was what girls felt when they liked a boy. He was cute. He was kind. What else was there?

My answer had given Marc the idea that we would try to stay boyfriend and girlfriend forever. He lingered longer than usual at my front door that night, almost giddy, though I didn't know why. As we stood on the porch, dodging the swarm of kamikaze moths that had gathered around the outside light, he laughed nervously. I still didn't know why. Aside from ducking away from the flittering moths, I was never nervous around him. Just comfortable. I thought that was important in a relationship, that I be nothing but comfortable. I even told all of my friends how great it was that I could be myself with him.

He leaned in like he always did for our quick goodnight kiss. I was ready to kiss him back. But as he held me tonight, he pressed me tighter to his pelvis and forced his tongue inside my mouth. I drew back, appalled, and wiped my wet lips. The exchange was so gross— even more gross than watching my brother slurp his food, and that was saying something.

"What're you doin'?" I cried.

"C'mon, Robin. That's how boyfriends and girlfriends kiss."

"Not me."

"But I love you!" he wailed.

I stared wide-eyed at him. As a polite Southern girl, I felt it would be rude not to say it back. "I love you too." I didn't really consider if it was the truth. Whether or not I meant it didn't matter.

"Well? If you love me, you'd kiss me like that." He was so certain. Where had he gotten this information?

What if this was one of those things in that *Your Body is Changing* book that Mom was too shy to give me? She had stood in my bedroom doorway several years ago, holding this light blue book with a drawing of a woman's uterus on the cover, at least I *thought* it was a uterus, and talked about how women and men make babies. But she was so nervous, with beads of sweat breaking out all over her face, and her skin turning deathly white—all of it happening so fast, like one of those diseases that kills you in forty-eight hours. I was worried for her. I had to make her calm down, so I told her I didn't need the book. I knew about the birds and the bees from what Peggy Hoolihy said at school. And everyone knew that Peggy Hoolihy had spent most of her high school years underneath the bleachers. She must know everything there was to know, right? Now I wondered if I should have asked Mom to give me that book anyway, even if she *was* about to pass out.

Summer was coming soon, and by fall we'd be in different states anyway. I knew this meant something big to him. So I leaned in and tried to kiss him his way. But all I felt was a wet, flopping eel running along my tongue and inside my cheeks. It was like getting a cheek swab for strep at the doctor, but more uncomfortable. I wanted it to stop. *Now*. After what seemed like a reasonable amount of time I managed to pull away, and I smiled as if it had been a pleasant experience. Judging from his dreamy face, I must have played my part well.

That was my first lesson in duplicity. I discovered I was good at it. For most of the summer, to avoid that kind of kiss again, I made excuses every time he wanted to see me. And when I did see him, I made sure it was at a group, family or church event, so he wouldn't try that kind of kiss there.

A few weeks ago, as summer was drawing to a close, we talked on the phone.

"I'm really gonna miss you," Marc said. He sounded upset, as if something was on his mind.

"Me too," I replied.

"I don't feel like…well, it doesn't seem like you really wanna be with me anymore."

"Why would you say that?"

"You never can go out with me." His voice was sad and kind of pitiful.

"It's not my fault I had summer jobs." *Yes, make him feel guilty for saying such a thing.* I was being so manipulative, I was surely damned to hell. Dad always said I was melodramatic, and now I was using my acting powers for evil purposes. I was sure to burn for eternity. Even so, it seemed worth the price to avoid having to kiss someone like that.

"No, I get that. I understand. I really do." Of course he did. How could he argue with helping schoolchildren learn how to read or coordinating all the food for the church picnics? After all, that potato salad wasn't going to make itself.

There was a long silence. "I have to go. My mom needs my help with dinner." I always found a way to get off the phone quickly.

So the last call before I'd leave for college was one I couldn't endure—an awkward maze with no easy way out. As the credits rolled for *Casablanca*, I sat back in the comfortable velvety chair and sighed. I loved film noir. Nothing in these films was as it seemed, particularly the women. They were mysterious creatures with power and beauty and that certain something that made the men fall at their feet.

Of course I couldn't imagine myself as a film siren or *femme fatale*. I wasn't as cool or confident. I worried constantly, always feeling a little strange compared to my friends. I spent my time deep in thought, usually thinking about things I couldn't control—the nuclear threat, violence in the Middle East or when *Saturday Night Live* was going to get funnier. I was inquisitive about the world and social issues, but all my friends wanted to talk about were boys. Not to sound rude, but my friends were boring. It was as if none of them cared about whether or not we invaded another country or why the price of gas was going up. They were content to live in their little suburban bubbles with freshly cut grass and think only about getting a ring. I'd have to accept being different.

I didn't even dress right, according to the unspoken laws of high school. Too often I wore blouses given to me by Granny Inez, who sewed them from ugly, old-lady patterns. I couldn't hurt her feelings or Dad's by refusing them. As a result I ended up going to school looking about forty years older than I was. For college, however, I packed only two of the blouses—to appease Dad. Then I said I didn't have any more room in my suitcase. When I could, I wore simple, button-down shirts tucked into jeans. I liked simplicity, not fashion trends.

I had my mom's hair, black like a crow's and shiny. I wore it long and straight. I didn't like the big eighties' hairstyle. When I heard someone say you had to spray it at the roots to get that wild look, I decided it was too complicated and worried that it could possibly make your hair fall out. Besides, I didn't have enough time in the morning to do that much hair preparation.

Boys told me I had pretty blue eyes, but I didn't think of myself as glamorous or poised or any of those things I associated with my mother. June Sanders was the most elegant woman I knew. She breezed in and out of rooms, balancing casserole dishes with ease. She always knew the right thing to say, except for talking about sex, and she stayed amazingly calm, even when Dad flew off the handle. I tried for a long time to be like her, then gave up, realizing it wasn't possible.

Whenever I felt insecure, which was nearly every day of my high school life, I looked to the poster of Bette Davis hanging in my bedroom. She served as sort of a guardian angel who reminded me I didn't have to fit in. Bette didn't seem to care what anyone thought of her. She didn't live to please other people; at least it didn't seem so. Being a pleaser myself, I looked up to someone like her.

At home, it was a constant struggle between who I was and who my parents needed me to be. They had expected me to go to college at Dad's alma mater, Florida State, and major in political science like he did. Mom hadn't finished college, so she agreed with Dad. The trouble was, here in this house of white walls and perfect décor, everyone knew their place. My dad knew politics and farming, Mom knew cooking and decorating, and my brother Kenneth knew football and tinkering with cars or anything with an engine. To them, I was an enigma, someone who daydreamed too much and watched too many movies.

When we first talked about what I would major in, Dad stared me down across the dining room table. "You can't major in film! There are no jobs!" He always looked like a general determined to win a battle.

"But…" I managed to say.

"She likes movies," Mom said softly, adding a few points to my side.

"Life is not a movie!" Dad thundered. And that was that. His opinion was reinforced by the crucifix hanging on the stark, white wall behind him.

When I registered at FSU, I was able to slip two film courses into my schedule. Mom promised to tell Dad in her own way. It would be our little secret for now.

* * *

We lingered in front of the big house in Atlanta that I'd called home for the past eighteen years. It was really an estate, but Dad called it a farmhouse. We owned more acres and horses than I could count.

I took it all in, in one sweeping glance, my happiest memories of childhood flashing before my eyes, then looked back to the expectant, slightly anxious faces of my parents.

Mom squeezed all the breath out of me. "Call us when you get there."

"I will."

"Jesus, Mary and Joseph!" Dad yelled. "Let the girl breathe."

I noted only two cars in the driveway. "Isn't Ken coming by?"

"He had to work today," Mom said apologetically.

"Everybody's got a screw loose at that garage." Dad shook his head. He didn't really like his son working with guys who he thought were just one step up from being white trash. In truth, he was still nursing a grudge, mad that Ken didn't want to stay closer to home and work the farm.

I tried to hide my disappointment. I'd miss my brother a lot. In his own quirky way, he was, most times at least, the sanest and most honest one of the family. He called things as he saw them.

I took a deep breath and picked up my last suitcase. Then, with a full tank of gas and my neatly rolled-up poster of Bette Davis in the backseat, I took off down the road. As I watched Georgia pine trees disappear, soon to be replaced by palm trees, I could almost hear the words: "Fasten your seat belts. It's going to be a bumpy life."

CHAPTER THREE

Lara's call came soon after the news broke. "I told ya, you can't run for office nowadays," she said in her raspy tone. "There's nobody without some stain. You gotta be Jesus to make it past the research. Goddamn Internet."

Lara Denning was Robin's press secretary, a woman so full of herself that she believed she could manage anything, including the earth's rotation.

"I don't have any stains!" Robin fired back. She tried to sound calm, as if it were all a nonissue. She paced her bedroom and spoke softly. "This is untrue. Once it's confirmed as a lie, a desperate last-ditch effort by my opponents, it will be over."

"Oh, honey, this is me. In politics, perception is reality. You know that. As far as Georgia is concerned, you're already a flaming lesbo. Wait a minute. Can lesbians be flaming? Or is that just gay men?"

"I don't know. Really, *I don't know*. Because I'm not part of that lifestyle. And what do you mean by…?"

"They've done flash polls in Georgia, South Carolina and Tennessee. You lost, sweetie, thanks to Twitter."

"It's a nonissue."

"You think it was Graham?"

"Probably," Robin replied. "I don't know."

"Whether it was or not, that's got to be our strategy," Lara said. "Pin the smear campaign on him. Make him look like a garden-variety, dirty politician. And you're an innocent, ethical leader." Then after a pause, she added, "Nobody really likes Graham anyway. They'll buy it."

Graham Goodwin, named after evangelist Billy Graham, was in second place behind Robin. Rumors swirled that he'd had a facelift and hair plugs. He also had two artificial knees from playing college football. In fact, it was possible that nothing about him was real. *Literally.* It would have made sense for Graham's team to dig up some dirt and conveniently leak it right before the final debate.

Robin hung up the phone, pondering Lara's advice. She undid her silk scarf, her trademark accessory, and placed it in the closet with the rest of her vast collection. In fact, she owned more scarves than shoes. Tonight's color was a flaming cranberry. As much as she hated to admit it, she wouldn't even get a haircut without Lara's approval. It had been Lara's idea for her to keep a streak of gray in her hair near the top. She'd told Robin that too much gray would make her look like a witch, but just enough would make her appear wise. Sure enough, all the magazines had commented on how her gray strand was being copied by other women, who were all trying to look wise.

"Lara Denning," Tom chuckled, buttoning his pajama top. He never could take Lara seriously.

"Yes, she's giving me the game plan."

"A woman who emailed pictures of her bare ass all over the web. *She's* the one you trust to manage your image."

"That was years ago," Robin insisted. "When she was young and drunk." She brushed her hair vigorously as she always did when she was worried. "I don't know, Tom. You think they're right?"

"That you're a lesbian?"

"Be serious."

For the first time Tom saw a glimmer of uncertainty in her face. In a way, he was relieved to see it. It meant that she was, in fact, human.

"Do you think this scandal could bring me down?" she asked.

He exhaled. Softly, he asked, "Is it true?"

"Don't be ridiculous!" she exclaimed.

Tom's mouth twisted into a growl. "Not so ridiculous, Robin. If it weren't for Kendrick, this wouldn't be a real marriage at all."

Years of memories hung heavily in the air between them, countless nights of sleeping alongside each other but not together, of forced kisses and the sadness that Tom wore like his suit, always clinging to him. She tried not to see it, though she knew it was true.

They hid it well, but theirs was primarily a marriage that looked good on paper. It was all part of a long-term strategy. To be a sure thing during this neoconservative era, Robin knew she had to win the heart of the South. Tom Rutherford was perfectly cast as the prominent, but not too prominent, good-looking, but not too good-looking, companion who wouldn't overshadow her. In a courtroom, he was most disarming, using his laid-back, almost lethargic attitude to catch defense attorneys off guard. Then he'd go in for the kill. But in his private life, he was actually averse to confrontation, doing anything he could to avoid it.

When Robin chose a political career, she had ridden in on the coattails of her father. Because the Sanders name carried so much weight in Georgia, when she and Tom married it was agreed she'd keep her family name. No one questioned her decision, not even Tom. In fact, he was the most agreeable conservative husband she could have asked for. Why then did everything feel so wrong?

She watched as he slumped on the bed. Surely he didn't want to talk about this *now*? This wasn't the time to examine their marriage. Her head was going numb from all the stress. She couldn't handle hearing how many years he'd waited to see that special light in her eyes when she looked at him. She would never be that woman, the one who couldn't wait to throw her arms around her man when he walked through the door at night.

What good would it do to talk about it anyway? She knew how sad she made him feel. She also knew about his liaison with Darlene McFadden, one of the lawyers in his firm. It was inevitable but…okay. In a way, it took the pressure off her. He wasn't even careful about hiding his trysts with Darlene anymore, sometimes even meeting her at the mansion. Maybe he wanted to be caught. Or maybe he wanted to see Robin get upset, to find out if she cared.

"A real marriage?" she repeated defensively. "Does every ambitious woman have to lose her husband because her success is too much for his ego?"

"Ambition? This isn't about your ambition. It's about sleeping next to the ice princess night after night. Can you blame me for wondering? If you were…it would almost make sense."

"You know how I feel about that lifestyle." She slammed the bathroom cabinets in search of a night cream she'd never find.

"Yeah, you've made it the centerpiece of your campaign."

Robin didn't hear the tone of suspicion in his voice. She was too caught up in concocting plans for damage control, weighing and analyzing all of her options.

"Yes," she answered flatly. "That's why they want to use this salacious, fabricated scandal to bring me down. How ironic: the God-fearing woman is really a queer! Come on, Tom. Isn't it obvious? It's not even creative."

She had a point. "So what are you going to do?" he asked.

"I don't know yet."

* * *

In the early morning hours, when Tom was snoring violently due to a deviated septum, Robin gingerly pulled back the covers and climbed out of bed. She hadn't closed her eyes all night. Rather than waste time sleeping, she tiptoed downstairs to the library, anxious to see the news reports, to hear what they were saying about her. She checked her phone, then the TV, flipping through channel after channel, hearing the same recycled speculation. Apparently, Adrienne had made an off-handed comment to a reporter in Boston, where she now lived, and the reporter had run with it. No one had since questioned her further. But her name was now all over the news. Robin couldn't find any new information, only the same outrageous story being told a hundred different ways: "Rock musician Adrienne Austen claims she had a lesbian affair with the governor when they were in college. The GOP isn't likely to nominate their front-runner now."

Then Robin changed to a channel that made her pause. There on the screen was a current photo of Adrienne. It was heart-stopping—the familiar, pointed smile, now with a few more lines around her eyes—a grown woman's face. Her hair was medium length and styled in a modern way. She looked good. She seemed happy. And she still had that little girl grin.

Something about seeing how she looked now brought it all back to Robin—memories so real, so vivid, the kind that made you cringe if you lingered on them too long. Even after all this time, the memories were still there, waiting to be found again. They flooded into the room and threatened to drown her.

CHAPTER FOUR

My little burgundy Toyota was no match for the hurricane force winds that welcomed me as I crossed the Florida state line. A wall of rain suddenly fell from nowhere and blurred the entire landscape. It was a blinding, wrath-of-God kind of storm—the kind that made me wonder when I'd last prayed. My family never missed a service, except for last week… As bolts of lightning took turns stabbing at my car, I was too frightened to notice the irony of the rain pummeling a highway sign that read: "Welcome to Florida, the Sunshine State."

I flipped on my hazard lights and pulled under a bridge to wait out the storm. I stared despondently at a map that was crinkled beyond recognition. I had managed to find 90 West just before Lake City, so I knew I was going in the right direction. I decided that Tallahassee couldn't be that far away.

I checked my face in the rearview mirror for the umpteenth time, comparing myself to airbrushed actresses. What if the Florida sun caused me to age beyond my years and I came back home looking like one of those leathery-skinned, Palm Beach women who wore white lipstick? I pressed the creases of the map and folded it neatly, placing it back inside the glove compartment. Whenever I was nervous, I liked to make things neat and tidy; it gave me the illusion of control.

Suddenly, the clouds parted and a blinding sun emerged. I marveled at this surprising weather as I pulled back onto the road. It wasn't long before university buildings popped up over the tops of palm trees in the distance.

When I finally stepped out of the car, billowing steam rose from puddles of rain on the pavement. Still wearing the denim jacket I'd put on at home, I lugged my biggest suitcase toward the stately red-brick dormitory building I'd been assigned to live in. It loomed over me with dramatic arches resembling those of a medieval castle. Inside was the musty smell of the past and pencils, a smell I'd forever associate with college. I scanned rows of students, standing in long lines like refugees, their belongings at their feet.

Eventually, I shuffled myself to the head of the line labeled S-Z and an acne-covered guy handed me a key to my room for the year. It was on the seventh floor at the end. "We're booked full," he informed me. "So no room transfers."

He stared at me a little longer than at the other students who had passed in front of his desk. But I wasn't interested in flirting. Finding the room was all that mattered now. This took about ten minutes. That's when the full horror of his words hit me.

CHAPTER FIVE

With its barren white walls and white tile floor, the dorm room looked like a fine place to die or have a last meal before going outside to be shot.

My thoughts tended toward the macabre, especially during times of stress. And my first day of college was no exception. "Oh my God." I set my suitcase upon one of the naked twin beds, the one on the left. As if it mattered.

The walls were made of cinder blocks, and the beds had wafer-thin mattresses. I'd somehow have to find a way to decorate this prison cell so that it didn't look like a prison cell.

There was a knock at the door. It was probably my soon-to-be roommate. When I opened the door, I saw a husky older woman whose shadow eclipsed me. Her look was stern, her hair a mousy color with no texture—like it was some fuzz that was glued onto her head. She was poised and ready for combat. "I'm Lydia. The RA."

"Excuse me?"

"Resident Assistant," Lydia shouted. Her manner was gruff, but natural, as if she spoke to her own mother that way. "I patrol the hall, make sure nobody's doing anything against regulations."

"Oh. I'm Robin Sanders." I extended my hand tentatively. I was used to people recognizing my family name at home. But here I was a stranger. It made no difference to Lydia whether I was a Smith, a Sanders or a Rockefeller.

Lydia distractedly shook my hand, then poked her head in the room. "Your roommate not here yet?"

"No. It's just me so far." I offered a slight smile, fascinated by Lydia's odd brown and orange, seventies-style clothes.

"I'll come back when she gets here. I have a few things to brief you on." With that, she took off like a bullet down the hall. Shortly I heard the muffled sounds of her banging on a neighbor's door, probably terrorizing her too. I closed my door and locked it, vowing not to open it again for anyone. My roommate would have another key anyway.

I couldn't stop thinking about how empty the room was. Standing there in its starkness, I felt a fear I'd never felt before. Fear *and* freedom. The room was a blank canvas, and I'd have to fill it. This would be the first time I'd make my own decisions without having to consider my father's opinion. Where to study, what to eat—I was the only one here whose opinion mattered. Growing up in a household with as dominant a personality as Jimmy Sanders, I rarely felt in control of my own life. Here I would explore what it was like to be truly on my own.

The room was much smaller than I expected. It wasn't even as big as my bedroom back home. There was one small, grimy window opposite the door, and the head of each bed rested against the wall where the window was. There were two tiny desks and dressers beside the foot of each bed, on opposite walls.

Using my jacket sleeve, I wiped some of the film off the window, slowly revealing a view of the football stadium. Then a smoky voice startled me: "You expecting a cold front?"

I whipped around to see who was speaking. She was someone who could have been plucked right out of a music video, sporting long, wild, blond-streaked hair, cut-off denim shorts and a clinging white, sleeveless shirt. Standing a little taller than me, she was definitely stunning. When she turned slightly, I saw a small tattoo on her right shoulder. I couldn't make out exactly what it was, probably a skull. She was a perfect nightmare.

"Oh, not exactly. Hi." I answered self-consciously, quickly trying to wiggle out of my jacket.

"Hi," the girl answered, extending her hand to my only available arm. "Adrienne Austen."

"Robin Sanders."

Our eyes locked, and momentarily I forgot where I was.

"Like the Colonel?" Adrienne was joking. I didn't get the joke at first. "The fried chicken guy?"

How witty. I lifted my face haughtily. "It's Robin Camille Sanders."

"Didn't your parents like you?"

"Excuse me?"

"Sounds kinda snobby. I like your little accent though." She was judging me already.

I didn't have an accent that I knew of. My dad sounded like he was from the South, and I knew I didn't sound like that. Something about this girl made me feel very defensive, like I needed to protect myself… though from what, I wasn't sure.

"So you're my roommate?" she asked.

"I don't think so. I'm probably not staying." I'd beg for a transfer if I had to.

"Aw, come on. Dyer Hall's worse." Adrienne glanced out the window.

"Nothing could be worse."

"Have you seen Dyer Hall?" Adrienne beamed with a lopsided grin and flashing, inquisitive eyes. They were almond shaped, and the color of two perfect little coffee beans.

I watched incredulously as Adrienne stuck a cigarette in her mouth and lit it. After a moment, she glanced at me, as though she had forgotten I was there for a moment. "I know. I put 'nonsmoker' down on the form, but I do sometimes. I don't have to in the room if you don't want me to."

How strange. A polite Hell's Angel.

"It's fine," I lied, slumping on the edge of my bed. I didn't want to make waves, not on the first day. I'd never known anyone who had a tattoo before. In movies, people with tattoos were always the bad guys, violent mafia types who dunked people's heads in toilets. Until I could find another place to live, I was going to be as nice as possible. If this girl was as dangerous as she looked, I wanted to keep from ending up on the local news.

"So where you from?" Adrienne asked, taking a puff and seating herself in one of the desk chairs.

"Georgia."

"Ooh, that's fucked up."

"Thank you." Not even a minute had passed, and I'd been insulted at least twice already. I wrinkled my nose like a rabbit and huffed to myself.

"Nah, just kidding," Adrienne said. "I had an aunt who lived in Georgia once. She said Kansas is worse." Her twinkling eyes danced in amusement. Was she laughing at me?

"Are you always this tactful?" I asked, trying hard not to take myself too seriously, but finding that impossible.

"I'm usually much worse." Adrienne's easy smile was pointed at the corners. It was the cutest smile I'd ever seen. I tried not to think about that though.

"Where are you from?" I asked awkwardly, trying to appear casual.

"A small town east of here. Just a dot on the map." Adrienne studied me. "Don't you ever get out in the sun?" she asked.

I looked down, suddenly self-conscious, all too aware of my pasty white skin. I couldn't help but notice Adrienne's smooth, bronze legs. "Well," I fumbled, "I'm not exactly the outdoorsy type."

"Robin Camille," Adrienne repeated with fascination. "Anyone ever call you RC, like the soda?"

"No, and I'd appreciate it if you didn't."

"No problem, RC." Adrienne blew out smoke and crossed her legs.

With that one gesture, she actually scared me. It wasn't a mortal-danger kind of fear, but a fear for my mortal soul. All those years sitting in church, listening to what I was *supposed* to do...only to discover now that nothing mattered to me as much as getting another glimpse of this unusual girl. I was going to hell for sure.

"I asked you not to call me that," I said.

"If you don't want to get your ass kicked, you might want to loosen up."

"Are you threatening me?"

"No," Adrienne said. "I just mean you should chill out."

I ignored her and began unpacking.

"Seriously," she continued. "You stay this uptight and other people might kick your ass."

I carefully took each article of clothing out of my suitcase, pretending to be consumed by this chore. Something about this girl brought out the strangest feelings in me. Everything was so confusing all of a sudden. Heat was rushing to my cheeks, and I didn't know why.

Relying on routines comforted me. So I sorted my earth-tone clothes according to shade, trying not to be unnerved by the eyes I felt upon my back. Everything about Adrienne seemed to be laughing at me. Every insecurity I'd had since childhood came crashing in on me like thunder, while I tried to maintain a calm demeanor on the outside.

After a few moments, Adrienne left the room to get her things. As soon as I was alone, I exhaled and stared up at God, or the leaky stain on the ceiling. *Of all the dorm rooms in all the colleges in America...she had to walk into mine.*

"No room transfers." The words echoed in my mind as I tried to organize things in my dresser. I was so rattled I couldn't concentrate. I was mixing colored socks with white ones, T-shirts with skirts. God only knew where the underpants would wind up.

A banging on the door woke me from my haze. I opened it to find Adrienne, concealed by a tower of stereo equipment. "Can you...help me?" she said. Cords were twisted and wrapped around her hands. She had long, slender fingers with painted nails. I took a speaker off the top, revealing her deep brown eyes. Another speaker, and the rest of her face appeared. There was no way around it. Hers was the cutest face I'd ever seen. I looked away and set the speakers on her bed. "Sorry."

"I was knocking for like an hour," she exclaimed. She brushed her hands off on her shorts.

"Sorry. I...was distracted."

I got another glimpse of her tattoo. It was very small, like an ink smudge. She caught me staring at it.

"Know what it is?" she asked with an excited grin. If I didn't know, she obviously couldn't wait to tell me.

I leaned in closer. I could only make out what seemed like tiny music notes, maybe a miniature piano sheet.

"It's the first few chords of 'Rock You Like a Hurricane.'" She stared at me expectantly.

"Okay."

"You know, the song?"

I looked blankly at her and shook my head. "Doesn't ring a bell."

"You've never heard that song?" The judgment was loud and accusing. "Oh my God. It's on the radio all the time. What are you, Amish or something?"

"No." I decided to ignore her and continue unpacking.

As the minutes passed, Adrienne's side of the room was quickly transformed into a shrine to big-hair bands that I never listened to. When she said something about how great the Scorpions and Metallica were, I nodded as if I had a clue what she was talking about. I certainly didn't want to get my ass kicked over my ignorance of heavy metal bands.

On my side of the room, I hung only the black and white poster of Bette Davis. It contrasted sharply with the bare, white, cinder block wall. All that was left was to put away Granny Inez's blouses. My plan was to shove them into the back of the bottom drawer and forget about them.

"Whoa!" Adrienne held up the worst of them, the one with flower appliques all over the front. "Are you shitting me?"

"Shut up. It was a gift. I don't wear it."

"It looks great…for someone who's ninety-five years old."

"Shut up," I repeated, biting my lip to keep from laughing. It felt good to hear someone say aloud what I'd thought about those blouses for so many years. But how could I laugh with someone who was obviously making fun of me?

My mouth tightened. I was too distracted to think of any clever comebacks. Adrienne was like a Category 5 hurricane inside our room, and I was simply trying to stay alive.

She continued to hover over my suitcase. It reminded me of nosy people at the grocery store who stare at the items you place on the conveyor belt and who silently judge you for the giant bag of Oreos.

"Do you mind?" I snapped.

"You know," Adrienne replied, "I don't know you or anything, but you seem like you need to get laid."

I placed my hands indignantly on my hips. "Well, I don't know you either, but you seem like you need to be in prison."

She threw her head back and laughed. Were we bonding? I couldn't be sure.

"You hungry?" she asked.

"What?"

"I thought we'd go out to eat. You do have restaurants in the Plum State, don't you?"

"It's peaches." I was irritated. How could she not know that?

"Whatever."

Everyone knew about Georgia peaches, didn't they? It wasn't as if Georgia was in Sri Lanka. "Peaches," I repeated, aggravated at Adrienne's obvious lack of education and breeding. I couldn't respect a girl who tattooed her body and talked like a hooker and that's all there was to it, I decided.

Yes, I was in serious trouble.

CHAPTER SIX

The next day, Robin was scheduled to appear on every major TV news program. Peter Fordham sat beside her in the limousine, and Lara Denning was across from her, her platinum curls bobbing up and down. CNN was their first stop. As they made their way through Atlanta's morning traffic, heading toward the CNN studios, Peter was uncharacteristically silent. Clearly, he wasn't sure what to say or think or even how to act.

To Robin, he was looking more and more like a bird. His weight loss, which fluctuated with his nerves, made his pointed nose and chin seem even pointier. His mouse-brown hair had more patches of gray now, probably due to stress. He had a wife and kids at home, but he spent more time with Robin than anyone. His ambition almost rivaled hers, in fact, which was why she viewed him as an opportunistic leech.

"How are you holding up?" he asked her finally.

"Where's my Diet Coke?"

"I'm sorry. I forgot it. I guess I was distracted with everything."

"With what?" Robin was serious.

"Oh, honey, please." Lara glanced out the window.

"You know…" Peter fumbled for words. "*Everything*. It's got to be on your mind."

"The only thing on my mind is my inauguration speech." Robin was in full-throttle denial.

"One thing in your favor," Lara said. "The woman making the claims is a struggling singer. No doubt she could use the publicity."

"Uh-huh," Robin replied absently.

"So we know you roomed with her," Lara continued. "Any contact with her since your first year of college?"

"Of course not." Robin wrinkled her nose. "She wasn't the sort of person I wanted to call attention to in my past."

"You could say that," Lara pressed.

Robin glared at her. "And sound like a complete snob?"

"Got it," Lara said. "I published the statement on your website. Your gratitude for your supporters, you haven't changed your commitment to them, blah, blah, blah. I'm telling you, though, hon, people don't read web pages unless they have lots of big pictures." She fluttered her hands to demonstrate.

Robin glanced out the window, trying to focus on what she was going to say. She ended up instead trying to imagine how it might have happened: Adrienne in a crowded bar, taking a drag on a cigarette and saying something sarcastic like, "Yeah, Robin Sanders isn't queer. Right. And I'm Mother Teresa." Or something equally damaging, delivered in the sharp, sarcastic tone that Adrienne did so well. And who had supplied that photograph? Her mind raced. It must have been taken the night of the bonfire…

Robin held her head high in the backseat. She wasn't the same scared girl she had been in college. She'd grown into a woman who could make a scathing remark with a smile. Adrienne would regret messing with her.

The limousine zoomed straight to CNN. Afterward, she'd be boarding a private jet to hit major media markets, from Los Angeles to New York, casting the widest net possible for damage control.

* * *

Benny Rhodes launched his CNN interview with a sharp attack. "A lesbian affair in college! How do you expect your campaign to recover?"

"I'm actually disappointed in Mr. Goodwin's political team," Robin said under the glare of studio lights. She sat comfortably, looking incredibly relaxed, like she was discussing the weather. Her composure left the interviewer looking more rattled than she was.

"Graham Goodwin?" Rhodes asked, a little disoriented.

"Yes. If I'd known he'd be desperate enough to tell stories about me, I would have told him about the time I slept with my second husband's twin brother."

Rhodes searched his notes. "I didn't know you had been married before."

"I wasn't. That was *One Life to Live*." Robin smiled. "When you can't find any skeletons in the closet, you have to invent one."

Rhodes nodded. "Well played, Governor." He smiled in spite of himself.

* * *

Lindsay Vaughan was next. She was looking particularly serious today rather than her normal genial self. She was super-prepared with a stack of notes a mile high. Lesser candidates would have been tempted to flee or cry. Not Robin Sanders.

"Governor Sanders," Vaughan began in a tone that sounded somewhat patronizing. "The cornerstone of your campaign has been your stance against gay marriage and gay rights in general. Is that not true?"

"Which is why this is the perfect Hail Mary pass for Mr. Goodwin's team. He's attempting to make me look like a hypocrite."

"Well, wouldn't you say that this undermines your credibility a bit?"

"It could perhaps. *If it were true.*"

"According to FSU records, Adrienne Austen was your freshman roommate in college."

"Yes," Robin said. "That's all that's true about this story."

"Let's say it is a false claim to sabotage you. How do you know it came from Graham Goodwin's team?"

"Ms. Vaughan." Robin laughed, as if to say she knew better.

Vaughan had obviously suspected the same thing. When she smiled knowingly, Robin knew enough to keep her mouth shut and let her wrap up the interview. There was nothing more to say.

* * *

Robin had almost succeeded at diffusing the scandal when she sat down for her last interview of the day. It would be with Roger Craft. A national news anchorman known for his cerebral approach, he seemed to be the last journalist left on television who still tried to be objective.

Logic was his default switch; this alone shook up most politicians. Even President Ellis had only done one interview with him during his first four years as president. Craft had reserved Robin's interview for his special nightly program, *The Full Story*.

Craft folded his hands and eyed her the way he did every guest, putting her in his hot seat. Robin was determined not to be deterred from her position. All day long she had deflected the spotlight from herself to the "pathetic political team of Mr. Goodwin," a phrase that almost made her laugh every time she uttered it.

"Governor Sanders," Craft said, "by now everyone has heard the rumor. We, of course, wanted to know the full story. So we invited the woman who claims she had an affair with you to come on this show tomorrow night."

Robin was slightly alarmed but didn't show it. "It's unfortunate what people are willing to do for their fifteen minutes," she said, repeating a line she'd used successfully throughout the day. She glanced around the studio as if bored. "I must say I'm disappointed, Roger. I thought you were a serious journalist. Ms. Austen is a struggling musician and this has no doubt given her band quite a boost. Why else would she go on TV to slander me?"

"She declined our invitation."

Robin's eyes widened. She had definitely not expected this response and the surprise showed in her voice when she finally said, "A last-minute attack of conscience perhaps?"

"It doesn't appear to be fame she's after," Craft replied. "In fact, I hear her band already has quite a following."

"Good for her," Robin said. "It's a shame then that she's willing to damage her own reputation for Graham Goodwin."

"Excuse me?"

She was back on track. "I'd hoped Graham's team would have stuck to the issues. It's what America wants."

"Mr. Goodwin hasn't commented on this," Craft said.

"Mr. Goodwin hasn't commented on this because, as I'm sure we all agree, he knows nothing of this trumped-up scandal." She winked at the camera, back in control and on her way to another public relations victory. "Seriously, I understand. To show there are no hard feelings, I'll even offer him a position in my cabinet when I'm elected." She smiled again, and a flock of live tweets fluttered in, praising her self-assurance and overall greatness. Many of her fans had no idea where she stood on the issues, but they blindly followed and praised her anyway.

Their time was up. Robin removed her microphone the second the cameras stopped rolling.

"I hope you understand," Craft told her. "I had to ask the question." He seemed apologetic, as she turned her back to him, stepping off the stage.

"Of course I understand," she said in a perfectly polite tone that sounded more like the kiss of death.

* * *

Adrienne not wanting to pursue this with interviews made her seem like an ethical person who was telling the truth. That didn't make Robin look good at all.

As Robin met her staff in the studio, she was confused by the contradictory facial expressions of Lara and of Peter, who was reading a text that had just come in.

"The signs are good. Real good," he said, scrolling to the next message.

"Like hell," Lara said.

Robin brushed her away and continued toward the exit.

Peter ran alongside her, still reading tweets. "Those that like you still like you, and some like you even more for standing up to Roger, the 'sexist pig.'" He made air quotes.

His constant chirping became white noise in the background. Robin's gaze was distant, unfocused. She was trying to get her bearings, as Lara confronted her.

"Robin, we've got to nip this in the bud. No, torch all the buds before this crap trumps the last debate." Lara's brows were lowered to an angry V shape as she blocked Robin's way. "I'm not kidding around. I mean, who doesn't go on TV these days? It makes that bitch look like a saint. Everyone wants publicity! Hell, I'd give my right tit for more publicity myself."

Robin nodded distractedly as she made her way to the car.

"We've got to squash her before Florida!" Lara called after her.

* * *

Peter stayed outside the limousine to take a call. Inside the car, Lara eyed Robin suspiciously. She wasn't going to let this rest. "Tell me," she said. "Think of me as your lawyer or priest."

"I'm not Catholic."

"This is only your career," Lara said acidly. "I'm going to give it to you straight. The more honest you are with me, the more I can help you."

Robin's mouth tightened.

"C'mon," Lara continued. "Lots of girls experiment in college. If you did, it's no biggie. We just have to make the little incident go away."

Robin rolled her eyes. *Little incident.* If only Lara knew…

"You could've had a slutty pajama party," Lara continued. "Tried your first pussy. It happens."

Robin recoiled, seeing Lara suddenly as just another of the contemptible, faceless people who wanted to be the first to hear the juicy gossip…and spread it.

"Not going to tell me?" Lara persisted.

"I already told you," Robin said. "We were roommates. Nothing more."

CHAPTER SEVEN

After spending several minutes brushing empty cigarette packs and ashes off the passenger's seat, I climbed inside Adrienne's black Camaro—or trash can on wheels—and sank into the car. I felt like I was sitting on the road.

Adrienne turned the key and revved up the engine, flashing me a sly, teasing smile. "Better than a vibrator, huh?"

I offered a weak smile and pretended to know what she was talking about. Adrienne cranked up the radio—which was tuned to a heavy metal station, of course. She could see the look of cluelessness on my face. So she explained: "It's the Scorpions. 'No One Like You.'"

"Oh."

"God, you don't get out much."

Always judging me. My irritation faded when my eyes caught the flash of the thin gold bracelet dangling from Adrienne's wrist as she switched gears. Another flash drew them down to a tiny anklet that sparkled against the smooth golden skin of her right leg. Strangely, I liked watching her. A little too much. I quickly glanced out the window.

"What kind of music you like?" Adrienne asked.

"Dance. Some classical."

"That's fucked up." Adrienne swerved into another lane, and I forgot to breathe as the golden arches of McDonald's got frightfully close. I saw the headline: "Jimmy Sanders' Daughter Killed by Ronald McDonald."

Adrienne probably didn't fear death. Most likely it never crossed her mind. She drove as though she thought she was immortal. Luckily, she managed to direct the car back into the lane and away from the curb where we would have definitely hit the McDonald's sign. *I should've driven.*

"Really fucked up," she muttered at my apparent lack of good taste in music. Obviously, it was still bothering her.

"You know that saying about honesty being the best policy?" I said. "It isn't true."

She laughed, switching gears, which jolted us in our seats. As we sped down the road, I could see dusk beginning to change colors across the sky. Streaks of deep mustard and pink merged with neon lights and silhouettes of palm trees. I felt like I was in a movie tonight, that everything was larger than life, even gas station signs. And strangely, the sound track to the movie would be some heavy metal song that, even more strangely, I didn't exactly mind.

"You got a boyfriend?" Adrienne asked.

I was surprised it had taken her this long to ask the question. Girls like her always wanted to know things like that. "No," I replied. I didn't want to open myself to more criticism about Marc and me.

"You're lucky," Adrienne said. "They're pains in the ass. I'm still with this guy from my high school. But now I'm in college, I wanna have some fun, you know? Some guys get so possessive."

"I know. I had a boyfriend in high school." It slipped out. I wanted her to think we had something in common. "He acted like we were married."

"You only had *one* boyfriend?" There was the judgment again.

"So? What's the big deal?" Why did this girl make me feel as if everything about me was wrong?

"Nothin'."

I tried to change the subject. "So why isn't your boyfriend going here?"

"'Cause he's a big dumb ass."

"Gee, that's nice." I looked at her, then caught my breath, suddenly grateful for the darkness. My heart was pounding hard in my chest. Why did she have to look so good? I glanced again out the window, feeling as if I'd just stolen something.

She swerved into a nearby parking lot.

"You tryin' to kill us?" I wailed, vowing never to get in a car with her again.

"Relax, RC! Live a little." Adrienne scooped up the keys and climbed out of the car.

This was ridiculous. I had nothing in common with this person. Why was my heart pounding so hard when I was around her? It made no sense. If anything, she infuriated me. One minute she made me feel like some backward, clueless person, the next she made me feel like Hobson, the butler in *Arthur*. Like I was the sensible, responsible one inexplicably put in charge of someone who was likely to knock over a fruit stand.

The strange feelings I was having must have been related to nerves. It was, of course, my first day at a university. And she was just… too much to handle on top of that. I decided then and there to make arrangements for a room transfer in the morning. If I had to use my father's clout, then so be it. I would not stay and subject myself to this…person.

Tonight, though, I had no choice but to follow her into a mostly empty doughnut shop. A single waiter, not yet college age himself, wiped the counter in front of one man who was sitting and smoking at a stool.

We sat at a booth near the window, where I began nervously rearranging silverware.

"Are you like obsessive compulsive or something?" Adrienne asked, studying me.

"No. Why?"

"You've moved that like four times." She gestured to my fork and spoon, which I immediately released in order to begin tapping a glass of water that was sweating as much as I was. I guess the water had been left by a previous customer. None of the tables had been cleaned off yet. Of course she had to pick some dive where they were so short-handed we had to sit amidst other people's garbage.

Unfortunately, I was too aware of the deep chestnut eyes studying me with great intensity, so I began chattering to change the subject. "I thought we were going to a different sort of place," I said. I looked around the shop, everywhere but at her. To Adrienne, it probably seemed as though I'd never had a doughnut before, that it was beneath me.

"I love doing breakfast for dinner. You do have doughnuts in Georgia?"

"Of course!" I exclaimed. "It's not a foreign country, you know. Just because you've probably never been out of Florida."

She lit up a cigarette, never taking her eyes off me. "You know, maybe you should take up smoking."

I laughed. "Right. My aunt's a smoker. She's ninety-eight pounds of nerves."

"Do I make you nervous?"

"No," I lied. "Not unless you're planning to drive us off a cliff later." My sarcasm always came out to protect me.

Adrienne grinned at my joke, then took out a pair of reading glasses and opened a menu. "Ooh, I want the jelly-filled."

"Oh, no. Chocolate-glazed. And a big glass of milk." I snapped my menu shut and unexpectedly met her eyes. They were almost hypnotic, with long, sensuous lashes. I felt the heat rush to my cheeks again. Was I blushing? I struggled out of the awkwardness by glancing away and pretending the moment didn't exist. I looked around the shop frantically. "If he'd ever come over here."

"He must be very busy," she joked.

"I'm starving. Aren't you?"

"Oh yeah. I was so nervous about meeting you, I didn't eat all day."

I was surprised. "*You* were nervous? No way."

"Yeah. So?"

"I never would've guessed it." I imagined that. Some of the things she said…it never occurred to me that she might be insecure.

Adrienne leaned forward, tapping the ashes into a tray. "Well, we're gonna be livin' together. I had to make sure you weren't a psycho."

"Like you, you mean."

Adrienne smiled broadly, sitting back in the booth. "And that little accent of yours. It's really cute."

It was official. I was blushing. I wondered if it showed.

"So," she continued, "have you ever fucked?"

"Have I *what?*"

"Come on. They *do* have fucking in Alabama."

"*Georgia.*" How dare she forget. I scooted my fork in strange patterns. "No."

"No, they don't have fucking in Georgia, or no, you've never fucked?"

My eyes darted nervously around the quiet restaurant. "Will you be quiet? And stop saying that word."

"What word? *Fuck?*" She seemed to be taking great pleasure in tormenting me.

"Please!" This was not a conversation that civilized people had. *Adrienne was crass and rude and…*

"Fuck you, Mary Poppins."

"Fuck me? *Fuck me!*" I was purple. Just then, the only other patron, an older man, walked past us, hesitating at our table and giving me a look of disgust, or possibly interest, on his way out the door. I shriveled up like a raisin, turning my shoulders in as if I could make myself smaller and eventually disappear. When he left, I glared at Adrienne. "You made me say 'fuck' in public."

"I don't see what the big deal is." She crushed her cigarette, her eyes never leaving me. "Well, you gonna tell me or not?"

"I don't think it's necessary to continue this inappropriate conversation." I was pleased; the words had glamour and sophistication written all over them.

She grinned. Obviously, I amused her. "I'd hate to be… inappropriate."

"Not that it's any of your business, but I'm a good Christian and I'm going to wait until marriage." I spoke with conviction, although deep down I knew it was easier to play the role of a good Christian when there was no real temptation.

"Oh, geez," Adrienne spat. "Don't do that. You'll be all dried up by then."

I couldn't believe that anyone in real life talked like this. "Shut up!" Where was Bette Davis when I needed a stop-you-dead-in-your-tracks retort?

"I could never wait that long." She rested her chin in her hand. "So tell me, why are you so uptight?"

"I'm not uptight!"

"It's the church thing, right? Or did you have some childhood trauma? See somebody naked at a young age?"

"Shut up!"

"Wait. Was it one of your parents you saw naked? Was that it?"

"Will you just shut up?" My eyebrows raised to my forehead.

"Hey, it scared the hell out of me too. It's okay."

"What are you talking about?"

"My dad had gotten out of the shower—"

"I don't want to hear this."

"He didn't know I was there. I was like seven, and I accidentally walked into the room, and it was like, what the hell's *that?*"

"Look, I didn't see anybody naked!"

At that precise moment, of course, the waiter popped up. I wanted to sink under the table and die.

"Yeah," the boy said in two octaves. "Most of us try to keep our clothes on here." He replaced the old glasses with two fresh glasses of water.

I held my forehead, staring down at the table.

"Could we just get one jelly-filled and one chocolate-glazed?" Adrienne said, looking over at me. "A coffee and a—"

"Milk," I said.

The waiter pulled a pad out of his back pocket and scratched something down. "Is low fat—"

"Fine!" I exclaimed to Adrienne's great amusement.

When the waiter scurried away, she covered her mouth, pretending not to laugh.

"You're such a bitch," I said. "You knew he was coming."

"Not really." She took a sip of water. "I swear I wasn't really looking at him."

My face must've been the color of a strawberry. I said jokingly, "I do believe you're a bad influence on me, Adrienne."

"Me? You're the one shouting 'inappropriate things' at everybody."

As we each recalled the moment, waves of tension-spilling laughter overcame us. In spite of myself, I couldn't stop laughing. It was one of those gut-splitting, can't-catch-your-breath-for-hours kind of laughs that I thought would never end. "You're terrible," I said in between spasms.

There was something about Adrienne. Despite all her tough talk, there was a shy girl underneath who had to say shocking things to cover up how scared she was. I could see that now. But painting her as a crude, rude, immature, tattooed monster somehow made it easier to be around her. I guess I was as strange in my way as she was.

After a few minutes, when we calmed down, Adrienne stared at me again, curiously. "So why are you here? You've got a lot of schools in Georgia."

"It's my father's alma mater. He's Jimmy Sanders." I waited for some kind of recognition. "Jimmy Sanders? He's a state representative in Georgia. He's been on TV many times," I said proudly.

"That's it," Adrienne replied. "I didn't buy the good girl act. Now I get it. Your dad's a politician, so lying runs in your family."

Did she mean to be this insulting? Or did she have one of those disorders where she had no control over her mouth?

"Adrienne, I take great offense to that."

"Honey, I'll bet you take offense to everything."

Before I could craft a scathing reply, the waiter returned with our drinks and doughnuts.

I was sure that to Adrienne I appeared to be this tightly wound nutcase, self-conscious to a degree rarely seen in the human species. I bet she wanted to see what I'd be like, completely undone with no inhibitions. I was going to have to disappoint her, because that was something *she* was never going to see. When the waiter left, Adrienne asked, "What's your major?"

"It's supposed to be political science." I shrugged my shoulders, still fidgeting with the silverware. "What I really want..." I stopped myself right there. Someone like Adrienne would just make fun. Or would she? "I want to make films. I have a plan. I'm going to make my first film by twenty-five. Get a cabin on a lake. Have a husband named Brian. A dog named Truffaut." I thought a moment, losing myself in the daydream. "But see, I don't really like dogs, so I'll probably just get a little one. That way, it won't really count as a dog."

She smiled at me. "You're a trip."

"Why? What?" Instantly, I returned to my defensive posture, my shoulders elevated to my ears. "What?"

She watched me with great interest. "That's cool. No, really. It's so great that you have...a plan." She seemed sincere. Suddenly, I didn't regret sharing it.

I relaxed a little. "What about you? Now that I've told you my life story, what do *you* want to do?"

"I don't know yet." Some of the powder from her doughnut lingered on her lower lip. It was only a dusting, but I was distracted by it.

"You have a..." I pointed to my own mouth to indicate the location of the powder.

"Huh?"

"Some doughnut..."

She took my hand and made me touch her face. "Get it off."

So I moved my thumb across her lip and brushed the rest from her chin. Her skin was so soft, so...I yanked my hand away as if I'd just stuck a fork in a light socket.

"So you don't know yet?" I repeated, trying to act like a normal person.

"I like music, but my dad says I can't make a career out of it."

"Wow, sounds like my dad."

"He's not okay with you being a film major?"

I smiled sheepishly. "Yes and no. Mostly no. I think my mom is more supportive of that."

"My dad really pisses me off." Her gaze turned sad, reflective. "He thinks I should be a lawyer or something he can be proud to tell his friends about when they get drunk on the boat." She shook her head, as if remembering something uncomfortable. I didn't want to pry. "You need good grades for shit like that. I always got by on C's. It wasn't 'cause I couldn't do better, but 'cause I didn't care, you know?"

"What about now?"

"I don't know. That's what I hope to find out." She seemed earnest. "Geez, I never talk this much to anyone." She smiled so warmly, even shyly. "You're easy to talk to."

"I wish I could say the same," I joked.

She threw a napkin at me.

The time seemed to pass so quickly; I wished I could stay longer in front of my plate of crumbs.

When we got the bill, she grabbed it immediately. "Have you met your Brian yet?" she asked.

"Not yet."

"When the right guy comes along, if his name isn't Brian, you gonna kick him out?"

"Yes." I laughed. "No, I just like that name."

The waiter picked up the cash Adrienne left and smiled at me. "Come back and see us. With or without your clothes."

She laughed, and I smiled awkwardly at him.

Walking across the parking lot, we dodged puddles of rain that had poured, unnoticed, while we were inside. I followed Adrienne's swift boots, and all of my senses seemed heightened. I realized I'd never forget this night—the runny reflections of light on the street, Adrienne's cute smile and the way her long hair fluttered in the breeze when the windows were rolled down. I'd have to rethink the room transfer idea...

"He liked you," she said as we crossed the parking lot.

"Who?"

"That *guy*. C'mon, couldn't you tell?"

"I didn't notice."

She put her arm around my shoulders. "Stick with me. I'm gonna make a worldly woman out of you yet."

"Yes, I already feel born again." Even with my armor of sarcasm, I knew that I was falling into a huge abyss without a safety net.

CHAPTER EIGHT

"She called," Peter had said. His face was ashen. "She wants to talk to you."

His words played over and over in Robin's mind as she returned to the governor's mansion. She told him she'd get back to him. She had to buy some time, figure out how best to handle the situation. The idea of talking to Adrienne again after more than twenty-five years…

Her stomach was rippling with nerves. The butterflies in her stomach did more than flutter. They were acrobatic, traveling-circus butterflies. She kept telling herself to breathe as it had said to do on a yoga CD she'd purchased and watched once while eating a piece of cake. Unfortunately, breathing wasn't changing the way she felt. There had to be a spare Valium in the bathroom cabinet. No, white wine was the better choice. She knew she needed to think this over carefully, but she couldn't do that with a clear, fully present mind. There was simply no way to deal with Adrienne Austen in reality, to meet her head-on with all of her faculties intact. She was a person who fit better in the realm of fantasy, in swirling dreams where you're flying above the ocean or floating through outer space. She didn't belong in Robin's practical world and the mundaneness of day to day… Adrienne had always seemed larger than life. How strange it would be to meet her again in the real world. Robin poured the wine with shaking hands. Suddenly, the calm, careful politician was replaced with the self-conscious schoolgirl. This wasn't happening…

* * *

Dinner that night was unusually quiet. Tom's heavy-lidded, red eyes fought to stay open. Servants fussed around the table, refilling their wineglasses and trying to serve everything at a table that was much too long for a family of three.

Kendrick, their thirteen-year-old daughter, picked at her food, her long, dark hair falling past her shoulders and into her peas. When she wasn't hiding behind her hair, Kendrick had her mother's features, especially those dramatic, ice-blue eyes.

Robin raised the bowl of peas to the servant.

"These aren't the kind I like," she barked.

"It's the same ones you had Tuesday."

"I don't care," Robin argued. "I can tell. These are fuzzy inside." She scrunched up her face like a child. This was what she did in times of crisis—ignore the elephant in the room in favor of some insignificant detail. "I like the kind that pop in your mouth with a burst of sweet butter." She handed her plate back to the annoyed woman who had served her dinner.

"I've told them a million times," Robin grumbled. "You'd think they could remember a simple request."

"Will you stop with the goddamn peas!" Tom roared.

"Language, Tom." Robin sipped her wine, casting judgmental eyes on him, then taking a brief glance at Kendrick.

"I've heard worse," the girl grunted, not looking up.

"How is school going?" Robin asked, doing whatever she could to distract herself from the memory of Darlene's sweet perfume, which she had smelled the moment she came inside the mansion, and the fact that Tom was getting plastered. Maybe Darlene had broken it off with him. Maybe it was only a fight. Whatever it was, she didn't think she could handle one more ounce of drama tonight.

"Same as usual," Kendrick said. "Sayin' shit about you."

There was an uncomfortable pause as Tom scooted his chair away from the table and stormed out to the wet bar for something a little stronger than wine.

"I'm sorry," Robin said. "I wish my job didn't create these opportunities for people to hurt you."

"I'm used to it." Kendrick seemed pretty well adjusted for someone who most likely walked through school hallways with people pointing at her and whispering every time her mother made news. While she was certainly attractive enough to break plenty of hearts, she didn't seem to have a very big social life. She kept to herself. She had a way of shrugging off the world, not at all like her mother when she was a teenager. Young Robin had cared very much what the world thought of her. Kendrick, on the other hand, walked around like nothing could touch her. "That woman they've been talking about, Adrienne Austen? I know her."

Robin almost choked on her wine. "You know her personally?"

"No, I've got her CD. Her band's really cool."

"You've heard them?"

"Yeah," Kendrick said, matter-of-factly. "It's Eye of the Storm."

"What is?" Robin was confused.

"The name of the band?" Kendrick said in a perfectly annoyed teenager tone.

"Well, that's certainly apropos," Robin muttered to herself.

"Huh?"

"Nothing."

Tom returned with a fresh drink, obviously whiskey straight up. Robin watched him carefully as he tried to appear steady, scooting out his chair. She set her embroidered napkin on the table and cleared her throat. "Kendrick," she said calmly. "I roomed with Ms. Austen during my first year at college. But she wasn't the sort of person I wanted to call attention to in my biography. Can you understand?"

"No." Kendrick looked up and flipped her hair out of her face. "If I knew someone like her, I'd totally say I knew her."

"You don't understand," Robin explained. "They're saying things that aren't true."

"I know that." A slight smile broke across Kendrick's face. "You can hardly say 'darn,' let alone get it on with another chick."

Robin wanted to laugh at her daughter's teenage logic, but the refined mother in her prevailed. "I didn't raise you to talk like that."

"Oh, lighten up," Kendrick said.

"Watch your tone, young lady!"

"I have to agree with her." Tom laughed. "You do need to lighten up. You used to be a lot more fun." His smile was taunting, masking his pain.

"I am plenty of fun!" Robin insisted. "But y'all need to know when to put a cork in it."

They all laughed together, something they hadn't done in a while. After the laughter, though, all that remained was the scraping of forks against fine china and the tension hidden behind their chewing.

When she had her own family, Robin insisted they have dinner together every day that she didn't have official duties, saying it was "family bonding time." Because that was what she knew. Respectable families ate dinner together. It certainly wasn't because she actually enjoyed it. When she was growing up, the dinner table was the place where everyone was least honest, saying anything to appease their parents so they could hurry up and be excused. But dinner inevitably ended with her father yelling and someone crying, usually Robin and sometimes her mother. Acid boiled up in her stomach in recollection. Happy memories.

Robin's eyes darted to Kendrick, wondering what she was really thinking. She knew her daughter was exceptionally intelligent, razor-sharp, in fact, like herself. She appeared to take things in stride, but Robin knew that acting also ran in the family, so she wanted to be sure that Kendrick was really as fine as she claimed to be. She would check on her when she went to bed.

As the dishes were cleared, Robin kept hearing what Peter had told her: "She wants to talk to you."

No. Robin was the governor, after all. She didn't have to talk to anyone she didn't want to. So she opted for the safe way out and decided she wasn't going to talk to Adrienne.

CHAPTER NINE

When we returned to the dorm room that night, there was a sheet of paper taped to our door. It was from Lydia, the RA. She wasn't pleased that we hadn't stayed to be "briefed" on whatever it was she was going to brief us on. The sheet had a list of things that weren't allowed in the dorm—smoking; sex; drinking; drugs; pets, including but not limited to hamsters and fish; leaving hot plates and curling irons plugged in—the usual. Adrienne ripped it off the door as we went inside.

"She's fucking nuts," she said.

"Oh, did you meet her?" I asked. "At first I thought she was my roommate."

"No wonder you were so freaked when I got here." We shared a smile. Lydia was like no one in my, or apparently Adrienne's, life experience. "She stopped me in the hall when I first came in. All this shit about hurricane preparedness." She laughed.

"What exactly is that about?" I asked.

"You don't need a meeting about how to prepare for a hurricane," Adrienne explained. "It's no big deal. You just tape your windows and get a six-pack to wait out the storm."

Something told me these weren't official tips.

"Of course," she continued. "I'm from central Florida, so we really don't get many of them. She'll probably tell you all this stuff about getting extra batteries, canned food, a can opener. If something happens, I'll get the stuff." She smiled at me like she was my protector.

When I looked around the room, I realized that I didn't see a bathroom door. "Where's the bathroom?" I asked suspiciously.

"Out there," Adrienne replied casually, throwing her keys on the desk.

"Out where?"

"Down the hall."

"You've got to be kidding."

She shook her head. "Geez, you really are a little princess."

I raced down the hall and saw the familiar public restroom symbol, the circular head with a triangle underneath that indicated the dress that all women supposedly wore. Either that, or we were supposed to have bodies shaped like triangles.

I pushed open the offensive door to find four bathroom stalls, four sinks across from them and four shower stalls, two of which had flimsy, mildew-covered curtains hanging on rusty rods. The other two had no curtains at all!

"Oh no," I breathed, no, *panted*, my eyes wide with shock. Who would even consider taking a shower without a curtain? Those had to be for the exhibitionist girls who wanted everyone to look at them, like the ones in the high school locker room. I always tried hard not to look at those girls. Sometimes I couldn't help it. They were so distracting, though. Even if I closed my eyes, I'd open them and find myself face-to-face with a bare torso or belly button or something farther south that would surely lead me to hell. I'd feel so badly for seeing anything, I'd want to rush to church immediately and pray away my guilt.

When I returned to the room, I paced the floor and kept exhaling with my hand covering my mouth. I must've looked like Norman Bates in *Psycho* when he's just realized he's murdered a woman in the shower.

"I can't do this," I exclaimed. "I can't handle public restrooms!" I was a step away from breathing into a paper bag, too caught up in my own drama to notice there was another crisis already in progress—Adrienne was kneeling on the floor with a wadded up tissue in her hand.

"You'll handle it," she replied. "At least it's not coed."

"You don't understand. I nearly failed gym class because I wouldn't change into shorts in front of the other girls."

"Nearly?"

"Yes. The coach let me write a paper detailing the benefits of cardiovascular exercise instead."

I suddenly noticed that Adrienne was looking for something underneath the desk. I didn't have to wait long to find out what it was. A giant Florida-sized roach emerged from underneath the desk and scurried across the floor. I screamed and jumped on my bed. "We have roaches!"

"Calm down. It's just a palmetto bug."

"I don't care where it's from! It's a bug!"

"Just be glad it's not the kind that flies."

"What?" I couldn't imagine such a thing. I might as well be going to college in South America.

"Oh yeah," she said, clearly relishing the moment. "Some fly right at your head."

"You've got to be kidding!"

She rolled her eyes and laughed. "You're hysterical." With sharp precision, her boot caught the traveling bug. The resulting crunch was more than I could stand.

"I think I'm going to throw up."

"Nah. You don't wanna throw up in a public restroom. Someone might hear."

I glared at her. The bug wasn't the only vile creature in the room.

"Could you get me another tissue?" Adrienne was impatient.

Slowly, reluctantly, I skirted the crime scene and headed for the door. I returned with fresh tissues in hand, offering them to her from a distance. "I'm sorry," I said. "But that bug's so ugly it makes me want to cry."

Adrienne looked up. "Now, c'mon. How would you like it if someone said that about you?"

I shrugged. "They probably do."

"I doubt that." There was a twinkle in her eyes that made heat rush to my face again. I lowered my eyes and everything was quiet.

That night, I lay wide awake in my bed, so distracted by the scary feelings I was having about Adrienne that I even forgot about the palmetto bugs. Was this going to be a year of sleepless nights?

CHAPTER TEN

I'd never showered in a public place before. In fact, I was one of those girls who couldn't even pee in a public restroom if another woman was in the stall next door. My first morning before class, I went into the bathroom and waited for one of the showers that had a dingy shower curtain. The water had just stopped running in the one on the end, so whoever was using it would soon be out. Understandably, nobody wanted to use the curtainless ones.

A girl who looked as nervous as I was slid back the curtain and, clutching her towel, rushed by me without making eye contact. Juggling a basket of shampoo, soap and razors, I stepped into the shower carefully, trying to decide where to hang my towel. The tiles were already wet, and I could almost feel the mold and bacteria slithering over my feet and up my legs. I hung the towel gingerly over what I was certain was the contaminated curtain and curtain rod. Then as quickly as I could, I turned on the hot water, which was lukewarm now.

I soaped up as quickly as possible, fearful that someone might walk in on me. Or worse, that Adrienne might come in. Adrienne was probably one of those girls who had no boundaries about nudity. The night before, I'd made sure my back was to her while we dressed for bed. But she seemed like the type to strut around naked just to get a reaction. Or one of those spring break girls who flashes crowds from motel balconies. I bet she did that. I shuddered, angry with myself that the thought made me angry. What was my problem?

To avoid accidentally flashing a stranger myself, I was sure to make lots of throat-clearing noises. That way if anyone who came in and wondered, in spite of the already running water and mushroom cloud of steam billowing from its top, if the shower was occupied, they would know beyond a reasonable doubt that it was. It was the fastest, most stressful, heart-pounding shower ever taken in the history of showers.

I wrapped myself in my fluffy, but slightly damp towel, imagined getting toe fungus and hurried out of the shower room. Struggling to hold up my towel, I flew down the hall, my eyes fixed on the thin industrial carpet beneath my feet. I felt like some kind of streaker. It was like the dream you have that you're naked in public. Only I *was* naked, with only a towel between me and the leering public. When I got back to the room, Adrienne left to take her turn in the shower.

As I hurried to get dressed before she came back and walked in on me, I thought about my father's description of when he was in the infantry, where there had been rows of commodes with no walls or doors and guys were just passing the toilet paper roll to each other, like passing the salt at a table. Dad liked to talk about things that made my mom uncomfortable, especially after a few drinks, just to see the expression on her face. That had been one of his favorite stories.

While Dad did his best to act like he had been okay with those kinds of facilities, I knew that I definitely was not. This type of living arrangement wasn't suitable for me. This was the way people lived in Third World countries. Why did they even bother giving us a bathroom at all? I wondered angrily. Why not just have a trough behind the building where everyone could pee? It was all so gross and undignified. I'd come from a house with six bathrooms, not a straw hut in the jungle. If I was a princess, as Adrienne called me, then so be it. I wasn't supposed to be squatting in public places or committing acts of indecency every time I took a shower. This was all wrong.

CHAPTER ELEVEN

That night, Robin knocked on Kendrick's bedroom door.

"Come in." Robin could hear the apprehension in her daughter's voice. She was probably bracing for a conversation about body changes or menstruation.

"Hon," Robin began. "There's going to be more talk over the next few days."

"Please," Kendrick said. "I don't care what they say. I know you don't like puss–" She stopped herself before her mother's eyes caught fire. "I know it's not true," she said softly.

"You shouldn't be talking like that."

"It's how everyone talks at school."

"I don't care how they talk at school! You need to show that you have class, that you're a cut above."

"Yeah," Kendrick grumbled. "Might as well just put a big target on my head."

Robin's mouth turned down in moderate disapproval, but she nodded, understanding what her daughter meant. "I'm sorry."

Unbeknownst to Kendrick, that frown was also the expression Robin had given her doctor when she learned she was pregnant. While having a child was part of her plans, the timing was terrible. She had been working on tougher legislation for domestic violence and sexual assaults. A girl she'd known in high school had been attacked walking home from school one day. Hardly anyone wanted to talk much about it. And when her assailant was finally caught, his jail sentence was so light that to Robin it seemed he might as well have gotten a mere slap on the wrist.

Growing up in a male-dominated household, she hadn't heard much about issues that affected women. It was understood that she couldn't go downtown at night by herself, while Kenneth could. This had struck her as spectacularly unfair. Instead of joining in her frustration, though, her father and brother seemed to shrug it off. Even her mother seemed to think that it was just the way the world was.

But Robin had a chance to do something about it now. She had worked so hard gaining support for these bills; she wanted to see them through. She didn't want to appear at state senate meetings with an expanding belly, because she knew that what her male peers said and what they thought were two different things. She could see it in their eyes when they nodded politely at her in the halls of the state capitol. They saw her not as a woman who cared about her career, but as someone only two steps away from being covered in strained peas and baby puke.

"You can say times have changed all you want," Robin had told Tom. "But you still have to play with the boys if you want a career. You can't be seen as someone who's going to quit her job the first time there's a skinned knee and stay at home to take care of offspring." And she had really used the word "offspring." It was the only way she had been able to cope with what was happening to her body and her head.

She managed somehow to not only deliver a healthy seven-pound baby girl but also get her bills passed, even if they had to be slightly diluted to please everyone. To demonstrate her down-home family values, she brought the baby along for the photo op when she signed them.

She then had taken Kendrick home and handed her over to the nanny who basically raised her during her baby and toddler years. Robin couldn't wait to get back to the office to work on issues she cared most about. "You can be a father and a lawyer," she'd said to Tom, "and nobody expects you to choose one or the other. And if you chose being a lawyer, no one would bat an eye or call you a bad father."

Standing now in her teenager's bedroom, its walls covered with posters of brooding musicians she'd never heard of and her desk strewn with worn-out Shakespeare plays, Robin was proud of the young woman Kendrick was becoming. She wished she knew her better and were closer to her. She had struggled with that for most of Kendrick's childhood. Every now and then regret over the years she'd lost slipped in, but Robin had learned to put it out of her mind, like she did with anything she didn't want to think about too much, anything that interfered with her ambition. She knew she'd made mistakes, but she'd never apologize for having goals. Nor would she ever join one of the support groups that encouraged career women to feel guilty, or to cope with their guilt. She saw flyers for them all around town—"How to Have It All," "What's Wrong with Having It All?" and "Split in Two and Suffering." She despised the idea that women should feel ashamed for pursuing their dreams with as much drive as men did.

"Whatever you may hear," Robin said carefully, "it isn't true."

"How many times are you gonna say that?" Kendrick asked with a smile.

Robin looked warmly at her daughter. She hoped she would grow up to be like her, at least in all of the ways she liked. She prayed that unlike herself, Kendrick would be honest about who she was, no matter what. Robin started to leave. "Don't forget to read your *Bible* after your studies."

Kendrick saluted her.

"Don't be disrespectful, or that video game will stay in the store."

Kendrick smirked. "Nah, you'll get busy, then get it for me anyway to buy back my love."

"Come here!" Robin ran to her and mussed her hair until they were both laughing. When they calmed down, Robin sighed. "Oh, you precocious thing! I love you, Ken."

"I know."

Robin closed the door and paused in the hall for a long moment. What would her daughter think of her if she knew the truth?

CHAPTER TWELVE

Dr. Paul Gentry paced the auditorium stage, scratching his black beard, not really looking at us as we feverishly took notes. He seemed to be a pillar of composure, but he held his chalk like a cigarette, which made me wonder about his personal life. I couldn't imagine him as a smoker. He was so neat and clean. His scrawny neck poked through a white shirt that was impeccably starched, and his gray suit was so perfectly tidy it could have still been on a hanger in a store. "Film Appreciation," the words he'd scribbled on the board two weeks ago on the first day of class, remained on the blackboard, reminding us what he was trying to teach us.

"Film is a conscious art," he said. "Meaning that every character, every scene, right down to the last detail, is put there to move the story forward. Everything is there for a reason."

I smiled to myself at the truth of that statement. The predicament in which I found myself wasn't an accident at all. Somewhere deep, deep down in the craters of my mind I'd known that this time was going to come, that one day I'd no longer be able to block out the memories of those schoolgirl crushes, no longer be able to convince myself that they were part of a strange phase that the *Your Body is Changing* book probably said was perfectly normal, not permanent and nothing to worry about. Then again, knowing Mom's discomfort about all things sexual, I never got to read *Your Body is Changing*.

I bet my guardian angel was knocking back martinis with her angel buddies at this very minute and having a good laugh about the ignorance and confusion that had kept me tossing and turning for days now.

Dr. Gentry passed out a list of approved films we could check out from the film library in the Performing Arts building. The one that immediately caught my eye was *Desert Hearts*, about a woman who goes to Reno to get a divorce in the 1950s and falls for a female casino worker. I'd seen a write-up about it in *Seventeen* magazine—a short piece about the shocking content of this new movie about lesbians. Somewhere in my mind, I'd filed it away under "Things to See Later When I Wasn't Living Under the Same Roof as Dad." Maybe when Adrienne went home some weekend I could check it out and rent the VCR in the lobby…

Later that afternoon on the way back from class, I spotted Adrienne heading up the hill to our dorm. There were so many hills in Tallahassee; it was the San Francisco of Florida.

"Hey, stranger!" I called to her in a playful tone.

Adrienne whipped around and smiled as she recognized me. Her long, highlighted caramel hair and twinkling dark eyes caught the sun as she stood there. She looked like a model in a magazine. Her deep red, silk shirt—the top buttons opened just enough to reveal her tan skin and long neck—clung to her chest. It was an image I knew I would always remember, like a favorite photograph you kept in your pocket even when it got tattered and creased.

I rushed to catch up to her, and Adrienne said, "You're just in time. I was gonna order a pizza."

"Oh, sure, make me fat." I bumped her arm, teasing her. Although we'd begun like two anxious cheetahs sizing each other up in a cage, we'd quickly developed a familiarity that made us seem as if we'd been friends a long time. There was also an unmistakable spark between us, which made me nervous as well as excited. I was feeling giddy, my head floating somewhere up in the ozone as we walked together, feeling the warm, late afternoon breeze. The campus was so welcoming with rows of pink and orange hibiscus lining the walkways, everything flowery and friendly, matching my mood.

My excitement only grew with the revelation of every new detail, like seeing Adrienne in different light or shadows, revealing each new expression as a dramatic close-up, as in a movie. Even the thrill of how a different color shirt could contrast with her face—it was another thing to look forward to each day.

Inside the dormitory, Adrienne stopped at the sight of a chubby girl with cropped hair, walking in the opposite direction down the hall. "Oh God," she whispered, gripping my arm. "That's *her*."

"Who?"

"The girl who…" she said, hesitating before pushing the elevator button. She spoke in hushed tones and waited until we were the only ones in the elevator. "She's a queer. She cornered this other girl in the bathroom and tried to kiss her. She's a total freak."

"How do you know she did that?"

"The other girl told everyone. She was pretty freaked out." Adrienne watched the floor numbers light slowly as the elevator rose. "I don't blame her."

My stomach sank to my feet, and I wasn't sure why. After all, I had nothing in common with that girl in the hallway. A heavy sensation spread over my body, as if Adrienne's contempt had been injected into my heart. Did a minute pass? Maybe two minutes? When we got to the seventh floor, I followed her slowly down the hall and into the room.

Adrienne slung her keys on her desk, at least I thought so. I heard the sound of them clanking against wood. When I looked up, she had the phone pressed to her ear.

"You want pepperoni?" she asked.

"That's fine." I unzipped my backpack and distractedly pulled out books. I wasn't very hungry.

CHAPTER THIRTEEN

In the wee hours of the morning, when the whole house was quiet and peaceful...this was Robin's favorite time. She could be alone with her thoughts, away from cameras and her increasingly annoying staff.

She climbed out of bed, careful to avoid a well-known creak in the floor. She couldn't wake Tom anyway. His breathing rumbled on, low and steady, like an idling motorcycle. She envied his ability to sleep.

Making it safely out of the bedroom, she slipped down to the library in her bathrobe and slippers, clicked on the light and turned on the computer at her favorite cherrywood desk. In the shadows were bookshelves stacked with Southern authors, a popular feature of the mansion library. Carson McCullers was her favorite of these authors, though she couldn't remember the last time she'd relaxed with a good book.

Robin had looked at the clock before she came down but couldn't remember now if it was three o'clock or four. It didn't matter; she knew she'd never be able to fall back to sleep. The curiosity was too much. She had to know. She had to see. Internet search history be damned. Planning to delete the evidence of her search afterward, she navigated to YouTube, where she typed "Eye of the Storm."

Adrienne's band appeared on the screen, performing to a large crowd at Boston's House of Blues. The video had been recorded by someone in the audience. The quality wasn't half bad, except for the occasional jerk down to the floor then back up to the stage. Adrienne was wearing a black leather body suit with a jacket that she eventually took off. Her voice was full and deep, even soulful. She owned the stage and the crowd, just as she had at their college parties, when everyone had gathered around her like magnets drawn to steel. Sometimes Robin would watch in awe, as she did now, captured by the idea of Adrienne, an otherworldly songstress singing a haunting rock ballad.

In this moment, Robin forgot her own iconic status. Now she was a vulnerable, ordinary woman…or a lovesick college girl. She caught herself smiling as Adrienne stopped dramatically, head down, while the drums did a solo. Then she turned, sweat from the hot lights glistening on her neck, her lips turned upward in a teasing smile. The smile Robin knew.

Robin sat back, watching, with her hand over her mouth.

There was a close-up of Adrienne's slender fingers working the strings of an electric guitar with such abandon; she had definitely mastered the instrument she couldn't play years ago.

As a woman in her late forties, Adrienne was more fully realized and more self-possessed, if that was possible, than she had been at eighteen. Her eyes, always sparkling and brilliant, were now filled with more experience, more genuine passion. Robin imagined the things she'd experienced since their time together. No doubt she'd had her heart broken. She'd lived life. There was something so undeniably sexy about *the woman Adrienne*, crooking her finger at someone in the audience, smiling and enjoying when people, male or female, reached out to grab her leather pants. Her ambiguous sexuality on stage made her accessible to everyone. It all made sense, Adrienne the rock star. It was inevitable. Her magnetic presence on stage, her attitude, was already like that of a rock icon. It was only a matter of time.

Robin admired her for staying on course toward this career path, especially at an age when so many women were either more settled in their careers or home life. And by this time, it was all too common to give up on the wild dreams of youth. Then again, Adrienne never seemed to lose her wild side. It was part of her.

A sense of regret, of loss, surged through Robin. She closed her eyes a long moment and waited for it to pass.

* * *

The sprawling backyard terrace was Jimmy Sanders' favorite spot at the governor's mansion. There he could have the illusion of privacy and kick back with his favorite cigar and a scotch.

Abigail, her hair freshly bleached, sat by his side. She was a nervous, wafer-thin woman, always nibbling at platters of raw carrots or crackers and never gaining any weight.

"Politics ain't what it used to be," Jimmy growled.

"I know." Robin smiled tiredly at him.

"You need nerves of steel, the way they spread all that garbage about you. I don't think my old ticker could take it." He patted his chest.

"I can handle it, Daddy." Robin crossed her legs and held her head high, the most dignified posture she could muster. Honestly, she could withstand anyone's judgment but his. He'd always called her "Daddy's little girl," whatever that meant exactly, and she tried to live up to that.

"I have no doubt you can." He winked at her and swirled the ice in his glass. "You know, I was no fan of John Kennedy, but even he got a private life without everything havin' to be out in the open. That's the problem now. Everything's in the open. I saw a talk show with this doctor, I guess he was a doctor, askin' a lady in the audience about her bowel movements. On national television! Doesn't that beat all hell?"

"What for?" Abigail squeaked, reaching for her martini.

"Somethin' about the color," he replied. "If it was the wrong color, you had cancer. I don't know."

Abigail turned in her seat, now desperately worried. She munched a whole cracker. "Well, what color was it?"

"I don't remember!" he exclaimed. "That's not the point."

"Daddy," Robin said, "I'm not letting some nobody destroy my career."

"Course you won't," he said. "Especially not some queer. They do these unnatural things and expect everyone to applaud when they do one of them parades. If Jesus came down today, he'd put a stop to them parades!"

Robin lowered her eyes; her face remained hard.

"I wish you remembered what color," Abigail persisted. "My cousin had colon cancer."

"Good Lord, woman," Jimmy said. "You can Google it. Everything's on the damn Google."

Abigail glanced away, clearly dissatisfied. Then her eyes fixed on Robin. It was obvious she'd been dying to ask her something since the scandal broke.

"Who is she anyway?" Abigail asked. She could hardly contain her curiosity now, as she nervously picked at the plate of cheese and crackers.

"Someone I knew at Florida State."

Jimmy perked up. "I do recall you goin' through a wild period down there. You came home hatin' Reagan."

"I never said I hated him."

"You were goin' through your teenage rebellion," he chuckled.

Robin's porcelain face flushed crimson. "I never had a rebellion," she corrected. "Maybe I should have."

He laughed. "I know it's not true, sweetie." He touched her knee.

Robin took a sip of white wine and gazed out at the endless, rolling countryside. "The truth is, she was not the sort of person I'd associate with today." She chose her words carefully, too aware of Abigail's eyes on her. They felt more intrusive than reporters' questions. "I never thought it was important to mention her. All I can do is wonder why she'd say such an outrageous thing."

"Oh, you know why," Abigail sighed. "She wants money from you."

"They say she's in some band," Jimmy said. "So unless she's on that *American Idol* show, I don't think she's makin' much."

"*American Idol* is for solo singers," Abigail corrected.

"Then she's definitely not makin' money." Jimmy didn't keep up with pop culture, and the only bands he knew were either country or groups from the fifties. If he hadn't heard of it, he was convinced it couldn't be very successful.

"Apparently Kendrick is familiar with her band," Robin said. "It's called Eye of the Storm."

"What's that again?" Jimmy squinted.

"The band."

"Such a silly name," Abigail said, sipping her drink.

"Well," Robin sighed. "No one can ever have too much money."

Amidst the turmoil, Robin felt peaceful sitting under the hanging Spanish moss, the grand oaks watching protectively over her just like the trees on the farm had when she was a child. It was a living Monet painting, where there was no unrest, no judgment, only quiet for miles. Here she could take comfort in the sound of distant crickets—as long as they stayed in the distance, of course—and the pink lemonade sun in the afternoon. No matter where she traveled, there was no place quite as pretty as the South.

Jimmy smiled at her. "My darlin', you've got the truth on your side. And the truth will always set you free."

Robin smiled faintly. She wondered if the disgrace and pain she was feeling would eventually spread through her body like a disease and eat her alive. The morbid thoughts always found their way in...

When Jimmy went inside to refill his glass, Abigail bubbled with anticipation. She leaned closer, aching to tell Robin something.

"You know," Abigail said so quietly, almost in a whisper, "there was a girl in school who used to hold my hand." She sat back, her mouth wide with the expectation of Robin's reaction.

Robin smiled politely.

"Not like how girls sometimes hold hands, you know," Abigail continued. Obviously, she thought she wasn't making herself clear. "It was at times when you just didn't hold hands. And I felt, you know, sort of funny. She was a very cute girl, if I recall." She giggled and gestured in her nervous hummingbird sort of way. When she didn't get much of a response, she cleared her throat defensively. "Some girls kind of experiment in college, you know."

"Oh, well," Robin replied. "I'm sure *some* do."

She stared out at the majestic oaks, thinking about Peter's urgent message the day before. She would give him her answer today. There was no way she was going to meet with Adrienne. Absolutely no way. Of course it didn't matter to the press. Minnie Douglas's gossip column would talk about no other subject besides "Did she or didn't she?" It was getting unbearable. No, she decided. That was final. Besides, talking with her would only dignify the rumors that were swirling around. No, she had to keep a distance, for political reasons. The more she rationalized, the better she felt.

CHAPTER FOURTEEN

I couldn't understand Adrienne's attraction to heavy metal music. The singers were always angry and snarling, the drums boomed, and the guitars... If a million bee stings could be heard, they would sound like those guitars. Sharp and insistent, sometimes dragging out the sting. The more I thought about it, the Scorpions and their *Love at First Sting* album kind of made sense. It scared me that it made sense to me. Without a doubt, something in the songs felt very dark and aggressive. When I heard heavy metal for the first time, I almost liked it, maybe because it was the opposite of everything I knew.

"How can you not have heard this before?" Adrienne asked in her usually judgmental way. "Does your family live in a cave?"

"Yes, yes, they do," I said sarcastically. "There's no music or TV, so we have to read by candlelight and carve things on the walls for fun."

"I believe it," she said.

Back at home, my dad preferred country music, while Mom enjoyed Bach and Beethoven. I'd grown up taking piano lessons not because I had talent, but because my parents thought I should have some kind of lessons. I had no natural gift for music, but I learned to appreciate the classical pieces I was playing. I was a rare high school girl who could detect the differences between Chopin and Mozart,

Haydn and Brahms. Skid Row and Megadeth just hadn't been on my radar. Until now.

Watching as Adrienne turned up the stereo, relishing her heavy metal world, I saw a wild party girl, the kind of person who was up for anything. And that scared me. I didn't take any of my own actions lightly. They were always seriously thought out, right down to the map I'd made of rest stops from Atlanta to Tallahassee. This girl, on the other hand, might do something on a whim. *This girl could hurt me.* I knew it instinctively the first night we met.

As soon as Adrienne discovered that we got cable TV in our room, she immediately switched on "Headbangers Ball" on MTV. I was studying for my Western Civilization class and made the mistake of looking up at the screen. I'd never paid much attention to music videos, but this one was hard to ignore. Scantily clad women were being rounded up and thrown into a cage by the men of a rock band.

"What is that?" I asked, a definite edge to my voice.

"It's Mötley Crüe," Adrienne answered matter-of-factly, strumming an air guitar at her desk in front of an open textbook she wasn't reading. The girl never studied.

"I mean, what is *that?*" I pointed to the screen.

"Oh, you don't like that kinda thing, do you?"

"Do *you?*" I replied.

Adrienne smiled. "I don't have a problem with it," she said.

I slammed my book shut. "If that doesn't bother you, then you do have a problem."

"Hey, why should it bother me? It's not *me* up there."

"It's not you up there," I repeated, shaking my head in disbelief.

Adrienne squirmed. I could see that I made her defensive. "If these women wanna be in this video, it's their right. Who the hell are you to judge?"

"I'm a *woman*!" I gathered my things and left for the library. The atmosphere in the room had started to suffocate me.

* * *

Apparently there was some rule that film teachers had to have beards. Kyle Perkins, who taught film production, had a ragged, fuzzy gray beard that hadn't been trimmed for decades. His eyelids sagged worse than his pants. He also had that film teacher scowl—the one that meant he'd been doing this for years, had gotten nowhere and was generally kind of disappointed with his life.

On our first day, he'd given us a speech he must've given to every class that had come before: "It's not too late to withdraw from this class! You can still get out and get a real major! Something with a future!" He looked out at the wide eyes and gaping mouths in the small, predominantly male, class of hopeful film students. "LA is nothing but a cesspool of politics and plastic surgery." He smirked beneath his fuzzy beard. "Don't go there. If you do, you'll die penniless and alone. For those of you without the common sense to leave, let's begin."

I'd been taking meticulous notes. As I wrote down "penniless," I heard the weirdest noise—a distinctive laugh that could have been a type of horn used in some exotic country. It was emanating from deep inside the nasal cavities of a boy, seated in the back, who was dressed in spandex shorts and a blazing pink tank top. "Ahh!" He laughed for what seemed like a whole minute. I thought it would never stop.

"What's your name, in the back?" Perkins asked.

"Andrew," the boy managed, catching his breath. "Andrew Bennington." He announced his name like we should all remember it because he was going to be famous. I admired his confidence.

"Andrew." Perkins raised an eyebrow. "You might wanna see someone about that, son."

Some students laughed, while I scowled at the teacher. A man in his position shouldn't be making cracks like that.

A couple of students dropped out after the first day, but for the following weeks, our number stayed the same. We only had this class once a week, so it took longer to get to know the material, not to mention the other students. I'd never had a class where our first assignment wasn't due for weeks, and the final film wasn't due until the end of the second semester. But I soon understood why. Before we could make our first short student film, Perkins had to teach us all the features of a camera, how to get a particular shot, even how to set up a tripod. Today he had run in and without a word to us scribbled "F-stop" on the chalkboard. Then he looked over his shoulder.

"I'll admit I'm disappointed," he said. "Usually I weed out more of you starry-eyed types as it gets more technical." He shook his head. "You guys…" He held his fingers on each side of the bridge of his nose. Did he have a headache? "I wish I could give you the benefit of my experience. But you have to make the same stupid mistakes. No one can tell you." He looked up at the lights, half-smiling, as if he were talking to God. He was having some sort of epiphany. I, on the other hand, was thinking about dinner tonight.

Adrienne had left me a note before she went to class that morning. She wanted to meet me at the on-campus grill, The Meat Grinder. No doubt she wanted to talk about last night. She was probably mad at the way I stormed out. I raised my chin proudly. I had stood up against the objectification and degradation of women. I preferred to spend my evening at the library anyway. It was quiet; I didn't have to listen to that noise she called music.

"...may God have mercy on your soul," Perkins said, apparently finishing a moving speech. Thankfully, I had missed most of it. "Excuse me a minute." Seeing someone outside the door, he exited the room.

"Somebody needs more fuckin' fiber in his diet."

The words came from Carol Munson, one of only two other girls in the class besides me. I couldn't help but laugh at her comment. I'd noticed her immediately in my other class, Film Appreciation. She'd walked into the auditorium as if she owned it. Wearing a flowery sundress, sneakers, a nose ring, bright red lipstick and a black Annie Hall hat, she seemed like someone who knew where she wanted to go in life, but who had a tendency to keep slamming into brick walls. Her dress was misbuttoned; it seemed either sloppy or intentional. I knew we'd be instant friends.

In the small room in which Film Production class was held, Andrew's laugh cut the silence. He couldn't stop laughing, and some others joined in.

A guy sitting behind Andrew with a bandana on his head punched him in the back. "C'mon, man. Quit actin' like such a fag."

Andrew turned around, the smile gone from his face. "I guess I'm your type then." He swiveled back around, and not another word was said.

A few years ago, when Boy George referred to himself as a "drag queen" on TV, the American public nearly fainted in shock. Even though the guys in big-hair bands had long hair and wore more eyeliner than most women, in 1989 it was still assumed that everyone was straight. When anyone branded someone else with terms like "fag" or "dyke," it was the equivalent of an automatic scarlet letter, not considered something to be proud of, even if there was an occasional parade.

I watched Andrew. I liked his fiery retort. He didn't act like a helpless person, and he had to be braver than I was to wear those spandex outfits. I smiled to myself, watching the guy behind him make indignant grunting noises to save face. But he didn't bother Andrew for the rest of the year.

CHAPTER FIFTEEN

Governor Sanders gave speeches all across the South over the next few days, selling out stadiums like a rock star. For this series of rallies, she wore her brightest red scarf, the one that of course meant she was more patriotic than her opponents, in addition to the flag pinned conspicuously on the lapel of her black suit jacket.

During one of these packed cheer fests, this one in Birmingham, Robin looked out at the crowd, and the expectant faces and clapping hands froze in place, then resumed as if in slow motion. Everything was quiet. It was like one of those weird out-of-body experiences in the movies. She could see herself, not as who she was, but as the person everyone else saw. There on the stage, an iconic figure full of poise and power that the scared teenage Robin had never had. *If they only knew.*

She thought about the long, strange, treacherous road she'd taken to get to this place—and about how she almost changed the course of her life with a dramatically different detour so many years ago.

Was it hurt and humiliation that had led her to this place? Only she knew, but she didn't know if she could separate the truth from the self-delusion. Clearly, it had been fear that sent her running back home, back to the comfort of the familiar. She understood the values her parents had, understood why they believed the things they did. She'd seen how their faith helped them through her mother's illness.

If only Robin had had as strong a faith as her father, maybe her mother's death wouldn't have been so unbearable. Holding her mother's tiny hand in that awful powder-blue bedroom, waiting for her eyes to open, hearing her father say how God was taking her home—Robin felt her insides churn and knew that nothing would ever be right in the world again, because her mother wouldn't be in it. At that moment, there was no God. There was no religion. There was only the empty bed where someone she loved so much was supposed to be. The pillow was still creased from where her head had lain. Now there was nothing, only the stale air trapped inside the room.

Later, when she had trouble getting through impossible times in her life, Robin had tried to wrap herself in religion and wear it as armor. She'd heard someone say that in hard times you should act "as if" until you really feel a certain way. She tried that when she shouted about God. She tried that at her wedding when she was stuffing Tom's face with a piece of white cake. But acting "as if" had never made it so. Not for her anyway.

In the limo after the rally, Robin stared ahead calmly and quietly, enjoying the cheering outside. Maybe she and Adrienne had something in common after all—a love of the stage, and attention.

Robin's greatest satisfaction in this campaign had come from her ability to throw so many Republicans off balance, pushing back hard on laws that negatively impacted women, laws which were often proposed by her own party. Some people supported her simply because she was so full of surprises. In an age of candidates who were merely mouthpieces for their parties, she was somewhat refreshing, if not infuriating to the LGBT community. Unfortunately, the new conservative movement that was making her a star was also fueled by antigay rhetoric, making it impossible for her to speak against something that helped her rise to the top.

As they traveled to their next stop, Robin caught Peter watching her. On his face was a mixture of awe and confusion.

"Governor," he began carefully. "Do you think it's a good idea not to take her call?" Of course he was talking about Adrienne.

"Yes," she replied curtly. "The subject is closed."

He folded his hands in his lap and looked down. No matter what he really thought, he'd keep his mouth shut for now. She was his ticket to the top, and he'd sell his own mother to get there.

"I had a cousin, Laken," she said, staring ahead. "He lived with another man. Course I was too young to know what that was. Laken was my mother's nephew and my cousin."

Peter leaned in, hanging on her every word. She rarely spoke of her private life, so this was a special treat for him.

"No one ever talked about his male companion," Robin continued. "But you knew, the way they were with each other. They acted like my parents did. The day Laken died, everybody said it was from pneumonia. A forty-year-old man who can't fight off pneumonia?" Her dismissive shrug couldn't hide a painful truth that was weighing on her. She'd long ago placed the past, Laken's and her own, in a vault inside her mind and locked it tight, never expecting to want to reopen it one day.

Peter's eyes filled with concern, but she ignored him. She didn't see him as a confidante. She simply wanted to talk, and he happened to be there, that's all. In reality, she saw him as nothing more than a political parasite.

"It was like he never existed." Robin's gaze was now far away. She was looking at old home movies in her mind, the kind where the only sound is that of a rattling projector. And there was Laken, hiding behind his seventies-style mustache, holding a toddler-size Robin on his knee.

"He's in old family albums. But when my father gets to one with him in the picture, he never says anything about him, just flips the page. I doubt Abigail even knows who he is."

Peter rubbed his hands together, trying to make sense of this revelation. "You're not changing your mind on…that issue?"

She laughed a hearty laugh, amused by his transparency. "Oh, Pete. You're about as smooth as a bull on roller skates."

He didn't know whether or not to smile. Not originally from the South, he didn't know what to make of her little "down-home" analogies. Usually they involved grits. This was a new one. Did it mean a yes or a no?

"You think because I had a gay cousin I'm going to vote for gay marriage?" She turned to face him.

Peter shook his head.

"You know, Laken always said I had pretty eyes." She looked out the window, smiling to herself, as if it was the only compliment she'd ever believed.

They reached their destination.

* * *

In truth, it wasn't political issues that motivated Robin Sanders, but her need to be in control of some aspect of her life. The young girl growing up on a farm near Atlanta saw a mother who lived and breathed cooking. And Robin wasn't much of a cook. She wasn't much for the farm animals either. Every time she tried to help her father, she got hurt. Like the time she was helping to feed an older horse. Aside from occasionally flipping his tail, he wasn't that active. But Robin stood in the wrong place at the wrong time, and he stepped back, his hoof breaking her foot. Farming clearly wasn't for her.

She needed to find a way to get out from under her father's thumb, as well as something to satisfy her insatiable ambition. Ironically, the quiet girl from Atlanta finally found the platform where she could have all the power, like her father, in politics.

Somewhere along the line—she couldn't pinpoint exactly where or when—her conscience had been swept away by the wave of compromises she'd made to get where she was.

Now she could look at the issue with a sort of detachment. But every time she called people a sin, she seemed to lose a piece of herself. That was why she traveled with enough antacids and migraine pills to put down a horse. Maybe on some level, the voice inside that knew of her duplicity sickened her to her stomach.

Politics was all about compromise, she'd remind herself. If she had to make a few statements here and there to get what she wanted, then so be it. If she was able to get a bridge repaired, an organization more funding, all of her compromises, she reasoned, were for the greater good. It was the only way she could keep doing what she was doing and stay sane.

Besides, in time she might, *might* be able to soften her position on certain issues. So many people often did—but that could only happen after her father was dead. By then she'd have all the clout and influence she'd ever dreamed of.

Robin knew she was a coward. But more than anything, she wanted to be heard. And if that meant chunks of her soul falling away with every step up to the next stage, then that would have to be okay. A big bloody mess, but okay.

The governor gave speeches from Nashville to Savannah—covering the most red-hot cities where people were all so eager to hear her message. But the Atlanta speech was going to be the most well attended of all of them. People were coming from all over to hear her, and everyone seemed loyal in spite of the scandal. Maybe they admired her for appearing at all instead of hiding out in her bedroom, stuffing her face with ice cream. Of course, that was not her style. And everyone was about to know that for sure.

They got to the arena with only minutes to spare—someone had neglected to check if the Braves were playing a home game and adjust travel plans accordingly—and Robin settled herself backstage to prepare. She was going to close her eyes for a minute or two, shut out the noise, meditate for a moment and envision what she was going to say and do.

First, though, she popped a Valium in her mouth and washed it down with a swig of bottled water. This rally appeared like all the others—tens of thousands of screaming supporters, signs waving in the air, and a giant American flag hung behind a well-lit stage at night. It wouldn't be a rally like the others though. And it would take more than a pill to help Robin Sanders get through it.

CHAPTER SIXTEEN

"*Auteur* is French for author," Dr. Gentry explained. "Do you know why they call a director an auteur?"

No one answered, not because we didn't know, but because most of us were too intimidated to speak.

"Because a true auteur makes the same film over and over again. In each one, he reveals his world view or *weltanschauung*."

"Gesundheit," Carol muttered under her breath.

I smiled, glancing over at her. Film Appreciation followed the Production class. So today I took the opportunity to sit a little closer to the girl I thought I might have something in common with.

Dr. Gentry continued, "You'll note the rape scene was clearly a metaphor for his view of society out of control."

"Oh, please." Carol sighed loudly.

"Yes, in the back." He pointed at Carol.

"Well," she snapped. "I think that's bullshit. Not every rape scene is a metaphor. Sometimes it's purely gratuitous."

Some of the class rumbled with comments, while others chuckled. Dr. Gentry tried to quiet them. "Everyone is entitled to their opinion. However, I do believe it's more complicated than that. Anyone else?" He turned his dismissive face away from her and scanned the class.

I was completely outraged, looking at Carol, who, seemingly undaunted, was sipping a soda. She didn't notice, but I was studying her with the intensity of someone who longed for a kindred spirit. Deep down, I was always outraged when women's voices were dismissed, because I suppose I saw myself as someone whose voice was always quieted at home.

When class was over, I approached Carol as she was gathering her books. "He completely disregarded what you had to say," I said. "I think you had a very valid point."

At that moment, the bags under Carol's eyes seemed to vanish, and she smiled brightly. "Carol Munson," she offered, extending her hand.

"Robin Sanders."

"Sanders? You're not related to that guy in the news, are you? The one who's trying to ban curse words from public schools?"

"Guilty."

"That's fucked."

I frowned. Maybe she wouldn't be a kindred spirit after all. "I'm actually very proud of him for standing up for his beliefs, no matter how unpopular. It's always easy to do what's popular."

"Good luck enforcing a law like that." Carol impressed me because she actually watched the news and seemed to pay attention to the issues.

When I'd first arrived at the university, I had studied the crowds of Greek clubs, football players, girls who wanted nothing more than to date football players—and I only found those I could identify with in the film or drama departments, those who had strong points of view, who were misfits in some way, as I saw myself. Whether it was Carol's Annie Hall hat or Andrew's animal-in-heat laugh, no one in my film classes would have fit in with any of the other groups. And even though I dressed conservatively, I knew in my heart I couldn't be a sorority girl. Oh, I could look the part, but I couldn't feel it inside. My mind was always moving me in other directions and usually not toward the same places where everyone else seemed to be going.

Carol and I walked around the campus in the thick, sticky air. "I gotta be honest," Carol said. "When I first saw you, I thought you were some rich fuckin' snob. No offense."

"None taken. I don't think." I laughed nervously.

"Then I thought you might be a slut. You kinda look like my cousin, and she's been ridden more times than my Harley."

"It's funny how we use stereotypes to keep others at a distance." Ironically, I realized I'd done exactly that with Adrienne. After all, she was far less threatening if I imagined her as an empty-headed party girl.

"Whoa." Carol stopped and stared at me. "You're serious?"

"Uh-huh." She was staring at me like I didn't have any clothes on. "What?"

"Never mind."

We resumed walking.

"I live on a farm back home," I said. "And my dad's always sayin' not every pig is a slob." That was his way of saying not to stereotype, I guess.

Carol looked weirdly at me again. Maybe she was regretting this conversation.

"Didn't it bother you? What he said?" I had to know.

"Nah, he's an asshole." We stopped again under a sprawling oak with hanging Spanish moss. Carol set one foot on a bench and lit up a cigarette with nervous hands. "I've taken him before. Failed his class three times so far."

"Are you serious?"

"No, his tests really suck."

"Great," I quipped sarcastically.

"Every semester, he tries to make an example out of something I say. The little fuck."

"Why do you take it?" I asked.

"'Cause he's a damn good teacher, the prick. Probably the best I've ever had."

I marveled at how she could admit that he was a good teacher in spite of her frustration. It was clear on the first day that Film Appreciation was going to be an intense course. At first, the auditorium was filled with students who thought it would be a breezy elective that would enable them to sit back and watch movies the whole time. What they didn't realize was that the movies were going to be analyzed, some frame by frame, and that long essays would be required to explain the themes and vital elements of each one.

They also assumed we'd be viewing popular Hollywood movies. While some were included, there were many more films from around the globe—French, Eastern European—all with subtitles and more complex, unfamiliar ways of telling a story. For some, just the word "subtitle" made them break out in a sweat. By the second class, I had no trouble finding a seat in the much less packed auditorium.

I shook my head, as we trudged across the grass. "Why do you think so many girls don't care about sexism in film?"

"Today's girls are idiots," Carol exclaimed. "Their bra-burning mothers had the right idea. But they did too many drugs, so their kids are fuckin' zombies."

"Interesting theory."

"It's not a theory. It's the truth. Everyone in the sixties messed up their genetic codes. The next generation's brains were compromised. I read it in a magazine." Carol had a way of stating everything as if it were the gospel.

"Oh."

We continued walking together under a clump of threatening clouds.

CHAPTER SEVENTEEN

That evening, I went to the on-campus grill to meet Adrienne for dinner. Our argument last night about the sexism in heavy metal videos must've really made her mad for her to leave me a note with a meeting place on it. Would she be carrying a gun to shoot me? Of course not. That was paranoia. After all, a restaurant was a public place.

I walked into The Meat Grinder and scanned the blazing red walls, which were covered with artsy black and white photographs of bare body parts. It seemed a little racy, but I reminded myself that I was now a college student and a long way from Bible school. I soon found Adrienne standing in a long line at the counter, straining to read a chalk-scribbled menu.

"Hi," I said.

"Hey."

"I'm surprised you wanted to meet me." I stuffed my hands in my pockets.

"Why?"

"I don't know." I shrugged, but of course I knew why. Adrienne made me feel like an activist who would tie myself to trees or something. It bothered me. Why should I feel the need to curb my opinions when I was around her?

"Can we get hamburgers?" Adrienne asked.

"Yeah, it's the first one on the board. Can you see it?"

"No." She strained so hard to see the menu that she almost fell on the person in front of her.

"Put on your glasses," I said.

"I don't want to."

I smiled to myself as I realized that she was embarrassed to be seen wearing her reading glasses. I liked knowing a secret about her. It made me feel good…special…confused.

"What?"

"Nothing." I smiled. This wasn't exactly the conversation I'd imagined when I came here tonight.

"Is there a chicken sandwich?" Adrienne asked.

"No, that would be the duck à l'orange."

She shot me a dirty look. "Bite me."

When it was her turn, she said, "I'll have a chicken patty sandwich."

The counter guy looked at me. "The Cobb salad," I said. I'd heard stories about the "Freshman Ten," and I swore I wasn't going to come out of here with an extra butt.

"We'll bring 'em to you," the guy shouted over the noise.

As we moved through the tightly packed tables, I said, "How do they know where we're sitting?"

"They do this all the time. They have a system." I could tell she had no idea what she was talking about.

We took a seat beside a photo of a woman's bare torso. Adrienne looked at it a long moment. "It's pretty."

"Yeah," I replied. "What happened to the rest of her?" I often made jokes when I was uncomfortable.

"I understand what you're saying…about the videos." In a rare moment, Adrienne seemed absolutely serious.

"Really?"

"Well, yeah. I just never looked at 'em like that. I mean, I don't take that stuff as seriously as you do."

I was too serious because I thought about what the image meant? Having an opinion meant that I didn't have a sense of humor? That I was uptight? Adrienne made me feel this way more than anyone I'd ever met.

"Well," I responded, "you never see men dressing that way. And they sure as heck wouldn't be put in a cage."

"Oh, I'll bet some have done that," she said. "Some guys like freaky stuff."

"That's not what I—"

"I know." She grinned. "I guess I'm not…as political as you."

No one had ever called me that before. It would be my dad's dream come true. "Political?" I repeated.

"Don't get me wrong," she said. "I get pissed off at a lot of things, like how guys still have the power. I mean, how many female rock bands do you see?" She took her chicken sandwich from the waiter.

I tried to hide my surprise. She had a brain to go with that face. *Darn.*

"You should do something about it," I urged. "Start your own band."

She laughed. "Yeah, right. I can't play anything. You know, I always wanted to play guitar, but my mom said girls should learn piano. I hate piano. She made me take lessons for two years! Could be worse, I guess. At least I can read music."

"I was forced to take piano too!" We laughed. "I couldn't get beyond a very basic song called 'Tuba Tune.' It was awful. I said, if I can't play like Chopin, I might as well hang it up right there." As I got my Cobb salad, I could tell she was still watching me. She was always watching.

I proceeded to drown my lettuce in the ranch dressing they'd placed in a container on the side. Honestly, the salad was merely an excuse to have the dressing. So much for avoiding the "Freshman Ten…"

When the laughter subsided, I said, "I have a confession. I don't completely dislike every heavy metal song I've heard. Actually, I like a few of them. It's strange."

"No, it's not."

"Well, yes, it is. For me, I mean."

"You mean because you're so uptight?" She winked at me.

"Shut up."

"Or because you're too good for the music of us common folk?"

"Bite me." I surprised myself. I guess she was rubbing off on me, a scary thought.

"You wish." After a pause, she asked, "Which one's your favorite?"

I thought a moment. "That song about being alone again?"

"Oh, 'Alone Again.'" Adrienne nodded.

"That's the title?"

"Yeah."

"Of course it is," I laughed.

Soon we were both laughing. When I dared to meet her shiny brown eyes, they were crinkled up above her full cheeks as she laughed. She had the most joyful grin I'd ever seen. And in the dim light, her eyes seemed to dance as she looked at me. My face flushed with heat, and I tried to cool myself down by sipping my soda. I wasn't sure how I would survive the year.

CHAPTER EIGHTEEN

The Atlanta crowd loved Robin Sanders, roaring with applause at every point she made.

"Who says the rich don't understand the poor! I know all about poverty!" She stood, dripping with Cartier jewelry. "My Aunt Clara slept on a dirt floor!" Everyone cheered, as if they were happy about Aunt Clara's dirt floor. In truth, her Aunt Clara had run off with a hippie group during the seventies. She had lived in a camp out in the woods and often slept on dirt. But that detail wasn't important now.

As the crowd reached a fever pitch, Robin was hoarse with promises: "I will never raise taxes! Ever!" If she could have thrown in a free car for everyone like Oprah, she would have.

"I'm here today," she continued, "not just as a candidate, but as a concerned citizen. Whoever takes office next has to return this country to traditional values and stop unnatural unions from becoming law." She looked down for the first time during her speech. Though the crowd cheered in response, these words felt a little thicker in her throat tonight.

After the speech Robin shook hands and signed autographs. She was exhausted from smiling, from handshakes, from trying to appear the picture of grace no matter what her detractors were saying. Peter was right by her side, guarding her, listening in his earpiece to every new development. He took her arm. "Lara says your poll numbers are back up." He was beaming. She offered him a smile, knowing that all was right in his world.

Though Robin felt somewhat fatigued, her fans had kept her energized throughout the night. She signed glossy photographs of herself all the way down the front row of the audience. She was especially gratified to see young girls looking to her, as if they could run the country someday too. When Robin reached the end of the row, though, she was handed a different photograph, a blown-up color photo of her younger self with Adrienne Austen in college. She looked up, startled.

There she was. An older, more radiant version of the girl she remembered, Adrienne Austen the woman was, as ever, stunning. Her eyes were intense, fixed on hers. And her amused smile brought everything back in an instant. "Make it out to Adrienne," she said, raising the photograph.

Robin sometimes wondered what she'd say if she ever crossed paths with Adrienne again, but whatever she'd thought about was quickly forgotten once she met those familiar almond eyes.

The governor momentarily lost her composure, as cameras snapped, capturing the moment. She knew Peter could tell from the look on her face that this woman had meant something to her. He immediately whisked her away to the limousine and glanced over his shoulder. Two other members of the governor's entourage were escorting Adrienne to her car. She was going to get what she wanted—a visit to the governor's mansion.

Robin watched through her limousine window as cameras flashed at Adrienne. She was dressed to the nines tonight, like one of those glammed-up sirens in film noir movies—just before they put the final bullet in their former lover's body.

Quickly catching on to who she was, reporters began shouting questions at her. "Did you have an affair with the governor? Are you trying to win her back?"

Robin watched as Adrienne ignored them and glided to another limo waiting with escorts on all sides. Like Robin, she had a way of moving as if nothing could touch her.

As Robin's car began to move, Peter said, "I never worried about the outcome of this election…until now."

Robin was obviously shaken. She decided to make use of the full bar in the backseat. "Where was security? How could she just pop up at my rally?" She was livid, her voice scratchy.

"Save your voice," Peter replied, pouring himself a vodka tonic. Then he checked his phone. "She's been staying at the Hilton downtown." He was breathing funny, running his hand through his now sweaty mop of hair, growing more agitated.

"She's following us?"

"Yes. You really need to put this thing to rest. Either now, or she screws it up for you in Tampa." Of course he was referring to the final debate. He was really scared. "I saw you with her," he said quietly. "If a guy like me can see it…"

"There's nothing to see," she insisted, staring out the window.

CHAPTER NINETEEN

"You got plans tonight?" Adrienne asked, tapping off the ashes of her cigarette.

I coughed. "I told you, smoking will kill you. Or me."

She rolled her eyes.

"Tonight? I'm not sure," I said. "Why?"

"You wanna party?" she asked.

"Party?"

She now rolled her eyes so far back they seemed to disappear into her head. "C'mon, you know, *party*. Some guys I know were gonna get six-packs and just hang out and listen to music."

I thought a moment. My first impulse was to say no. A "get-together" with her could only lead to a raid later by campus police. I was sure of it.

There was a knock on the door. Adrienne opened it and let in this girl I'd seen sometimes hanging around the student union. She was a human Barbie with hair that was sprayed up and teased out like an exotic plant. And the way she dressed…a good wind could blow off her flimsy tank top. Maybe that's what she wanted to happen.

I stared at her with obvious disdain before reminding myself to be polite.

"Hi," the girl said, popping her gum.

"Hi," Adrienne responded. "Uh, Nancy, this is Robin."

"Robin?" Nancy repeated. "Like the bird?"

"Yeah, like the bird." I'd never had to explain my name before.

I could tell instantly that Nancy didn't really care if I was there or not. She was more interested in Adrienne's cigarette pack. "Oh," she said. "Can I bum a few? I'm all out."

"You're always out," Adrienne complained, handing her the pack and lighting one for her. They had a familiarity with each other. Nancy must've been among the party crowd that Adrienne sometimes talked about. I didn't like her.

Then *he* arrived. This had to be the famous Sean Voight. Adrienne had mentioned him a few times in a giddy sort of way. So I knew he meant something to her. I instinctively disliked him even more than Nancy.

"Hey." Sean came into the room with a kind of redneck peacock shuffle.

"Hey," Adrienne replied with great interest. "Sean, Robin. Robin, Sean." It seemed important to her that we meet. I didn't know why.

"Hi," I said politely. I examined him like a specimen under a microscope, trying to identify any possible reason why this boy held such a fascination for her. He sported tattoos and ambiguous facial hair on his chin. The hair on his head was long and greasy brown. There was nothing special about him as far as I could see.

Adrienne turned to me and said, "They're gonna hang with us tonight."

"Uh," I stammered, desperate for a way to escape. "You know, I have to get to the library tonight. A lot of studying." I shrugged apologetically.

"You sure?" Adrienne looked disappointed. "It'll be fun."

Nancy popped her gum again.

"Yeah," I answered. "Maybe some other time. Nice to meet y'all." With that, I hastily grabbed my books, stuffed them into my backpack and left.

CHAPTER TWENTY

The library, illuminated with lights, looked like the Emerald City from the darkness outside. In spite of the heavy air choking me, I walked into the building with a sense of purpose and rising excitement. After meeting Sean and seeing how enamored Adrienne was with him and probably with boys in general, I'd decided to confront the strange feelings I'd been having. They went back farther than I was willing to admit. Back to high school, in fact. That was when I found *Curious Wine*.

I had been shopping at a nearby mall, and, after a long day of trying to find enough decent clothes to balance out the unfortunate wardrobe that Granny Inez had been building for me, I wandered into a bookstore and browsed my way into the section labeled "Gay and Lesbian." There I picked up a book called *Curious Wine* by someone named Katherine Forrest. The blurb on the back said it was about two women who fall in love at Lake Tahoe. After glancing around the store to make sure no one I knew was there, I rushed up to the counter, head down, and quickly purchased it.

When I got home, I stuffed the book underneath my mattress. I couldn't wait until after dinner to go upstairs and read it. And I did. In one night. I stayed up so late I could barely keep my eyes open the next day in school. But it was worth it. I spent the day dreaming about the two women in the cabin and what it was like for them…something about the story really drew me in. That sensual scene in the upstairs bedroom…it was quite a departure from my nightly *Bible* readings growing up. One night I was in the world of Corinthians, and the next minute, enjoying some perverse, delicious encounter at Lake Tahoe— and Tahoe was starting to look better and better. Another reason I worried that I was going to hell.

I couldn't fathom something like the scenes in Lake Tahoe ever happening to me. None of the girls I'd seen who called themselves lesbians seemed to be anything like me. The girl in the dorm who spooked Adrienne—she seemed nice, but she dressed like my brother. I couldn't relate to what I thought a lesbian had to be. It was all so confusing, this strange world of women who intrigued and scared me at the same time.

I reread *Curious Wine* off and on for the rest of the school year. I knew I couldn't take it to college with me in case my roommate saw it and got the wrong idea. And I couldn't leave it at home in case my parents found it and got the wrong idea. So as much as it saddened me, I threw it out in a Dumpster downtown, far away from school or any place where it could be traced back to me. I felt like some sort of criminal.

It was time to read it again. In the library I went to the Gay and Lesbian section in the stacks and searched for *Curious Wine*. Sure enough, there it was. It had become one of the most popular books in the genre, so it was no surprise to see it there. I pulled it out and sauntered over to the Psychology section to peruse it. I was a cliché, standing there reading lesbian literature in a section devoted to Freud and his "poor women without penises" books.

I opened the book to the place where I knew I'd find my favorite scene. I was so excited to read it again that tears welled up in my eyes. I scanned the pages hurriedly, with a certain paranoia, as if the lesbian police were going to storm in at any moment and announce to the world that I was one of them. I'd then be taken to an undisclosed location where I'd be forced to play softball and wear corduroy, both of which I wasn't particularly excited about—further proof I couldn't be a lesbian!

"Hi." The voice startled me out of my skin. I spun around to find Andrew Bennington, dressed in bright yellow spandex shorts and a white tank top. He was definitely proud of his bare, fuzzy skin.

"Oh, hi," I said, with some relief. I remembered him, but he misinterpreted the blank face I gave him as I tried to gather my composure.

"I'm in your Film Production?"

"Yeah, right," I said. "The *laugh*."

He sighed dramatically. "I get so much grief for that. It's genetic." He was so full of life and himself that he hadn't noticed at first what I'd been reading. Now a passing glance at my book stopped him. "Ooh, I hear that's a good book. My best friend Sara loves it."

Involuntarily, I snapped it shut. "Oh, really?"

"Yeah, look, sorry to bother you." His hands were very expressive as he spoke, like he was playing a game of charades. "I was wondering if I could ask you a huge favor."

"Sure."

Though he sounded like he was going to ask me to give him a kidney, he only wanted to borrow some of my notes. "You look like you take great notes."

"Oh?" I replied absently. "Looks can be deceiving." I smiled and handed him my notebook.

Andrew dropped it and bent over to retrieve it, pushing his backside into my face. "Whoa," I laughed. "Way more of you than I want to see!"

"Ahh! You're so funny!" He stood up and slapped my arm. Something about him seemed to me like an old friend. "I haven't mastered the f-stop thing. Everything is coming out blurry."

"I know what you mean."

"It's pretty confusing," he continued. "I don't know. And the teacher hates my guts."

"He hates everyone's guts."

"Ahh!" Andrew's laugh drew some attention in the library. I was a little embarrassed. I looked around, over my shoulder. Then Andrew held up my notebook. He cleared his throat and said softly, "Thanks for this. I'll get it back to you tomorrow." He winked at me and walked away.

Relieved at his departure, I exhaled and turned back to the Psychology section, where I shoved a few more "secret" books for later reading. If workers at the library weren't too conscientious, the books would still be there tomorrow.

All was quiet and still, as I walked back to the dorm. Regal palm trees against a moonlit sky appeared like postcards I'd seen in tourist shops. It was a sharp contrast to the scene I witnessed when I got back to the dorm room. The aftermath of the party reminded me of what a nuclear holocaust might bring—corpselike bodies lying in weird positions across the floor, the rank odor of warm Budweiser swirling up my nose, a Marlboro fog still hovering in the air and towers of beer cans rising up like monsters out of the trash can and teetering dangerously.

Adrienne and Sean, the redneck peacock, were entwined on Adrienne's bed with their clothes on. My dislike of Sean intensified. It was not intellectual; it came from a place deep in my gut. The sight of them together was like a hard punch to my stomach. I winced at the filled ashtray on my nightstand. With a sleeping body blocking my closet door, I gingerly climbed into my own bed with my clothes on.

* * *

The next morning, a half-asleep Adrienne frowned at herself in the mirror as I fixed my makeup.

"What time is it?" she asked. Her mascara had smeared into her hair, her eyes were pink and unfocused. To me, she still looked beautiful.

"Eight thirty," I said. "The bodies rose from the dead about an hour ago and left, thank God."

She shuddered. "Could you…just…shhh?"

I leaned into her ear and shouted, "Hung over?"

"Bitch." Adrienne pushed me away and opened her closet, staring at her clothes disdainfully.

"What was that? It looked like Armageddon when I came in last night."

"I told that fucker he wasn't sleeping over," she grumbled, pulling out a pair of jeans.

"Who?"

"Sean."

"Oh, the one who was sleeping with you?"

"We didn't sleep together," she snapped defensively. "We had a fight. I told him to leave. But he was too wasted to go anywhere."

"You don't owe me any explanation."

"No, it's cool. I just wanted you to know what happened." She smiled faintly at me before disappearing to the showers.

CHAPTER TWENTY-ONE

Security at the governor's mansion that night was the tightest it had ever been, as everyone awaited Adrienne's arrival.

Robin waited in the library. She sat rigidly in her favorite high-back leather chair, unable to relax, knowing that the one person who could unravel her carefully crafted persona, not to mention all her future plans, would soon be there. Vaguely aware of the occasional pop and crackle from the glowing fireplace, a necessity in the drafty mansion, she settled back into the leather cushion cradling her head and remembered a time when nothing else had mattered but Adrienne's impression of her.

Why had she been so drawn to the most dangerous person she could have met? She'd never know the answer, only that Adrienne was the one she had always longed for in the hidden recesses of her mind, in places she'd never share with anyone, especially not her husband. She could hardly even share it with herself!

Peter lingered in the doorway. "Governor? If you need anything, I'll be right outside."

How comforting, she thought sarcastically.

She heard the front door close. Moments later she saw Tom passing in front of the archway that led to the library. He was just getting back from work. He nodded to Peter, pushed past him and entered the library, closing the door behind him. "You really think this is a good idea?" he asked.

"Word certainly gets around." She rose from the chair. "You're home late."

"A lot of work at the office." He poured himself a brandy. She noticed how the amber liquid rippled in the light. It was actually kind of pretty. Sometimes she could find beauty in unusual things, at the oddest moments. Here she was, balanced on a tightrope between her career and the reemerging desire that had haunted her all these years. She knew she could just as easily fall off into oblivion as to make it safely to one side or the other. And yet here she was, pondering her husband's drink and attempting small talk.

"Security out front," Tom said. "They told me you're meeting her *here?*"

She nodded. "That's correct."

"You know the place is going to be swarming with the media."

"Peter assures me the second car is taking a more circuitous route, to avoid being tailed. We're taking every precaution we can to keep this discreet."

"Discreet?" He laughed. He gulped the rest of his drink. "Be careful. Her only motivation is to bring you down."

Robin nodded, but she wasn't really listening.

He smiled bitterly to himself. "I'm going to go up and check on Ken, see if she needs help with her homework." In quick strides he made it to the door, then paused, turning around. "She *is* pretty." With a slight, knowing smile, he turned the knob to leave.

"Tom…" She watched the door close behind him.

Going to the flat screen, she switched it on and saw what Tom must have seen. A still shot of her face upon seeing Adrienne in the Atlanta crowd was being splashed all over the news. Ann DeMarco, looking stern with her slicked-back, auburn hair and black-rimmed glasses, was commenting on it.

"Clearly, Governor Sanders did share a room with Adrienne Austen in college," Ann said, "although it still remains unclear whether or not they had more than a friendship."

On CNN, Jay Savage was interviewing one of Robin's opponents in the Republican primary, Jerry Johnson. He too was from Georgia and liked to talk about his days as an SEC coach.

"I just think the whole thing's distasteful," Johnson said, scrunching up his face. He had at least a pound of pancake makeup on and his pepper hair had been sprayed so much it wouldn't have moved in a tornado.

"Do you think this rumor that keeps dogging the governor will have a negative impact on her campaign?" Savage asked.

"I'm not a betting man," Johnson responded. "But…"

"They say her poll numbers are still quite strong."

"That may be. But I think where there's smoke…you know, too often some of my less fortunate colleagues have been caught doin' the one thing they said they were against. It happens all the time."

"Like your gambling problem!" Robin exclaimed as she shut off the TV. She needed a moment of peace anyway. She turned away from the screen, toward the windows that now flashed with headlights. Her heart began to pound…

CHAPTER TWENTY-TWO

I loved Florida skies. At the end of each day, as I walked up the hill toward the dorm, I'd notice the wisps of pink cotton candy clouds floating overhead. They were only a temporary distraction, though. What I was most interested in was seeing if the light was on in one particular seventh-floor window—the one on the end. When it was, my heart beat a little faster and my feet got lighter as I ran up the steps to the towering building. The front desk staff must have thought I had some kind of condition. Every time I went into the lobby, panting and sweating, I had to stop to catch my breath. Not wanting Adrienne to see me like that, I'd stop in the bathroom to freshen up before entering our room. I started tying my hair back more, because the humidity would make strands of it stick to the back of my neck.

Most days, Adrienne wasn't in the restroom. But on the rare occasion when she was, I would nod, duck into a stall and wait for her to leave. It was a bizarre way to live, but I'd become so accustomed to my strange rituals, they had begun to seem normal.

I was losing the emotional war I was fighting in my head. I knew it every day, my face sometimes betraying my thoughts, my feelings. Mundane moments of everyday life rippled through my mind like treasured photographs. The way Adrienne turned around when I called her name, the inside jokes we began to share, simply studying beside her quietly—there was no work of art or piece of music that could hold my attention quite like this. No Chopin piece could rival her voice, especially her throaty laugh. This was the stuff girls in high school wrote notes and poems about. This was the reason why they etched certain initials in the margins of their notebooks. It all made sense now, like one of my senses had now been turned on and couldn't be switched off.

I'd lie in bed and remember the comfortable nights with Marc back home. I realized that Adrienne made me feel anything *but* comfortable. The constant butterflies in my stomach whenever Adrienne was near—that must have been what it was like for Marc. I'd feel a pang of guilt, then roll over to erase it.

My trips to the library grew more frequent and urgent. I eventually read all of the top-secret books I'd stashed in the Psychology section.

One night, when there was autumn frost on the Spanish moss and shrubs around campus, Adrienne returned to the room fresh from her shower wearing only a pink terrycloth towel. "Did you turn the heat off again?" she exclaimed, rushing over to the thermostat.

"I was hot," I said.

"You're always hot."

"You're cold when it's sixty degrees! You don't know what real cold is."

Adrienne closed her eyes. "Twenty degrees. I know." She turned the heat on and took a seat at her desk, studying beside me. Her long, wet, curled hair dripped down her exposed neck... My breathing became shallow. Droplets of moisture glistened on her bare, broad shoulders... My thoughts were wild horses; I tried to focus them on my book.

What a cruel world—forced to read about the political structures of China and India—when all I could think about was gently placing my lips upon her shoulder...so smooth, so soft...and gliding my mouth lightly across her skin, gathering beads of sweet water with my lips, caressing her skin with my face.

I wiped my eyes and exhaled loudly, suddenly remembering where I was.

"You okay?" Adrienne asked.

"Yeah. Just Comparative Politics."

"Is it hard?"

"Getting harder."

CHAPTER TWENTY-THREE

"Robin." It was *her* voice.

Without looking up, Robin poured two glasses of white wine.

"You know I'm a beer drinker," Adrienne said. Robin raised her head and met those caramel eyes, now with a new line or two around the edges. They only made her even more striking. She noticed that Adrienne was wearing a simple but glamorous black dress, something she'd never seen her wear before, with black hose and heels, not the casual boots she used to favor. She actually heard the faint sound of her heels clicking on the marble tiles before she entered. Adrienne's slight smile was intimate, familiar. "This is fine." She took the glass, briefly touching Robin's fingertips, watching her with obvious curiosity. "You look so different now. It's not your face. Maybe the clothes."

Robin self-consciously pulled at her blouse. She'd removed her scarf and the blazer of her pantsuit, feeling they were too formal now.

"Please, no small talk. Why are you doing this?" Robin was intense, her eyes like steel.

Adrienne searched her face as though she was trying to solve a mystery. "You're a liar."

"You mastered the art of hypocrisy quite well yourself." Robin swirled the wine in her glass, careful to avoid Adrienne's eyes, now glistening in the dim light. She looked almost delicious.

"I was different back then," Adrienne said.

"So was I." Robin came closer. "You should know, Adrienne, I won't allow anyone to destroy my career."

"Should I be worried about getting out of here alive?"

"This is not a joke."

Adrienne looked oddly at her. "So it's true. Politicians *are* scary." She walked over to a window and peeled back part of a curtain to reveal the black, starless night. "What the hell happened to you anyway?"

"*Me!*" The governor was off the hinges now. "You were the one who…" For just a moment she felt a splinter of the pain she'd suffered over this woman. But she clenched her jaw and made a dismissive gesture, as if nothing that had happened between them was worth talking about.

Adrienne set down her drink. "I've changed, Robin."

Hearing her say her name again…she felt her all over again—her laugh, her soft skin, her irreverence—and she suffered all over again—in a single instant. She felt a perverse pleasure in the pain of it all. Maybe it reminded her she was still alive. But a desperate voice inside reminded her of her faltering campaign, not to mention the damage this would eventually do to her family.

"How exactly did this leak occur?" Robin asked.

"It was a casual conversation in a bar," Adrienne replied. *Just as Robin had suspected.* "This guy asked if I knew you, and I said, 'oh yeah,' and winked. I might've added a few other words. Like 'in the Biblical sense.'"

Robin closed her eyes. "Oh, Adrienne." If she'd been anyone else, Robin would have been tempted to throw her through the window.

"It was an accident," Adrienne said.

"How did they get that photo?" Robin asked.

"I honestly don't know." She seemed sincere. "They wanted me to go on all these shows, but I wouldn't. Not until I talked to you first."

"How admirable," Robin said sarcastically. "What do you want from me? Money?"

Adrienne seemed offended. "I don't need your money."

"Don't you? I hear you're playing in a band, no recording contract…awfully risky for someone your age, don't you think?"

Adrienne let out a bitter chuckle. "I'd almost forgotten that self-righteous bitch tone you get."

"Let's be honest." Robin set down her drink. "This scandal certainly gave your little group some publicity, am I right?"

Adrienne stepped closer. "Get one thing straight. I never meant for this to be public. But now that it is, let's get real. The first time I saw you on a morning show, talking about unnatural unions, I spit out my coffee. What the hell was that?"

"I don't owe you an explanation."

"Yeah, you do," Adrienne snapped. "I'm gay, and you're an affront to all gay people."

"So you're calling yourself a lesbian now?" Robin raised an eyebrow. "Well, I guess you *have* changed."

"Fuck you. The little Southern belle routine is getting really old and boring."

"Don't presume to know me. It's been over twenty years."

"Twenty-seven years and four months." Adrienne traced her glass with her fingertip. "I still remember how you taste."

Robin tried to maintain her composure. "I don't agree with that lifestyle."

"Bullshit. You *were* that lifestyle. You wanted it, and you got it."

"Stop it! Just stop it!"

Was Adrienne playing with her? Trying to get a rise out of her?

Peter barged in when he heard Robin's raised voice, but mostly because he was nosy. "Everything okay?"

Adrienne turned to view him, an eyebrow arched. "Who's this?"

"Peter, please, give us a minute."

"Okay." He eyed Adrienne; it was obvious he was threatened by her in more ways than one. He kept watching her as he backed out of the room.

Robin exhaled deeply. "How can you visit me twenty-seven years later and think you know anything about who I am? You know how much a person can change in that time?" Even as she asked the question, Robin knew that she herself still imagined Adrienne as a snapshot frozen in time, never changing, always the party girl she used to know. She had no idea what Adrienne had gone through in the years between.

"Of course I know," Adrienne said easily. "Look at me. I used to think I had to make out with a whole football team to be comfortable with who I am." Unlike the governor's minions, Adrienne held her ground and unnerved Robin with her strong sense of self.

After all these years, Robin Sanders was nothing but a well-rehearsed paper doll. And Adrienne was the only other person besides her who seemed to know it.

"What do you want from me?" Robin asked quietly.

"I want you to admit it. That something happened between us."

She wanted validation? *How ironic.* The tables had turned. Robin took a deep breath. "Yes, something did happen between us." Her eyes filled. Just saying the words aloud unleashed an unexpected flood. "Just remember who broke whose heart!" She tried to catch her breath. "You hurt *me!*" She grabbed her pearl necklace to collect herself.

Adrienne pulled her cell phone from her purse and touched the screen. "That's all I needed." The phone had been clipped to the outside of the small black purse, so inconspicuous, Robin hadn't noticed it.

A sickening sensation overtook Robin as she realized it wasn't validation Adrienne was looking for, but a confession. Tom was right. All she had wanted was to bring her down.

"Adrienne!"

It was on video now, potential fodder for YouTube or the highest bidder.

Her former roommate turned on her heel and started for the door.

Robin had been a fool for this woman once, and now, her weakness for her was about to cost her everything she'd worked so hard for.

CHAPTER TWENTY-FOUR

"Yes, yes. I like it fine." I nodded on the phone with my father, even though he couldn't see me.

"How is that political theory course coming along?" he asked.

"Fine." The truth was, I was really bored talking about Aristotle, conservatism and foreign policy. But some of the students in my classes were very passionate, and I could see them as young replicas of current senators. Their next stop out of college would be Capitol Hill for sure. In many ways I didn't feel like I fit in with that crowd at all.

"I hope you're giving it your full attention, not gettin' distracted by anything silly." Of course he meant that my political science major was more important than my other classes.

"No, but I did take some electives. You said I was allowed to do that."

He groaned. "Your mother told me." He wasn't pleased.

"There's just one," I lied.

"Your other classes come first, you hear?"

"Of course."

"What's your favorite class?"

"My favorite? Um, I'd say the role of media in politics. That's a good one." It wasn't a complete lie. I could easily see how important the media was in shaping social attitudes. It seemed the ones who could master the media could practically rule the world. That kind of power, of course, was intriguing to me.

"Sounds good." Dad was pleased to see me following in his footsteps, or so he thought. He'd been trying to groom me for the role for years, dreaming that I'd one day go farther than he did. But Mom had to keep reminding him that it was *my* life, not his. "Your mother is sending you a care package. Just a few things, some packs of your favorite tea…I don't know what else. June, quit talkin' to me when I'm on the phone! I can't have two conversations at once! Robin, you'll just have to check your mail. I don't remember what all she put in it."

"That's fine, Daddy."

My parents were still snipping at each other when I hung up. When I turned around, Adrienne was watching from her desk. "He doesn't know you're majoring in film, does he?"

"No, and he doesn't need to." I went about my nightly routine, which began with a series of facial moisturizers. Apparently my skin was as tight as my nerves lately. I wouldn't look at Adrienne, who was wearing her favorite nightshirt, a faded cotton Seminole football T-shirt with gold stripes on the sleeves. It clung to her breasts just enough to make me blush whenever I looked at her.

A slow smile broke across her face. "I like that you lied to him. It means you're like, you know, normal." She laughed. "It seems like something he's gonna find out eventually, though, don't you think?"

"Maybe by then I can change his mind." I stared in the distance, worry creeping over my face. I'd had this conversation with myself many times. But obviously, I hadn't thought it through very well, not like my usually planning self.

"Will he be pissed about it?" she asked.

"I don't know!" I finally looked at her and tried to avert my eyes away from her shirt. "What are you anyway, the morality police?"

"I'm not that much of a hypocrite." Adrienne put on her reading glasses and resumed writing a paper. I assumed it was homework, though I rarely saw her do it.

"I don't want to talk about it," I said quietly.

Adrienne held up her hand. "I got it."

I kept watching her as she wrote. "You think it's bad?" I asked.

She removed her glasses and faced me with a slight smile. "No," she said softly. "I don't think it's bad at all. It's important to have dreams."

"You sound like you know."

She lowered her eyes. "There are some…interests I have."

"Oh God," I said. "You want to sell drugs."

"No, dummy!" She threw her pen at me. After a pause, she said, "I never wanted to be one of those conventional girls, the ones who find their husband and get the house with the pool. Or the ones who work nine to five for some jackass who never appreciates what they do. Then they retire after they're really old and wonder what it was all for."

"You've really given some thought to this." My smile was one of amusement, though I wished it wasn't. I liked hearing her thoughts, and I didn't want her to feel shy or that I was laughing at her.

"Yeah, well." She started to turn back around again.

"I think it's great that you don't want a traditional job," I said.

She looked at me, and for a split second, she seemed like a young girl searching for approval. "You do?"

"Yes, I do."

We smiled at each other. I think we recognized that in a very real way, we were alike. There was a rebel lurking inside both of us.

CHAPTER TWENTY-FIVE

The next night, Adrienne slipped a tape in the VCR. She seemed giddy, as if she couldn't wait to show me. "Sean let me borrow it."

"Let me guess. More heavy metal videos?" My head was buried in a textbook.

"Not hardly."

When I glanced at the screen, there was a naked woman lying on her back on a white mattress. Her legs were spread wide open, leaving nothing to the imagination. Her hand rubbed and swirled between her thighs, as her hips thrust up and down.

I gasped. I couldn't look away, so I watched with my mouth hanging open in disbelief. I'd never seen anything like this on a TV screen before.

The woman on the tape seemed to be aching with pleasure and really enjoying being watched. Her hand started rubbing faster and faster, her fingers caressing herself, then a finger or two slipped inside…

I could hear Adrienne's breath catch in her throat. "Whoa," she finally sighed.

I don't think I breathed for several seconds. Then the screen went black.

"What was *that*?" I resumed breathing again.

"Porn." Adrienne jokingly pulled the neckline of her shirt back and forth, as if in need of some air. "Is it stuffy in here?" She laughed.

"And you wanted to watch it?" I was still in shock.

"Don't start. Sometimes porn is hot. Usually Sean's videos have couples fucking."

"That's what you do at his apartment? Watch porn?"

"Sometimes." Adrienne wanted to see my reaction. But I gave nothing away. "You don't like it, I know."

"I didn't say that." I surprised myself, and maybe Adrienne too. I went back to my textbook, but there was no way I could care about the political structure of China right now. I could tell that Adrienne was intrigued by my comment, but she said nothing more.

That night as we lay in bed, I remembered my past school crushes. I'd never thought of them in a sexual way—I was drawn to a pretty face, wanting to stare a little longer than I should, I guess. But that was all. I'd never thought of the other puzzle piece, and tonight I had been strangely aroused by watching a stranger pleasure herself. I didn't believe I could get excited by anyone I didn't already know, let alone a faceless woman on a screen. Try as I might, I couldn't even recall the woman's face!

Was I no better than a sexist guy, appreciating women only for their bodies? This thought disturbed me. No, I answered to myself. I deeply admired several women in politics and world leaders who fought against injustice. *There. My feminism was restored.* Able to relax again, I tried to close my eyes and go to sleep. But the conflict churning inside wouldn't go away.

My religion, my inner self and now even my inner feminist all seemed at odds with this emerging awareness. They were now arguing and exploding inside my head like an episode of *Meet the Press*.

Nighttime was the worst. Just knowing that Adrienne was there, so uncomfortably, dangerously near…

In the darkness, I thought I heard her bed sheet rustling. I looked over at her bed, which was illuminated by a sliver of moonlight. Though her eyes were closed, she seemed to be moving her hand under the covers.

I wasn't going to get any sleep tonight. Again.

CHAPTER TWENTY-SIX

Robin was desperate. "What do you want?"

Adrienne hesitated by the door. "Change your stance on gay rights."

"You know I can't do that. That's why people have voted for me."

"They voted for a lie." Adrienne turned around. Her face was determined, even more mysterious in the floating shadows from the firelight.

Robin momentarily lost her bearings. Then she gazed directly into the eyes of *her*, forever her rival, her undoing. She couldn't help but notice the glow from the fire upon her, accentuating the features of her face. "You never did have any scruples."

"You're going to do it because this…" She held up her phone. "This shows you to be a liar and a homo. I'm not sure which is worse to you."

"You really are a ghastly woman!"

"Ghastly!" Adrienne mocked. It was as if they were in the doughnut shop all over again. "Where are we, Victorian England?"

Robin gripped the edge of her desk for support. "You want money?"

"I told you what I want."

"I can't and I won't."

"You can and you will."

"This is blackmail, Adrienne."

She smiled broadly. "I prefer to think of it as forceful persuasion." She started toward the door again. "Anyone lays a hand on me, I'll file charges." She stopped right before opening it. "If you don't do this for me, you'll find out what a real scandal is."

"I'd sooner drop out of the race…"

"Do what you have to do." With that, Adrienne left.

Robin was paralyzed, listening to the click of the door closing and the distant echo of Adrienne's heels all the way out the front door.

Peter popped his head in. "Everything okay?"

Robin nodded. But it wasn't okay at all. Nothing would be okay again from this point on.

* * *

So Adrienne wanted to destroy her. Robin stood frozen under the archway, a swarm of staff members flanking her on all sides. There was Jeannette Fishburn, a veteran speechwriter, and, of course, Lara Denning, who waved the others away. "She needs her space, everybody. Go home! Get some sleep!"

Peter gave her the look of death; Lara was treading on his territory. "That's right," he said, clearing his throat. "Everyone out!"

But Jeannette wouldn't be deterred. She blocked Robin's way with notepad fresh in hand. "Governor, you'll need to make some kind of statement about your meeting with Ms. Austen."

"That's an understatement." Lara was usually annoyed with Jeannette.

Though she could write first-rate speeches, Jeannette was, to someone like Lara, too mousy and forgettable to work in politics. But even though Jeannette blended into the background much of the time, Robin knew she was someone not to underestimate. In fact, Robin was very good at trusting her intuition about people—except where Adrienne was concerned.

Robin's eyebrows raised. "Why would anyone know about our meeting?" She glared at her seventh advisor. Maybe it was time to contemplate hiring the eighth one.

"I'm sorry, Governor," Peter said softly. "There was a guy from the *Journal-Constitution* hiding in the bushes. He totally fooled security."

Robin groaned and tore across the room, toward the stairs. "Is it too much to ask for everyone to do their jobs around here?" Her voice had a tinge of hysteria, the kind of sound that suggested she was coming unglued. She climbed a few more steps, then rested against the banister. She didn't feel well and she knew she didn't look it either.

Unfortunately, Jeannette had no sense of good or bad timing. "Governor Sanders, please. We need a statement we can release to the press, or more questions will come up. Surely I don't have to tell you we don't need the distract—"

"You want a statement?" Robin thundered. "I'll give you a statement! I'm giving a press conference tomorrow!" She stormed up the stairs, leaving her staff to bicker amongst themselves.

Before she could reach the top of the stairs, Robin could hear Peter responding to something that Lara had said: "That may not be wise with the state of mind she's in."

She reached the top floor and started making her way down the long hall. Feeling dizzy, she kept moving forward, the demise of her campaign, her career flashing in front of her eyes. It was always Adrienne, her weakness, her blind spot. Did everyone have someone in their life like that?

Robin chastised herself for her lack of judgment. Once again, she had been so entranced by Adrienne, so distracted and thrilled at the idea of seeing her again, so busy noting every detail of her face, her clothes, trying to imagine what her life had been like for the past twenty-seven years, that she had lost control. Once again Adrienne had gotten the best of her. There was nothing she could do now.

Fleeting thoughts swirled in and out of her head. *Why didn't the security detail check Adrienne for recording devices?* If only she'd stayed in control like she did with everyone else, she'd have been able to zero in on exactly what Adrienne's intentions were after all these years. *Why had Adrienne remembered exactly how long it had been, down to the month?* If she had stayed focused, she could have owned the situation. Where Adrienne was concerned, though, she always seemed to lose herself. And this time, it would lead to her downfall. She was sure of it.

Kendrick's bedroom door was ajar. Usually she kept it closed at night. Even though Robin knew it was sometime after midnight, she crept toward the door to check on her.

As she pushed the door open, she was surprised to see Kendrick, still wearing her brown hoodie from school, sitting up in bed, listening to music with her headphones.

"Ken, honey, you should be in bed." Robin came inside.

Kendrick was momentarily startled, then slowly took her headphones off. "Technically, I am."

Robin smiled tiredly. "Okay, smarty-pants."

"I couldn't sleep," Kendrick said quietly.

Something was wrong. Robin sat on the edge of her bed. "I'd ask you if it was about me, but you always say it isn't."

"You remember Christy, from math club?"

"Yes. She's the only friend you mention by name."

"She's my best friend," Kendrick said. "*Was* my best friend." She stared down and pulled at a string on her bedspread.

"Uh-oh. What happened?"

Kendrick shrugged like it didn't matter. But her face was shrouded in despair. "Stupid shit. Everyone at school is sayin' stupid things."

"What kinds of things?"

Kendrick couldn't look her in the eye. "They're sayin' that my mom's a lesbo, so I probably like girls too. Christy doesn't believe it, but when we hung out together it was just...weird. I guess her mom doesn't want her hanging out with me anymore."

"I'm so sorry." Robin reached for her and wrapped her arms as tightly as she could around her daughter. "This will blow over. I promise." But she knew she was making a promise that it wasn't going to be possible to pull off for a while. She privately cursed Adrienne.

* * *

"Everything go okay?"

Tom rolled toward her the moment she climbed into bed. "How did it go?"

"About as I expected," Robin said. She looked at the clock. Why did he have to be awake at one in the morning? He always fell dead asleep at ten. Why was he in the mood to talk now? Why couldn't she have some peace and quiet, to suffer in silence like a normal person?

"What did you expect?" he asked.

"I needed to face her—to prove to everyone I won't back down from my enemies." It sounded good, no matter how absurd at this moment. She stared up at the ceiling, remembering Adrienne and the loud music she'd always associated with her. The music rang in her head that night. The anger and violence of it... She wanted to listen to it right now.

"What's next?" he asked.

"I don't know, Tom. I really don't know."

CHAPTER TWENTY-SEVEN

"What do you think of Sean?" Adrienne asked me.

I'd been reading about subtext in film. The book said that the best film scenes featured dialogue spoken by people who aren't saying what they really mean. "He's nice," I replied.

"He wants me to go away with him for the weekend."

"Really." I looked up from my book.

"Yeah. We're going to Destin."

"Yeah?"

"It's a pretty beach. Really white sand."

"Sounds great," I said, thinking about all the things left unspoken, at least by me.

"Yeah, but it's a major drive, so we'll have to cut class Monday."

"Oh, like you haven't done that before," I teased.

"Yeah." The way she stared off into space, I wondered if she really wanted to go. "They say the beach there has some of the whitest sand in the world."

"You're a Florida girl," I said. "Haven't you seen all the nearby beaches?"

"My hometown is in *central* Florida. I've seen a lot of swamps."

I smiled at her and nodded. She'd been pretty mysterious about where she lived. I'd decided I wouldn't ask too many questions and wait for her to tell me whatever she wanted to.

I watched as she pulled her suitcase from the closet. I'd be grateful for a long weekend away from her. I'd have the room all to myself, and I'd spend the whole time trying to figure out whether I was gay or straight.

* * *

The first day she was away, I had long debates with myself that never reached a verdict. I pored over Adrienne's back issues of *Playgirl* magazine, which she'd stuffed under her bed, and I stared at the centerfolds, particularly those rubbery appendages, which I'd only ever seen before on Greek statues in a museum. I stared and stared until they didn't make me jump anymore. It was no use. My feelings were nagging at me, only getting stronger. Eventually I found myself pulling Adrienne's leather jacket off the hook on the back of the door and holding it to my face, inhaling the soft scent of her. *What was happening to me?* I quickly hung the jacket back up, praying she would never have it dusted for fingerprints.

On Sunday afternoon, I took a long walk around campus. I resolved that I was, in fact, straight and just hadn't met any guy who was as exciting as Adrienne. As images of girls I used to know in high school zoomed into my mind, I batted each one away—the girl with a dazzling smile and long black hair and how my heart had fluttered whenever she walked past my locker, the beautiful basketball player who asked if she could borrow my pen and I suddenly forgot how to speak. Could it be I went to school with exceptionally gorgeous girls? Maybe everyone else noticed them too.

I still felt unsettled. Each beautiful, but troubling memory, locked away in the secret vault in my mind, my own private Pandora's box, was floating out now. The contents weren't supposed to be revealed under any circumstances or only after I was dead. I was the daughter of a prominent politician, and my every move was considered a reflection on my family. For that reason alone, I had no choice but to ignore this wild attraction to someone of the wrong gender.

Maybe I was bisexual. That would be better. Then I could keep up a noncontroversial public life and no one would have to know about this other side of me. It was perfect.

Of course, there was one little problem. Boys. They were good friends, and I liked how they said what they meant. I understood them. But the kind of thoughts I was having…they weren't thoughts I ever had for boys. Whenever I'd kissed a boy in school, it was no different than kissing tree bark. Well, I imagined it was no different. I'd never actually kissed a tree. But I knew that back in my neighborhood in Atlanta, I'd get in less trouble for kissing a tree than for kissing another girl. Memories of Marc's wet, sloshing tongue still gave me shivers. And not in a good way. I'd have to learn to think of something else whenever I did it. Kissing was overrated anyway. I'd made my plans. I was going to have a husband, dammit. If I was lucky, maybe I wouldn't have to kiss him too much.

By Sunday night, my decision was made. I'd live a straight life, and all this terror would go away. I felt better already, just like Jan on *The Brady Bunch* when she decided her black wig was a perfect fit. I sat up in bed, studying, beneath the watchful eye of Bette Davis, who, by the way, wasn't buying any of it.

On Monday, I sat through biology class with my mind everywhere but in the room.

"Cellular mitosis…" I pictured Adrienne the day I called to her outside. Just the way she turned and smiled at the sight of me, with her long, sandy-streaked hair and dark eyes flashing like the devil's. I sometimes wondered if I wasn't the William Hurt character in *Body Heat* and Adrienne was Matty Walker, alluring and cunning, inviting me in only to lure me to my destruction. Because even when she smiled, something always felt a little dangerous about her.

"Chromosomes cannot be clearly spotted in the nucleus…" Adrienne had a smile I could dive into and stay in forever. "Next we have prophase and prometaphase…" And the way her lips pointed at the corners. If I could trace those lips with my fingers…

I struggled to win my inner battle. But as everyone gathered their books, I knew deep down I was losing. I wandered listlessly around campus, taking brief note of the clumps of palm trees with concrete cut around them. I wondered about the boy-girl couples I passed, how certain they seemed to be about each other.

Surely there was a boy I hadn't met yet who could give me some of these feelings. It was a big world, after all. Maybe he was out there. I had to believe… That was it. I decided. By the time I reached the room, there was no way I was a lesbian. The verdict was in. I slammed down the gavel. Case closed. I pulled out my *Bible* and read it frantically before I could change my mind.

That evening, I styled my hair and put on my finest silk nightgown, a straight girl who was casually awaiting her roommate's return. When I wasn't checking my appearance in the mirror, I sat upright against my pillow, pretending to read. Waiting. Just waiting. The minutes stretched out like years. *Where was she anyway?*

Finally, long after ten, a key clicked in the door. Adrienne burst in, freshly tanned, with a beaming smile and those dark eyes. "Hey!" she exclaimed with outstretched arms. She sat at the edge of my bed and wrapped her arms around me.

I was surprised by the nearness of her, realizing we'd never hugged before. As with most things, I tried to reason through this. Adrienne had been gone on a long trip, so a hello hug seemed acceptable. Her arms were so warm and silky in her sleeveless white T-shirt, which clung tightly to her.

The jury was sent out to deliberate on my straightness again. I nestled against Adrienne's soft neck and held my breath. It was a hug that would take center stage in my mind for many days after, though it lasted barely a second or two.

"Wait." She released me and proceeded to dig through her bag. She pulled out a small bottle filled with what looked like sugar. "For you," she said, handing it to me.

"What is it?"

"Sand, silly. Since you couldn't be there, I wanted you to see how white it is."

"Thanks." She'd thought of me when she was away. Knowing that while she was with Sean, she thought about *me*...that meant everything. That was the most special little plastic bottle of sand in the whole world. I held the bottle reverently. "I'll treasure it," I said softly. The words came out without thought. This night was perfect.

"Guess what?" she said excitedly. "We did it." Now not-so-perfect.

"What?" A lump formed in my throat. I suddenly felt so vulnerable sitting there in my thin nightgown.

"Yeah. We did it, and it was so great!" She looked at me with such high expectations, so I had no choice but to construct a smile to survive the moment.

"That's great!" I exclaimed forcefully. My stomach was in knots. I wanted to die.

"I think he's the one," she added, squeezing my hands.

The lump in my throat began to grow. "Oh, Adrienne. Well, take a little time to get to know each other."

"Oh, yeah. Sure." She jumped up and began unpacking. I stared at the bottle of sand in my hand, watching the granules glitter as I turned it in the light. Then I set it on my nightstand, giving it a place of honor next to a picture of my family. I heard Adrienne's next words with the attention span of a dog: "Blah, blah, someone's throwing a party, blah, blah, Sean wants me to go…blah, blah…you should come, blah, blah…"

No, I thought. I preferred to stay by myself and wallow in self-indulgent misery and drama. If I couldn't spend time with her alone, it felt good to be miserable just thinking about her. That had to be a line from a song…

Moments later, she clicked on "Headbangers Ball" and my least favorite videos came on. I couldn't hide my disgust. I wasn't aware that I was actually sneering at the TV.

"What's your problem?" she exclaimed.

"Nothing. I just hate these."

"You really do get all worked up over nothing."

"It isn't nothing!" I shouted. "Forget it." *Empty-headed party girl. That's all she'll ever be.*

I clicked off my light and pretended to be going to sleep, which of course, was impossible. When I closed my eyes, I saw Sean Voight doing unspeakable things to her. What was it about him? His face wasn't exactly repulsive, although I didn't think he was as cute as Marc back home. Frankly, Sean was boring. He never said more than two words at a time. He never changed his blank expression. He didn't look as though a single thought was rolling around in his brain. And the patches of facial hair…they were the final straw. What about him did Adrienne find so attractive, enough to *sleep* with him? I couldn't bear to imagine it. What he must have done to her, how he must have touched her…I couldn't go there. Some things had to stay off-limits in my mind.

CHAPTER TWENTY-EIGHT

The betrayal was too much to bear. Robin sat in the kitchen, sipping strong coffee with a definite flavor of mud and waited for the sun to rise. As she pondered her options, the hanging clock that had been in her family since the Civil War ticked back and forth, almost like her heartbeat. She didn't dare go on TV and suddenly announce she was for gay rights. She'd simply have to withdraw from the race. There was no other choice. By now she was too tired to cry or even feel anger. Her face was frozen in a bitter half-smile; the master planner had not seen this coming.

She glanced again at the clock. Almost five in the morning. Robin had been ignoring her phone messages, but she knew that Lara would be coming over as soon as possible.

"Can I get you breakfast?" Marla, the housekeeper, with whom Robin had a love-hate relationship, was obviously surprised to see her in the kitchen at this hour.

"No thank you." Robin's eyes, even her smile, were kinder than usual. When the housekeeper left, Robin took another long, slow sip and returned to the dark bottomless pit of her thoughts.

One question dogged her: Whom should she tell her supporters to vote for now? Two of the other contenders for the Republican nomination, now third and fourth place in the polls, had been interviewed for their thoughts on the scandal. Their words played over in Robin's head. First was Myron Welles, always dressed in gray and believed to be too wealthy to reach regular people.

"Well, I think the whole thing is just deplorable," he'd said in his Mississippi drawl. "Here she is, parading around with this woman while talkin' about the evils of homosexuality. That's hypocrisy at the highest level. I've been married to my wife for thirty-four years. Heck, I'll even bring my weddin' album to the debate!" He'd chuckled as he straightened his gray tie.

She couldn't stand him. Her stomach was sick at the thought of him taking the lead.

Next was Jerry Johnson, the former coach and state senator from Alabama, also originally from Georgia. He had only served one term. So instead of calling attention to his inexperience compared to the other candidates, he presented himself as the good ole boy you could go shoot a deer with. He was hoping to be a last-minute surprise front-runner in the wake of this mess.

"I don't see how you can enforce the laws you wanna make if you're already breakin' 'em." He'd laughed in his high-pitched voice as microphones were shoved in his face. He was reputed to have arranged for his football players to get lighter sentences when they were accused of sexual assaults just so they wouldn't miss any championship games.

Definitely not Jerry Johnson.

Then, of course, there was the man in second place, Graham Goodwin. He'd been closing in on her numbers since the beginning of the race. He represented everything she disliked. A former pastor, Goodwin liked to quote the *Bible* whenever it suited one of his opinions. He'd talk about compassion, then go on to suggest that poor people were poor because deep down they really wanted to be poor. He'd talk about honoring the nation's veterans, then say that programs designed to help them with PTSD and other issues were part of the "fat" that needed to be trimmed from the budget.

Robin rubbed her face and groaned. She despised them all. Maybe the incumbent Democrat Mark Ellis should be reelected. What if she endorsed him… She wondered how controversial that would be, whether it would help his chances or hurt them. If she was going to back out of the race at this late date, she might as well go out with a bang. This was the lowest point she'd ever reached. All that work… only to have it end like this. She was still in mild shock, unable to fully process all that was happening.

Lara Denning barged into the kitchen just as Robin realized it was now five thirty.

"I came to see if you've come to your senses," Lara said.

Robin looked down, stroking her empty coffee mug.

"I've set up a press conference for ten—even though I don't even know what it's about," she continued, pulling back a chair for herself. "You think you might want to share that with me?"

"No," Robin said.

"What? Wha...what?"

"No."

Lara stared into the steely blue eyes across the table and sat back in her chair. She looked at Robin as if she thought she'd completely lost her mind and she wasn't sure whether to yell at her or get a butterfly net.

She lowered her voice. "What exactly happened last night?"

"Nothing to concern you," Robin replied. "I'll take care of the press conference."

"But Jeannette needs to know what to say—"

"You've all done an excellent job." Robin was too calm; it probably frightened Lara.

"We've *done* an excellent job? What does that mean?" Lara reached for her hand. "You're not dying?"

Robin smiled. "No, although..." She gazed off to a distant place. "No." She felt hollow, like there was only a shell of herself sitting there.

"Come on, this is bullshit! I can't work for someone who keeps things from me!"

"You won't have to worry about it." Robin said as much as she could without saying it.

When Lara left that morning, she had no better idea what was going on; Robin saw to that. This wasn't the kind of thing she knew how to tell those closest to her. It would be shocking to hear it first at a press conference. But that was the only way to keep them from trying to talk her out of it. She wouldn't be able to tell them why she was doing what she was no matter how hard they pressed. She would take her secret to the grave.

CHAPTER TWENTY-NINE

Garnet and gold uniforms moved the ball down the field to the cheers of everyone in the stands. Carol and I stood and screamed at the top of our lungs. "C'mon! You son-of-a-bitch!" I yelled.

"Listen to you!" Carol shouted back. "That's my line."

"I was going with the moment."

"Oh, fumble."

"No," I argued. "That was an interception." We sat down with the rest of the disgusted crowd.

This was the most important game of the season, against our biggest rivals, the Florida Gators. Whenever they were in town, the whole Seminole world was on high alert. Sometimes the excitement could get out of hand. It could even be dangerous, depending on what colors someone was wearing. I knew of the rivalry, but it was quite another thing to experience it firsthand amidst the out-of-control fans on both sides. I myself got swept up in the highly charged atmosphere. In the stadium parking lot, we pointed and hissed at every bright blue and orange bumper sticker we saw. It gave me a good excuse to unleash some of my frustration and, who are we kidding, my rage.

Watching the game, I was relieved that Dad was too busy with his work in the state legislature to come down. Usually, he hated to miss a homecoming game. Lucky for me, he couldn't manage it this year. I imagined my parents meeting Adrienne, wondering what they would have thought of her or what she would have thought of them.

Back in reality, I noticed everyone around me still grumbling about the last call.

"It *was* an interception," I insisted.

"Whatever," Carol said. "Who the fuck cares?"

"Well, it seems like you do now."

She smiled sheepishly. "Well, how could you not? Look at his tight little pants. I'm not proud, you know." She held her hands up like she was squeezing someone's butt. "I just wanna squeeze 'em, you know?"

She was referring to her on-again, off-again relationship with one of the tight ends. Of course, the irony of the position he played wasn't lost on me.

"Yep, your tight end has a very tight end," I joked. "And you're turning into a major slut." Chomping on popcorn, I looked around the stadium distractedly.

"With any luck. Aw, he waved at me."

"He has something in his eye."

"No, he doesn't." Carol glared at me. Then she added, "Trust me, I wish I didn't like him. He can be a total asshole. But face it, as women we're screwed. You can't deny biology."

Just then, I saw Adrienne and Sean walking hand in hand down the bleachers to their seats. "That's my roommate," I said.

"Wow," Carol exclaimed. "She's a hottie. Lotta hair."

I smiled to myself. I hoped Carol wouldn't see. "Yeah. She spends hours on it."

Carol eyed my popcorn greedily. "You gonna eat all that?"

I was distracted by the vision of Adrienne laughing at something Sean said, so I absentmindedly handed the bag to Carol. I watched Adrienne push her hair back behind her left ear, the one that had a hoop pierced through the top. I'd never seen an ear piercing that wasn't in an earlobe. There was something sexy about that top piercing, and the way she smoothed her hair behind her ear, exposing it. I felt a shove. "What?"

"I said it needs more salt!" Carol screamed over the crowd.

"Sorry!" What did she want me to do? It's not like I kept salt packs in my purse. That was my mother. Now I was annoyed that Carol jerked me out of my thoughts.

"I'm just sayin'!"

* * *

That evening, I returned to the room to find Adrienne sitting up in bed, reading a paperback. I rarely ever found her with a textbook. "Hi," I said.

"Hey." She flipped a page.

"Did you have fun at the game?" I asked.

"Yeah. I thought I saw you."

"I thought I saw you too." I set down my backpack.

"Who was that girl you were with?" Adrienne's question surprised me. Was she jealous?

"Carol," I answered casually. "She's in film."

"Oh."

I reached for a bottle of soda out of the miniature fridge. When I stood up, I caught a glimpse of Adrienne taking a pill and throwing it back with water. "Hung over?" I asked.

"No. Birth control."

My heart sank. "I didn't know you took that."

"Only about a month now. Don't tell anyone."

"It's none of my business." I looked away, feeling like a fool. The only saving grace was the fact that no one but me knew exactly how big a fool I was. It was a secret I'd take to the grave.

"Oh my God," Adrienne said. "You won't believe what he did!"

I purposely checked my watch. "Oh no! I'm late!" I exclaimed. "I'm sorry. I promised Carol I'd study with her." I grabbed my bag and almost made it safely out of the room.

Adrienne held my arm. "I was hopin' you could party with us tonight."

"I promised Carol," I repeated. The more I said it, the more it sounded true. "I really have to go."

But Adrienne wouldn't let go. "Wait, please." Her plea seemed so earnest, I stopped. "What is it?" she asked.

"What's what?" I had to give an Oscar-winning performance now.

"You don't like my friends."

"I never said that."

"You don't have to." The hurt in her eyes, the tone in her voice, was clear. "You can't possibly have that much to study."

"You'd be amazed. Of course I know the concept of studying isn't something you're familiar with." The haughty snob took over whenever I was threatened or embarrassed.

"Fuck you!"

"I'm sorry. I didn't mean that."

"C'mon!" she thundered. "Level with me. I can tell you don't like Nancy. And I *know* you don't like Becky."

I released my backpack. "You want the truth?"

Adrienne nodded.

"Really?" I repeated.

"Yeah."

"They act really stupid when they're around guys. I hate that."

"You're so arrogant."

I flipped my hair and thrust my chin into the air. "Maybe I am. I don't care. But I think girls have to show they're just as smart and strong as guys, or we'll never be taken seriously."

"You're such a *feminist.*" The word slithered off her tongue like a snake.

"Have you ever looked up that word in the dictionary?" I asked in a most condescending tone. "It means someone who advocates equal rights for women. What's wrong with that?"

"They want everyone to think like they do."

"You know, I don't give a shit what you think." My own words shocked me, and probably Adrienne, but they felt good. I decided to start saying "shit" a little more often. "I've seen corncobs back home with more sense than you."

"You wanna be an uptight bitch your whole life?"

"If you're the alternative!" I grabbed my backpack again and slammed the door behind me. I rushed down the hall, but I couldn't outrun my tears.

CHAPTER THIRTY

Rachmaninoff crackled on the turntable. The aroma of brewing hazelnut coffee floated in the air. Carol's dorm room was a lot messier, but I could breathe here. I watched the needle bounce up and down on black vinyl. "I haven't seen one of these in years," I sighed. But my casual chitchat was eclipsed by the sadness in my eyes. And Carol saw it. Of course she would; she was highly perceptive, like some advanced life form—a life form whose fuzzy brown hair kept sticking inside her glasses, but advanced nonetheless.

"You gotta really dig to find 'em now," Carol replied, trying to straighten up papers to no avail.

I stood in the middle of clutter—piles of *Newsweek*, papers, junk food wrappers. Rows of candles were lit under the window like in a church. And on every wall were posters of classic films—*Dial "M" for Murder, Gone with the Wind, Casablanca, The Searchers*. I looked up, trying to take it all in.

"Want some coffee?" Carol asked.

"Sure. Where's your roommate?"

"She's usually sleepin' over at her boyfriend's. It works out, 'cause I'd rather live alone."

"What about Mr. Tight End?"

"Uh…" Carol hesitated. "We had a little difference of opinion."

"Again?"

"He's always too aggressive after a game," Carol explained. "He can't admit that I'm right about everything, and he's always wrong." She smiled, seemingly undaunted by their rocky romance.

"Well," I said. "You're lucky your roommate's never around."

"You don't like your roommate?"

"I wouldn't put it quite that way." I squinted at the neon raspberry rug. "She thinks I'm uptight."

Carol poured the steaming coffee into a cup. "Yeah, well, she's got too much hair. Stereotypes are for lazy people."

"Yeah, she's lazy. God, she pisses me off."

"Look," Carol said, handing me the mug. "Most people don't get along with their roommates. It'll be okay. You can come over anytime you want."

"It's not that. Oh, God. Carol, I really need to talk to someone about something."

"Huh?"

I started to pace across the raspberry rug, tightening my sweaty palms into fists and breathing rapidly like I was about to give birth. "I really hope it's okay to tell you this. But if I don't tell someone, I'm going to explode."

Carol eyed me suspiciously and lit up a cigarette. "You can tell me anything."

I watched the smoke float in front of my face. "Won't you get in trouble for that?"

"Oh, please." She waved the smoke away. "Tell me."

"Okay. My roommate—"

"Is a bitch."

"Sort of, but not really. Actually, that would make it easier. I don't know. It's me." I threw my head into my hands and collapsed onto one of the beds.

"What's you? Speak English."

"I'm scared."

"What, she's stashing weapons?"

I laughed nervously, crouched over into the letter "C," holding my torso. "No. I'm scared of how I feel."

First, Carol looked confused. Then a slow smile broke out across her face. "I get it! You got the hots for her!"

My face filled with fear. To hear it aloud… Was I that obvious? I touched my cheek to feel it burning.

"It's okay," Carol said. "I'm bisexual."

"What? You never told me that!"

"You never asked."

"Oh please! You only talk about guys."

"Well," Carol said, "your dad is a conservative Nazi, so I didn't know how you'd take it." I was greatly surprised at this new information. She continued, "It's true. My fifth-grade teacher, Ms. Kessler. A dead ringer for Susan Sarandon."

"Really." I sat in awe. I needed to process this.

Carol stared off into space. "That was the only time I ever liked math."

"I wish you'd told me sooner."

"I even stayed after class."

"I feel like I'm going crazy."

"I'm the crazy one. I turned into a little stalker. I followed her home from school once."

"That's sort of sweet. In a sick, twisted way." I laughed.

"So does she know?"

I raised the coffee cup to my mouth with shaking hands. "It's so screwed up. No. I wish I had the guts to tell her."

Carol pondered the situation a moment, slowly sucking on her cigarette. "I don't know that I would. I've seen that gang of metalhead fuckers she runs around with."

"I can't eat. I can't sleep."

"You're lucky. I gain thirty pounds." Carol tapped ashes off into a Styrofoam cup. "Every time I like someone, thirty pounds. A really big crush, forty pounds."

I managed a smile. "I wonder how you know, how anyone knows. I mean, I've never slept with a girl."

"You don't have to sleep with someone to know who you want to sleep with. It isn't rocket science, kiddo."

"I guess not. But God, Carol. I don't know how I'm going to get through this year. I mean, it's all I can do to just act normal."

"What's normal, anyway?" Carol spat.

"Acting like I'm happy while she dates this jerk."

"Well, in that case, normal sounds pretty fucked up."

CHAPTER THIRTY-ONE

Was Robin really willing to give up everything because this woman suddenly resurfaced in her life? As she tied her light blue scarf in the mirror, she was either not positive of her decision or simply too numb to feel.

When she came downstairs, she was startled to see Tom with Jimmy and Abigail, having their coffee in the living room.

She overheard her father saying to Tom, "You know what it's about?"

Tom answered, "No."

A hush fell over the room when Robin entered.

"Hi, Daddy," she said. "Abigail." A polite nod. She could see the questions on their faces. She could hardly look at them, especially her father. She couldn't bear his disappointment. A sick sensation came over her, as she began to doubt if she could go through with it.

"It's all over the papers." Jimmy's voice boomed.

"Your blood pressure, dear." Abigail patted his leg.

"Front page story about you talkin' with that woman last night." Jimmy set his cup down. The frown lines between his eyebrows deepened. "I can't imagine what in Sam Hill possessed you to talk to her. It doesn't look good. And at this late date…"

"I'm holding a press conference shortly," Robin replied.

"So Tom tells us," Jimmy said. "What're you saying?"

"I can't talk about it," she said firmly.

"That's just great," Jimmy exclaimed. "A surprise press conference." He patted his chest. "The old ticker can't take any more surprises, Robin."

"With all due respect, Daddy, it's my career." She folded her arms, refusing to let him make her feel guilty.

Abigail's eyes shifted back and forth. She was a bundle of nerves, but sipped her coffee quietly as the drama played out.

"Promise me one thing," Jimmy said, gesturing to Robin and Tom. "Y'all are stayin' married." Seeing Robin's puzzled face, he added, "It looks like you're my only hope for more grandchildren."

"Stop that," Abigail scolded him. "She's too old for that. She's in that age group where the risk goes up."

Jimmy seemed confused.

"For things…not goin' right." Abigail blinked.

"She might not be the sharpest tool in the tool shed," Robin said, glowering at Abigail. "But she loves you, Daddy. She's a keeper."

"Excuse me?" Abigail was offended.

Robin had no filter this morning. With everything that had transpired, she was too fatigued to keep up pretenses anymore.

"Dear, sweet Abigail," she continued. "I'm sure you weren't trying to call me old." If there was one thing Robin couldn't abide, it was any commentary about her age.

"Well of course not, dear." Abigail tried to smooth out her ruffled feathers.

"Now, Daddy, what do you mean about grandchildren?" Robin asked, taking a seat across from her father.

"I'm afraid we got some unpleasant news," Jimmy said. "Kenneth and Sheila are callin' it quits."

"What?" Robin rubbed her temples.

"You got your migraine pills?" Tom asked. He was always very solicitous of her.

She nodded. "How can this be?"

"It's true." The crease over Jimmy's brow was now a crater. She could tell he was sad and anxious.

"It can't be," she said. "You know Kenneth. He just likes to stir the pot."

"Afraid that's not the case this time." The way Jimmy didn't look at her, the way he rubbed his knees nervously…it was true.

She couldn't believe it. Kenneth and Sheila had been inseparable since their first day of high school. There was nothing in the world that would tear him away from the waif-like girl with fudge-colored hair who wore a ton of foundation to cover her freckles. She doted on him, adored him. If it had been another century, she would have followed him into the throes of some medieval battle. What could possibly have happened?

Jimmy finished his coffee with one final gulp and set it down roughly against the fragile china dish. "Would you believe he blamed *me*?" He drew shapes on his knees with nervous fingers. "As if it's my fault!"

"What do you mean?" Robin asked, her eyes darting to the somber-faced Abigail, who waited quietly for him to tell the story.

"It seems he always liked this other girl," Jimmy said helplessly. "Said she wasn't someone he could bring home to us. He said he married Sheila 'cause me and your mother liked her! Can you believe that? I thought that boy had more of a spine than that."

Robin stared at him a long moment. "Well, Daddy, you were very strong in your opinions. I'm not saying this is your fault, but would you have approved of this other one?"

"I didn't even know her!" he insisted. "Your flaky brother never gave me a chance. You didn't keep stuff from me 'cause you were afraid what I'd say, too, did you?" He asked the question, but didn't really want an answer.

"Course not," Robin lied.

Jimmy kept rubbing his hands together. "He says he loved Sheila, but was never 'in love' with her. Doesn't that beat all hell?"

Abigail took Robin's hands. "We hope this doesn't hurt you in any way."

Robin glanced at Tom, who was obediently silent. "Of course not," she said.

"I think she'll be fine," Jimmy told Abigail, "as long as it's not her gettin' the divorce. It's only her brother." He didn't hear how the words sounded. "You can understand the concern, though," he added, facing Robin. "Divorces don't happen to good Republicans." He half-smiled, but it was clearly no joke to him.

"Everything will be fine," Robin said as much to soothe herself as them.

"Thank God you and Tom have each other," Jimmy said. "You can be strong for one another, no matter the outcome of this damn election." He stood up and hugged his daughter a long time. "Elections come and go, but your *husband*, the one who stands by you, that's all that matters."

She heard his words as the eighteen-year-old girl again, being strongly advised about how to live her life. This made the looming press conference now even more ominous.

CHAPTER THIRTY-TWO

Governor Sanders took her place behind a podium that seemed to shrink as she stood there. She wished it could shield her from the flashing cameras and expectant faces. Among them were the wealthiest endorsers of her campaign. They would feel betrayed. This was political suicide…

It was time to begin. The press room fell silent.

"Ladies and gentlemen of the press," Robin began. She looked down, which was uncharacteristic of her, and gripped the podium as a life raft. The room began to spin, she was about to hit the floor…was she fainting?

She abruptly raised her head and looked around her quiet office for a moment. The press conference hadn't yet started, but her visions of it seemed frightfully real. In this darkest of times, she had no idea how she was going to say the words that would end what could have been a brilliant career. With a bitter smile, she thought to herself that maybe it was karma.

The state capitol was buzzing with reporters and frantic staff, who were preparing the North Wing for this highly unprecedented event. All morning long, the media had been speculating that this press conference may or may not be connected to Governor Sanders' meeting with Adrienne Austen the night before.

Lara Denning burst into the governor's office and made sure the door was closed and locked behind her. She marched toward Robin's desk and began with something it seemed like she'd rehearsed: "Look," she said, "I know you like this off-the-cuff, unrehearsed thing you do…" She paused to collect herself. "And it's been good. It's made you popular, but…it's too late in the campaign to surprise everyone. At least *I* should know what's coming. Can you throw me a bone here?"

"I know you're concerned." There was that calm Robin from earlier this morning. She was going to give another patronizing response.

"You've got a staff out there that's really nervous. No, scared! You're scaring the fuck out of me too." Her voice revealed her panic. "We're so close, we can taste it. But if you're not going to work with us…what's the point in us being here?"

Robin folded her hands. "That question is about to be answered." Her stare was distant, unfocused. She seemed a shell of herself, with none of the fighting spirit Lara expected to see.

"What's with these cryptic comments? Is this the goddamn *Da Vinci Code*?"

There was a soft knock. Lara went over to unlock the door. It was Peter.

"No luck," Lara told him.

But Peter had other news. "Governor? You have…a visitor."

Adrienne Austen pushed her way past Lara and Peter into the office. Robin's eyes were wide with surprise. "Leave us alone," the governor told her staff.

They angrily ambled out of the room, waiting as long as they could before closing the door. There was muffled conversation outside the room. No doubt everyone thought there was a connection between this woman's appearance and the press conference.

"Your security people like their pat downs," Adrienne said. "I should have had 'em buy me a drink first." She brushed off her jeans, which were slightly faded, and a rust-color shirt was tucked inside, the top two buttons undone.

The governor rose to her feet and came around to the front of her desk. "How dare you show up here! You want to destroy me. You're getting your wish. Is that not enough for you?"

"I don't want to destroy you," Adrienne said. Her voice was softer; the tension from the night before was gone.

"Get out."

"I came to apologize."

"Apologize?" Robin was dumbfounded. "For blackmailing me? I'm sure you've already sold that video, haven't you?"

Adrienne pushed her hair over one ear, revealing a tiny diamond at the top. She lowered her eyes. "There's no video." She held up her phone. "It's a new model. It's so complicated, I don't even know how to text on it yet."

"You were bluffing?" Robin's mouth fell open in disbelief. "My career is on the line, and you're playing some childish game?"

"I wanted to shake you up a little," Adrienne said. "Get you to think about who you were, what you're doing." Adrienne shifted in her boots, apparently trying to think of what she wanted to say. This was a very different woman from the demon in the black dress.

Robin's eyes narrowed to black lines of mascara, cold and venomous. She was not going to leave herself vulnerable to this woman again. Her posture was confrontational, with arms folded tightly across her chest. "What do you want, Adrienne?"

"I heard you were doing a big press conference, and I wanted to stop you if it had anything to do with—"

"Why did you come to the rally?" Robin interrupted. "Why did you want to see me last night?"

"I had something I wanted to say to you," Adrienne replied. She didn't make eye contact. "But then you got up on your fucking high horse…you were so cruel…I wanted to make you suffer."

"You've already achieved that. Every time you show up in my life." Robin retreated behind her desk, her voice thin and tired. "Why should I believe you won't go on national TV and reveal my secrets to the entire country?"

"Because I love you." Adrienne blurted it out, then shrugged it off, as if it were an affliction beyond her control. She was surprisingly resigned and calm about it. "I love you," she repeated softly, meeting her eyes just once before turning to leave. "I always have." She glanced around awkwardly; there was no more to say. "I have to go check out of my hotel. It was…good to see you again." The revelation was bittersweet, but she seemed earnest as she closed the door behind her.

When she was gone, Robin fell into her chair, stunned and spiraling down fast with no soft place to fall.

CHAPTER THIRTY-THREE

When I came back to the room that night, Adrienne was wide awake and worried looking. I didn't realize how long I'd been at Carol's. It was close to two in the morning.

"Where were you?" Adrienne asked in a panicky voice.

"I went out." I fell upon the bed, exhausted from the night's discussion.

"I thought something happened to you. Don't you know, this is prime rape and murder time?" She sounded like me.

"I'm sorry. I didn't mean to worry you." I kind of liked that she was worried.

"Well, you did. There are a lot of sick people out there. I should know. I went to high school with most of them." She sat on her bed and stared at me. I was too tired to feel uncomfortable. "I wanted to apologize."

I waved my hand. "Forget it."

"No, I mean it."

"You asked me to tell you the truth," I said. "So I did, and you didn't like what you heard. It's okay. I probably wouldn't want to know what you really thought either." I lowered my eyes, hoping she wouldn't tell me.

"I shouldn't have gone off like that. Becky *is* an idiot."

I shook my head. "I've been thinking. We don't have to be friends. You just have your life and I'll have mine." I was oddly resigned; I think it worried her.

"Whaddaya mean? I said I was sorry."

"I know. It's not that."

I could tell that Adrienne was confused. She was squinting, straining to understand. "Well, what is it then?"

"Nothing. I just don't think…we need to hang around so much. You know, having lunch…"

Adrienne came over to sit beside me on the bed. "I'd rather hang out with you than my party friends."

My heart thumped wildly inside my chest. She was the devil on my shoulder—drawing me closer and at the same time stabbing me with a pitchfork. Only she didn't seem to realize it.

"Party with me this weekend. Please?" Adrienne's plea was impossible to ignore. I knew I'd eventually say yes.

* * *

The next Saturday night, in Sean's dark on-campus apartment, everyone swarmed like moths to the blue stereo light. Sean slapped the back of his scrawny friend, Boyd Matthews, who resembled any member of a heavy metal band. His big hair looked like he'd plugged himself into a light socket.

"This is Boyd," Adrienne said. "Boyd, Robin."

I chose to wear a simple, short-sleeved white knit top. It fit a little too snugly over my breasts, but I was running out of short-sleeve shirts to wear. It also helped that Adrienne had told me it looked good on me. Right now I was regretting my decision to wear it, because Boyd's gaze lingered on my chest as if I were a centerfold. I crossed my arms to block his view. *Gazius interruptus.*

"Hello," I said politely, glaring at Adrienne. "Can I have a word with you?"

She smiled a giddy smile. "Am I in trouble?" To Boyd she added, "It'll be the third time this week."

She followed me outside, where we argued like a couple of Rottweilers.

"Are you out of your mind?" I yelped.

"What? He's just someone to hang out with tonight."

"He's looking at me like I'm a steak."

"Have some fun. You never know what might happen." Then she held up her hands. "I know he doesn't seem like your type. But you never know."

I exhaled dramatically. "What could we possibly have in common?"

"You've got to stop closing yourself off from people. Look at us. We have more in common than you thought." She grabbed my shoulders. "Listen to me, if something happens, great. If not, let yourself have a good time. No big deal."

"You ever notice how something bad always happens after someone says 'no big deal'?"

Adrienne smiled with an arm around my shoulder. "Think of him as fun."

"Is that how you think of people?" I regretted the question as soon as I asked it, because I wasn't sure I really wanted to know.

Adrienne paused, considering her answer. "Not exactly." She seemed momentarily awkward, which was strange for her. "It depends. Some guys are just for fun. You can always tell who the serious ones are."

She escorted me back inside, to the hazy den of wolves, where Boyd thrust a can of beer into my hands. I took it apprehensively.

"Go on," Adrienne said. "It doesn't bite."

"You never had a drink?" Sean smirked to his buddies. This was the most interest Sean had shown in me. He seemed to enjoy me as an object of ridicule. For a guy like him, it was always those intellectual girls who were the most fun to take down a few pegs. I could see it all over his not-completely-shaven face.

I wrinkled my nose, slowly bringing the can to my lips. "I've never had beer."

Adrienne turned to Sean and said, almost proudly, "She's like Sandra Dee."

"Shut up," I squealed, taking my first sip. "Ugh." I swallowed loudly and scrunched up my face like a raisin.

Adrienne laughed. "You don't like it."

"Fizzy…yak pee."

Adrienne laughed harder, turning to Sean. "She's very dramatic."

Sean was already bored. "Could we?" His heavy-lidded eyes indicated that he was either sleepy, stoned or looking for something more than another drink.

But my next sip seemed to hold Adrienne's interest more. She watched me with sparkling, laughing eyes.

Boyd leaned against me, grinning. "A few more and you won't taste a thing," he said.

"Now there's a goal." I didn't try to hide my sarcasm. It kept me feeling safe in the midst of my fear. I held up the can in a mock toast, to the sounds of cheers all around. I pinched my nose and gulped it down.

When I allowed myself to surrender my cognitive abilities, I felt good. Thinking was overrated anyway. Adrienne was right. I thought about everything too much. I breathed in the smoke like perfume and swallowed the beer until it started to taste not quite as disgusting. After a little while longer, all of my anger and frustration cracked through the walls, released in the screaming guitars of the Scorpions, as long as I didn't listen too closely to the lyrics. The appeal of it all was now clear—to let go of fear and get in touch with your inner badass. Now *I* was the femme fatale, until I took a puff of Adrienne's cigarette and coughed my lungs raw. Not pretty for a femme fatale. I'd never once seen Bette Davis choke on her cigarette.

Beer cans piled up, as well as ashes in the ashtrays, and the fog engulfing the apartment got so thick, you would've thought we were in a sauna. Through the clouds of smoke, I overheard parts of conversations—Nancy telling Becky how cute some guy was. I figured if I kept drinking alongside everyone, I wouldn't feel so different.

The song on the radio changed to my favorite slow ballad, "Alone Again." Pairs of feet moved slowly on the carpet. It was too dark to tell if anyone was really dancing.

Boyd guided me to where others were dancing in the living room. I pretended to be interested in what he was saying, all the while watching Adrienne, who was sitting and smoking beside Sean. As Sean inched closer to kiss her, Adrienne turned her head, tapping ashes off into an empty can, looking up at me. The way her eyes met mine, I couldn't tell if it was the fog in the room or my foggy head, but she seemed to be gazing at me the way Boyd was. Maybe it was what I wanted to believe. Adrienne's black, button-down shirt opened at the top as she bent down, revealing the skin of her upper chest and neck, which I imagined had to be so soft…

So I danced. And danced. I thought I might be a regular at these parties, it was so much fun—as long as *she* was there. While Boyd and I danced, I looked over his shoulder. Again I caught Adrienne watching us. Adrienne arched back, letting Sean kiss her throat. Everything was wrong. The world was going in reverse. Upside down. Biology was wrong. Penises and vaginas, birds and bees. Nothing made sense in my drunken mind. Was the earth really round? Was it the beer talking? After a few beers, I'd begun to feel like a famous philosopher. With each drink, I was getting closer to solving the mysteries of the universe.

It was then when I clasped my arms around Boyd's neck tightly and kissed him hard in front of Adrienne. When I came up for air, I saw that she was watching. *Mission accomplished.* I smiled to myself with satisfaction. Bette Davis would have been pleased. To any normal bystander, it was all very absurd, but my reality had long passed absurd in this world of swirling smoke and the fizzy swill I kept pouring down my throat and pretending to enjoy.

When it was time to go, Adrienne assured me that we were close enough to the dorm to walk. So of course it took us forever to get back, but I didn't really notice. We kept hanging on to each other all the way back, though we weren't sure why, except that neither of us could stand on our own. I liked that I could be this close to her and it was okay. In this twisted reality, it made sense for us to be tangled up, two pretzels in denim shorts, with our arms wrapped around each other. Neither of us could balance, so we kept laughing about it. For someone who had never done a daring thing in her life besides adding pickles to the potato salad at the church picnic or sneaking out to shoot pool with my brother, this was the most fun I'd ever had.

We stumbled into our room, still laughing. I headed straight for my bed, falling backward onto the mattress, which was thinner than a potato chip, with one arm behind my head. Adrienne turned away from the closed door, looked at me and said, "You'll never fuck him."

"What?" I raised up unsteadily on my elbows.

"I said, you'll never fuck him." She had a predatory stare as she walked slowly toward me.

I lay back down. "You don't know what I would or wouldn't do." How dare she think she knew…oh, who was I kidding?

She moved closer, a shadow in the darkness, then her face was suddenly, strangely close, her lips just above mine. The next thing I knew, our lips were touching. It was so soft, and so alarming. I felt her lie all the way down on my bed, her deliberate movements exciting me, as I anticipated what she was going to do. I closed my eyes and felt her lips touch mine again, moving slowly, sending shock waves through my body. I couldn't believe she was doing this. She raised up, looking amused, as if she could tell how much I wanted her. The truth was, I'd always known it would feel this way. And I wanted it all, whatever it was, something I dare not allow myself to imagine, not even in my daydreams. My breathing suspended, I felt her cheek brush against mine. I could feel her warm breath, the heat of her body so close. Like something I'd always known would happen yet so surprising at the same time, this night would change my life. Nothing I'd ever experienced before could compare to this. She was finally here, not across the room, the temptation I couldn't touch. She was inviting me to touch her, and I was too excited to be scared, even though I was. Running her hand through my hair, she gazed at me, an unmistakable look, her mouth parting a little before she kissed me again. Both of us were feeling brave, uninhibited, as each kiss was deeper than the last. Her lips were so soft and melting, and her soft face—it was nothing like Marc's scratchy stubble. With boys, everything seemed aggressive and forced. When Adrienne's kisses grew more urgent, even possessive, it only excited me more. I was beginning to understand the difference and what that difference meant. Adrienne unbuttoned the black shirt that I had been eyeing all night, and she lowered herself onto my body. The room was quiet, with only the creak of the bed…

Kisses like melting butter along my neck startled me with their intimacy. I held her face in my hands and kissed her mouth again. "You know what I want?" she whispered.

I shook my head. I laughed as she threw off a couple of stuffed animals, clumsily breaking up the moment. Then we stopped laughing.

She lifted my shirt over my head, and my mind was cleared of all thought as her hands glided along my bare shoulders. I could sense her excitement, as though she'd been wanting to do this for a while, her fingers so slowly tracing along my chest, my collarbone. Then she kissed my neck. I leaned back, still a little dizzy from the alcohol, but amazingly alert now that this was finally happening.

After undoing zippers and buttons, she moved her nude body sensuously over mine, both of us savoring the softness and tingling heat of our skin. I closed my eyes, smiling to myself in the dark. I held her tightly to me, with my legs wrapped around her torso. I wanted to feel her all over and never let go.

Her hand moved lower, reaching between my thighs, her fingers opening me. I stirred anxiously as her face moved down, tracing silent kisses along my hips, my thighs.

"How do you know what to do?" I whispered.

"I don't know." Her voice was quiet. I could almost hear her smile in the dark.

As she glided her lips and tongue along the warm, secret place we both knew, I spread myself further open, offering myself to her. I surrendered to the pleasure, and terror. I lost control and welcomed the chaos, moaning from deep in my throat. I made sounds I didn't even recognize.

My senses scattered like fragments of exploding light. I was aware of Adrienne's beautiful smile in a foggy haze, her naked, muscular thighs and silky bronze skin that I had longed to touch from the first moment I saw her.

She held me quietly in the darkness, the two of us wrapped in a swirling, cotton sheet, my heart still pounding from a few moments before. It wouldn't be long before I was the one on top, gazing at her, ready to return the favor. My inexperienced hands glided down her body, instinctively knowing where they wanted to go. Then she guided me down between her legs. I felt mostly terror, knowing that this was taboo. But my body moved without thinking, and next thing I knew, she was making sounds I'd never heard her make before. I watched her neck arch back, her eyes closed, her clenched hands tearing the sheet off the mattress. The power of her release was so great I felt it with her, and I held her trembling body tightly, stroking her hair. I would never forget this night and what it meant to me. Somehow, though, in the midst of the intimacy we had shared, I felt only momentarily safe in her arms.

CHAPTER THIRTY-FOUR

I awoke to harsh, morning light that scolded me for last night's fall from grace. It wasn't a dream. Adrienne was still there beside me. I stared in awe at her bare back, with the sheet curling provocatively below her waist, the curve of her hip so delicate like the statue of a goddess, but somehow more perfect.

Then I thought about the pastor back in Atlanta, Reverend Butler, how he'd told me to repent just for saying "shit" when my brother tracked cow manure onto my bedroom carpet. For this, he'd surely damn me to hell. Did anyone ever admit to something like this? I wondered. Touching Adrienne's flowing caramel hair on the pillow, I decided it was none of Reverend Butler's business.

Such a sensuous, forbidden encounter—I lay still, intoxicated by the memory and wondering if the person next to me felt the same. I almost didn't breathe. Now I knew for sure there was a heaven, or at least a really perfect hell.

She stirred under the covers. She was waking up. I closed my eyes and pretended to be asleep. I lay stiffly, awaiting the next touch, the next caress, wondering what her smile would look like in morning light so close to me, wondering how she would look at me now that we had this intimate knowledge of each other. But she threw off the sheet abruptly, rose from the bed, grabbed something from her closet and left the room.

Minutes later when she returned, I saw that she'd taken a shower. She dried her damp hair with a towel, and was already dressed. She then grabbed a trash bag and began sliding empty cigarette packs into it, when she saw that I was awake. "You're still in bed?" Her question felt more like an accusation.

I stared at her, expressionless. "Yeah. I was just thinking about last night."

Her body stiffened, and she laughed nervously. "Yeah. Look, I'm sorry. I should never have had that many beers."

A paralyzing sickness settled in my stomach. "Oh, right. Me neither." The words came out to protect me before I had a chance to think. "I've never had beer before."

"I know. I'm sorry." She smiled awkwardly and checked her watch. "Damn, I gotta go." She searched absently for her books, stuffed them into her bag and flew out the door. She never studied at the library, especially not on a Sunday.

I stared at the closed door, devastated, before groping for my clothes. Suddenly, the goddess statue beside me had crumbled into a heap of dust.

CHAPTER THIRTY-FIVE

"Are you out of your mind!" Lara chased Robin all the way back to her office. When the door was closed behind them… "What the hell was *that*?"

"An announcement." Sometimes Robin simply enjoyed watching Lara fly off the rails.

"You didn't say anything!" Lara exclaimed. "You care about the environment? Fine. But you support creating more oil jobs. Remember? What the hell? You basically talked in a circle."

"Isn't that what politicians do?"

Lara backed out of the room. "Not you. The reason you're ahead is because you're not like that. This, whatever this was, I don't know. It was a confusing mess."

"I sent a message to environmental groups, to let them know that I don't plan to torch the planet."

"It came off like you're trying to please both sides." Lara sighed. "When you try to please everybody, you end up pleasing no one."

"Especially you." Smiling, Robin came around her desk and held Lara's shoulders. "It's going to be all right."

"How do you do that?"

Robin stared blankly.

"How do you drop a pile of shit in there," Lara said, "that I have to clean up, by the way, then act like it's no big deal?"

Her answer was a slight smile as the governor turned away.

"I have to convince Jeannette not to quit now." Lara huffed to herself. "I should've retired to Bermuda years ago…" She muttered all the way out the door. She scurried down the hall, still talking to herself like a crazy person.

With the press conference out of the way, there was a sense of relief among most of the governor's staff, although an uneasiness remained.

"It's a matter of trust," Peter explained awkwardly. Minutes later, he sat across from the governor's desk, trying to make his case without losing his temper. He'd seen what happened to his predecessors, and he wanted to keep his job. "There is talk about all the secrets…"

"Talk?" Robin laughed. "As if we don't have enough to worry about out there." She gestured toward the window. "Now I have to be concerned about the loyalty of my staff? Let me know who isn't on board with my campaign, and I'll be happy to let them go."

"No, Governor, no. It's not like that."

"Well, then what is it like?" She stood up and went to the windows that were streaming in afternoon light. "I told you, I was warding off what I saw as a potential issue, with the environment, but I think it will no longer be an issue." Her fingers glided along the rim of her scarf, her thoughts drifting to what Adrienne had told her, hearing the words she said and the way she said them. She couldn't stop thinking about her.

"Governor, to be frank…there's a thorn in our side that's not going away. " His words surprised her. "We've gotten word that Adrienne Austen is going to do interviews. We need to address this right away."

All the color left Robin's face. Was Adrienne going to betray her anyway? Robin didn't know what she was capable of. Remembering the past, every time she trusted Adrienne she got hurt. What if nothing had changed? "Interviews?"

"The first one is going to air tonight on CNN," he replied. "Lara wants to have a statement ready, depending on how it goes."

"I need to go." Robin grabbed her jacket and headed for the door.

"But Governor!"

* * *

Robin slowly untied her light blue scarf and stood in front of the full-length mirror in the bedroom to appraise herself. She touched her neck, her chest, examining the older skin, though still unblemished. She traced a few new lines on her neck; the cool air felt good on her skin. She took a deep breath, enjoying the feeling of no scarf around her neck. She glanced at all the scarves in her closet. Lara had told her to always wear one after an interview Robin did where she'd worn one. Since more people had seen that interview, Lara told Robin that she should keep wearing them so it would become a trademark, something to make her stand out. But now they were beginning to feel confining.

Hearing noise downstairs, Robin rushed to change into a more comfortable outfit—a simple shirt and pants. She knew she needed to talk to Tom and Kendrick before they heard anything shocking on the news. She didn't trust anything Adrienne was going to say. So much for Adrienne "declining" to be interviewed. She could only perceive this move, made without letting her know what she was planning to say, as a betrayal. As she buttoned the last button of a crisp, white shirt, a wave of fear rippled through her body. How could she tell her family? What would they think of her, knowing that she'd deceived them? Especially her daughter, who she wanted so much to look up to her. And Tom, would this be the final nail in the coffin for their marriage? Never mind what might happen to her career…

She descended the staircase, her palm moist on the banister, her head starting to spin. Though Robin had never fainted before, there was a first time for everything. She was struck with a sharp, sickening sensation—the thought of her father learning her secrets on live television. She almost couldn't breathe. She started to feel the stairs move underneath her feet, until she saw Tom in the living room, which prompted her to stay alert and focused. He was very dapper looking in a gray, pinstriped suit. He'd just set down his briefcase to ask Kendrick how school was. Both of them stopped their conversation when they saw her.

"You're home early," Tom said.

"I need to speak to both of you," Robin said somberly. Her voice was different, odd.

They followed her out to the backyard terrace where they could be away from the probing eyes and ears of the housekeeping staff.

"I can't change clothes first?" Tom complained, loosening his tie. He removed his jacket before sitting in one of the patio chairs.

"No, this is important," she said. It was also only a half hour before *The Jay Savage Show* would be airing on CNN. She tried to stay focused, but noticed Kendrick's gloomy face as she slumped in the chair beside her. "How was school?" she asked.

"Sucked."

"I'm sorry about that." Robin cleared her throat, preparing herself. It was better they hear the truth from her, not from a stranger on a news show. She owed them that much. She said, "I have something to tell both of you."

"Another woman came forward?" Tom joked, though there was a smear of bitterness on his face.

"No," Robin replied, offended that he would make such a joke in front of their daughter.

Her mother's deadly serious face got Kendrick's attention. It was as if she could tell this wasn't going to be some banter about one of her mother's opponents. This was going to be serious, like death-in-the-family serious. She brushed the hair out of her face and watched her mother closely.

"I have to tell you…" Robin's voice cracked. Neither Tom nor Kendrick had ever seen her so vulnerable. The strength seemed zapped out of her, replaced with raw nerve endings. "I haven't been honest with either of you. I was afraid…if you knew the truth…"

Tom closed his eyes, opening them slowly, as if he knew what she was going to say.

"I'm sorry I lied to you." Robin couldn't look at either of them. "I was ashamed. It's not something I'm proud of."

"What?" Kendrick interrupted. "You smoked once and inhaled? What?"

"I did have an affair," Robin said. "With Adrienne Austen." She still couldn't look at them.

Kendrick tilted her head, making sure she heard her right. "No way!" She was almost smiling. To her, it was probably a little exciting to learn her straitlaced, conservative mother once had a wild side.

"Yes," Robin answered reluctantly. When she raised her eyes to meet Tom's, she feared what he must have been thinking.

"Can you excuse us a minute, Ken?" he asked.

"Yeah." Kendrick came over and kissed her mother on the cheek. "It's okay, Mom. Even if the dweebs don't vote for you, I still love you."

"I'm sorry about your friend." Robin felt responsible for everything her daughter had been going through. But like Scarlett O'Hara, she'd have to think about that tomorrow.

"Screw her," Kendrick said, then corrected herself. "I mean forget it. I'm not talking to her." She gave her dad a quick kiss, then looked at her mother again. "I still love you," she repeated, then left.

Before Robin could collapse in tears, Tom reached for her hand. "You know that goes for me too," he said.

She shook her head. "Tom…"

"Don't say anymore. I thought maybe…"

"I don't deserve your kindness," she managed to say.

"You're human." He traced his forefinger along his chin, a gesture she noticed he did in times of stress. "I don't care what you did in your past. But…I do care if this affects us now. Does it?" He dared to look at her, even though he probably feared her answer.

"You deserve more."

He shifted in his seat. "You don't love me? Or you can't love *any* man?"

"Don't make me hurt you. Please." She rubbed her face, grateful for the shield of her hands. She couldn't stand to see his grief-stricken face and to be the cause of it. Ruthlessness in politics was easy; she could sign a bill and never have to see the despairing faces of the people who would be harmed by it. Now, being the executioner who had to sit across from the one being executed was a different story. "I don't know. Things are confusing right now." She was sincere, her shiny blue eyes pleading with him not to ask her any more. He really loved her, and that was the worst part of all.

"Whatever happens," he said, "I'll be by your side. Divorces don't happen to good Republicans." He smiled faintly, repeating her father's words.

"I don't want this to hurt your reputation," she said carefully.

He didn't understand.

"She's going to do interviews," Robin explained. "I'm not sure exactly what she will say." Her face was pale, worried.

"That's why you told us." He nodded, realizing her confession wasn't completely a selfless act.

"I thought it better if you heard it from me than on the news." She saw his disappointed smile and had to look away.

He rose from the chair and left her to contemplate this dramatic turn of events. As she looked out at the pastoral, endlessly green landscape, she wanted to stay in this peace as long as possible. But just as the green was eventually swallowed up by the horizon, she too would have to go inside and face whatever forces were going to swallow her up as well. When this was over, what would her life be like? She couldn't imagine…

CHAPTER THIRTY-SIX

I lifted heavy hand weights in the university's weight training room, alongside a bunch of sweaty muscle guys. I didn't care that the room smelled like dirty socks. I didn't care that some of the guys were gazing at me like sleazy nightclub singers. I didn't care about much of anything, just lifting each weight to my chest—again and again. I hoped the pain of lifting would overtake the pain in my heart. But it didn't. So last night was something Adrienne had to apologize for. I was her drunken mistake. Of course. What else could I have been? As I replayed the night over and over, with flashes of moments so real, so honest, there was no way she didn't feel something too. She had to. I was overcome with humiliation, alternating between anger and confusion. I hated her. Or maybe I loved her. They were the same anyway, right?

Andrew, my friend from film production class, ran on a treadmill beside me, while a radio played the local heavy metal station. "This music is so vile," he spat.

"And juvenile," I added with pleasure and an extra dose of "snob." I huffed. "Just like the people who listen to it."

He marveled at my determined lifting. He kept glancing over at me. "God, girl. You're fired up!"

But he misunderstood. I wasn't an athletic person. Bending over to tie my shoes was about as strenuous an activity as I ever wanted to do. Weight lifters had too many visible, unattractive veins, so I wouldn't be doing this full-time. And joggers could drop dead of a heart attack at any time. It was a proven fact, according to my mother, whose biggest daily activity was beating eggs.

Of course today was different. Somehow I didn't care if I had a heart attack. My heart was already broken.

* * *

The same group of students always hung around the film lounge between classes, sort of like the regulars in a bar. Carol was a permanent fixture on one end of the couch, sprawled out and smoking in her floral-pattern sundress like a lump of flowers.

Seated beside her today was Gina Chi, the only other female in the film program—a New Age girl dressed in organic materials and sandals. "It's a Bergman film," she commented as Carol waved her away. "It's set during the time when people were dying of the plague. The symbolism is really great."

"Fuck symbolism," Carol fired back. She crossed her arms like a spoiled child who wasn't getting her way.

"It's about people whose lives are filled with pain."

"Well, why the hell do *I* have to suffer?"

I could hear them before Andrew and I walked in with our gym bags.

"Where the hell were you guys?" Carol demanded.

"Some of us were training for the Olympics." Andrew shot me an all-knowing smile and scurried off to the bathroom.

"Where's he going?" Carol asked.

"Restroom, I think," I answered, noticing the matchbook that fell out of his gym bag. I picked it up.

"Good idea," Carol said. "We should pee before we sit through five hours of the plague."

"It's not five hours," Gina argued, rolling her eyes.

I turned the matchbook over in my hand. It read: "THE COBRA." On the back was a picture of two snakes entwined. I eyed it curiously. It wasn't anyplace near campus. I tried to guess where and what it might be. It seemed like some sort of a club.

Gina was still agitated with Carol, so she tried a new audience. "Bergman is a master of depicting pain and suffering."

"Oh, like he's cornered the market," I muttered in a way that caught Carol's attention. She knew something was wrong.

"What is it?" she asked.

"Never mind." I glanced away, grateful to see Andrew rounding the corner. It was amazing how fast guys could go to the restroom.

"I want details," Carol persisted.

Meanwhile, Gina dove into a book, ignoring everyone. She muttered something about how we didn't appreciate real art.

I handed the matchbook back to Andrew. I tried to be delicate, but I was obviously curious. "Is this…a men's club?"

He smiled secretively. "No, we get quite a few ladies in there too. You should come with me." He winked at me as another student walked by.

"Two minutes, guys," the student called. "Can't put off the inevitable."

Of all things, why did it have to be a Bergman film? I was already feeling dark and hopeless. I gave Andrew a sideways glance as we made our way to the auditorium. Was that wink because he knew my secret? Was it written on my face? The hard part about this situation was that I was so completely self-absorbed with my own lovesick drama, that I was convinced it was and should be very obvious to everyone. On the other hand, unless everyone was a mind reader, I could've simply appeared to be another brooding film student. I wouldn't be the first. All the film majors wore black and walked around, making sarcastic comments. But I wondered if Andrew could sense others like him, like the "gaydar" I'd heard about in some of the books I'd read. Was I so obvious I was causing his gaydar to ping?

In the dark auditorium, Carol and I sat in the back. The last thing I wanted to do was contemplate the mysteries of death in black and white. My eyes kept blurring, and I'd try to casually wipe a stray tear away from my face so that Carol wouldn't notice.

But she noticed everything. As we watched a man playing chess with Death, I felt Carol reach for me in the dark. She took my hand and gave it a reassuring squeeze.

CHAPTER THIRTY-SEVEN

TVs were set on CNN throughout the mansion. Robin watched and waited in the library, armed with a glass of brandy. She tried to brace herself for what seemed like an inevitable bombshell interview.

Jay Savage appeared stern in all of the promotions for tonight's broadcast. "The mystery woman from Robin Sanders' past comes forward." Or "Rock musician finally breaks her silence about her relationship with Governor Robin Sanders."

There was no light at the end of this particularly dark tunnel for Robin.

When she first saw Adrienne on the show, she appeared calm and relaxed, undaunted by the build-up and obviously frothing anticipation of the anchorman—not to mention everyone else in America and on Twitter.

"Did you have a relationship with Robin Sanders?" Savage was known for cutting to the chase, and he wasted no time tonight.

"Yes." Adrienne nodded, a slight smile broke across her face. She was dressed more conservatively than usual, wearing a black pantsuit with a white shirt and small gold hoops in her ears. Her hair was smoother, not quite as wild, but still with blond streaks. Robin could tell it had been cut before the interview.

"Was the relationship romantic in nature?" he asked.

"Robin was my roommate in college," she said. She seemed very confident and self-possessed, not at all a tool of one of Robin's opponents wanting fifteen minutes of fame. She was clearly not like the picture Robin had tried to paint of her. "We lived together for a year."

"Did you have an affair?" Savage pressed.

"No," Adrienne said. "We were friends, nothing more."

"What about the rumors that—"

"I was joking in a bar, and a reporter misconstrued what I'd said." Adrienne was unflappable, even believable.

Robin's heart was pounding so hard, she had to consciously remember to breathe. She wasn't going to betray her. If anything, she was *helping* her? Robin's mind raced to the three words Adrienne had said to her. Now more than ever, it seemed to be true.

Tom poked his head in, then made a beeline for the wet bar. "The woman can keep a secret," he said knowingly. The room was too dimly lit for her to see if there was pain in his eyes. If there was, she couldn't bear to see it. The idea that she could have spared her family any knowledge of her affair...somehow, clearing her conscience did not make Robin feel better. If anything, it probably raised more questions for Tom.

"Yes." She turned back to the screen, waiting for him to leave.

When the interview was over, another news show came on, showing the current poll numbers. Robin remained in the lead, and support for her was only growing now that this "wrinkle" had been ironed out satisfactorily.

She ignored the call from her press secretary. She didn't want to discuss positioning and preparing for the final debate at this time. She needed to be alone. But she had to take the call from her father.

"Good news," Jimmy exclaimed into the phone.

"Yes, Daddy. I know."

"I told you, when you've got the truth on your side, the Lord will protect you."

"Yes." She listened as he did most of the talking. Though her mind drifted off at one point, she understood that he now apparently could return to his gun club without being asked a lot of questions. "I'm happy to hear that."

When the call was over, she slumped into the creaky, leather high back chair and pondered the situation. Everything was looking good for her campaign now. She was back on track to the most powerful position in the country. This was good news. So why did she feel so heavyhearted? She sat, unable to move, except to cut off the TV. All she could do was stare into the flames in the fireplace, envisioning the time when her life had fewer complications. At the family farm, her biggest worry was how to make an excuse so she wouldn't have to milk the cows. The sweet smells of magnolia and honeysuckle...when she could excitedly put on her first pair of shorts for the summer once the mild, warm breezes began to blow in...those were now times she longed for.

Tonight she seemed like a stranger, even to herself. No matter how many speeches she gave about the unnaturalness of these feelings, behind blue eyes now marked with crow's-feet, she still carried with her the eighteen-year-old girl who longed for something she didn't want to tell anyone. Adrienne Austen was the tumultuous storm that rained on her life and ruined her peace of mind. And every time she resurfaced, Robin, like a flimsy piece of patio furniture in a hurricane, was twirled around and dumped in some strange place with no idea how to get back to what was familiar.

The governor was slowly beginning to see that she wasn't supposed to be the same as she was before she went off to college, that change was something to count on, to hope for, no matter how scary. Though Adrienne and her music seemed dark and dangerous, it was only because Robin feared walking through the door to a life that she'd heard was wrong and evil ever since she was a child. If only Robin could have opened the door, reached out for what she really wanted, maybe her life would have been different. If only. But she didn't. So now she found herself in a hollow, echoing mansion with the world safely tucked away outside, and admirers who only admired her for what they thought they knew about her. It was lonelier and scarier than any place Adrienne could have left her.

CHAPTER THIRTY-EIGHT

"She was called Bloody Mary for all the executions she ordered, obliterating everyone who stood in her path." I was reading my history book, but was too distracted by Adrienne's phone conversation with Sean. Her flirtations, her giddy laughter, twisted the knife in my stomach deeper.

I cast a fierce eye in her direction, repulsed by the jealous anger welling up inside of me. I never wanted to become one of those girls who spent all of their time lamenting over some object of affection. I'd thought of my life as too big and important to waste time on such things. That's why I ignored the girls in high school who spent half their days in the bathroom, crying over boys. Who called, who didn't call, who looked at another girl a certain way…it seemed like such a waste of time. But now here I was, reduced to shards of self-pity, catching fire again and again with each word my roommate spoke. I'd become one of *those girls*.

"What about tomorrow night? I really wanna see you." Her laugh broke my heart again. When she finally hung up, she opened a textbook and sat at her desk. Waves of silent tension rippled through the room. "You know," Adrienne said, removing her reading glasses. "You should give Boyd a call. It seemed like you guys really hit it off."

That was the final straw. "Oh, I am." Two could play this game.

"So," she said. "I guess he wasn't the bad guy you thought?"

I didn't understand what she meant.

She smiled. "How you probably judged him 'cause he's a friend of Sean's?"

"Yeah," I replied distractedly.

* * *

Two girls, a blonde and a brunette, ran through the woods near the campus. I yelled, "Cut!" Unscrewing the tripod, I felt the choking heat melting my face, as well as my sanity. As the two girls approached, I wiped my forehead. "That's it for today. We'll meet back here tomorrow. Same time."

As the girls walked away, Carol hovered over me. "Acting majors," she muttered, adding mockingly, "'What's my motivation?'"

I managed a weak smile, but was obviously upset about more than the amateur production. Though it was clear I wasn't a master of technical skills, I couldn't make myself care more about this project, what with my world coming to an end and all.

"You ever gonna tell me what happened?" Carol persisted.

I continued twisting the base of the tripod. "It's a real mess," I said.

"Hey, kiddo, it's me here."

"We slept together."

Carol's eyes bulged out of her head. "Wow! Well, I guess now you know how she really feels."

"Not exactly. We were drinking, and the next day she acted like it was a mistake."

"Oh, I hate that!" Carol exclaimed. "Using alcohol as an excuse. That's crap. Lots of straight girls get fucked up and they don't even kiss another girl. Trust me on that." She was so loud, I'm sure the people across the parking lot now knew the sordid details of my sex life.

"So you think she's lying? About it not meaning anything?"

"Who the fuck knows? You've got two possibilities. She was either really into it, but got scared the next day. Or she really is straight and really got drunk."

"Why can't my life just be normal?"

"I'd say it's pretty interesting."

We walked across deep green grass. I tried not to think about the swarms of red ants eager to spread up my ankles. I walked faster at the thought. I'd heard about the lethal wildlife down here, just waiting to kill you every time you went outside. "You better not say a word to anyone," I warned.

"Who am I gonna tell?" Carol tried to look innocent.

I stopped. "The thing is, I'm acting like such a...such an asshole now. I was trying to make her jealous with this guy—"

"That's what I'd do."

"You would?"

"Hell, yeah. If you really want to find out how she feels." Carol was such an eager spectator; all she needed was a bag of popcorn.

"Isn't this nuts?"

"Don't sweat it. You haven't done anything wrong. Just don't sleep with him unless it's for the right reasons."

CHAPTER THIRTY-NINE

On board the private jet, Peter helped himself to a vodka tonic, while he reclined in one of the leather swivel chairs. This was the good life that he could certainly get used to.

"Governor Sanders," he began in that annoying tone she knew meant he was trying to be delicate. After so many years together, they were somewhat like a married couple, able to decipher each other's tone of voice.

She ignored him, distractedly staring out the window when there was nothing to see. Her eyes were tired. She sat tensely in her perfectly matching blue suit with pearl earrings.

"Excuse me?" Peter persisted.

Robin was immersed in the clouds. They stretched for eternity, unaware of time or the insignificant lives and laws of human beings. She envied them for just *being*, not able to be pushed or pulled to suit anyone's demands. Maybe she was just craving the freedom she knew she couldn't have.

"Why did you want to come here?"

She smiled peculiarly at his question. "Unfinished business."

The jet banked to one side as the lights of Boston twinkled below.

"Must be important business," he said coyly. "And so you know, all instructions were carried out."

She nodded. "Good."

An intern seated between Jeannette, the speechwriter, and Lara, nervously arranged her iPad and notebook on her lap.

"What're you doing?" Lara asked.

"Taking notes."

"There isn't time. You should be paying attention, not taking notes." Lara was especially hard on new people. She was so impatient, she was probably the worst person to train anyone.

Peter chuckled to himself. "It's been a long time since we employed Zelda."

"Zelda?" The intern repeated.

"She's our decoy," Lara explained.

Zelda was the code name for a woman who, with the right wig and dressed in a suit and scarf, could be a dead ringer for Governor Sanders. That afternoon, "Zelda" had conspicuously paraded out of the capitol, surrounded by security, got into the governor's limousine and traveled to the mansion.

"We use her to throw off the press when we need to keep the governor's whereabouts secret," Lara told the wide-eyed young woman. As she started to write "Zelda" in her notebook, Lara slapped her hand. "No notes. Doesn't your generation know how to listen anymore?"

"Zelda," the intern repeated softly to herself. "That's interesting." She seemed excited to know this inside information.

"Not really," Lara said. "The woman's an alcoholic. We really need a new Zelda."

"No, she isn't," Peter argued. "She has a slight balance problem when she walks. Could be an inner ear thing."

Lara laughed. "Right."

"Lara," Robin scolded, her eyes darting to the intern. "We don't need to talk about her."

"Oh, c'mon," Lara said. "We're not the CIA."

Robin glared at her, then motioned to her to join her at the back.

"I didn't want you to bring any interns along!"

"More secrets with you! What kind of business are we doing?" Lara dramatically raised an eyebrow. "You're not taking anybody out, are you?"

Robin patted her shoulder. She liked her acid-tongued, fiery friend.

"Want to tell me why we're in your dad's plane?" Lara asked.

"I want to keep this little 'mission' under wraps." Robin returned to her seat.

Lara followed, now more curious than ever, although she had a pretty good guess. The governor's staff was getting used to being kept deliberately out of the loop lately, although they were still complaining about it to each other.

Robin buckled herself in, trying to regain a sense of peace in the clouds. She wanted to pretend she wasn't surrounded by this traveling circus she called a staff.

There was a call from Tom. As soon as she saw his face on her phone, she took a deep breath.

"Yes?" She turned toward the window.

"Hi." His voice was very reserved and quiet.

"Is everything all right?"

"Where are you?" He seemed agitated.

"I'm taking care of something." She nodded at Peter.

"Unfinished business," Tom suggested. He let out a labored sigh. "I have to tell you, Robin. I'm not sure I can do this."

"Do what?" she asked carefully.

"Keep playing the doting husband. I've been thinking about what's good for me, something I don't think I'm doing enough." This didn't sound like him at all.

Robin had taken for granted the idea of Tom still by her side. Especially with Graham Goodwin's camp gaining on her, she knew his presence was vital to her campaign. "Have you been talking to your lawyer friend?" Of course she meant Darlene.

"No," he answered firmly. "I've supported you with everything. But you can't even tell me where you are tonight! It's like I'm living with…with…"

"I'm doing what I have to do. You'll have to trust me."

There was a bitter chuckle on the other end. "Trust you," he repeated. "I have to ask you straight out. Is the affair over? With that woman?"

"Of course! I told you." There was a long silence. Robin was distracted by a shape she thought she saw in the clouds, the silhouette of a woman.

"When you said I deserve more," he continued, "that was the worst thing you could have said, especially if you wanted me to stay."

"You want me to force you? Threaten you?"

Peter and Lara exchanged glances.

"Of course not," Tom replied. "But you never say anything that makes me want to stay."

"I can't talk about this now." Robin lowered her voice.

"Of course you can't."

"Really," she said almost in a whisper.

Her staff pretended they weren't listening to every word, as she hung up. Jeannette's eyes were wide, shifting to the others on the plane. But nobody looked up.

Robin glanced out the window and searched the clouds again for the shape she thought she had seen. But it was gone.

CHAPTER FORTY

I flopped on Carol's futon to discuss my warped plan. I couldn't bring myself to return to the claustrophobic dorm room right away. And even though Carol's place smelled like strong clove cigarettes, I could breathe easier here.

"You want to go out with him to make her jealous," Carol said. "I got it."

"Isn't it mean, though? Leading him on?"

"Jesus, girl. You got way too much of a conscience. How much do you read that *Bible*?"

I rolled my eyes. I hated it when people made a joke out of my faith. There was nothing wrong with believing in God and trying to live a good life. Nothing at all. The question was, could it be that what I'd done with Adrienne was against God's plan? Or could we actually make sense together? In the bigger scheme of things, was it really okay, in spite of what Reverend Butler used to say? Maybe Reverend Butler was an idiot.

I made a quick stop in Carol's bathroom before returning to "the pit of hell," as I started calling it. When I washed my hands, I couldn't help but notice endless rows of pills in the cabinet left open above the sink. How much medication did she take?

I came out, not realizing how much I was fidgeting. I felt guilty for being so self-absorbed. "I'm sorry to go on about myself all the time," I said. "What about you? Are you okay?"

Carol was the most perceptive, intelligent person I'd ever met. She knew in an instant that I'd seen her meds. "I have to take a lot of stuff. My head's a little screwed up."

"Screwed up?"

"Yeah," she answered. "You ever wake up in class, not remembering how you got there or what clothes you put on?"

I slowly shook my head. She was scaring me.

"Try it sometime," she joked. "It's a lot of fun."

"So you mean…"

"I get blackouts. They told me it was schizoaffective disorder. That's why it's taking me a little while to graduate." For the first time she seemed insecure, unable to look me in the eye. "Bipolar, mood swings, you name it. The trouble is, the side effects of the meds are worse than the condition!"

That explained why Carol failed so many tests. She seemed too smart to make such low grades. But now it made sense.

I reached out to her, to give her a hug. "I didn't know."

She pulled back fast. "Hey, no pity party. I'm fine." She paused a moment. "But there is something you can do. You could tell your dad to quit cutting the budget for people like me." Then she muttered, "Thank God I don't live in Georgia."

"What do you mean?"

She smiled ironically. "You really don't know, do you? When I wasn't at school, I had an apartment, thanks to HUD. Guys like your dad believe people like me *choose* to be on disability."

"That's not true."

"If it were up to him, I'd be homeless and couldn't afford my fuckin' meds!" She was so angry she was biting her lower lip. "Hell, I wouldn't even be able to go to school!"

"But Democrats always want to raise taxes," I argued, remembering what my dad had said. "How can that be good for you if you're struggling as it is?" I knew that Carol was pretty much on her own. Her father had died, and she didn't see her mother in New York very much. She seemed like such a lost soul.

She laughed bitterly. "You've been brainwashed by Republicans."

"Don't do that. We're all people."

"Keep telling yourself that."

Dad had always told me never to talk politics or religion with people unless I knew we were on the same page. He said it was a sure way to make enemies. I was beginning to see that he was right.

"Telling myself what?" I asked.

"Look, everybody wants to fix the economy. But nobody likes to hear anything they don't like." Seeing my blank expression, she continued, "No one wants to take medicine. They only want sugar. So you tell 'em no taxes ever, even if it throws the country down the fuckin' toilet. That's what your daddy does." Her tone had become very angry. Here it was; her mood was about to turn ugly fast.

"Okay, look. I guess I can see the positive and negative on both sides." There. That was a nice diplomatic way to escape the volcano.

"You should go into politics then," she said. "Then you can talk out of both sides of your mouth and fit right in."

I could see this wasn't a good night to talk about this. "Well, anyway, I'm sorry I didn't know about your…situation."

"I don't go around telling everyone. They'd look at me differently."

"I won't."

She held open the door for me. "Good luck with that guy or the roommate. Just don't do anything too stupid or I'll have to kill you. And since I'm not stable, you know I will." She winked at me before giving me a quick hug good-bye.

I was relieved that we were still friends.

CHAPTER FORTY-ONE

The next night, the stage was set. I would go with Adrienne to Sean's apartment, where Boyd would also be. A double date where no one goes anywhere. I was uneasy, but held fast to my plan.

It was another hot and sticky evening, the kind that suffocates you until you find life-saving air-conditioning. We traveled along the sidewalk toward the on-campus apartment, neither one of us saying very much. We wore shorts and light tops, but I still felt the heat sticking to my skin.

"Hey." Sean handed us a couple of beers. He and Boyd had obviously chugged back a few already.

"Hey." Adrienne slid her arms around his neck, giving him an extra friendly welcome.

I remembered I had a part to play, so I did the same with Boyd and topped it off with a deep kiss. I pulled back, ignoring his lovesick, or lustful, expression and glanced around the living room. Now without as many people as there were the night of the party, I could see the apartment layout. I noticed there were two bedrooms and a bathroom down the hall. If Sean lived here by himself, he must have let his buddies come around and use the other bedroom for more private "parties" like this one. I felt light-headed. I held Boyd's shoulders and steadied my balance. Thankful for the air-conditioning blowing at full speed, I took a sip of beer and tried to hide the inevitable sneer of disgust that followed that first sip.

"I made a mix tape," Boyd said with a smile. He crouched down in front of the stereo and ran his fingers with expert precision over the buttons to get to the right song.

"None of that 'Gene Loves Jezebel' shit," Sean warned.

"Aw, c'mon, man." Boyd frowned and fast-forwarded the tape.

"'Desire,'" Adrienne said. "That's what they sing, right?"

Sean nodded.

"I like it." She winked at me, so all I could do was turn away. I watched Boyd as if he was the most fascinating creature I'd ever seen.

All the songs Boyd had picked out for me to listen to merged together into one angst-ridden guitar. Of course I was intensely aware of Adrienne and Sean, beside us on the couch, making out. I couldn't look. Or listen.

After a few beers, I started to come on strong, sitting in Boyd's lap and kissing him fiercely. I was vaguely aware that Sean and Adrienne were moving away from the living room.

Now it was me and Boyd on the couch. I ran my fingers through his long, blond hair, and imagined he was Adrienne as I kissed him hard, over and over. My lips were on fire as I fantasized, holding his face as I wanted to hold hers. It helped that he had long hair. But the fantasy ended abruptly when he guided my hand down to the rock in his crotch. Knowing I had to play my part, I cupped it in my palm, making excited moaning sounds I'd heard in movies. It was a long way from my church back home. I put on a really good show for Adrienne, until I looked up and saw that she was gone. She and Sean were both gone.

"Where did they go?" I asked.

"I dunno." He wanted to keep kissing.

I looked around in between kisses. They weren't in Sean's bedroom; the door was open and it was eerily quiet.

Oh no. I was alone with Boyd. This wasn't part of the plan. Apparently, I hadn't thought it through. How can you make someone jealous if she's not there to see it?

"Let's move this party," Boyd muttered, biting my earlobe.

I knew he meant the other bedroom. But I never intended to go quite this far just to make Adrienne jealous. Was I insane? I'd have to think fast.

"Come on," he breathed in my ear. His sweaty, musky smell turned my stomach. It was a pungent odor mixed with cigarettes and days-old beer from bottles scattered about the apartment.

"Oh shit," I sighed. I gave my best look of disappointment. "I felt something. I, uh, I think I just got my period." Yes. That was perfect—the phrase no guy wants to hear before sex.

But he was so ready. "Huh." He had to think a moment. "I'm not one of those guys who cares about that. Really!" Unfortunately, he didn't seem like other guys, which would have made it a little easier. The nicer he was, the crueler I felt. I was using him. I was worse than the meanest femme fatale.

"Thanks for saying you don't mind," I said. "But I do. I just don't feel as pretty."

"But you are! You're so hot!" He was practically begging. Even his blond frizzy hair, getting frizzier from the heat, seemed to be begging too, as it blew upward in front of the air conditioner.

"I'm so sorry. I can't tonight." I gave him a quick good-bye kiss and started for the door.

He jumped up and grabbed my arm. "Are you shitting me? You're leaving?" Suddenly, he switched back to the guy I could picture hanging around with Sean Voight. He pinned me against the wall, by the front door. "Tell me you're not just a cocktease, are you?"

Now I didn't feel quite so bad about using him. *Cocktease.* I wasn't familiar with the term, but it wasn't hard to guess what it meant. "I don't know what you're talking about," I replied. "Of course I want to be with you. Just not tonight, okay?" That's it. The nicest, most polite way to leave a bad situation. Even though it was a lie, he didn't know that. What if I had cramps? Diarrhea? What if *I* didn't feel well? It was always about whether the *guy* was happy or not. It seemed that way with most things.

He held the doorknob behind me. I started to get scared, then scanned the room for objects I could use to strike him if he didn't take no for an answer. There was a kitchen knife on the table; the kitchen was visible from the living room. I could pretend to change my mind and want to do something kinky on a kitchen table, then cut him right in the stomach. I would have to do it if it came to that. I did watch *20/20*, after all.

"Okay," he mumbled. "I'm…sorry. Geez. I was just so…you look so…I was thinking you might be messin' with me."

"Would I have kissed you like that if I didn't want to?" How easily it all came to me—the deceit, the manipulation. I was a natural. All I needed was a long cigarette and a Siamese cat on my lap.

"Okay." He kissed me again. It was the most awkward kiss I'd ever have to endure, and that was saying something, because every kiss I had with boys had been awkward. I couldn't break away fast enough. But I had to do it convincingly, with all the fake disappointment I could muster. "When it's, you know..." he mumbled. "Over? Your period, you know. I really want you." He moaned into my ear, about to stick his tongue inside when I jerked away.

"Yeah, oh yeah," I lied, vowing never to return.

Finally, I opened the door to freedom. The muggy Florida night air...I'd never been so grateful to breathe in the thick humidity. There was a full moon glowing down on campus. I stared up at the sky and wiped my mouth hard.

* * *

When I returned to the room, Adrienne was there, finishing a Stephen King book.

"Robin?" She seemed surprised that I had come back.

"What are you doing here?" My eyes were glassy and unfocused.

"We had a fight."

"Oh, well thanks for leaving without a word. I didn't exactly enjoy walking on campus alone at night."

"I did try to tell you I was going! But you guys were all over each other. I guess you didn't hear."

"I guess." I moved listlessly to my bed, my mind screaming, as I swore I'd never do that again. It was such a close call. I could've ended up as some statistic. I felt sick, thinking of what that would've done to my parents.

Adrienne came over and sat at the edge of my bed. She took my hand in both of hers. "Are you all right? What happened?"

I wanted to tell her that I'd slept with him just to make her jealous, to see what her face would look like. But I couldn't. "Nothing."

"You okay?"

I shook my head and felt hot tears slip off the sides of my face onto my pillow. "No."

She stroked my hair and looked at me with the same tenderness as the night we spent together.

"Why do you care anyway?" I sniffed.

"What do you mean? Of course I care," she said. "Honestly, I was kinda surprised you liked him."

I sat up on my elbows. "I don't like him. Wait. What did you say?"

"I was surprised you liked him."

"Why?"

"I didn't really think he was good enough for you."

"What about all the stuff about me calling him?" I screeched. "How I should give him a chance? What was that?"

"I don't know. I say a lot of shit."

I hated her. Of course there was a slim difference between love and hate, about the width of a razor's edge. And that's exactly what I was balancing on. I rested my head in her lap, letting her run her fingers through my hair. Her touch felt so good, so comforting, even though I hated her tonight. Neither of us said anything. Slowly I drifted off to sleep.

CHAPTER FORTY-TWO

When Robin and her staff checked in to the hotel, she took Peter aside.

"I have something to take care of," she said.

"I know," he replied. "I'll have Donny bring the car—"

"No cars. I'll be in contact."

"But Governor..."

She scurried toward an elevator at the far end of the hall, which took her up to her room. The woman who emerged from Robin's hotel room was dressed in plain jeans and a flannel shirt, covered by a long, black wool coat. She wore a knit hat pulled down around her ears. It was a good disguise; no one had ever seen Governor Sanders dressed like this. But her outfit served more than one purpose. As a Southerner, her blood was too thin for a Boston evening in autumn. She had to be prepared.

Robin fled across the street, dodging the glow of streetlamps, staying in the shadows and away from curious eyes. There was a feeling of excitement, exhilaration, surging inside of her as she crossed Boylston Street, following the map on the paper she'd stuffed in her coat pocket. She needed to find Commonwealth Avenue. Block after block...it was a confusing city with diagonal streets that seemed to lead to nowhere. She caught a glimpse of a cobblestone side street with old houses that looked like they hadn't been updated since the Pilgrims' arrival. Finally, there it was. Her heart pounded faster when she came to the street. She turned up the collar of her coat to keep off the chill from the nighttime breeze blowing off Boston Harbor. It was a different world up here, a long way from the scent of magnolia trees, the sway of royal palms and the warm Florida nights she and Adrienne used to share.

* * *

Adrienne Austen lived in an old Victorian brownstone in the heart of the city off Commonwealth Avenue. Her sprawling condo had bay windows that overlooked a park with statues of great feminist icons—Lucy Stone, Abigail Adams and Phillis Wheatley. The irony was not lost on Robin, who, for a long time, had tried to get Adrienne to see the objectification of women, how it had become so normalized, especially in the heavy metal videos they'd watched together. But like so many of her passions, Robin came to accept the things she couldn't change, and she compromised like crazy, hoping that someday, if elected to the most powerful position in the country, she could introduce some of her ideas that might be considered radical by her constituents. But for now, everything she believed, everything she cared about, all took a backseat to her ambition—she'd grown to love and nurture it most of all.

* * *

Robin passed a wall of mailboxes in the empty lobby, then took a long flight of stairs up to Adrienne's apartment. Robin had asked her brother Kenneth to call as a favor to her, rather than one of her staff members. She distrusted them with this delicate situation; it was too tempting for information to be leaked. But she trusted her brother. Even though they hadn't spoken in a while, he agreed because, as he'd told her, she sounded desperate on the phone. So he communicated to Adrienne that Robin only wanted to talk, and that she'd be alone—no security, no annoying advisors. Adrienne told him that she hoped Robin was in good shape. As Robin huffed breathlessly on the fifth-floor landing, she realized what Adrienne meant. Robin hadn't been the most physically active. She always said she never had time to exercise and couldn't imagine herself as one of the "jogging presidents."

"Take up golf," Lara had told her. "It's not that active."

Robin had given her a sideways glance.

"Seriously," Lara continued. "You drive around in a buggy all day. How tiring can it be?"

"It's a golf cart," Robin corrected.

"Same thing."

The door to Adrienne's apartment opened while Robin was still making her way down the hall.

* * *

"Surprised isn't quite it," Adrienne said, taking Robin's coat. "When I got the call, I thought you'd hired someone to kill me."

"Not yet." Robin scanned the living room, taking note of the bay windows and the breathtaking nighttime views she had. There were streaks of orange in the sky, just over charcoal brushed clouds creeping closer, and twinkling streetlights below. "Your band must do pretty well."

"We have sort of a cult following."

Robin wouldn't admit that she'd seen her band online. She tried to appear whimsical. "Is it heavy metal?"

"Heavy metal has…fallen out of favor." Adrienne sounded as if she were trying out the words. "But it still influences rock, and the music we play. You didn't come here to discuss music genres, did you?"

"I might have," Robin said. "I can be unpredictable."

"So I see," Adrienne said. She was cautious with her. "Can I get you something?" she asked.

"No." With hands clasped firmly behind her back, Robin stepped further inside, noticing built-in bookshelves stuffed with feminist authors, some of whom she knew, and newer lesbian romances she wasn't familiar with. Her eyes fixed on the beaten-up guitar case in the corner of the room. She still had it.

Robin curled her hand around a random Roman column in the center of the room, another detail adding to the charm and character of the place. "This must cost a pretty penny."

Adrienne pulled bottles out of the refrigerator of a small kitchenette set off with a counter and barstools. "One of my friends has a few properties," she replied, matter-of-factly.

"I imagined you lived with five other people over a garage." Robin smiled, but it didn't seem like a joke.

"Because I'm in a band?" Adrienne asked with a smile that suggested she knew something Robin didn't. "We do okay. You may have heard of us. Eye of the Storm?"

"Excuse me?"

"That's the name of my band," Adrienne said.

Robin nodded, not revealing that she already knew.

"Why did you come?" Adrienne asked. The pleasantries were over.

Robin noticed photos of Adrienne and an unknown woman laughing together at a place with boats in the background. Her chest surged longingly, seeing a quick snapshot of the road not taken and hearing all of her silent regrets.

She looked at a larger photograph above the mantel. It was Adrienne and the same woman from the boat picture, a woman with dark hair and clear blue eyes like Robin's.

"Well?" Adrienne wanted an answer.

Robin let out a long, slow breath. "How could you tell me you love me?"

Adrienne came back to the living room, holding two bottles. She shrugged. "It's the truth. I don't have a problem with the truth."

Robin strode across the living room floor like she owned the place. "You lied on TV because you love me?"

Adrienne paused, leaning against the column. "That's why you're here? Because I said I love you? I didn't think it mattered."

Robin took the beer she didn't ask for. "Of course it matters. You drop a bombshell like that…"

Adrienne gazed at her, her smile turning up at the corners. "After all these years," she said, "I realized it was true. Hard as I tried not to, as much as you pissed me off…it's true. I love you."

Robin was uneasy. She set her beer on the coffee table and sat on a plush, though small, couch. "I don't know what to do with that," she said. She didn't make eye contact with her.

"I'm not asking you to do anything," Adrienne said. "Don't get a big head. I loved my partner."

Obviously, the woman from the boat picture…

"Her name was Jenny," Adrienne continued. "We were pretty happy for a while. It was sort of on-again, off-again. Then she got sick."

"I'm sorry."

Adrienne nodded. "With you," she said, "it was always there. I'd see you on TV or hear your name on the news. God, you pissed me off! But I couldn't help it. You're like a disease with no cure!"

"Gee, thanks."

"Why else would I go against my better judgment?" Adrienne came closer to her. "Your heart doesn't listen to your head. It's fucked up."

Robin smiled knowingly. How true that had been for her when they were in school together.

"It's hopeless," Adrienne said. "I'll meet someone else, but you know how sometimes you think about how…just before you die, there'll be that one person you'll think of right before the end? For me, I know it's gonna be you."

Robin had had the same thought years ago, but she wouldn't admit it. She stood up, pretending to be interested in the décor. Being here in this apartment with her, now a stranger, and yet feeling something so familiar still between them—she wondered why she had really come. Had she wanted to hear Adrienne say those words again and to be sure she meant them? She hadn't planned what she would do once she heard her say it.

Adrienne smiled to herself. "You'll probably fuck up the whole country, but there it is. I couldn't hurt you if I wanted to."

"You mean *again*? You couldn't hurt me *again*." Robin's voice was sharper than a knife. Her wounds were now showing.

"Yeah." Adrienne lowered her eyes.

Robin took her seat on the couch again. "I love my husband," she announced abruptly.

"Good for you." Adrienne made herself comfortable in a chair across from her and crossed her legs.

Robin glanced at her, taking brief note of Adrienne's black stockings and heels underneath her skirt. Through the stockings Robin could see something she hadn't noticed the other night. Adrienne had some kind of new tattoo, almost like a snake or serpent-type creature, swirling up her calf. Still the wild child in the way she dressed and in her attitude, Adrienne would always be her temptation—the poison apple she couldn't ponder too long.

She was lost in the sight of her, vaguely aware of the hum of traffic noise below.

Adrienne sighed. "I really should thank you. If it wasn't for you, I would've kept running for a long time. I'll always be grateful to you for that."

Robin didn't know whether to laugh or cry. Instead her mixed emotions came out in an inaudible, awkward chuckle. "How ironic," she sighed. "You're thanking me for something…"

"Your whole campaign is against?" Adrienne hung on the verge of a laugh, her lips turned upward. "Seeing you again," she said, "I figured you'll suffer more living a lie than having some nutcase call you out."

"I am not living a lie!" Robin would have been more convincing had she not shouted it quite so loudly. She set down her beer and rose to her feet. "It obviously meant more to you," Robin lied. There was that fear again, protecting her like an old friend.

"It will eat away at you," Adrienne said. "You already look older."

The governor could take anything but that. *She looked older?* Now she was furious. And she didn't know whom she was furious at— Adrienne or herself, for coming here in the first place.

Robin walked purposefully across the hardwood floor and stopped, face-to-face with the person she pretended meant nothing to her. They stood in front of each other, moments stretching like hours, until Adrienne held her face in her hands. "I'm not trying to hurt you," she said.

Robin lowered her eyes. "I want you to know," she said. "You broke *my* heart. Remember that." She went toward the door as Adrienne let go.

"I was a scared kid," she told Robin. "Years ago, when you told me you loved me…everything was so intense. I was afraid."

Robin released the door handle, frowning at the memory. They weren't kids anymore. It was time to tell the truth, at least while no cameras were around. "You weren't too scared to parade around with that boyfriend of yours."

As soon as the words slipped from her tongue, it was obvious to Robin, and probably to Adrienne as well. Robin remembered it all, every hurtful detail. Even more obvious to Robin was the awareness that her feelings weren't confined to the past. They were with her still, even now. She'd heard about how a first love never completely leaves you, but she'd done everything she could to be the exception, to remain above it all, as if she'd never experienced any of it.

Adrienne would never know how Robin ran home to Georgia and remade her identity as the Southern belle who dated boys at Emory. Or how she threw herself into her books. How she went to church more times a week than she needed to. How she did everything to be the perfect daughter for her parents. And how she locked the year at FSU away in her mind and thought she'd thrown away the key. She thought she had come so far, only to find herself unchanged in the presence of the woman she couldn't forget, the woman she still loved.

Robin turned around slowly. There was no point in pretending anymore.

"I know I really hurt you." Adrienne ran her hand through her blond-streaked hair in the familiar way she used to. "I'm sorry. I guess we both did what we had to do at the time."

"I guess we did."

Adrienne's eyes were bright, intense. "So what now?" she asked with a slightly awkward smile.

"I'm doing what I have to do." With that, Robin opened the door and went to the stairs. In spite of her recent realization, Robin couldn't let herself succumb to her feelings. She could feel the hollowness inside of her expanding with every step she took. She reached the first landing quickly.

"Say hi to your husband," Adrienne called. Her voice was cold, like a slap in Robin's face.

With white knuckles Robin gripped the banister... "Adrienne, there comes a time for everyone, a sort of crossroads, where you can see the right path and the wrong one. I know what's right, and I have to follow what I believe is right."

"I agree." Adrienne folded her arms in judgment, standing in the doorway, looking disappointedly at her on the stairs. She had to have been wondering why Robin bothered to come here at all.

"Good-bye, Adrienne," Robin said, like she was finally closing this chapter of her life once and for all. Even though it seemed over, she had to wonder if it was really over. It had taken her years to push everything down. Now that it had all come bubbling back up, how much longer would it take to push it back down again? Would she be able to now?

As she took another step, she tried to seal up the door to what seemed like someone else's life.

CHAPTER FORTY-THREE

The green Gulf of Mexico glistened in the hazy morning light. In spite of the turmoil, of course I had agreed to get out of town with Adrienne for the weekend. Falling in love was like that—anger, then willingness to do anything no matter how irrational. I was convinced I was no longer in charge of my brain. The outing gave me the idea, no matter how stupid, that I would try to broach the subject neither of us had been able to talk about. During this trip, I was somehow going to find out if I was alone in this relationship, if it was a one-way street that only led to a dead end. Of course, if she told me she only thought of me as a friend, one whom she happened to have sex with, it would be a very long, awkward ride back home.

Before we left that morning, Lydia the RA blocked us in the lobby. "A storm's headed this way." Her brow was crinkled. She seemed to thrive in times of impending catastrophe.

"We won't be out long," Adrienne reassured her. Then in the parking lot: "Who the hell does she think she is? The Gestapo?"

We doubled over with laughter until we saw Lydia guarding her post at the glass door of the lobby. So we quickly climbed into the car and sped out of the parking lot.

Adrienne's little Camaro zipped down the highway as we headed west. We listened to a heavy metal station, and I was proud to recognize many of the songs. I even liked them, the ones with not-so-offensive lyrics. My hand beat against the door along with the drums.

"I love this one!" I shouted, singing as much of the words as I could to "Rock You Like a Hurricane." I glanced at the little notes tattooed on her upper arm. "This is so great!" Until I heard the words more clearly than ever: "What does he mean? *'Give her inches?'*"

Seeing my horrified face, Adrienne replied, "He's talking about a ruler. He's going to give her a ruler!"

I shook my head as she laughed at me, as usual.

"You like a lot of misogynistic songs," I said.

"There you go with the big words again. Focus on the song, not the words." She turned off onto an exit.

"It's hard not to because he's screaming them at me!" I kept shaking my head. The whole world was going to hell.

With the windows open, I could immediately smell the salt air of Panama City. The excitement, the anticipation of the beach and this place I'd never been—the air seemed to crackle with electricity.

We passed run-down tourist shops and seedy motels, each a different pastel color reminding me of the 1950s. A bit tired-looking compared to how it had been in its heyday, Panama City was still situated along some of the prettiest stretches of beach I'd ever seen.

"The sand is almost as white as Destin," Adrienne told me. When she winked at me, my chest rippled inside.

Waves crashed as we strolled side by side looking out at the sea. It was every shade of green, sparkling in the light. We found a spot on the beach away from clumps of tourists and screaming children who smelled like sunscreen. Adrienne wore a sleek, black bikini, and I was covered from head to toe in a cotton wrap covering a one-piece, old lady bathing suit, topped off with a white hat and a gallon of sunblock. I looked like a giant tampon.

Next thing I knew, the balmy breeze seized my wrap and threatened to pull it off completely. I tried to gather it in, as it blew backward.

"Why do you always cover yourself up?" Adrienne asked.

"I don't want to give the birds a free show."

"It's Florida, for God's sake. You gotta show a little skin."

"So I can get skin cancer?" But the clouds had already begun to gather. There wouldn't be much sunlight for long. "I'm convinced. Florida is a weird, hostile environment," I declared. Just then, drops of rain started to fall upon the sand while the sun was still shining. "Look at this! It's not supposed to rain when the sun's out! What is that?"

"It does that."

"Isn't there some law of nature that says that can't happen?"

"Not here," Adrienne laughed.

"It's a bipolar state."

"Haven't you ever felt sad even when you're happy—at the same time?"

I smiled faintly. "No comment." I hated it when she got poetic, especially on days when I wanted to dislike her.

Our eyes locked. How weird it was to never talk about the only thing that was on my mind ever since our night together. I allowed myself quick glimpses of Adrienne's curvy body and remembered what it felt like to touch her skin. Her bathing suit bottom had relaxed a little and was sliding down her hips just enough to make me forget to breathe.

"Hey, what're you thinking about?" Adrienne came closer.

"Nothing."

"Yeah, you are."

"It's nothing important." Thank goodness she didn't have the mystical gift of mind reading.

Adrienne took my hands, and electricity shot through my body. *Just go away.* "Why don't you give me a chance and tell me?"

I looked away, suddenly fascinated with washed-up seaweed. Adrienne held my chin and turned my face toward her. "I see you staring off all the time like you're deep in thought or something. You think I don't see?" Her lips turned upward in a smile. "Can't you trust me with your deep, dark secrets?"

"How do you know they're deep?"

"Everything about you is deep."

"You think so?" I laughed to myself. If only she knew…my deepest thought lately was her bathing suit accidentally coming off.

"You never like to watch anything fun on TV," she continued. "All you want is the news. And you're always arguing about the economy with the guys on TV—who can't hear you, by the way."

"So you think I'm insane."

"You said it, not me." She kept smiling, leaning closer to me. It almost seemed as if she wanted to kiss me.

We started laughing as rain began to fall. Even more threatening clouds seemed to congregate directly above us.

"You think Lydia was right?" I asked.

"She's crazy."

"About the storm?"

"We're fine." That wasn't an answer, so I knew we were in big trouble.

The rain fell harder, as she scooped up wet sand and threw it at me. I tried to hurl it back at her in retaliation, but all I managed to pick up were gray clumps that couldn't hold together long enough to throw at anyone. In no other circumstances would I enjoy being outside in a rainstorm, with wet mushy sand working its way into every crevice of my feet, toes, hands and God knows where else.

When the weather cut the trip short, it reminded me of my original plan. Would I be able to find my inner braveness? As we traveled back, dark clouds followed us, casting a long shadow on the car. It looked like the end of the world was coming. Maybe it was. If I couldn't find my gutsy side, I'd never be able to live with myself. I watched the intermittent windshield wipers swipe at the rain until it fell so hard that everything was a blur.

"Adrienne, can I ask you something?"

"Sure."

I thought carefully before crafting my words. "What if you wanted to tell someone something, but you weren't sure how to say it and really weren't sure how they'd take it? What would you do?" Surely Adrienne would know by now what I was going to say.

She smiled. "You do like Boyd!"

"No!" I guess it wasn't that obvious to her after all.

"You said nothing happened that night." Adrienne grinned. "But you wanted it to, didn't you?"

I looked out the window. The wind brushed whitecaps across the water. "No."

Adrienne didn't believe me. "You've gotta tell him. You don't have a chance if he never knows how you really feel."

"What if he, and I'm not saying it's him, really doesn't think of me that way?" I'd never been so scared, teetering on the edge of a storm, wondering what the crash of thunder would feel like.

"So?"

"What if he's really *offended* that I like him that way?" The whole discussion seemed ridiculous, but her homophobic comments were just too frightening for me to risk putting myself out there. If things went badly, I'd be stuck in a small room with her for the rest of the year. I had visions of Adrienne pointing me out to her party friends as the girl who put the moves on her and that ugly sneer she had when talking about the girl on our floor, the "freak" who kissed another girl. There was too much at stake. If Adrienne had really been too drunk, she might become hostile if she thought I had deeper feelings for her. The space we shared was too small for that kind of problem. She might be uncomfortable and think that I was going to stalk her when she took a shower or something. If things got so bad that I had to transfer, how would I explain it to my parents?

"Offended?" Adrienne looked peculiarly at me as the rain let up a little. "You really don't give yourself enough credit. You're really cute. And he seemed to be into you."

"You think so?"

"Oh yeah." Our eyes met for a moment, as she placed her hand over mine.

"The road!" I was distracted by another pocket of torrential rain up ahead. Wind seized the car and jerked it from side to side. I closed my eyes. "Just tell me when we're on the other side of this."

CHAPTER FORTY-FOUR

The wind was relentless. It jerked the car around so much I started praying to myself. I muttered a few phrases under my breath.

"What is that? Voodoo?" Adrienne teased.

"Shut up. Haven't you ever prayed before?"

"Yeah, once." Her face became hard like stone. She stared at the road, expressionless. "I prayed something would happen to my dad, so Mom and I wouldn't have to put up with his shit anymore."

"You prayed for him to…"

"Die." She glanced at me to see if I was shocked. "That's right. You think I'm a bad person now?"

"Nooo." I was careful in my response.

"He went through this time when he drank every day. He'd slap my mom around, and I knew it was a matter of time before he turned to me. But I wasn't going to take it. I got a spare hammer from the garage and kept it in my bedroom, planning how I'd hit him with it if he ever came after me. But he never did. It got so bad, though, Mom had enough and she left. Not a word to him *or* me."

I could tell from her face that her mom's departure had hurt her deeply.

"So yeah," she said. "I've prayed before."

"I'm sorry. I never saw you as the praying type." Then I remembered that she was living with her dad now. "How is he now?" I asked carefully.

"He doesn't drink as much. When he gets bad, I lock my door." She was so matter-of-fact. I wanted to say the right thing, but I couldn't think of anything. I also realized how silly I must've seemed to her, freaking out over bugs and public restrooms when she had much more serious things to deal with.

Then a crack of thunder and flash of lightning seemed to bounce right off the hood of the car with one powerful strike.

"What the hell was *that?*" I leapt out of my seat. "We should've listened to Lydia! We knew a storm was coming, but no! *You* had to go to the beach!"

"Oh, will you get a grip?"

"I'm sorry, but I don't feel like getting electrocuted today." Lightning and the possibility of death were *not* silly things, I decided.

Everything blurred across the windshield as more buckets of rain descended, along with some hail. She strained to see the road as long as she could before pulling into the nearest convenience store, where we could wait out the storm.

Once inside, I watched the gray windows streaked with water and still more rain shooting down like bullets across the glass. Everything seemed so angry. Maybe God was punishing us. Shivering, we took cover in the back aisle behind the Ding Dongs and Twinkies.

"Do they have to blast the air conditioner like that?" I kept whining as I tried to wipe my arms dry.

"It's Florida." Adrienne put her arm around me. "Sorry about this," she said.

"It's okay," I said, realizing I was being a baby. I had to get over myself. Mother Nature could be a bitch, and there was no changing her mind today.

The wind blew so hard against the glass windows and doors, it sounded as if they might burst. I jumped with each new startling sound. Even the worst thunderstorm back home never sounded like this. More people rushed in from outside, trying to take cover near the ice machine or behind the counter. We stayed in the back, the farthest away from the glass.

"They should've put tape on the windows," Adrienne said.

The water level began to rise until it was above the ankles of people running on the other side of the glass. I slid down the Twinkie-stuffed shelves, grabbing my knees.

"You okay?" Adrienne asked, crouching down beside me.

"Yeah," I answered. "Twinkies will save us." There it was again—the sarcasm that tried to mask my fear.

She touched my face. Her fingers ran down my cheek so slowly, I felt it as a caress. "You had some mascara," she muttered. "It was running." It really didn't make sense, but I didn't care. "So you like Boyd?"

"What?" I'd forgotten our previous conversation.

"Boyd, you know. You were telling me how you feel."

"I'm sorry," I said. "I'm kind of distracted with the end of the world out there." But she really seemed to want to know. "It's not exactly him," I managed. "I think you know who it is."

The next crash of thunder hit and the lights went out. People in the store stayed pretty quiet, mesmerized by the view outside.

"No, I don't," Adrienne said quietly. "You never talk about anyone."

I was in that place where I had to decide if it was better to hide behind the Twinkies in fear or face the lightning. "It's *you*," I said finally in a big exhale, not looking at her. In the next moment I felt her arm around my shoulders, pulling me closer. When I looked at her, she was staring at the ice cream in the freezer straight ahead. It seemed she couldn't look at me, either. "Well?" I was going to push the issue; I shouldn't have to go it alone anymore. "It's been so weird, the way we've never really talked about that night, you know?"

"It seemed like a dream," she said, still not looking at me.

My head went numb. A dream is something that isn't real, something you can wake from that has nothing to do with reality. Was that really what she wanted? To see it as something unreal? Of course. Everything she'd done since that night proved it.

Dream. I analyzed the word in my mind. It was funny. You go through life hearing a million words that don't mean anything. And suddenly one word takes on the greatest meaning of all. *How exactly did she mean it?*

I sat back on my heels and tried to breathe. "I'm sorry," I said. "Believe me, I don't want to feel this way. But to me, it was more than a dream. It was real."

"It was real to me too."

I was confused. "You don't regret it? You seemed like you wished we hadn't…you said you drank too much."

She finally looked at me. "I had to say something. I thought you'd freak out." Then I saw a look I couldn't read in her shiny, brown eyes.

It may have been fear. She pulled me closer and we held each other a long time in the back aisle as the rain poured.

The counter clerk saw us and said, "It's going to be all right, ladies. You're not going to die or anything."

We pulled apart and realized that the storm had let up. Of course he thought we were doing a final embrace because of the weather. *Hysterical women.*

She stood up to check the windows. I watched her with a mixture of relief and elation, not to mention the ever-present fear. What did this mean? What would happen now?

The ride back was unusually quiet. Obviously, we both had a lot of thinking to do. I had trouble hearing my own thoughts with the heavy metal tapes that she kept putting in, one after another. I looked out the window at the passing tropical scenery, so oddly calm after the storm. A purple sky was spreading overhead as the afternoon lingered on. Alice Cooper screamed about a woman he'd better not touch, someone he wanted to get closer to but couldn't or shouldn't. *How apropos.* I tried not to listen, but the music was mimicking every thought I had.

Then I realized…there was still the issue of Sean. Was I nothing more than a fling, or the dreaded experiment in college that so many girls later admit to? I remembered how Adrienne had told me that while she was in college, she just wanted to have some fun. What if I was her fun? I sat perfectly still and said nothing for most of the ride home.

When we returned to the dorm, students were crowded into the lobby, watching the weather on TV. Lydia was the first to confront us.

"I warned you two about the weather!" she exclaimed. "Why would you go out in this?"

"It was fine this morning," I explained. "We thought we'd be back before it hit." Lydia believed me. I think Adrienne was impressed that her do-gooder roommate could be such a cool liar.

"Well," Lydia said gruffly. "You need to stay in now. It's mandatory. A Category 3 is churning in the Gulf." Her gestures were very dramatic. "We're just getting the outer bands."

"You mean this isn't the storm?" I exclaimed.

"No, it's not." Lydia's hands were on her hips.

"Oh, for God's sake," Adrienne sighed. "We're in a brick building." She glanced at the TV screen. "It's heading west anyway."

"That may be!" Lydia snapped. "But guess where the most dangerous side of a hurricane is? Where we are, the east part. We'll be getting fierce winds and rain all night. So you two better hunker down."

We laughed all the way back to our room.

"Hunker down!" Adrienne mocked her, throwing her keys on the desk. "Let's be sure to 'hunker down.' Jesus, does anyone really say that?"

"Apparently she does."

We laughed harder.

As rain pelted the window of our tiny room, I cracked open a beer. The devil on my shoulder wanted to lose control again. "Let's have a hurricane party," I said excitedly.

"The girl who doesn't party?" Adrienne's mouth broke into a slow smile. "Don't you have to study?" she teased.

"I can't go to the library tonight," I said, taking a sip. "The drill sergeant out there would kill me." To be honest, I wanted to re-create the situation that had resulted with her in my bed. The part of my brain that wasn't working would have done anything to make it happen again. *Take that, Reverend Butler!*

She laughed, pulling out a beer for herself. "She's probably called in the military to guard the doors." Ever since our conversation in the convenience store, Adrienne seemed odd around me. Maybe she was nervous. "I could call Nancy upstairs."

I took a step toward her, setting my beer can on the desk. "That wasn't the kind of party I had in mind…unless you're scared." I slid my arms around her neck, suddenly feeling bolder than ever. This time it wasn't the beer talking.

Adrienne backed away. I stood, dangling, in the middle of the room, feeling a lump swell in my throat. She took my hand and sat me down on my bed. We sat side by side against the wall, under Bette Davis, with our legs tucked up beside each other. The seconds that passed might as well have been a hundred years. I watched as she traced the sharp edge of the opening of her beer can. "I'm not scared," she said.

"Really?"

She lowered her eyes. This was the first time I'd seen her look really vulnerable. I thought I understood so much more about her now. "I just…"

"I'm not your type," I teased. "You think I'm too uptight."

"No, I don't."

"Yeah, you do!" I laughed. "And it's okay. But I'm not."

"I know! I'm starting to think you're the wild one of the two of us."

"Not hardly." I dissolved into giddy laughter, shaking my head more times than necessary. "You have that honor."

* * *

Under the watchful eye of Bette Davis, I was just an eighteen-year-old girl in love. It was innocent and frightening in ways it didn't have to be, other than the usual terror of falling in love with someone who never made you feel sure you were standing on solid ground.

"It's just that..." Adrienne struggled. "I'm not queer, you know." She looked at me with a pained expression.

My face, my entire body, spread with the heat of embarrassment and humiliation. I had to somehow scrape my pride off the floor. "It's okay," I said. When I looked at her again, I was so busy concentrating on how to look cool and undaunted by her revelation that I didn't even remember her face or what she said next. There was only an ache inside, a pain stronger than any I'd ever known, getting stronger inside me. "Excuse me." I had to go out to the bathroom where I could let it all go. The last thing I wanted was for her to see me cry. That was something I'd never, ever show her.

CHAPTER FORTY-FIVE

Robin paused on the stair, realizing that Adrienne hadn't closed her apartment door yet. Then another thought surfaced—the possibility that this chapter of her life didn't have to be closed if she didn't want it to be. There was such freedom in opening herself to the idea of joy, pure joy, and possibility, again. She climbed the stairs, ignoring every thought that tried to pull her back down. She met Adrienne in the doorway, took her face in her hands and kissed her like it was the end of the world.

Adrienne pulled back. "Do you know what you're doing?"

Robin nodded, still lingering on her lips, her chin, and thinking only about everything she wanted to do to her. She wouldn't deny herself, not now. As she tried to pull her tighter to her, Adrienne stopped her again.

"Because I don't play games," Adrienne said. "Not anymore."

Robin kissed her again, holding her tightly so Adrienne wouldn't change her mind. Then Adrienne held her hands and led her inside.

* * *

Adrienne's bedroom was decorated as warmly, as invitingly as the rest of her apartment, which shouldn't have been all that surprising to Robin. But it reminded her that Adrienne was, in fact, an adult. There wouldn't be posters of hair bands on the walls. Robin smiled to herself, grateful for the passage of time and warmed by the memory of the girl she used to know. They fell upon a down comforter, and Robin couldn't hide her smile.

"What?" Adrienne traced her mouth and searched her eyes.

"Remembering." Robin's smile was bigger and more joyful than it had been in years. She felt slightly self-conscious as Adrienne continued tracing the features of her face. She imagined what Adrienne must have been thinking—her drooping eyelids, sagging cheeks. Of course Robin imagined them so much worse in her mind.

"You're beautiful," Adrienne said, almost in a whisper. Hearing Robin's sharp intake of breath, like a gasp, Adrienne took her into her arms and kissed her so deeply, urgently, erasing all thought, all reason from Robin's mind.

They peeled off each other's clothes in a passionate fury, years of ache and desire, too long unanswered...for Robin, it felt like her last chance to be free.

She held Adrienne's face gently as she laid kiss after kiss on her soft, yielding mouth, kissing her cheeks, her eyelids...

Adrienne laughed at the frenetic kisses; it was as if Robin only had seconds to live and was getting every last bit of pleasure she could find in this life. There was a sense of frenzy, as they reached for each other with eager hands. Adrienne's bronze skin wrapped around Robin's pale, porcelain body, intertwined in a raw, sensual dance. Robin was unapologetic and bold, the way she caressed the round fullness of Adrienne's breasts, something she'd imagined—and remembered— for so long. The feel and scent of her skin, it was so familiar to her, so perfectly intoxicating. As Robin mounted her, Adrienne's hands were cupping her backside possessively, then gliding slowly up to her shoulders, in awe of her.

They moved so easily together, as moonlight cast its spell of shadows and made more perfect the imperfections of the day.

Like an old movie, the moon's streaming light gave Adrienne's face a gentle, Hollywood glow. Robin stroked it, yearning to see every expression as she touched her.

Adrienne felt her longing and answered with caresses almost too unbearably real for Robin, making her want more.

As the hours ticked by, Robin's insatiable desire only grew. She held Adrienne's strong thighs and pushed them apart, driving her wild with thrashes of her tongue, her lips. Robin remembered *Curious Wine* and the Emily Dickinson poem it referenced: "I had been hungry all the years...my noon had come to dine..." The feel of Adrienne's raised hips, quivering, convulsing...she was so utterly lost in the moment, she almost didn't hear her begging her to stop. She slid up the length of her beautiful, bronze-like body and held her.

"I'm sorry," Robin whispered.

"Don't be, please." Adrienne tried to catch her breath. "I haven't been...treated like that in years." She laughed. "It was so good I need a cigarette. And I don't smoke anymore."

Robin could feel her cheek in a smile against her chest, her heart still thudding so fast.

The night seemed to stretch out with no end, with Robin losing herself next, shuddering, as Adrienne enjoyed her, with expert fingertips never losing contact with her breasts and her whole writhing body.

Before long, the light shifted behind the window curtain, a silent warning for Robin. As Adrienne slept, she checked her phone. Peter's voice mail messages reminded her of the reality waiting right outside the door. No matter how long she stayed here, she couldn't shut out the world forever.

She hurriedly grabbed her clothes off the floor. With one step of her foot on a creaky floorboard, Adrienne began to stir in the bed. She raised up slightly on her elbows and looked at the clock.

"It's early," Adrienne said. "Can't you stay for breakfast?"

"Oh no," Robin answered. "I have to get back to the hotel."

She knew she needed to leave before dawn broke, before her identity was revealed to everyone on the street. And she knew she couldn't be seen arriving at the hotel; it would only spark another scandal.

"Oh." Adrienne's face fell as the reality set in for her. She threw off the sheet, tempting Robin with her nude body lying there. "I guess you have to go back to being a big, self-righteous right-winger."

"Don't." Robin sat on the edge of the bed. "Don't ruin it."

"Ruin what?" Adrienne sat up. "What's there to ruin? What is this?"

"You've given me a wonderful memory. But that's all." Robin glanced at her bare breasts, then looked away. She rushed to gather the rest of her things. Sadly, she had to accept that her joy couldn't last forever. There was too much at stake.

Adrienne bolted out of bed and followed her to the living room. She seemed to enjoy how uneasy she was making her, the way Robin couldn't even look at her.

"Could you please put some clothes on?" Robin was obviously uncomfortable.

"You didn't seem to mind last night. In fact, you preferred me without clothes." Adrienne purposely straddled a barstool by the kitchen counter, revealing the still glistening wetness between her legs.

Robin ached but turned away to pick up her coat from the couch. "You knew this wouldn't be able to last," she said. "We can't make more of it than it was."

"I told you I don't play games."

Robin turned to face her—Adrienne's arms were folded over her breasts and her legs still wide open...

"What do we call *this*?" Robin said, gesturing to Adrienne's pose.

"Touch me one more time," Adrienne said. "If you can and you still leave, I'll believe it's over."

Robin approached her slowly and reached for her face. But Adrienne took her hand and drew her finger along the velvety, wet center of her. Adrienne's breath caught in her throat. Robin couldn't stop stroking her once she'd begun. Adrienne kissed her so hard that everything in Robin's head began to swirl.

Minutes later, Robin was undressed again, and they were slow dancing in the living room, their hearts pounding. Robin's whole body felt like a flowing river of peace, relaxation, an exquisite pleasure she hadn't experienced in so many years.

* * *

Adrienne wore a long, soft button-down shirt as she fixed them coffee. Robin, back in her flannel shirt and jeans, reclined on the couch, watching her tanned legs with admiration.

"You know," Robin said, "I used to look for the light on in our window when I came back from classes. I'd get excited to know you were back...with your reading lamp on." She smiled to herself at the memory.

"I have a confession too," Adrienne said, handing her a steamy mug. "I used to sit at the window and watch for you to come up the hill."

Robin broke out in a slow smile that quickly turned to sadness. She only took one sip of her coffee before she said, "You know I can't stay." She knew she was now going to have to outrun the sunrise if she was going to make it back undetected. It might still be possible. "It's been so...wonderful." Words failed her, but everything she felt was in her deep blue eyes, which could barely hold back the flood as she made her way to the door.

"Yeah." Adrienne followed her, waving her hand like nothing mattered. "I don't know why I've been so nice to you. You'll probably win, you know. And now, after this, can you say with a straight face that what we are is unnatural?"

Robin stepped toward her and held her face in her hands. "Nothing has ever felt so natural and right in my whole life. The worst part is, I'll never be sure if I'm doing the right thing, leaving you."

"The worst part is I know you're doing the wrong thing, and I have to let you go." Her caramel eyes were shinier than Robin had ever seen.

There was some peace in knowing that Adrienne did feel the same, but it also made everything more difficult, even tragic.

Robin held her one more time.

"Wait!" Adrienne pulled away and went to the bedroom to get something from her nightstand drawer. She came back, holding a wrapped gift in the shape of a small rectangle. She gave it to Robin and closed her fingers over it. "Don't open it until before the debate. It's for good luck."

Robin looked at her suspiciously. "You're wishing me luck? Wouldn't you prefer to see me lose?"

"Well, yeah. But take it anyway." Adrienne laughed, then held a smile, a loving, genuine smile that Robin felt deep inside.

"Thank you," Robin whispered, kissing her on the cheek. "I don't know what it is, but thank you."

They both laughed awkwardly, neither one able to face the magnitude of this moment, like the time they said good-bye at school. Some moments were too filled with emotion to be able to move through easily. And if Robin let herself feel completely, it would be too much to handle. If it was a final good-bye, neither of them wanted to say it.

It would be Robin to break the awkward silence first. "I guess this is good-bye."

Adrienne nodded quickly, almost businesslike, her smile dissolved. She took a deep breath. "I don't like 'good-bye,'" she said. "How about 'so long'?"

Robin nodded. "So long." She gave her a long hug, then turned and left.

CHAPTER FORTY-SIX

I spent Thanksgiving in a walk-in clinic in Tallahassee. My nose was stuffed and itchy, throat scratchy, and I felt really tired. I'd planned to go home for the long weekend, but Mom got nervous when she heard me on the phone.

"You need to rest," she said. "You could get a fever and pass out on the highway and get yourself killed!" She was the master of the worst-case scenario.

So against my wishes, I stayed in Tallahassee. At the clinic, I sat across from an older man who seemed full of despair. His head was down, his hand covering his forehead. Next to him was a Betty Boop tote bag. I knew it couldn't have belonged to him, so I figured his wife was the sick one. Sure enough, a white-haired lady came out and motioned him over to the counter to pay the bill. He dutifully rose, carrying the Betty Boop bag. It was cute how couples that had been together a long time sort of merged into one entity. That tired-looking man now owned Betty Boop.

My thoughts were drifting all over the place when they called me next. I was examined by a gray-haired doctor with a bored expression, who I knew would have rather been playing golf than looking up my nose.

"You have allergies," he said after less than two minutes.

"Are you sure?" I asked. "I mean, I've never had allergies before."

"You can get them any time in your life."

"Are you sure it isn't the flu or walking pneumonia…" I wanted it to be something serious to keep me away for Thanksgiving. I was still fuming that I was going to miss my mother's raisin stuffing. Everything about this year was wrong!

"You're not from here, correct?" he asked, looking over the form I filled out.

"No."

"Well, Florida has lots of flowers and plants that don't all agree with everyone. Your body is reacting to something in the flora or fauna."

Then get rid of the flora and fauna. The problem wasn't with me.

I assumed my uppity posture. "So what does this mean?"

"You'll need to see an allergist and get shots." He wasn't much for delivering news gently. He probably told people who were dying: "You're dying."

"Shots?" I repeated.

"They'll test to see which things bother you." He rolled his chair closer to me, looking annoyed. Obviously he was going to have to explain biology to a patient. Darn. "Your body has an immune system, right? It attacks allergens, or what it considers foreign invaders. Your immune system is hyperactive and trying to keep out what it thinks doesn't belong."

"Sounds like me."

"You're a college kid, right?"

I nodded.

"Didn't they cover this in high school?" He was snarky, and I was immediately offended.

"You don't have to be rude," I said quietly.

"In the meantime," he said, ignoring me, "take a decongestant. You'll be fine." He waved me out with his sun-damaged, leathery hand.

Since I'd already missed half the weekend, I opted not to go home. I'd see everyone at Christmas anyway.

It was weird, though. The campus seemed haunted with virtually no one else there, except kids who were foreign exchange students who didn't celebrate Thanksgiving or the ones who were trying to study extra hard to become the valedictorian.

I went to the Performing Arts building and checked out a copy of *Desert Hearts*. I excitedly read the description on the back and brought it back to the dorm room. That night I curled up with a box of tissues, watching my first-ever movie about two women falling in love, while sniffling and sneezing through most of it. As the credits rolled, I didn't have much doubt left about who I was. But I still wavered as to how I could possibly live my life admitting such a thing, being from a prominent family in a conservative place.

Luckily, Carol didn't go home that weekend either. New York was too far for her, so she saved her plane ticket for Christmas. I stayed at her place on the last night, before Adrienne would be coming back, just for the company. Carol and I sat up and watched old movies together. The latest was a Barbara Stanwyck film noir classic, *Double Indemnity*.

"See, my roommate would hate this," I said. "She rolls her eyes at anything that's in black and white."

"She sounds like an idiot."

"Yeah." But my face was still dreamy, I guess. My sneeze interrupted my thoughts and shook the roof.

"Jesus! Tissue?"

I nodded, and she handed me a box of Kleenex from the bathroom.

"You're so lucky to have your own bathroom," I said.

"You always say that."

"It's a luxury, a private bath," I muttered. I still wasn't used to my dorm setup, "I know, I know. I'm whining."

"Yeah, knock that shit off." She muted the TV. "She told you the deal, right?"

It took me a moment to realize what she was talking about. "Adrienne? Yeah, I guess."

"No *guess*. She told you. She flat-out said she wasn't queer."

I wrinkled my nose. "I don't like that word."

"It doesn't matter! You know what she meant!" Carol seemed frustrated.

"Is it the Tight End?" I asked. "Is that why you're so…so…"

"Bitchy?" She finished my sentence. "Partly. But I'm done with him. I know when to pull the plug. You need to know that too."

"I get what you're saying, but…"

She touched my thigh. I didn't think twice about it at the time. "You need to be with someone who appreciates you." She was unusually kind, nearly sensitive. It was alarming.

"Thanks." I looked back at the TV until she unmuted it.

* * *

When Adrienne came back, I asked her how her Thanksgiving was, which seemed like normal conversation to me. But she was hostile about it.

"Okay," she said. "Whenever my dad and I are alone, it's…totally awkward. And the turkey was dry 'cause he can't cook." She unzipped her suitcase. There was more going on besides the turkey, I was certain.

"Want to talk about it?" I asked.

"No." She started unpacking, then stopped abruptly, letting out a long sigh. "See, we get in this fight all the time. It's the same damn thing. If I even hint that I might wanna study music, he goes off, like, do I want to live in a shack? Do I want to not know where my next meal is coming from…shit like that. Then I get depressed and wish I never brought it up."

"You could take some electives," I suggested.

"Like you, you mean."

"No, I'm flat-out lying. You could really take a class here and there, and see how you feel about it."

She paused and smiled at me, then resumed unpacking. I hoped I made her feel better.

For the next couple of weeks, we were immersed in finals. Yet there was that nagging feeling I had, wishing we could have another party. Ironically, when Adrienne used to beg me to "party" with her, I'd say no. Now all I wanted was for her to ask me again. But oddly, she seemed content to study and do the things we came to school to do. I didn't like it. Though I got her message about not being queer, I didn't want to believe it. I kept the hope alive that she wasn't being completely honest. It was the only thing that kept me going.

* * *

It wasn't long before holiday lights were strung around all the dorm windows. The party had begun early that evening, with empty beer cans scattered around our room. Despite what she'd told me, I was certain that in her less guarded moments, I could make it happen again. Maybe it's the certainty that comes from obsessive love, when you need to believe someone feels what you do. I'd always considered myself a pretty logical person, but maybe this is what happens when you fall hard for someone. Maybe I was on the road to a padded cell…I didn't care.

I felt pretty tonight in my black turtleneck, but thought Adrienne was even more beautiful in a fuzzy, oatmeal-colored sweater. I wanted to run my hands all over the softness…of that sweater. Tonight, our last night before Christmas break, I envisioned a party that would end up with us curled up on one of our beds, a perfect last night before I had to go back home where I'd be tempted to repent. So I tried to see if Adrienne wanted to spend more time with me. When she took another beer out of the fridge, I asked for another too. I knew that Adrienne was like a cat I was trying to hold that was restless and ready to slip out of my arms at any minute. But when something feels so good, you want to ignore any signs that say otherwise, even if they're flashing in neon letters.

The sun was starting to go down, so Adrienne lit a small tree decorated with miniature beer can ornaments.

"Where did you get *that?*" I asked.

"Don't make fun. It was a gift…from Sean."

I folded my arms.

"Don't look at me like that," Adrienne protested, shaking a stubborn light that wouldn't turn on.

"I didn't know you were still seeing him."

"Yeah," she answered. "We hang out sometimes." She seemed defensive.

We both stood with arms crossed, regarding the tree. "Whaddaya think?" Adrienne asked.

It's the tackiest thing I've ever seen. "It's…different."

"You hate it."

"Hate is a strong word."

"Oh, geez!" Adrienne threw her hands up in the air. "It was a gift. I can't take it down."

"No, it's okay. It's your room too." I tried to be polite, though why I didn't know.

"You're such a liar." She smiled, finishing off her can in record time. She came closer, and I set down my drink. She held both of my hands and looked in my eyes with a mixture of wonder and fear.

I raised my hand to her face, running my fingers down her jaw, to her neck. She closed her eyes; she seemed to enjoy being touched. Alarm bells sounded in my mind as I wondered if she'd soon pull away.

"Sometimes," she said, "I feel confused about you."

I couldn't help but smile. I wanted her to be confused. I touched my lips to hers in a light, gentle kiss. But she jerked back.

"Crap! He'll be here in a minute!" she exclaimed, looking for something.

"*He's* coming?" All the blood left my body. An icy chill blew into the room.

"Yeah. You have plans tonight?"

You were my plans. "Not really. I might go hang out with some friends."

"I owe you an explanation." Adrienne was very serious.

"Save it."

"No, listen!" She held my arm, which I yanked away.

"I don't want to listen! I don't want to hear any more about him, okay?" I hated who I was becoming, and it was all her fault.

She ran her hand through her hair. I watched in awe as she came a little undone and was secretly glad to be the reason for it. "I feel all these things about you. I'm not trying to lead you on...but...I can't figure it out."

"Stay with me tonight," I said. I couldn't go a whole month suspended like this. I looked intently into her eyes, hoping my silent plea would persuade her.

Then came the inevitable knock on the door that ruined everything.

Still looking at me, Adrienne opened it. It was Sean. "Hey, we gotta hurry," he told her. "I'm parked in the tow-away."

"Keep your pants on!" She was obviously torn. "Will you be okay?"

"Sure." I averted my eyes, scared she might see my tears.

It wasn't long before Lydia made her presence known. "Somebody's parked in the tow-away zone, which is a violation!"

"I'm movin' it!" Sean barked, then pointed at Adrienne. "Come on!"

Adrienne turned to face me with outstretched arms and that infectious, warm smile. It was a smile that made me forgive all of her sins. "I guess this is it," she said. And what came next was more for the two people waiting in the doorway: "We'll have to catch up later. But if I don't see you, have a great Christmas!"

"You too." So she was spending the night at Sean's.

She wrapped her arms around me, hugging me so tightly I was swallowed up in her oatmeal sweater. I closed my eyes and breathed in the softness of her, wanting to stay that way as long as I could. For some reason, I couldn't stay angry at her, even though I wanted to. Oh, how I wanted to! When she released me, Sean yelled, "Let's go, Austen!"

CHAPTER FORTY-SEVEN

Behind double Gothic-looking doors embossed with two mirror images of cobras appeared a burly bouncer with muscles protruding from his tattooed upper arms. He was a human Popeye.

Standing in the dimly lit foyer, I squeezed Andrew's arm, wondering what I was doing here. Of course I knew. Nothing could be sadder than sitting alone in the dorm room tonight, imagining all of the things Sean was going to do to Adrienne. So of course I called Andrew, who told me there was a special holiday discount at his club tonight. I begged Carol to come with us. Though she insisted she'd been there before, which I thought was a lie, she reluctantly agreed to come later.

Andrew gave me a reassuring answer squeeze, which silently told me that all would be okay in spite of the fact that we were in a sketchy part of town, that there was no sign from the road and that this seemed like the sort of place that police would swarm at any minute.

The bouncer stamped my hand with a black ink smear of their snake logo. "Thank you," I said politely, which only made me seem more out of my element, if that was possible. I'd worn my black sweater with jeans, and my eyes widened at a group who seemed to be wearing the material you find on floor mats in your car. It was shimmering rubber or something similar, and some of them had heavy chains around their necks—not the kind of chains that could pass for a necklace, more like a chain-link fence.

"C'mon." Andrew grabbed my arm before I got us thrown out for staring and looking like I didn't belong, I guess.

We turned the corner and walked through a giant, carved mouth of a cobra. When we emerged on the other side, I saw a world that was beyond my imagination. It was a sprawling, dark and foggy club. A singer I'd later learn was Siouxsie Sioux shouted from huge screens, which wouldn't have made that much difference had I ever seen anything like her before. She was singing a song that was a cross between a dirge and a Broadway musical. There was nothing I could compare it to. But what struck me most was that she was the most self-possessed, confident female I'd ever seen. With black spikey hair and dark eye makeup that could only be described as demonic-looking, she moved and sang in a way that dared everyone to even try and not look at her. All of the music in this place was strange to me. There was a dance song that moved like a fast carousel, with spinning wheels in the video. And a group I'd learn was Sisters of Mercy—they were so tough and leathery, they made heavy metal bands look like cupcakes. Andrew called it "alternative" music—Erasure, The Cure, Siouxsie & the Banshees—all kinds of bands, all new to me, that I discovered in that one night. It was magical, really. How many times can you remember a single night when a whole new world is opened to you?

The club had dark corners and flashing lights, so it was difficult to see exactly how much space stretched out in every direction. I stood awestruck, watching dancing bodies—mostly same-sex couples—on a crowded dance floor as smoke and strobe lights twirled around them. Of course, the flashing lights made everyone appear to be better dancers than they were, a feature which I liked. Purple lights lined the steps up to the bar as on a cruise ship, and more couples sat scattered throughout the club at metal or chrome tables. It was very futuristic-looking.

"Want a drink?" Andrew asked, obviously trying to relax me.

"Sure, great." I searched for the ladies' room so I could pull myself together. The restroom was decorated the opposite of the rest of the place. It was like a Victorian hotel, complete with a chandelier, and empty except for the girl with melting mascara who stood in front of the mirror. Long minutes passed. I would have to fix my smeared makeup before setting foot back out there. The muffled music bounced off the walls, and something about the noise of music and crowds talking and laughing on the other side of the wall sounds scary when you're new to a place. I took a deep breath. I had to stop wishing I could share this night, this experience, with Adrienne. I had to erase her from my mind, even though I saw her on the dance floor, in the music videos, even in the weird sculptures that served as centerpieces on the tables. Another deep breath...and I pushed the door open.

When I came back out, Sinead O'Connor's stunning face filled every screen, singing "Nothing Compares 2 U" against a black backdrop. It was the most dramatic video, very unlike the heavy metal videos in our room. Through the fog I found Andrew perched at the bar, his eyes following a guy who was walking away. "Hey," I called.

Andrew waved dramatically. "How do we like it?"

"It's great."

"You know it's gay, right?"

"I kind of got that impression." I did an excellent portrayal of someone poised and comfortable with herself.

"Look," Andrew said, "if you ever need anything, I'm here to help. And I'd like to start with your hair and clothes. Ahhh!"

I smacked his arm. "Sorry. I'm not into spandex." I leaned against the bar, cradling the beer he got for me. "Thanks," I said, raising it to toast with his. "Who was that guy?" I glanced at the one who was walking in the opposite direction.

"He doesn't know it yet, but he's going to be mine."

I shook my head, laughing. "God, I wish I had your confidence."

"So who is she?"

"Who is who?" I did my best innocent face, but he wasn't as gullible as I hoped. "It's no one. Trust me. She's *absolutely* no one."

He grinned broadly. "Ooh, then I must know all about this absolute nobody."

"No, really."

"C'mon! I want all the sordid details!"

"There are none!" I shouted over the music.

"You must be in love if you're this upset."

He was a sage in spandex. Seeing that I wasn't ready to talk about it yet, he took my hand and escorted me out on the dance floor.

"Honey, we're going to have some fun!" He started moving his hips more than any straight guy I knew. Some of his moves looked like they might be illegal.

That night, I had fun. I danced under the lights and forgot about my hair, my face, how I looked to anyone else. The boys weren't scanning me because they were all gay and didn't care, and most of the lesbians seemed to be coupled off anyway. It was okay. It was fun—something I could get used to. I might even want to do it again.

* * *

An hour later, a slow song came on, so I decided to sit it out and wait at the only empty chrome table. I watched as couples made up of two boys or two girls danced so easily with each other, without ridicule or judgment. Here everyone was fine with everyone else. It was beautiful. There was no fear. And the way they held each other…I was so entranced by the scene, I hardly noticed when Carol showed up.

"They've got a bathroom that's too pretty to pee in," she said, taking a seat beside me.

"Hey, you made it." I helped pull out her chair.

"So where is she?" Carol asked.

"Where is who?" I watched as Andrew ordered more beers for us at the bar.

"The bitch." Carol didn't mince words.

"Shut up." I might have thought it, but I didn't want anyone else saying it.

"Where is she tonight?" Carol pressed.

"With her boyfriend."

"Of course she is. C'mon."

I winced. "Don't say it. Please."

"That she's straight?"

"She was almost with me tonight!" Of course I heard how pathetic that sounded.

"Maybe she's not straight," Carol said. "Maybe she's bisexual. But if the boyfriend trumps you, I say fuck her."

Just then, Andrew came over. "Hey, Carol!" He beamed. "Fancy seeing *you* here."

She waved her hand. "Don't get all excited. This isn't a date."

"Do you want it to be?" Quickly, he threw up his hand. "None of my business!"

She sneered at him. "Bite your tongue."

Did I miss something? I'd been too wrapped up in my own drama to notice anything, or anyone, else.

"So what're your holiday plans?" Andrew asked, changing the subject.

"I go home tomorrow," I replied. "What about you?"

"To Naziville?" he said, rolling his eyes.

I nodded with understanding. Why did the nicest people so often get more than their share of torture? It wasn't fair.

"It's okay," he continued. "I'm staying with some friends." He looked at Carol.

"Gotta go to Albany," Carol muttered. "My mom's all freaked that I haven't visited in a while. But she'll be planted on the couch the whole time, while my Gucci sisters squawk about their husbands. It's fucking annoying."

"Sorry," I said softly.

She seemed more agitated toward me than usual. Maybe she'd forgotten her medication. I was concerned about her driving with all the medicine she took and the side effects, not to mention the fact that she was drinking. But she told us all to leave her alone about it, that she had a license and that it was none of our business.

"What do you care?" Carol snapped.

"Hey," I retorted. "Why are you so hostile?"

"She's pissed at me," Carol informed Andrew. "'Cause I speak the truth." Then she mouthed to me: "The bitch."

"The truth is overrated," Andrew said.

"Amen!" I laughed.

"So Andrew," Carol said. "Did you ever pine over some psycho?"

I shook my head. "Don't start this."

"All the time, sweetie," he answered. "The worst was Jay in Denver. He didn't know I existed. I stood outside his window in a tank top and got frostbite in places, well, you know."

"What color was the tank top?" Carol asked.

I looked peculiarly at her. "What?"

"I'm serious," she continued. "What color?"

He replied, "Orange."

Carol sat back. "That was your first mistake."

"Aahh!" When Andrew laughed his trademark laugh, somehow all was right with the world. "Will I be seeing you here at the club again?" he asked me.

"Maybe." For a fleeting second, I thought about bringing Adrienne here. Then I pictured her heavy metal gang, and promptly dismissed the idea.

* * *

When we left the club, Andrew led me back to his car. We waved to Carol, who was parked on the other side of the lot. We didn't even get off the curb before a gang of college guys taunted us from the shadows: "Hey, faggot!"

Andrew kept walking through the parking lot. I turned around to see them, but I couldn't make out faces in the dark. "Why don't you say something?" I urged him.

"And get the shit beat out of me? No thanks." He fumbled for his keys.

"Are you a dyke?" Another guy yelled.

Rage and heat pulsed through my body. So this was the life that awaited me if I indulged my feelings and continued through the door I'd opened. Adrienne wasn't even here tonight. I had a choice. I could shut the door and get on with a normal life. Or I could, as Andrew so succinctly put it, get the shit beaten out of me. The choice seemed clear. It was time to run away from the snakes.

CHAPTER FORTY-EIGHT

"You're back, from wherever it was you were." Tom gave an uneasy smile.

But Robin wasn't back. Something had changed inside her, and she couldn't go back to being the person she had been anymore.

Tom saw it in her face. It was as if gravity was the only thing holding her to the earth at this moment. Otherwise, she was detached, almost robotic, a woman who still looked like his wife, but nothing more. He fidgeted in the chair that nobody ever used in their bedroom. He was dressed casually in his favorite polo shirt, obviously not working today. He struggled to confront her; she could feel the anger, the fear, rising in him.

"Are you going to tell me where you went?" he asked. "Or will I hear it on the news?"

She closed her eyes. Of course this had to be torturous for him. She'd been only fleetingly aware of the impact on him. Now she had to *see* it, something she'd never been very good at—seeing things she didn't want to—ever since her last day at Florida State. "It's not public knowledge," she said, setting her suitcase down on the bed. "I went to Boston."

"Boston?" His face reddened. "Who lives in Boston? As if I didn't know!" He jumped up and punched the hangers in the closet, knocking down as much clothing as he could, feeling contempt for the sequins, the designer fabrics, all mementos of this life of privilege and emptiness.

She shuddered at the sound of his anger. "Tom..."

"I knew this wasn't a marriage. You kept saying otherwise, so I thought I was being paranoid." He smiled ironically. "When you admitted the affair, I told myself, well, it was some wild college days. I had spring break in Daytona. Now?"

She could see the beads of sweat breaking out above his upper lip.

"It's more, isn't it?" His eyes crinkled as he tried to make sense of his life.

"No." She closed her eyes again.

"Tell me, does this woman still mean something to you?" His arms were folded. He appeared as though he were interrogating a witness in court.

"No...I don't know." She fell upon the bed, hunched over the edge. She didn't want to look at him or deal with any of this. All the way back on her plane, she had to endure the quiet faces of her staff, all speculating. All she could do was stare out the window, dive into the clouds...here she could only see Tom's darkened, heartbroken face. It was more than she could handle. She had a debate to prepare for, but her life was unraveling.

"Obviously she does." He stood over her, refusing to let her look away.

"I know about Darlene," she said calmly. As his eyes widened with rage, she added, "I don't blame you."

"Well, that's real gracious of you!"

She stood up and grabbed him by the shirt. "I don't blame you," she repeated until he stopped breathing so hard.

After a few minutes, they stood there in the perfectly decorated bedroom beside the matching linens and custom wood furniture, leaning against each other, their foreheads touching, as if anchoring each other. It was a solemn moment when neither of them knew what to do next.

"I know you're confused," Tom said, rubbing his face. "I know you're hurting." He grabbed her shoulders, facing her. "But we can get through this."

"No, we can't." It seemed so clear to her now...

"We have to. You need to get elected." He rushed to the closet to pick up the mess he made. It was like a switch was flipped and he instantly became someone else.

"This isn't fair to you, Tom." She knew he was right from a political perspective. But after Boston, she wanted to lift the veil, to be honest, especially with her family.

"No, Robin. It's fine." His eyes were remote. "It wasn't what I wanted." He tightened his lips. "I wanted you to be the *one*." He began changing into a suit. "But we work with the hand we're dealt. And we have a duty to each other. There's your reputation to consider and mine."

As he fastened his tie, it became clear what he wanted.

"You deserve more," she said quietly.

"We can revisit this after you're elected." He was almost chipper, the immediate change in his demeanor almost chilling. "In the meantime, I can sleep in the guest room if that makes you more comfortable."

"What about Darlene?"

"She understands the situation."

"It's my fault, Tom," she cried. "All these years, trying so hard to… you deserve better."

"Will you stop saying that!" he shouted, then donned a plastic smile again, trying to regain his composure. "It doesn't matter."

"Doesn't it?"

He shook his head. "We have obligations."

She noticed he was dressed in his finest black suit.

"What are you doing?" she asked.

"The family photo shoot? For the holiday card?" he replied. "Have you forgotten? You haven't forgotten about Kendrick."

The dig about their daughter left her cold, a flailing attempt at making her feel even guiltier. Of course, the holiday photo. Every year they had to do something more spectacular than the year before. They were running out of exotic backdrops already. This year they were planning on a simple waterfall setting. In order to do that, however, the nearby park had to be closed to the public for the photo shoot, and the photographer, who wasn't used to working with water, had begun complaining about getting moisture on his lenses. She wanted to tell him, and everyone, to go to hell.

When Tom left, she went into the walk-in closet, aimlessly looking for a suitable outfit. As she flipped through the line of suits, she thought about what Tom had said. For so many years she believed as he did, that it was necessary to play a role to get ahead in a political career. There didn't seem to be any way she could blend her dream career with her personal happiness. The two never seemed to connect. When she tried to explore solutions in her mind, searching for options, it was useless. They all led to dead ends.

CHAPTER FORTY-NINE

Most of my friends were Protestant. But I also had a few who were Catholic. They always talked about this place called purgatory. It's a place where nothing is good or really bad…kind of like Georgia. Now don't get me wrong. It's a beautiful state. But growing up, I always felt restless, as though I needed something more, and the quiet solitude of our ranch and surrounding countryside wasn't enough. In purgatory, something has to change in order for you to move on. Here, nothing would change. From the hazy green hills in summer to the spotted colors lining the highways in the fall, it would stay the same. In my town, a small suburb of Atlanta, there would always be the main strip, where high school kids rode around, checking each other out at the *Cheese 'n Freeze*, and the small movie theater that had been there since the 1950s. I used to like being able to count on these things. I used to take comfort in the warm childhood memories and sameness of my surroundings. But now, as I traveled north for the holidays, I knew I had changed. Today, driving through the place of my childhood, I didn't feel as welcome as before, not with this new knowledge of myself, not with church billboards every few miles, which seemed to shout at me, calling me a sinner.

Of course every teenager feels tortured and that her experience is singular and dramatic and worthy of a movie soundtrack. I was no different. After I crossed the state line, it was like I was in a Western; I could almost hear the music of danger, as though I was an early settler in hostile territory.

I passed church after church, with steeples rising up into a white, expressionless sky. Winter had cast a murky cloud over everything— yellow and brown grass, bare trees and icy patches left on the road from a recent storm. More billboards with *Bible* quotes… And a chain of "old-time" family restaurants. The photos of the family eating at the restaurant always consisted of a smiling mother and father, and two-point-five kids. Everything seemed a sharp contrast to some of the half-naked men dancing under strobe lights at the Cobra Club. Much to my great surprise, I felt more at home there.

I switched the radio from classical to a heavy metal station. I smiled inside when I heard a song I recognized: The Scorpions' "No One Like You." It reminded me of my first night at school. The flashes of neon lights across Adrienne's profile as she drove…and the smell of smoke even as she held her cigarette out the window… I'd never forget those things. I had to turn the station until I found some sleigh bell-type song, one that was so familiar I didn't have to really listen to it. After a few more miles, I turned onto the country road—winding toward our grand house. I imagined how Carol, and even Adrienne, would have snickered at such opulence. But why should I apologize for my family having money? I fought with them inside my head as I drove up. I thought about all the things Carol had said about my dad's policies. I'd never been more confused about things I'd once taken for granted.

The surrounding yard dusted with snow greeted me like an old friend. I pulled into the familiar gravel driveway and was suddenly grateful for the distraction of Christmas.

After a flurry of hugs from my parents, we assembled in the living room. Dad was trying to hide his interest in a news program as he dragged my suitcase across the floor. He kept glancing at the TV.

"How's your nose, dear?" Mom asked.

"Yeah." Dad had plunked into his velvet chair. "You're not contagious or anything?"

"No, it's allergies. I'm taking something." I wouldn't tell them that I'd been putting off allergy shots as long as possible.

Mom disappeared for a minute, followed by the furious sounds of dishes in the kitchen.

"Does she need help?" I asked, still tired from my trip. Always the dutiful daughter, I felt bad if I didn't ask.

"Nah, she's got it," Dad replied. "She'll kick you out if you touch anything, believe me."

"Kenneth's just pulled in," Mom announced, eyeing the driveway while carrying a casserole dish to the dining room. I couldn't remember too many times when I didn't see my mom carrying a casserole of some sort. "All right, time for dinner!"

"Just a minute, Mother," Dad complained, as he'd done for twenty years. He continued to stare with glazed eyes at the news.

"Oh, for Pete's sake, Jimmy! Can't you stop watching that for a minute?"

"That Reagan is the best thing that's ever happened to this country," he declared, clicking off the television.

"Oh, please," I groaned.

"What?" His eyebrows raised.

"I'm not voting Republican." I might as well have aimed a gun at everyone.

Dad turned to Mom. "See, she goes off to college and comes back a goddamn liberal!"

"Don't take the Lord's name during the holidays," Mom warned as she headed back into the kitchen.

"What's wrong with voting Republican?" Dad wasn't going to let that remark slide.

I debated as to what to say. "Maybe we should save this for another day."

"No." Dad wasn't going to leave me alone.

"We're talking about economics in class," I said. I didn't want to mention my conversations with Carol. "Reagan's policies seem to be protecting the rich and leaving the rest of the country to fend for itself. I'm not sure how I feel about it."

"Feel?" he bellowed. "I'd like a word with some of those damn teachers of yours."

"Oh, here we go," Mom sighed. Her silent hand signals weren't getting anyone to the table any faster.

"I'll tell you what you're gonna *feel* if you vote Democrat," he said. "We can afford nice things because I worked hard to get us here. Now if our taxes get raised for all these programs to help lazy people, then we might not have much money left. So you're gonna *feel* cheated that the government is taking our money. Or someday, *your* money."

I thought about Carol. It wasn't her fault she had a condition that required costly medications. But I stayed silent. I wanted to keep the peace and avoid another stressful holiday meal that hurt my digestion.

"It's not that simple," Mom argued.

"There's your mother." He shook his head. "She'd keep givin' the shirt off her back to the poor til she don't got any clothes left." He winked at her. "I love her compassion, though, even if she does get swindled all the time."

"I do not! It's called being a good Christian."

Just then Kenneth came through the door, wearing the same tan corduroy jacket I always remembered. He'd gotten a haircut, and his blond strands seemed a little darker. He was turning into a very handsome man.

"Where's Sheila?" Mom asked, the first one to hug him.

"She thinks she's gettin' the flu. She didn't want to make y'all sick." Kenneth took off his jacket, then gave me a big hug. "Sorry I didn't get to see you off before school," he said apologetically.

"I forgive you." I smiled at him. He was another one who was easy to forgive. Of course he wouldn't call or write letters the whole time I was away, but I knew he wasn't much of a writer.

Dad gave him a quick slap on the back, and my brother made a beeline for the table.

He had moved to Marietta with Sheila, his girlfriend of two years, and gotten a more "respectable job," as Dad put it, at a retail store selling automotive parts. Dad still held a grudge that Kenneth didn't stay and work the farm, that he had to pay "twice as much" to get help. But Kenneth let the guilt roll off his back somehow, and I wanted to ask him what magical spell he used to do it. Mom and Dad were anxiously awaiting engagement news from Kenneth, so they wouldn't have to keep dodging the issue of him living in sin around their church friends.

Slicing the turkey as he'd done every year, Dad rattled on about family values.

"What does that mean?" Kenneth asked, scooping a mountain of mashed potatoes onto his plate. "I mean, who isn't for family?"

"You'd be surprised," Dad said mysteriously.

Kenneth grinned. "I'm for dysfunctional families myself." He winked at me.

"Smart-ass," Dad muttered.

There was something so comforting about being back home with people I'd known my whole life. After all, they were my touchstones in the world, the people who had always made me feel safe in spite of their weirdness.

"So tell us about school, dear," Mom said.

"It's great." I was tempted to talk about Adrienne, but I didn't want my face to turn red or accidentally reveal anything that would result in yelling. So for the sake of my digestion, I kept quiet.

"How do you like the campus?" Dad asked.

"It's beautiful," I answered. "I went to this amazing place off-campus the other night…it was a club that played really good music and…I went with this friend of mine."

Mom's eyes twinkled with delight. "A *boy* friend?"

"Oh no." I laughed and tried to act like it was no big deal. "He's a boy, yeah, but he's gay, so, no…not a boyfriend."

A stunned silence fell upon the table. Mom jumped up to get some extra gravy. My dad dropped his turkey cutting knife. And Kenneth simply said nothing. It felt like all of the oxygen had been sucked out of the room. During this time in the 1980s, the only time gay people were mentioned was in news reports about AIDS or pride parades where the commentary wasn't exactly favorable.

Dad pointed his fork at me. It was a major moment I'd never forget. "You be careful who you associate with down there, y'hear? I don't wanna hear that my daughter is hangin' out with queers."

"But he's a nice guy!" I insisted. "You just don't know anyone who is."

"I don't want you gettin' any diseases," he said, plunging the knife into his turkey. "And you don't want to associate with them 'cause it reflects bad on you."

"Really, dear," Mom chimed in. "How do you expect to find a nice boy to marry if you spend time with…you know?" I knew she wasn't trying to be cruel; she just didn't understand.

"It's no big deal. We went out dancing once." I stared down at my peas. They were the kind that were fuzzy inside and made me feel like I was going to choke.

There was silence all around. Dad seemed to be coming out of his chair.

"Feel free to jump in here." He glared at Kenneth. "She listens to you."

"I hear they're good dancers," Kenneth said. "Maybe they can teach her 'cause she sucks."

I shoved my brother.

"Robin," Mom began, "if you continue to go to these...places... people will think you are, you know."

"You wanna bring shame on the family?" Dad said. "Keep hangin' out with queers. You don't know what you're gettin' mixed up in."

Now it felt like my parents were the enemy, giving me those same shivers I had in the club parking lot when the gang of guys harassed us. This wasn't the man who had taught me how to swim or the mother who had cut bubble gum out of my hair when a cruel wind had shifted my bubble over to the side of my head at age seven. My loving parents had been replaced with fearful, angry strangers, hissing and clawing at me from across the table.

"I guess I don't see the big deal," I said quietly.

"Your grandmother would turn over in her grave if she heard you talk like this," Dad said.

"She was cremated," Mom corrected.

"Well, whose fault was that?" Dad was now irritated and purple.

"Let's move on, Jimmy," Mom urged softly. Certainly this wasn't the conversation Mom had envisioned when I came home from college.

But a heaviness had fallen across the table. I lost my appetite. There was nothing worse than arguing with my parents. I was a pleaser at heart and never wanted to do anything to upset or disappoint them. That's why I instinctively knew it was up to me to salvage the family dinner.

"Just so you know," I said, "I wasn't planning to go back to that place anymore. I only liked the music they played."

"Well, you can hear music anywhere," Dad said, lightening up a little.

"Yes." Mom was very eager to ask Dad to name places in town where they played music.

So he launched into a long speech about exploring the town more and checking out this and that. I tuned him out, then slid a forkful of peas into my mouth. I chewed and chewed them but couldn't swallow. They seemed to expand inside my mouth. "I don't want anyone thinking I'm that way either." I heard myself say the words. I felt Bette Davis judging me. But it was a momentary, fleeting discomfort. It was so much easier to slide back into the familiar, the ways of home, of religion, of straightness.

My parents nodded with relieved smiles. The world was turning on its axis again.

I glanced at my brother, noticing how he didn't seem to mind challenging our parents. He didn't seem to care about keeping the peace. Then again, they didn't seem to get so angry at him either. When he told Dad that the farm was not for him, Dad reluctantly had no choice but to accept it. Somehow, though, I knew with something like being gay, it wouldn't be the same level of acceptance as changing jobs.

* * *

That night, I lay on my bed and stared up at the ceiling. I imagined what the dinner table would have been like if I'd told them I wondered if I might be gay. What I pictured was a nightmare—silverware flying, Mom breathing into a paper bag and Dad having a stroke. But especially the yelling. It would last for days. I was exhausted from simply imagining it.

What a strange, yet familiar, holiday it would be this year—with the frenzied unwrapping of presents, the sounds of Dad and Kenneth snoring in front of a football game and Mom baking Christmas coffee cake. She spent her whole life in the kitchen, and she loved it. It truly was her favorite room in the house, and not because of 1950s advertisements that told her she belonged there, but because she really loved cooking and baking. When she was not cooking or baking, she was looking for new recipes to cook or bake. I didn't really understand her, but I envied how clear her goals seemed to be and how she could let the day take her in whatever direction—without having to have a list of projects every morning. I was driven to a level my mother wouldn't understand. Every day, I felt compelled to achieve; my ambition was thicker than the Georgia mud. I'd inherited that from my father.

I was now suspended over my body, watching myself lying in bed, locked in a weird place where there was no way out. *But there was.* I didn't have to be subjected to taunting strangers outside back-alley clubs. I had all the power to stop these thoughts and choose the path I'd follow, the right path, God's path. I could follow Adrienne's lead and say the whole thing happened because we drank too much. Nothing more. After all, Reverend Butler always said that alcohol was the devil's brew and caused people to do strange things, usually things without their clothes on.

A dance song by The Cure, "Lovesong," played faintly in the background, reminding me of the Cobra Club. Before I changed the station to classical, I got a great idea. I found a blank cassette in my desk drawer and began making a compilation tape. Even though Adrienne and I had agreed not to get each other anything because we were both broke—I went along with that so she wouldn't hate me for having money—we never said anything about *making* a present. And I wanted to do this. I felt so excited. I waited for songs I recognized to come on the radio station, and I quickly hit "record" to get them from the beginning, hoping the DJs wouldn't talk over them. This was the most fun I'd have all Christmas.

CHAPTER FIFTY

The holiday break wouldn't have been complete without a surprise visit from Marc. He arrived unannounced one morning, wearing a black overcoat and holding a small wrapped gift.

"Marc!" Mom exclaimed with arms outstretched. "Come in from the cold right this minute!" She treated him like a son. "Robin! You have a visitor!"

Just the way she announced him—I knew who it was. I took a deep breath in front of my stereo, where I was still working on Adrienne's tape.

I came downstairs in a simple cranberry turtleneck and jeans. "Hi," I said.

Marc raised his face to see me on the staircase. He looked as though I was a leading lady in the movie of his life. It was far too much pressure. Only now I understood what he felt, why he kissed me the way he did. And I knew with certainty that I couldn't return those feelings.

"I'll leave you kids alone." Mom scurried down the hall. She was even more excited to see Marc, I think, after the previous dinner conversation.

"Hi," he said, gazing at me.

I came over to him, but I kept a safe distance between us. I was uncomfortable with the way he stared. I stuffed my hands into my pockets to give my arms something to do. After a moment, he presented me with a Christmas gift. I hadn't gotten him anything, and my face burned red-hot. "I'm sorry, I didn't know I'd see you."

"It's okay." He shrugged. It probably wasn't okay.

I unwrapped a small box and pulled up a silver bracelet with a charm that had our initials engraved in it. "Aw, that's so sweet."

"You think so?" His voice was suddenly hard and businesslike.

"Yeah. Thank you." I reached up to kiss his cheek, but he turned, and my lips bumped his chin. It was awkward, as I expected it to be, especially knowing that I'd spent all of last night working on a music tape for my roommate.

"You don't write or call," he said.

"Neither did you."

"I asked your mom in church for your address. She said she'd get it and forgot to give it to me."

"Oh." I held my head in shame. "Sorry."

"You didn't even think about seein' me over break. You really think it feels like we're in a relationship?"

I exhaled in frustration. Nervously stroking the top of Dad's velvet chair, I finally decided to let the pretense go. He wasn't a fool. It was time to stop treating him like one.

"No, it doesn't," I answered. "But we knew things would be different when we went to college. I'm sure you've met other girls."

"I've met some," he said. "But they aren't you. So I guess you found another guy?"

"Not exactly."

He threw his hands in the air. "What does that mean? Are you breaking up with me?"

"I care about you," I exclaimed. "I really do. But I think we should let each other experience life. I don't want you to feel committed to me."

"Thing is," he muttered, "I want to be. I love you."

I couldn't say it back. He started for the door. "Enjoy the bracelet," he said bitterly and left.

Hearing the door, Mom rushed back into the foyer.

"Robin," Mom scolded. "You didn't even offer to take his coat? Or invite him to stay for cheesecake?"

"Trust me, Mom. It wouldn't have been a good idea."

"I realized I forgot to get your address for him. Every time I saw him in church, I said to myself, 'I need to get that.' But I forgot." She was blaming herself for us breaking up, which I was sure she heard from eavesdropping in the kitchen.

"It's not your fault, Mom," I said. "It really isn't."

* * *

The last night before going back, I spent a lot of time in my room, even though I knew my parents wanted more time to visit with me. I didn't want to answer more questions. Dad wanted me to pledge a sorority, but I thought they were weird. The first week of school was Rush Week, where all the new pledges chose, and were chosen by, a sorority. I saw all these girls crying in the arms of total strangers because they were now wearing the same letters on their shirts. It was too weird for me. I told Dad I'd consider it, but I wasn't going to.

There was a knock on my door. "It's Ken."

"Come in." I sat up, surprised to hear his voice. He'd gone home after Christmas to take care of his sick girlfriend. I was glad he came back.

"Hey, Robbie," he said. His face was warm and familiar. He closed the door behind him and sat on the edge of the bed. "Mom and Dad wanted me to check on you."

I rolled my eyes. "Because I'm in my room?"

He nodded. "You know them. They want to make sure you're not...whatever they saw on a talk show." He ran through the list. "Teenage depression, pregnancy..."

"No chance of that," I laughed. "If they only knew..." It slipped out before I could censor myself.

"If they only knew what?" His face was relaxed. He didn't have the same expressions of my parents, who always seemed to be moments from needing a padded cell.

I looked at him intensely. If only I could unburden myself, share my secret with someone I trusted.

"Nothing," I said.

"Well..." He mussed my hair and got me to laugh. Then he looked at me seriously and imitated something our high school counselor used to say: "Now remember, dorms are for studying, not sexual relations."

I slapped him playfully. Of course his joke was aimed at my goody-two-shoes reputation. He'd gone to college for a semester, but decided it wasn't right for him. Again, he managed to tell my parents, who were very disappointed. I thought I'd rather have my eyes gouged out with hot pokers than disappoint them. But he switched to a vocational school, and they were eventually okay with that.

"Ken?"

"Yeah?"

"I don't know," I mumbled.

"Sure you do. What is it?" He could always see through me.

In his face I saw the boy I climbed trees with, went to Sunday school with, all those things that had once made sense. If I revealed myself, it would make me a stranger to him. What if he looked at me like Mom and Dad did?

"If I told you something, could you keep it secret from Mom and Dad?" I smiled awkwardly.

"Of course. You never told them mine."

"Huh?"

"They still don't know about the tattoo on my ass."

"That's right!" I remembered. Now I had some leverage. I laughed. When he was in high school, he went to a friend's party and got drunk. He came home with a tattoo of a cross on his right butt cheek, but couldn't remember how it got there. Since it wasn't in a spot where our parents were likely to see it, no one had to know. He was kind of proud of it, although I'd never seen him as the tattoo type. He wanted to tell me, though, and I swore I'd never reveal his secret. "So you kind of owe me, don't you?" I smiled playfully.

"This better be good." He lay across the bed with hands folded.

There was so much heaviness on my face, and I knew he could see it. I was carrying not only the weight of the world, but the universe and whatever other matter existed out there too.

"Hey," he coaxed. "It can't be that bad."

"Oh yes, it can." I got up to check the hallway, making sure no one was nearby. Then I locked the door. I came back to the head of my bed and took a deep breath. "It's my roommate."

He nodded. I could tell from his blank stare, he had no idea where I was going with this.

"I think…" I couldn't look at him and say it at the same time. So I looked at the floor. "I have a crush on her." I practically whispered it.

He looked surprised, but not in a horrified way, as Mom and Dad would have. "Wow." That was all he could say.

"That's it?" I snapped. "*Wow*?"

"Well…" He considered the situation thoughtfully. "You're not the kind of person I'd expect to…you don't seem like you've ever had a wild thought in your life. Remember when I'd want to go exploring some barn, and you'd say it was trespassing, and we'd get in trouble? That's how I see you, I guess. So…wow. What're you gonna do?"

"I already did." I looked away.

I heard a quiet chuckle. Maybe he was merely impressed that I'd done something wild.

"You…slept with her?" His eyes were wide with surprise.

"Yeah, but just once. Swear you won't say anything."

"I won't." After a pause, "Cool."

"No, this isn't some male fantasy thing. I think it's the real thing."

He looked strangely at me. "Does this mean you're queer?"

I shook my head. "I don't know what it means. But you can't say anything. Ever."

He crossed his heart. "I'll take it to the grave." As he started for the door, my throat swelled as if I'd soon cry. He turned around and said, "Whatever you are, you know I love you no matter what. You're my sister."

I jumped up and gave him the biggest hug. This was unusual for him. Kenneth had never been one for long or important conversations. Usually he'd grunt and I knew what he meant. I assumed most boys weren't big talkers until I met Marc. But I hadn't been around Ken in so long, maybe his girlfriend Sheila had forced him to talk more.

"I won't say a word, but you know," he continued. "It wouldn't kill Mom and Dad to wake up a little. I know a girl who got pretty pissed at something Dad said about unwed mothers. It was in the newspaper."

"Yeah, I guess. It's…so scary." Before he could leave, I said, "Give my best to Sheila."

"Uh, since we're tellin' secrets…" He seemed awkward, as he came closer. "I kinda said she was sick so Mom and Dad wouldn't get all…you know how they get."

I nodded. "Yeah."

"We've been havin' some problems. We're havin' a separation for a while. But we're not broken up or anything."

"Oh. I'm sorry."

"I'm not." He wouldn't look at me.

Kenneth and Sheila had been in a relationship since high school. It was hard to imagine them not together.

"I don't know if she's the right one. But don't say a word." His intense plea was understandable. Sheila's family had a lot of money,

Total Paid: $12.00

$0.00

$6.00
$6.00

Oakland Public Library
RECEIPT
Patron: YAMUREMYE, MONIKA
05-28-2017 3:46PM

INVOICE #: 759516
STATUS: OverdueX
DESCRIPTION: Southern comfort / Skyy.
AMOUNT OWED: $6.00
AMOUNT PAID: $6.00
BALANCE: $0.00

ICE #: 759517
OverdueX
reak point / by Yolanda Joe

Oakland Public Library

Main Library

Date Due Receipt

To renew, call (510) 238-3311 or visit
www.oaklandlibrary.org

05/28/2017
Items checked out to: **********9385
Money owed: $15.00

TITLE: Hurricane days / Renee J.
BARCODE: 32141041103866
DUE DATE: 06-18-17 00:00AM

and they were considered a perfect match as far as our parents were concerned. So I could see why he was reluctant to share this with them. "We'll probably get back together soon."

"Don't do it," I replied. "Not unless you really want her. I mean, this is your life. You had no trouble telling Dad you didn't want to stay at the farm."

"This is a little different."

"Make sure you're really happy, or don't do it," I repeated.

He nodded in a way that I could tell he wasn't really going to pay attention. I worried for him. I stared at the closed door a while after he left. A sinking, anxious feeling overcame me. School would be starting in a few days. I wondered if, living in the same world of limitations and expectations, Ken or I could do what our hearts really wanted.

I settled back into my pillows. I could hear the agitated voices of my parents downstairs, especially my father's because it was the loudest. The cold, hopeless sensation returned to my stomach. It was a nice dream while it lasted.

CHAPTER FIFTY-ONE

Ann DeMarco was too sharp a reporter to let go of a story when her instincts told her it was good. No doubt rumors had been flying that Adrienne paid a visit to the Georgia state capitol right before Governor Sanders' somewhat strange press conference. Robin suspected that Ann would be investigating more than anyone, to see if this affair was a misunderstanding as Adrienne Austen had portrayed it or if it was something more—a real love story.

As Robin rehearsed for the debate, she caught the end of a nightly news program with Ann DeMarco. Ann ended the broadcast with the teaser: "Did Governor Sanders come clean about her alleged college affair? Contact us on the 'Tweet Line' anytime. We'd love to get your tips. We'd especially like to hear from former college friends who can tell us if there's more to this story than meets the eye. Until then, have a great night."

Ann flipped a page on her desk and smiled a twinkling smile.

Robin was angry. Of all the top news reporters, Ann had never pandered to the ratings machine. This "Tweet Line" tip line was a new thing, however, and everyone on her network had begun to promote it. They were trying to be "more interactive." So Ann may have had no choice. Even so, Robin believed she had no friends in the media. They were all wild animals, looking to make their next kill.

Then in one loud exhale, Robin said, "Carol." She was the first person to come into Robin's mind, especially with her lack of a censor switch and habitually rude bluntness. There was no way to predict what Carol would say if reporters got to her before Robin had a chance to talk with her.

* * *

Lara accompanied the governor to a small psychiatric facility in Montgomery, Alabama.

"What are you not saying?" Robin asked after an unusually long silence on the private plane.

"I'm not saying that I think you're overreacting," Lara said. "I'm not saying that I think you're making everything too goddamn personal and that it's going to affect your standing in the polls. And I'm especially not saying that you should be focused on the biggest debate of your life in just a few fucking days. Not saying!" She held up her hands.

"They're sniffing around where they shouldn't," Robin snapped. "Carol hasn't done anything to anyone. She's in an institution, for God's sake. How dare they!"

"They haven't," Lara said.

"Not *yet*," Robin corrected.

Robin felt very protective of Carol. She was saddened that her career as a public figure could compromise the privacy of all her former friends.

"Honey," Lara said, "you've got to get your priorities straight. You of all people know it gets ugly at this stage."

"Not if I can help it." She heard how naïve she sounded, but for a moment, she remembered the spark of idealism she had when she first sought a career in public service. She smiled bitterly to herself. She used to think that her soul was a small price to pay in order to do some good.

* * *

Once inside the facility, Robin was left alone to visit her old friend in her room. She was first shocked at Carol's appearance—her unkempt, long and frizzy gray hair, cascading down her shoulders like a sixties' folk singer. She still had a nose ring, but no makeup. Her tired eyes had deep bags under them, and her dramatic weight loss left her cheeks slightly sunken and her arms like twigs. She knew that Carol's medications had terrible side effects, and her appearance was probably the result of years of those drugs. Even so, she felt a heaviness in her heart at the circumstances.

"Carol," Robin said, closing the door behind her. She was dressed in her designer suit and coat and looked very conspicuous in such a drab, depressing environment.

Carol was staring out the window, not looking at her.

"I'll tell you anything for a cigarette," she said.

"I can't do that," Robin replied.

"Then I don't know shit." Carol turned and saw that it was Robin. Her eyes widened. "Wow, if it isn't her majesty, the Nazi governor!" Carol always had a way of bringing Robin down to earth, and Robin was relieved, and a little worried, to see she still hadn't lost her edge.

"So you do recognize me!" Robin sat in the only chair available. It was a sterile, hospital-style room with a single bed, a nightstand and not much else. "Do you *live* here?"

"Hell, no." She sat against the metal headboard. "I've been in and out for counseling." She made air quotes. "They've put me on every kind of drug. I'm the rat they like to experiment on."

"I understand."

She appraised Robin in one brief glance. "My head's always been fucked. But not as much as yours."

"Okay…"

"You've made a career out of self-loathing." She laughed a sinister laugh.

"I need to ask you something," Robin said.

"Of course you do. Why else would you be here?" She could smile at her in a way that told her not to mess with her; she could see through everything and everyone. Unfortunately, she had little interest in anyone who wasn't there to talk about her. As far as she was concerned, she was the most important person anyway.

"I see how little it would take for you to divulge information about me," Robin said.

"The cigarette thing? Nah. They won't let me smoke anyway." Carol smiled tiredly; her eyes were glazing over. She was either heavily medicated or bored. Robin had to make sure that Carol wouldn't say anything to cause serious damage to her reputation. "Have any reporters visited you? Ann DeMarco?"

"No, and don't worry. I don't tweet." Carol was obviously still an avid watcher of news networks. "You really are a piece of work. I don't see you for decades, and now I can see the fear in your eyes…" She widened her eyes in a way that sent chills down Robin's spine. "Fear that I might say something about you and that heavy metal chick in college."

Robin shook her head. This wasn't looking good. Either she would say something to get revenge or be so drugged, it wouldn't matter. Of course, she could dismiss anything that was said by someone in a psychiatric hospital. The wheels began to turn. Yes, she could probably spin this. Part of her visit had been to evaluate Carol Munson's condition. If she'd seemed sharper, Robin would have been more concerned. But she could handle whatever came now.

"If someone like Ann DeMarco asked you whether or not I had an affair with another girl in college, what would you say?" Robin asked.

"I'd tell her it's none of her fucking business."

Robin exhaled. "Really?" She knew she must look visibly surprised.

"Really. Even though I should hang you out to dry…Hmm. Maybe I should say, if you get in office, we're screwed."

"If you feel like that, why would you protect my privacy?" Robin asked.

"Hey," Carol barked. "I might not like who you are, but I have ethics. Do you?"

"Right." Robin nodded politely. There was a long, uncomfortable quiet. They were obviously strangers now.

"I can't believe you found me," Carol said. "I've been off the grid." She gave Robin an explanation filled with a strong paranoia about the Internet and anything that became public information. "I pulled the plug on every social website, thinking no one could track me down."

"I have…people."

"Holy fuck." Carol laughed. "Who knew you'd get so big you'd 'have people'?"

Robin smiled in spite of herself. Something about being back in Carol's presence brought her immediately back down to earth. "It is kind of weird," she said with a smile.

Carol tucked her hand under her chin. "You know, I could tell 'em how you liked to go dancing."

"Dancing," Robin repeated. That seemed harmless enough, although Robin couldn't remember what she was talking about.

"Remember Andrew?"

"Oh, right, yes." That information wasn't too bad; many people had friends who were gay.

"Did you hear about him?" Carol asked.

"No."

"Of course not. You're too busy judging everybody. 'Being gay is unnatural'...give me a fuckin' break! Who the hell do you think you are!" Carol's anger was getting so loud, someone might come in.

Robin tried to calm her down. "I know. I haven't been...truthful."

"You think?" Carol shook her head. "Go on your computer and look up Andrew...what was his last name?"

"Bennington." Robin hadn't forgotten.

Carol was surprised at her memory. "Yeah, look him up. See what happened to him."

"Why don't you tell me?"

"Don't remember." She was obviously lying.

"All right then." Robin smoothed a single wrinkle across her skirt. She had to keep her clothes as tidy as possible, especially if she was seen in a place like this.

* * *

All the way back to Georgia, Robin refused to let Carol get inside her head and make her feel guilty about her success. She'd always been jealous of her and Adrienne anyway, Robin rationalized. How funny it was... Robin could forget where she put her phone, her keys, but she'd never forget the name of the boy with the laugh. Somehow he held a special place in her memory. Maybe she should get in touch with him too, make sure he still had her back.

CHAPTER FIFTY-TWO

Crossing the Florida state line, I wasn't the same girl who came down a few months before. I was resolved to remain cool when I saw her again, although my stomach did flip-flops with each highway sign that said "Tallahassee." Palm trees emerged on the horizon, frosted from an unexpected deep freeze.

How different the panhandle of Florida was from the rest of the state. It could actually get cold here—down to the thirties in winter. Fortunately, I'd packed as if I were still in Georgia, with what seemed to be a suitable number of jackets for various occasions. I remembered the night before the holiday break. *The oatmeal sweater.* I distracted myself on the tedious drive down the highway with thoughts of which clothes I wanted to wear—and in what order. Somehow, order gave me peace, especially when nothing else did.

The dorm room was empty. So, unfortunately, I had plenty of time, which wasn't good for someone like me. Too much time could turn my thoughts to monsters. I had to keep myself busy. I had enough time to buzz around, unpacking, fussing with my hair in the mirror, sipping a soda, fussing some more with my makeup, going to the bathroom because of the soda, coming back to the room to fuss even more.

Lydia, the RA, banged on the door, and I jumped out of my skin before answering it. She shoved a flyer at me. "Tips on hurricane preparedness."

"I thought the season was over."

"We, uh, had a little trouble getting everyone organized," Lydia explained. "So we want to do better preparedness drills."

"So these are tips for *next* season."

Lydia was defensive. No one had questioned her hurricane flyers before. "You goin' to a party? You look all made up." She must have decided to be less socially awkward this semester. But her attempt to make small talk only came off as creepy.

"No," I replied.

"Wait. Don't tell me. You're expecting some guy. That's it, isn't it?"

"You guessed it." I smiled as I closed the door.

I spent a couple more grueling hours waiting to hear the key in the door. "Hey!" Adrienne came crashing in with more suitcases than she had before.

"Hey! Need some help?"

"No, I got it." She dragged in one that seemed bigger than she was.

"You got a dead body in there?"

Adrienne caught her breath. "I forgot about your weird sense of humor."

When she was successfully inside with the door closed, she turned to hug me with more force than the one before the holiday, the one I remembered all December long. I was filled with joy at the sight of her.

When we finally pulled apart, she said, "It's so great to see you! It feels like it's been forever."

"I know, right?" I smiled shyly, often disarmed by her directness. "How was your Christmas?"

"It sucked. Don't ask."

"Okay."

"My dad had his new girlfriend over…the whole time."

"Oh. Sorry."

"How was yours?"

"It was okay."

"Did you get anything good? Like clothes without flowers on them?" She laughed hysterically.

"Bitch."

We were immediately at ease with each other again, almost comfortable. Then she said, "I really missed you."

"No, you didn't. You missed making fun of me."

"Well, that too." There was an awkward pause. "You know," she said. "I almost called you."

"Really?"

"Yeah. I don't know why, but I wasn't sure you'd wanna talk to me."

"Why not?"

"I thought you were mad at me, because of that last night."

"No," I assured her. "Not at all. Whatever I said, and I don't really remember, it was probably just because I was drinking." I'd rehearsed that on the way down. "How is Sean?"

"We had a fight."

"I'm sorry," I lied. "Hey, I got something for you."

"Me too!" Adrienne tore into her suitcase and dug around. "I know we said no presents, but I got this little thing…"

I pulled my gift for her out of the top drawer, the underwear drawer, of my dresser, where I'd hidden it underneath what she'd called my "granny briefs."

"Present time!" she exclaimed. Sometimes she got so excited, she sounded like a little kid.

When she handed me a crookedly wrapped, small rectangular present, her grin reminded me of a school picture she'd shown me once. In her smile I could still see the young girl with OshKosh clothes and uneven bangs grinning back at the camera.

I gave her the wrapped cassette tape I made with songs I was starting to like—The Cure's "Lovesong," Erasure's "A Little Respect." Sometimes when she switched radio stations, she'd hear one of these and say something like, "That doesn't totally suck." Also, I'd heard many of these songs at the Cobra Club, although I wouldn't tell her that. As I gave her my gift, I wondered if she was the type who would appreciate a homemade gift or if she preferred impersonal things from a mall.

When we looked down at the gifts we exchanged, we noticed they were about the same size. We tore into each other's presents, and laughed uproariously. She'd given me a homemade heavy metal tape with songs I'd said I liked: Scorpions' "No One Like You," Dokken's "Alone Again."

I couldn't stop laughing. This gift meant so much to me. It proved she was thinking of me over the holiday as I was thinking about her. But I kept the melodramatic sentiments to myself.

"We're psychic!" she laughed, hugging me so tightly. "I love it," she said.

"Me too. That's...yeah. Something I wouldn't have gotten for myself."

"You couldn't remember the bands!"

I nodded. "True. They say the best gifts are the ones you wouldn't think of for yourself or that you forgot you wanted, something like that..."

"Do you have to analyze everything?" She stepped out in the hall and carried a couple more bags inside.

"Geez, the room isn't big enough," I said.

In one hand she carried an old guitar case. She opened it on the bed. "My dad picked this up at a garage sale."

It was a beat-up guitar, just scratched enough to look cool, but one scratch away from being ready for the junk heap.

"He knows I want to play," she said.

"That's nice. Kind of like a peace offering?"

"I guess. But I've never had lessons." She seemed embarrassed.

"You could learn."

"I told you, no one in our town teaches it. They only have piano lessons." She rolled her eyes.

"What about the music department here?"

She lifted it up. "I'm going to show up with this thing?"

I smiled slyly at her. She didn't fool me. "You brought it back to school, didn't you?"

"Yeah, so? I couldn't have my dad see me leave it behind."

"You could've kept it in your car."

"What's your point, RC?" She put it back in the case.

"I told you not to call me that."

"Okay. My plan is to mess around with it where no one can hear me, like at the beach or a deep forest." She tried to sound dramatic.

"Whatever works for you." I laughed. As soon as I stepped out to go to the restroom, I could hear the muffled sounds of guitar strings being plucked. None of the notes worked right together, but they were each being tested. I smiled to myself.

* * *

While in the bathroom, I reminded myself to be cool and strong, like steel. I wasn't going to be humiliated again by someone who said she "wasn't queer." I bristled at the word. As I washed my hands, I stared in the mirror and told myself what I had to do. There was something about being around my family, realizing there was no future with Adrienne no matter how I tried to imagine it, all of it conspired to close the lid on the feelings I had—even if they were the happiest feelings of my life.

When I returned to the room, I caught her playing, and she winked at me. I knew what that look of playfulness meant. And I had to lay down the rules quickly before I lost my nerve.

"Whatever happened," I said, "you know, when we drank…it's in the past. I'm sorry if I made you uncomfortable."

"You didn't make me—"

"I'm not going to be drinking anymore."

"Oh, great," she replied sarcastically. "You went home and got born again, huh?"

"Not born again," I corrected. "I had time to clear my head and… that person I was…that…wasn't me."

"Well, I slept with somebody who looked exactly like you."

"I'm being serious. Why would you want to bring that up again?" After all, she "wasn't queer."

"Over the break, I missed you."

"I missed you too," I said carefully. The curiosity was killing me, so I had to ask: "What did you fight with Sean about?"

She rolled her eyes. "You know how guys get. They treat you like a prize. They think if you're their girlfriend, they've won you and they're entitled to keep you."

"How very feminist of you," I said, arms folded. *Who was this new Adrienne?* "So you said he didn't own you?"

"Something like that. Now I come back, and you tell me you don't want to have any fun anymore. It's going to be a great year." She was sarcastic.

I didn't want to be her fun. My blood was boiling. She must've seen confusion and anger on my face.

"No more parties," she explained. That was what she meant by *fun*.

"Oh. Yeah."

She shrugged. "I get it. I don't want to put you on the wrong side of Jesus."

"I take my religion seriously."

"And I take my lack of religion just as seriously." Her slight smile, bordering on a full laugh, made me laugh too, in spite of myself. I couldn't help it. Ripples of laughter filled the room. Did we laugh

224 Renée J. Lukas

to relieve tension? Of course I had to analyze and dissect everything to death. I remembered the first night in the doughnut shop. All we could do was laugh. It was as if we had to distract ourselves from the spark of electricity that was always there between us. Sometimes it was so intense, we had to pretend it wasn't there at all. Now I knew I wasn't the only one who felt it.

"You're awful!" I exclaimed, still laughing.

"I think I know what it is," Adrienne said.

"Huh?"

"It's from living in the South. You got a lot of preachers telling you not to do bad things. But it's in everybody's nature to do bad things. Being bad feels good." She flashed me that devilish grin that sent chills down my back. "Like in church. I'll bet they're always telling you not to have sex. But everybody has sex. So everybody's all confused, pointing fingers at everyone else when they're doin' it too. It makes you all look nuts."

"Hey, you're livin' in the South too."

"Florida doesn't count as the south. Don't you know that?"

"It seems pretty far south to me."

"Everyone down here is from somewhere else." Adrienne added, "Except me."

"Except you," I repeated with a smile.

"There are a lot of contradictions."

"Yeah," I sighed. "You got a few yourself."

She lowered her eyes. It was as if I'd tapped into something private.

"You ever go to church?" I asked. "You know, before you became all badass?"

She smiled. "My dad used to say that no good ever came from sitting for hours in a place where they told you how bad you are. I pretty much agree with that."

I laughed, thinking how she might have a point.

* * *

That night we ordered a pizza, sat in our room and talked. It was one of those nights I used to cherish. But now I had to be hard. No unnatural feelings or thoughts. I had to be tough. Remembering my father's words, I would have to be tougher than ever before.

CHAPTER FIFTY-THREE

That spring, I had to take a class in political debating. I dreaded it, but it was necessary. In high school, I had vomited every morning I was required to do any kind of public speaking, and this class would be nothing but that.

The first day I thought I'd die when I saw the auditorium-size class. I made my way up the stairs to find a seat somewhere in the middle—not too close to be called on too much, and not too far away to be viewed as a slacker. I found an empty seat and glanced around at the sea of strange faces.

"Hey, is this seat taken?" The question came from Chase, a tall, handsome guy with dark hair and a long neck.

"No," I answered. I was immediately aware of the girls in the class who watched me with jealous eyes because this particular guy had chosen a seat beside me. I could hear their whispering the moment his butt hit the seat.

What I did notice was one late student, who managed to scoot in just as the professor made her way to the front. The student was Terri, the girl from my dormitory—the one Adrienne had pointed out as being "queer." I watched Terri with great fascination as she made her way to a seat that was closer to the front. I'd never seen a girl cut her hair so short. It looked as though she'd shaved it in the back. I probably stared a little too long at her, but I found myself riveted to this girl who seemed to defy every social rule there was.

Professor Donovan was a young, slender woman in a black suit with inquisitive eyes that darted all around the room, waiting for us to get settled. She leaned against the podium, a slight smirk on her face as she got ready to tell us exactly how we'd be tortured this semester.

"As you can guess," she said, "you'll be doing a series of debates in this class. I want you to turn to the person next to you. That will be your debate partner."

Chase looked expectantly at me. I nodded and smiled. He seemed pleasant enough.

"The two of you will present two sides of an issue," Professor Donovan continued, "and the class will decide who wins the debate."

I was filled with a familiar sense of dread, the blood pounding in my ears. Luckily, my partner and I weren't scheduled to go in front of the class for a while.

* * *

"A petting zoo?" I screeched. "In this heat?" It would smell really bad. And in the muggy air, I could think of a million other things I'd rather do than go outside.

"Aw, c'mon. I heard it was fun." Adrienne never showed much interest in animals, except for a yellow lab she made friends with in front of the dorm one time. She held his paw and rubbed his back. She looked very comfortable with animals, but she didn't have any back home.

Of course I'd go along. I'd never resist any weekend activity that she suggested, especially when it included me.

"Is Nancy coming?" I asked tentatively, straightening my black, short-sleeved shirt. I'd never be a tank top kind of girl, but I'd bought a lot more short-sleeved shirts to survive the heat down here.

"No." Adrienne broke out in a smile, knowing full well the reason for the question. "Or Becky. Or Sean." She was right at home in a peach tank top, showing off her perfectly tan, sculpted arms. And those form-fitting jean shorts…

"I thought you two broke up."

She glanced away and grabbed her keys. "We're kinda on again. Sometimes he's great. Sometimes he's an asshole."

"Sounds perfect." My sarcasm was my default switch. I shook my head, following her out the door. It was my own fault. I made it clear there was no future between us. Of course Adrienne would go back to Sean. I really had no right to be angry. Or jealous. But of course I was.

"Did you ever have a family pet growing up?" I traced the car door handle as we rode down the highway.

"Not really," she said. "Well, yeah."

"It's not a trick question."

Adrienne laughed. "In our house, everything was complicated. My mom got us this dog. I don't know what kind. It was like a lot of breeds in one."

"A mutt?"

"Is that what 'mutt' means?"

"Uh, I think so."

"Well, yeah. A mutt. Barney. I really loved that dog. But I was only six or seven. When Mom and Dad got divorced, he got rid of the dog because it reminded him of her."

"Got rid of? You mean..."

"He found a farm somewhere," she explained. "He didn't have him killed or anything. But..." She stared down the road. "I was pretty sad."

"I guess you would be, to get attached and then lose it." Every bit of new information always made me feel closer to her.

"God, I *hope* he took him to a farm," she said. "He told so many lies, who knows?"

* * *

I was awed by Adrienne's ease with animals. Like Tarzan, she seemed to speak their silent language, compelling many of them to gather around her. It was the same with people. Everyone flocked to her.

"C'mon," she called.

I shook my head. "No, that's fine. I'll see them in *National Geographic*."

"It's not the same."

"Yeah, you miss that whole extra smelly dimension. You forget I grew up on a farm. They stink."

"You're supposed to be a country girl," she laughed.

But it was my brother Kenneth who usually tended to the outdoor chores, while I was allowed to stay indoors and help our mother. That was one time when I certainly didn't mind more traditional roles—because they kept me away from cow manure, flies, snakes and anything else that made me jump. There was a natural order to things—animals belonged outside and I belonged inside.

"Come here, Robin!" Adrienne called in a high-pitched voice, as if the fawn were talking. "Please come here and pet me. I'm really soft, and I'll try not to bite your ass off."

I rolled my eyes and laughed, still holding Adrienne's cotton candy. "She really is enjoying your hand there." I remembered Adrienne minutes before, swirling her tongue around and around the cotton candy. Some of the stickiness must have lingered on her hands.

"It's the cotton candy smell," she replied with a wink and a secret smile that stopped my heart with its intimacy. "Very alluring."

Just a wink and a smile. That's all it took. There was no one like her, no one with those lips, which always seemed to be on the verge of a laugh. There was just something about her that made me smile.

Then the stench of animal poop interrupted my daydream. No matter how cute an animal was, I was not getting near it. The first time my dad propped me up on a horse, it bucked me off, and I broke my leg. My uneasy relationship with the wild would continue whenever I saw a news report. Anyone who got too close to an unpredictable animal often paid for it dearly with a missing eye, a permanent scar or death. But the petting zoo was a fine place to be today, as long as I stayed on the other side of the fence.

I made an excuse and headed toward the nearest bench. While sitting there, I noticed a struggling caterpillar trying to cross the crowded pavement—determined to make it in spite of the stampede of human feet—a formidable obstacle indeed. He could so easily die, I thought, watching his tiny green body inching forward. At the same time, I was shamed by the plucky critter's courage.

"Hey, Robin! Check this out!" Adrienne called to me.

Swimming in her smile, I was hypnotized into following her. I bolted up from the bench, started toward her and in a split second, looked down and realized I'd just squashed the caterpillar.

Minutes later, Adrienne tried to console me.

"It's only a caterpillar," she insisted, rinsing her hands under a faucet.

"You don't understand!" My face had fallen to the ground.

"I don't get you at all. You're scared of a palmetto bug, but you're crying over a caterpillar!"

"Will you stop calling them palmetto bugs?" I protested. "They're roaches!"

"You're still nuts."

"What did you want me to see anyway?"

She shrugged as if she couldn't remember. "Oh, the baby goat was eating out of my hand."

"I took another life for *that?*" I stomped away, furious at myself, at Adrienne and the world.

All the way back to her car I was angry—angry that for a month I'd managed to keep my friendship with Adrienne as only a friendship and that she seemed to be okay with that. Not only was she okay, but obviously seeing Sean again. Even though I was the one who had laid down the law, I was still insulted that she would turn to him. If I wasn't going to have Adrienne, no one should. Of course it was irrational, but "rational" was no longer in my vocabulary.

"I don't know what your problem is," she snapped, opening her side door for me.

"You're my problem."

Adrienne stood there with her hands on her hips, looking at me in the passenger side. "It wasn't me who ended everything." She slammed her door and went around to the driver's side.

I stared ahead. I was embarrassed that she knew why I was so upset. I'd have to do a better job of lying. "I don't know what you're talking about," I said.

"The hell you don't." She punched the gas and we roared out of the parking lot.

CHAPTER FIFTY-FOUR

Robin would be the most gracious host, as usual, for her brother's visit to the mansion, even though she was exhausted from a sleepless night, and more than a little shaken, in the aftermath of her visit to Carol. Kenneth had been obviously surprised to receive the invitation, but she had missed him. He would be a welcome distraction, which she needed, now more than ever. She hadn't seen him in so long, she'd lost track of how many years it had been. She hadn't been sure he'd even agree to meet with her.

Kenneth arrived in a simple corduroy jacket and jeans, never one for formality. Robin appeared in the doorway, as glamorous as the woman she was on TV. If he was surprised to see her, he didn't show it.

"Ken!" She took both of his hands.

"Nice pad." He smirked, glancing at the high ceilings and chandeliers. "My apartment could fit in your living room."

"This isn't the living room," she replied. "It's a sitting area."

"So what do you do in the living room? You can't *sit* in there?"

"Of course you can." She smiled, seeing herself in his eyes. How absurd she must seem. She led him to a small room that was decorated like an upscale pub, with brown paneled walls and a pool table in the middle. She figured he'd be more comfortable here.

When they entered, he immediately grabbed a pool cue and chalked it. "Remember how I taught you how to play?"

"Of course." She took one too, then dusted chalk off her skirt. "Mom and Dad never knew."

Kenneth used to bring his little sister to his friend's house in high school, where he had a pool table in the basement. Since it was beside the garage, it always smelled of rubber tires and car exhaust down there, but she loved playing the game. It was the only rebellious thing she did, not telling her parents she was there. They most likely wouldn't have approved of an eleven-year-old girl going to a high school boy's house, even with her brother. They frowned on her socializing with any of his friends, whom her father called rednecks and, even worse, "older boys." But Robin always felt safe with her brother, and she liked having this secret with him growing up.

He racked the balls. "Cutthroat?"

"Sure." She smiled. "Dad told me about you and Sheila. I had no idea."

He broke first. "I'll take one to ten." He winked at her. They used to improvise the three-player game. Since the object is to sink the other player's balls and have at least one of yours still on the table, the person who had eleven through fifteen had a harder time winning. "It is what it is," he said and took a shot.

When he missed, Robin took control of the table, with more balls to knock out than he. She slammed two of his balls into the side pockets, then took aim at the next shot, her face deep in concentration.

"You were always dangerous on the side pockets." He shook his head, as she forced another into the left corner.

"Tell me," she said. "Did you ever love her?" Another ball sank.

The question startled him. After so long, he probably didn't expect a very deep conversation. Then again, they could seamlessly pick up where they left off as if no time had passed.

"I cared about her," he replied. He was much more guarded around her than he used to be, although he could tell that something was weighing on her mind.

"That's not what I asked."

As she took another shot and another, Kenneth laughed in spite of himself. "I never should've taught you. I created a monster."

Before taking his last ball off the table, she looked up at him with those intense blue eyes. "Did you love her?" She won the game without looking before taking the shot. "Cutthroat." Then she placed her cue neatly back on the wall.

"Man, you *are* scary." He hung up his cue and sat on the barstool. "No, I didn't."

She went around to the other side of the bar and fixed him a beer. He took it gladly. Much to his surprise, she joined him. She tipped each Corona upside-down, so the lime would float down perfectly in the yellow bubbles. He'd never seen her do this, so he watched in awe this stranger who used to be his sister.

"Dad said you always loved someone else," she said, recalling their conversation years ago, how she'd warned him not to stay with someone he didn't love. She wondered if he remembered.

Kenneth lowered his eyes, taking a sip of beer. "It's ancient history."

"Is it? Who was she?"

"After all this time, why do you give a shit?" The bitterness was finally surfacing.

"I do give a shit! I always have."

"You got a funny way of showin' it." He took another gulp.

"You're right, and I'm sorry. I know it can't erase everything, but I really am, Ken."

He said nothing.

"I'm making an effort here," she said in her haughty tone. "What about Christian forgiveness?"

"I'm not the one preachin' the Gospel everywhere." He took a breath, calmed himself down, then looked her in the eye. "I can forgive, but I don't forget."

"Fine. I'm not going to argue with you over words. I really want to know who this love of your life is."

"Why? What's it to you?"

"You're my brother." She stared at her frosty bottle, unable to meet his eyes because it was all too real.

"This wouldn't have anything to do with the love of *your* life? The one you had me call?" He had that all-knowing smirk that used to annoy her. "Oh, I know. And you never did a damn thing about it. Why should I?"

"It's another man?"

He laughed, brushing off the ice still clinging to his beer. Then he leaned against the bar. "Her name's Kathy, okay?"

Robin nodded, on the edge of her seat.

"She didn't come from money," he continued. "She lived in one of those housing projects on the other side of town. Her dad drank, her mom worked so many jobs she never saw her. So Kathy ran around with the druggies and...you know, the fast and loose crowd Dad warned us about." He laughed bitterly to himself. But his gaze was distant, she could tell he was seeing Kathy in his mind again. "But you know…something about her. She had reddish, like auburn hair, and I didn't even like redheads, so I told myself I didn't wanna like her. But her face…when she laughed…" He cut his smile loose and a look of anger set in. He took a final swig and set the empty bottle on the bar.

"The thing is," he said. "We'd get to talkin' and it felt like she got me. If I said I was kinda depressed, she'd ask me why or about whatever happened that day…usually a fight with Dad. If I told Sheila that, she'd tell me to snap out of it and get extra cheerful and say some shit about where we should register for the wedding, something like, 'Help me pick out wine flute glasses,' or some shit. I didn't care. But I knew…" His eyes narrowed to dark lines. "I knew that if I brought Kathy home…one look at her ripped jeans and denim jacket with the holes in it…they'd start askin' what her parents did, where she lived… I was a fuckin' coward and should never have married her! Like you and Tom."

Robin's jaw tightened. "You don't know anything about my marriage."

"I know everything about it, Robbie. Don't make the mistake I did, okay? Not goin' after what you really want, *who* you really want."

She wondered if Kathy had been the reason he broke up with Sheila at Christmas all those years ago.

"Why don't you find Kathy…when the divorce goes through?"

"She ran off to Texas with another guy, some asshole she said, 'who wasn't ashamed of her.'"

As he started to leave, he asked about Kendrick. "Where's my girl? I figure she's already in high school by now."

When Kendrick was little, she and Kenneth had a special bond. She was even named for him. He was the fun uncle who gave her horseback rides on his back before she was big enough to ride a real horse. But Robin's falling out with Kenneth, because of what he called her "extremist political views" and overall transformation the longer she was in public office, had kept Kendrick's favorite uncle away.

"She'll be sorry she missed you," Robin said.

"I'm sorry too," Kenneth said. "I didn't even recognize her on TV." He gave her a look that saddened her, as though he didn't know her anymore. "It isn't too late for you, even now," he said.

Robin felt an inexplicable sense of loss as he turned and left. If she wanted to reestablish a relationship with her brother someday, she knew she'd have to make more of an effort—if he was still willing.

CHAPTER FIFTY-FIVE

For me, courage was a funny thing. After all, how many people today would have been among those who sailed out to sea to prove the earth was round? And how many more would have stood at the shore, waving good-bye, uttering the words: "You're all going to fall off the edge of the earth, you idiots"?

I knew I wouldn't have gone on one of those ships, or the ones to the New World, even after it had been discovered. And that was exactly the point. That was also why I wasn't going to do well in Film Production. I had to take it for both semesters, which culminated in a final film project. To make a truly good film, I had to take a risk, to put something honest up on the screen. But I was too guarded, so my films looked like shapes trying to emerge through a kaleidoscope, but never fully formed. This, of course, drove Kyle Perkins crazy. "Why are there two girls running in the woods? What are they running from? What does it mean?"

In an age of music videos filled with images that didn't seem to belong together, like the Eurythmics' video of cows and cellos in the countryside, I told myself I was being avant-garde. "Why does it have to mean anything?" I asked.

"It always means something," he said, not fooled by my evasiveness. He sensed that I had quite a lot to say, but something was duct-taping my mouth shut.

Night after night, I pored through footage I'd taken in the woods near campus, trying to make a more cohesive story out of it. I knew that Kyle wouldn't accept anything less. I sat hunched over my film splicer with a tiny light on at my desk while Adrienne slept nearby.

"He's too literal," I complained to Carol as she lugged the tripod up the stairs of an old warehouse building.

"He knows you've got a story, but you're too chickenshit to tell it." She had a way of paring things down with the sharpness of a butcher knife. As we taped down cords and wires, Carol looked at me. "Doesn't it drive you crazy, the stuff your dad says?"

"What do you mean?" I was on all fours, trying to work the sound equipment.

"Banning books? He wants to erase fuckin' classics if they have sex in them! Everybody has sex. What the hell's his problem?"

I sat up, resting on my knees. I hadn't heard about this yet. "I don't agree with that."

"Then you've got to stop him." She was a mad tornado.

"You can't control what my dad says or does. You might as well try to pin mashed potatoes to the wall."

She set up the lights, muttering, "Damn Republicans."

"Will you quit saying that! Not everyone of a certain party all thinks alike."

"The hell they don't! Why do they always agree with every stupid idea he has?"

I stood up. "I agree with some things and not others. It's possible for people to have ideas that overlap. I hate all this two-party stuff, like you have to claim to be one way or another."

"So you'll be some fuckin' independent whose vote will never count and you'll screw it all up for the Democrats."

"Can we do this please?" I kept checking the time.

"Actors are flakes," she said. "They're gonna be late."

I wiped my forehead and examined the lights once more. Since I wasn't technically inclined, I was sure they were in the wrong place. But Carol, the authority on everything, insisted they were right. As for her arguing, I couldn't focus on politics while I was trying to figure out how to come away with a decent grade in this class. The last thing I needed was a low grade in an elective to pull down my GPA. Then

I'd never hear the end of it from my dad. So I ignored Carol's vitriol about Republicans and tried to focus. Of course I didn't agree with all of my dad's policies, but I didn't have the strength or energy to discuss it today.

When the two girls, who were both acting majors, finally arrived, I told them to kiss each other on the mouth. Everyone paused to collect themselves, including Carol. There weren't many depictions of a kiss like that in student films or even in the ones shown in class, except in one of the Swedish films. Even then, it was labeled "subversive."

So the girls slowly touched lips and caressed each other's faces. I shot it as up-close as I could, to get the image in the face of the viewer, so anyone watching it couldn't look away. Sure, it was literal. But it was raw. And *real*.

I was almost pleased with myself, then looked around to realize the actors hadn't arrived yet. Such a scene might only happen if I knew there was no way my parents could ever see it.

So the daydream was over. And I was still a coward.

The scenes I actually shot in the warehouse turned out to be the extreme opposite of Oscar-winning material, with fuzzy, blurred shots because I could never set my F-stop correctly, and even with Carol's help, some still had bad lighting. Worst of all, I settled for a story that wasn't inside me. That was my fatal mistake. It was hard for me to admit that I wasn't doing well in this class, especially since I'd made straight A's in high school.

* * *

"I want you to drop that course!" Dad hollered over the phone.

"I can't," I said helplessly. "It's too late in the year."

"Whatever possessed you to take it?"

"I'm sorry, Daddy."

That was the year I decided that film would not be the platform I was looking for, after all. A certain level of honesty was required of artists, to really put themselves out there no matter how embarrassing the truth might be. That was not a comfortable place for me. It felt too much like walking around naked in public.

* * *

Soon it was time for my political debate final. When I got to class and took my seat, I panicked because my partner, Chase, wasn't there.

Ms. Donovan arrived, and it was already past time for class to start. He was never late.

"Miss Sanders," she called from the front of the room. "I believe you and Mr. Drescoll are debating today."

"Uh, he isn't here, so…" I hoped it would be canceled. Of course it should be. After all, you can't have a debate with one person.

"Then *you'll* have to do it." Professor Donovan smiled. She had a booming voice that didn't require a microphone, not to mention a constant desire to challenge students whenever possible. To most of the class, she was perfectly annoying.

I stood up slowly. "You want me to do…both sides?"

"That's correct. Your topic is affirmative action and other antidiscrimination laws."

I walked down the steps to the front. This was ridiculous. What teacher would allow something so stupid? *There was no way…*in my mind I fought with Ms. Donovan all the way to the chalkboard.

"You want me to…?"

"Begin. Just take both sides." Ms. Donovan looked expectantly at me, like this wasn't the silliest thing ever. Then she spoke to the entire class. "If any of your partners should be absent, be sure to know both sides of the argument."

I could see whispering among the desks, probably everyone begging their partners not to be absent ever. I cleared my throat and stood behind one of the podiums that had been set up for the debates.

"Affirmative action is necessary to prevent discrimination in the workplace," I began.

Before I could interrupt myself, Ms. Donovan chuckled. "I'm only kidding! Who else had antidiscrimination laws?"

There was a show of hands. Ms. Donovan pointed to Terri, the girl from the dormitory. "You had the opposing argument?" Ms. Donovan asked.

Terri nodded, and the professor motioned for her to come up front. I watched as some in the class snickered. Terri stood, wearing a plaid men's shirt tucked into dusty jeans with a black belt. Her hair was cropped short, so short it was hard to tell exactly what color it was. It seemed brown. She walked with a swagger, her pudgy body swaying from side to side as she descended the steps with hiking boots clomping all the way down. Once she arrived at the opposite podium, she pushed up her black-rimmed glasses that had slid down her nose. I cringed inside; something about this girl bothered me for reasons I didn't understand.

"Okay," Ms. Donovan urged. "You take the second part."

"Affirmative action is unnecessary," Terri responded in a deep voice. "If we live in a country that's already supposedly free, we shouldn't have to have special laws protecting special groups of people."

"But you're ignoring the reality," I argued. "We may call ourselves a free society, but the fact is, discrimination is real. It happens every day." As I heard myself speak, my voice became stronger because I focused on persuading the audience. I stood taller, shoulders back, taking a more powerful posture.

"So where do you draw the line?" Terri shot back. "You protect this group of people, then this group. How do you decide who is protected? Why can't we leave it up to employers to choose the best person for the job?" A few in the audience clapped.

"Because," I replied, "we can't trust employers not to discriminate based on their own biases."

No matter how many examples I gave, I couldn't persuade better than Terri, who spun everything she said to suit her argument. Knowing that she was probably gay, I found it very ironic that she was arguing to *not* protect minorities. Of course, that side had been assigned to her. She may not have believed what she was saying, but she was very convincing. Very impressive.

After class, Ms. Donovan called me over to her desk. Knowing I'd lost the debate, and that was the only opportunity for a grade in this class, I felt defeated. I was already imagining what I'd say to Dad once he found out. I went to the teacher and stared down at my shoes.

"I'm giving you an A," Ms. Donovan said.

"Why?" I asked. "I lost."

"Doesn't matter. You're a natural. You need to work on your supporting arguments, but you have a real flair as a speaker. Don't forget that." She put her hand on my shoulder. It was a defining moment, trumped only by my sudden desire to be as good at the art of persuasion as Terri, the mysterious girl who convinced an entire class she was right. I really admired her for that. Not that I'd tell her that. Usually, whenever I saw Terri in the dorm lobby or around campus, I'd avoid her. And if I couldn't, I'd simply look away, pretending to be distracted by something else. I wasn't proud of that. But I was too much of a coward to ever say a simple hello.

All the way back to the dorm that day, the professor's words echoed in my mind. The next time I would win the debate. A new resolve came over me. This was what I was meant to do. It was an odd realization. I'd spent so long trying not to follow in my father's footsteps, only to find that I was most likely destined to do exactly that, and it was okay. With every step, I felt strangely powerful at the memory of myself at the podium. I was relieved that my Play-Doh legs didn't buckle and that I didn't vomit.

CHAPTER FIFTY-SIX

Adrienne was unusually quiet the next few days, and I was too immersed in my political science texts to notice. It wasn't until a knock on the door and Sean waiting in the hallway that I looked up from my textbook.

"Are we meeting for supper later?" I asked.

"I'll be at Sean's." She shut the door behind her.

I exhaled painfully, really missing her.

* * *

When Adrienne returned to the room that night, I was already settled in bed, about to go to sleep. "What're you doing back? I thought you'd be at his place."

"I couldn't. I got class tomorrow." She slipped into her FSU nightshirt, the one with football numbers on it.

"You go to class?" I joked, sliding under the covers.

"Shut up."

When the lights were out, the room was quiet, and no one seemed to be breathing. If our thoughts could be heard, the noise would have cracked the walls. But no one said anything. An hour passed. Maybe two. I wasn't falling asleep, but eventually I heard her soft, rhythmic breathing on her side of the room.

I pulled off my sheet and went over to her bed. I stroked her hair, watching her sleep. I smiled down at her, looking at the peaceful face, the only time she ever looked truly innocent. Then I bent down and kissed her forehead and, slowly, her cheek. Adrienne's eyes opened, but she wasn't startled; it was like she'd been awake the whole time. Then I gave her a soft kiss on the lips. That kiss led to another, her lips answering mine. It felt so easy, so…natural.

In the shower the next morning, I thought about what we'd done and how Adrienne seemed to want it too. They were only innocent kisses, I told myself, like a drug addict insisting she only *looked* at some heroin. I was so lost in thought I didn't realize how long I'd been in the shower. I was blinded by the cloud of steam.

When I got back to the room wrapped up in my white cotton bathrobe, I saw Adrienne all ready for class, looking like she was waiting for me to come back.

"What happened last night?" Her face was expressionless.

I was startled. "Well, you were there." I was scared she was going to tell me she'd been dreaming the whole time.

Adrienne grabbed her backpack, and the way she looked, I could tell she wanted to say something but didn't.

I held her arm, stopping her before the door. "I miss you." I touched the line of her jaw with my fingertips and before I reached her chin, she leaned down to kiss me. It was a kiss that told me she'd been very much awake last night. Our lips met again and again, as we moved backward, toward the bed…

"I missed you too." She dropped her bag and wrapped her arms tightly around my waist, encircling me possessively. I didn't mind.

We fell upon her bed, where I opened my robe, inviting her in. I couldn't get enough. I craved the feel of her silky body against mine. The way she moved, the way her breasts felt so soft in my hands. It was pure desire, washing over me. Where I came from, all the teachings back home, were all lost on me. It was as though I was living a double life.

Time and space were lost in that little room until we realized the morning sun had changed to a hazy pink afternoon sun through the window.

She woke from a long, peaceful slumber. As soon as she opened her eyes, she looked at me. I watched her in the pink light.

"I missed Western Civ," she said.

I started to laugh. "I'm sure you're heartbroken."

She smiled at me, holding my hand, watching our fingers intertwined. "It was just review. You can't make me miss the test next week, though."

"I'll try to restrain myself."

"You're such a liar!" Adrienne exclaimed, slamming me with a pillow, then imitating me: "We can only be friends. I was just drinking…you *liar!*"

Of course I thought about how she said she "wasn't queer," but I decided not to bring it up. We laughed and playfully smothered each other with pillows.

* * *

That's how it was for the rest of the winter. We were living in our own private, secret world, and no one else on the floor knew anything about it. Sean had stopped coming around, and I was starting to feel bolder about imagining my life in a new way. I still couldn't imagine broaching the subject with my father, or my mother, for that matter. But here in the safety of our dorm room, nothing and no one else mattered. I didn't have to think about my family or the reality waiting outside. I could just be. And I was starting to feel more empowered.

Sitting through my classes, I'd smile to myself just knowing I was going to see *her* face at the end of each day. It was really heaven on earth, something I'd never come close to experiencing in my careful life before, the life of a scared girl in a small Atlanta suburb.

CHAPTER FIFTY-SEVEN

Adrienne turned around, wearing a court jester hat. "You like?" she asked.

"Yeah," I answered. "It's definitely you."

She offered me a hat. "Come on. It's for the Mardi Gras party."

"No," I said firmly. "I don't do hats. No one in my family does hats. It's the shape of our faces or something. We look really weird in them."

She rolled her eyes. "I'd like to meet your family sometime."

"No, you wouldn't."

"Why not?"

"You'd say they were uptight. You think everyone but you is uptight."

"Because they are." Adrienne laughed and took off the hat, running her hand roughly through her long hair. "Tell me you're going to the party."

"When is it?"

"Tonight."

"I'll think about it," I stammered, feeling oddly jealous. Who would be at the party? I'd become accustomed to having her all to myself. But I had to relax and not become some possessive weirdo.

I lowered my shoulders and took a deep breath. It was only a party. Maybe it was her history with boys, one boy in particular, that made me so ill at ease.

Next thing I knew, Carol burst into our room without knocking. "Hey, kiddo." She plopped on my bed. We'd left the door unlocked, and Carol wasn't much for formalities.

Adrienne glared at Carol like an overprotective grizzly.

"Carol, Adrienne. Adrienne, Carol." I made the introductions, relishing Adrienne's curiosity and apparent jealousy about Carol.

"Hey," Adrienne said.

"Hey." Carol took a drag off her cigarette, looking unimpressed. "I would've called," she began, "but my phone's busted."

"What's up?" I asked.

"Some film people are getting together later," she said.

Bette Davis was smiling down on everyone. The tension in the room was palpable.

Adrienne looked at me, silently reminding me of my first party invitation.

"Where?" I asked.

"The beach," Carol replied.

"That's where ours is," Adrienne said.

"Oh, well sure," I said quickly. "I guess we'll all be there." A very diplomatic way to handle the situation, I thought.

"I doubt the film people will be hanging around the metalheads." Carol had no filter at times. It would be safe to assume Adrienne didn't like her much at all. So she did her own thing, sneering slightly while overhearing the conversation.

"I'm sure we can all hang out," I kept repeating, trying to keep Carol calm and from saying anything too provocative. Both Carol and Adrienne had super hot tempers that should never be allowed in the same room—another reason why I was all about keeping the peace.

"If you think so," Carol said sarcastically. "It's gonna be real crowded tonight, too many people for my taste. But I'll go if you go. They're doing the Mardi Gras bullshit there."

"Yeah, I'll go." I followed her to the door. "I'll walk you out."

In the hall, Carol glared at me. "I never see you anymore. Geez, I couldn't say two words to you without Hawk Eyes staring me down. What the fuck's her problem?"

"We're together now," I said quietly. "Nobody knows, so don't say anything."

"You and metal chick? For *real*?" Carol wasn't happy. She needed a minute on the couch in the lobby. "You're kidding me."

"No." I took a seat next to her. "I don't know why, but I sort of thought you'd be happy for me. At least I'm not confused about her feelings anymore." I chuckled awkwardly.

"Right." She seemed preoccupied. Something else was going on. "I don't know. I guess in a twisted way, I'd hoped she'd be as messed up as I thought she was. Then you'd come running to me."

"You wanted to be more than friends?" I asked.

Her cheeks reddened. She wouldn't look at me. "I don't know. I thought about it. Didn't you?"

"Yeah." Honestly, I had thought a few times about it, on those lonely nights in Carol's room, the only place that had seemed welcoming when I was full of fear. "Rachmaninoff Concerto Number Two."

"Huh?"

"You were playing that the first night I came over," I said.

"I don't remember, but sounds like something I'd play."

"You're the best friend I have," I told her. "I don't want to lose that."

"Oh, c'mon." She rose to her feet and wiped her hands on her extra faded jeans. "We don't have to get dramatic. I'll still be your friend. But I think she's all wrong for you."

"You're probably right." I smiled one of those dreamy smiles that Carol knew she couldn't penetrate.

"Don't let her mess with your head," she warned.

Still smiling…

"Okay," Carol said. "I got it. Promise me you'll still talk to us little people at the party?"

I laughed. "Of course. You're all my friends. I don't like any of the girls she hangs out with anyway."

"That's a good sign," she said sarcastically.

Before I could respond, she was out the door.

CHAPTER FIFTY-EIGHT

At the Mardi Gras party, students gathered around a smoldering bonfire at a nearby beach, while a group of shirtless boys played volleyball. Some college kids, concealing their beers, sat together on the edges of lounge chairs that had been scooted together. Adrienne waved at her party crowd as she and I climbed down a steep sand dune. I always struggled to get traction in the sand and was one step away from falling on my butt. I was never what you'd call graceful in outdoor settings.

Nancy, one of Adrienne's party friends, aimed a camera at us. "Say cheese!" she yelled.

Adrienne and I put our arms around each other and smiled big smiles with the bonfire flames shooting up behind us.

"Hey, how you doin', girl?" Nancy was already a little drunk. She put an arm around Adrienne as all of us made our way over to the lounge chairs. "It's been like forever!"

"I know!" Adrienne exclaimed. She opened the cooler nearby and immediately offered me a beer.

"No," I replied sharply. "I don't want one."

She cracked open the can and took a swig, noticing Boyd seated among the partygoers.

"Crap," I muttered, noticing him too. "I don't want to go over there."

"You're such a diva." Adrienne winked at me, handing me the can while she lit up a cigarette.

I noticed the flash of light from the tip of her cigarette against a backdrop of color-streaked sky, stripes of raspberry and orange sherbet over an ocean that, like me, was getting more agitated as the sun went down.

I kicked at the sand, already covering my flip-flops. "I'm not going over there." I'm sure I sounded threatened because I was.

"So don't." Adrienne waved at some of her other party friends.

I didn't really care. To me, Nancy, Becky and the others were a bunch of girls who liked to hang on each other and giggle and get as wasted as possible. I felt a bizarre satisfaction in knowing that Adrienne was the one I came here with tonight and the one she'd be leaving with. It didn't matter if we had our separate social groups.

As it grew darker, the ocean disappeared, replaced by sounds of crashing waves. The sand was cooler and silky, brushing over my bare feet as I took off my flip-flops and tried to find Carol in the crowd. Smoke from the bonfire smothered the salty smell of the air, as I caught glimpses of faces in the flashes of light.

Suddenly there was Boyd's wounded face. I remembered how I'd just run out of the apartment without a look back or another word. But he'd become too aggressive, and that memory tempered my guilt somewhat. He came closer. His hair was longer, frizzier, and his cheeks more sunken. He could have easily been shooting some drug; he looked as though he was wasting away.

"'I really want to do it!'" he mocked. "'Of course I want to!'" His high-pitched, terrible imitation of my southern voice made me sick to my stomach.

I stood my ground, holding my head high. I felt strong. And besides, we were surrounded by people. He'd never catch me alone again. "Boyd," I said sternly. "Some things aren't meant to be, like you and me." Then I resumed walking.

But he followed. "There never was a 'you and me.'" He climbed over the small hills of the beach unsteadily. "Was there?"

For a moment in the dark, I saw pain on his face. He lashed out at me because he didn't know what to do with his hurt. I had given him hope I shouldn't have.

"I'm sorry," I said. "It was my fault. I...had feelings for someone else, and I was trying to get over...him."

"Huh." That seemed to make it worse. "You're just a cocktease!" he shouted to save his pride or ego or whatever else he was clinging to besides his beer.

I tried to be kind, I reasoned. At least I tried. "Whatever." I moved on, coldly leaving him in the shadows.

Still searching for Carol, I turned, and over my shoulder I saw Adrienne on the edge of a lounge chair, laughing with Nancy and Sean. The hairs on the back of my neck stood on end. Every inch of my skin felt cold in spite of being so near to the bonfire.

"Hey, kiddo." It was Carol, standing a little too close to the soaring flames.

I motioned her over. "Let's get away from this, okay? It's too… fiery."

She laughed at my description, and we moved closer to the water and darkness. Only a sliver of moon lit our way, and it took a while for our eyes to adjust.

"How's your girlfriend?" Carol asked.

"Fine, I guess."

"You guess? Where is she?"

I didn't want to tell her. She'd have all kinds of rude things to say. I had a persistent, sickening feeling that I might be a character in a story where I was the only one living the story. One-sided feelings, one-sided thoughts. Even in our most intimate moments, how honest was Adrienne? She sometimes seemed like she was holding something back. Could I really trust her? When I gestured to the lounge chairs illuminated in bonfire light, Carol zeroed in immediately on the fact that Adrienne was now talking to her former boyfriend. And I had a strange sensation, wondering if we really would be leaving this party together.

"It doesn't mean anything," I insisted.

"You sure about that?"

Sean took off his shirt, inching closer to Adrienne. She was in her party mood, her charismatic smile drawing in everyone around her. She seemed to be at the center of the group the moment she arrived. She gulped down another beer, apparently enjoying the attention.

Without his shirt on, Sean was even more repugnant. Never mind that my visceral hatred of him sprang from deep-rooted jealousy, I also just plain didn't like him. I sensed something sinister, maybe it was his angry eyes. Even when he was trying to be nice, his eyes still looked like those of something evil, dark and empty. I'd seen it before in some guys. And I saw it in him. They were entitled to everything—

and *everyone*. His friends had the same look in their eyes, and several of them were out tonight, looking for girls to take to one of their private parties. I knew the scene all too well.

I made sure that Adrienne caught a glimpse of me and Carol walking together by the shore. She glanced in my direction, but she didn't leave her party crowd. Carol and I took a long walk, away from the noise and the lights. Everything was calmer under the moonlight, with nothing but the sound of waves tumbling over our feet.

"I shouldn't have come," I said. "I'm really not up for this."

"All the dumbasses she hangs out with?"

I smiled. Her bluntness sometimes made me feel better. "I guess."

"It's okay. The film crowd is down this way, unless I lost my sense of direction, which is entirely possible." She looked around, unable to tell if anyone was up ahead.

As we walked, we heard sounds of something going on, voices getting louder, until we could tell there was some kind of fight. Then an unbelievable scene suddenly unfolded right in front of us.

A gang of boys, some I recognized as friends of Sean's, were beating up Andrew and kicking sand in his face. They were wearing jester hats from the Mardi Gras parade that afternoon. "Fuckin' faggot!" I heard them yell. They were the same ones who had been waiting outside the Cobra Club that night.

"Stop it!" I screamed, running at them full speed. I nearly halted when I came face-to-face with the tallest one, who was standing on the edges of the gang, watching in amusement. "Get away from him!" I shouted.

Carol tried to pull me back. "You gotta be careful with these fuckers."

But I felt brave; I didn't care if they carried knives or if this was a secluded enough part of the beach where they might feel like they could get away with anything. It didn't matter. All I knew was what was right and what was wrong. In the nighttime light, it was really clear.

The gang proved more cowardly than we expected. At the first hint of trouble, the boys disbanded and were quickly swallowed up by darkness. I dropped to my knees beside Andrew, whose face was bloody beyond recognition.

"Oh my God. He's hurt." Carol came up behind me.

"Go get help!" I commanded.

She took off, while I gripped Andrew's hand. "It'll be okay," I repeated. I wasn't sure of that, but I hoped he'd be able to hear me.

CHAPTER FIFTY-NINE

After the ambulance pulled away, Carol and I ran back to the center of the party. We found Gina Chi and told her what had happened.

"We can follow him in my car," Gina said. She'd been Carol's ride anyway, but I would have to find Adrienne and let her know.

"Give me a minute," I said, trying to find my way through the crowd. Most of the lounge chairs were now empty. I looked up toward the parking lot and was surprised to see her Camaro still parked in its space. I heard the strumming of a guitar melting into the wind. When I looked closer, I saw Adrienne sitting in the sand, plucking the strings of her acoustic guitar. I could actually make out a tune; it was as if she'd been secretly practicing. She stopped when she saw me.

"Hey, check it out." Adrienne smelled like beer. Her words ran together without the usual pauses of a sober person. "Can you believe someone was gonna toss this? At a garage sale..." She played a few more notes to show off.

"Yes, I know. You told me."

"Where you been?" she asked.

"One of my friends got beaten up," I said.

"Shit!" Adrienne rose unsteadily to her feet and dusted the sand off her backside.

"Yeah, so, I was going to go with Carol and Gina over there…" I gestured to my two friends standing near the bonfire. "We're going to the hospital."

"Oh." Adrienne looked worried.

"Are you okay?" I could see that she wasn't.

"I was hoping you could be my designated driver." She laughed, mocking herself, her head obviously cloudy.

"Where are your friends?" I asked.

"They went back to Sean's place."

I'd wondered if she was going to go back with him too. Maybe I feared it all night. "I guess I'm surprised you stayed," I said.

"I wasn't going to leave without you," she exclaimed. "What the hell kind of person you think I am?"

"Sometimes you can…" Now was not the night to have a rational conversation. "I'll drive you back."

I asked my friends to check on Andrew and told them I'd be by in the morning.

"She didn't go with her boyfriend?" Carol remarked.

"No," I said. "I've got to get her back to campus."

Adrienne hiccupped behind me.

"Got it." Carol's glare was judgmental. I watched as she and Gina headed up to the parking lot.

"Call me if you have any news, okay?"

"Yeah!" Carol waved, her back to me.

Adrienne and I got to the car, then fumbled for what seemed like forever with the heavy guitar case and managed to get it back into the trunk.

In the car, we turned the stereo up way too loud, but the kind of loud you want when you've had too much to drink. I tried to turn it down a notch as I figured out how to roll down the windows of her car. Down the highway, the salty wind made its way inside; it would forever be a scent etched in my mind whenever I thought about this time and place.

"Why did you think I'd leave you?" Adrienne asked.

"You seemed kind of cozy with Sean." I wished I hadn't said it as soon as I'd said it.

"I'm not with him anymore. You know that." She took my hand.

We came to a curve, and I jerked my hand away. "I need both hands on the wheel!"

She laughed. "You drive like my grandma."

"Good. She's probably a safe driver."

"She's barely tall enough to see over the dashboard."

"Shut up." I took comfort in what Adrienne had said. Maybe I could learn to let myself relax about what we had together. But right now, my first worry was for Andrew. I wondered how serious his injuries were. Maybe the bruises looked worse than they were...

"You seemed all cozy with that film chick." Adrienne lit up another cigarette.

"Carol?" I was snapped out of my worries.

"Whatever." She tapped ashes out the window. Even though it was a totally disgusting habit to me, the way Adrienne tapped the ashes was kind of sexy. I didn't know exactly why. Maybe it reminded her of the women in film noir. Or maybe Adrienne could read a phone book and still be sexy. It was probably the blindness of first love where everything she did had a singular, awe-inspiring quality to it.

"I like it when you're jealous." I smiled, noticing a few stars popping out to guide my way.

"I'm not jealous, not unless you got a thing for nerds."

"Don't call her that." There was nothing nerdy about Carol. If anything, she reminded me of an artsy New Yorker who owned a gallery that made news for its controversial exhibits of penises or severed heads. Yeah, she was absolutely that type. Sometimes she wore black-rimmed glasses, but the nerd stereotype was ridiculous.

"Did I upset you?" Adrienne seemed to be trying to pick a fight.

"I just don't like labels. You like to do that, you know. You call everyone something." I imitated her: "'She's a slut. He's a jock.' You know, there's more to people than what you see on the outside."

"No kidding," Adrienne laughed. "Look at you, Miss Prim and Proper. Who would know?"

"Know what?"

"That you like pussy!" Adrienne wailed drunkenly.

I tried to remind myself that she wasn't really herself tonight. But I was upset anyway. Why did she have to take something good and make it sound like something from one of her porn movies? Unless it didn't mean the same to her...always the doubts creeping in. "Do you know that some of your buddy's friends beat up my friend tonight?"

"What buddy?"

"Sean!"

"He's not my buddy." She paused dramatically. "He's an asshole."

"You got that right. His friends called Andrew a faggot!" I slammed harder on the gas.

"Okay! I'll talk to him. I know he can be an asshole, but I can't control everyone he hangs out with. Who's Andrew?"

"Why do you hang out with Sean? Why doesn't that bother you?" I found myself in a familiar argument.

"I can't solve everything, and neither can you." She pointed her cigarette at me. "You better realize that, or you're gonna die of high blood pressure or something."

"That ship's probably sailed already." I pulled the cigarette out of her mouth and threw it out the window.

"Oh, for fuck's sake! Will you get a grip?"

"My really good friend was beaten within an inch of his life tonight, and I'm here because…because…you're too shit-faced to drive!" I swerved; I was driving faster than I normally did, feeling angry about everything. When I finally got to the city limits, I slowed down. It wouldn't be good if we were stopped. If Adrienne said one word, it would be all over. I could see my parents' faces as I told them I spent a night in jail for drinking and driving. They'd never be able to show their faces in church again.

"So sorry to put you out! Hey…" Adrienne grabbed my shoulder, pulling me out of my daydream. "I'm sorry about your friend. I really am. It's not my fault it happened, though, just because I used to date Sean."

I said nothing for a while. "You're right," I finally answered. I was holding her accountable for something that didn't matter anymore.

We turned into the dormitory parking lot. Carol called to assure me there wasn't any point in going tonight. They had him stabilized, and he was asleep. So she and Gina left and went back to campus too. I wouldn't get to the hospital until the next morning.

"Thanks for letting me know." When I hung up the phone, I saw Adrienne fast asleep in bed.

I came over to her bed and pulled the sheet up over her, even though she was still wearing her clothes. I looked at her, reminding myself how nice it was that she didn't leave without me. I wondered why I expected that to happen. I was grateful it didn't. I took a tissue and wiped the runny mascara under her eyes. Nothing stirred her awake, even as I brushed the hair away from her face. I sat for a while, just looking at her, and the bulky guitar case that now took up half the room. I listened to her steady breathing. I took off each of her shoes gingerly, so as not to wake her. But she had already started snoring, lost somewhere far away.

In that moment I knew I loved her. And I knew that love wasn't only like what they described in poems or what you heard in songs. It was about the messy things too, wiping mascara that's run down her cheeks, seeing the beauty of her face even when she was hungover with pink, puffy eyes…wanting to protect her even when I knew she wouldn't take care of herself. Love was very inconvenient and annoying, and it felt so inevitable and permanent, as if no matter what happened from this point on, I knew I'd always love her.

CHAPTER SIXTY

Andrew lay in the hospital bed with a few cuts and bruises decorating his pale face. He stared disappointedly at the elevated television. "It's Cher, you idiot!" he hollered at a *Jeopardy* contestant. "Stupid straight guys," he muttered to himself.

I knocked on the open door and entered cautiously, afraid of what I might see. I had gone over it in the hospital elevator on the way up here—if he had a missing eye or something hanging that shouldn't be hanging, I'd pretend not to notice it.

"Hi," I said.

Andrew's face lit up. "Hey! Come in!" he said. "So tell me straight, so to speak. Did they mess up my face? The nurses won't let me look."

Relieved to be able to recognize him, I said, "No, not really. Just a few scratches. You looked worse last night." I took a seat beside him. "I'm so pissed!" I exclaimed.

He closed his eyes and shook his head. "Channel that energy into something positive—like a new wardrobe. Ahhh!"

"I don't believe it. You're making jokes. How can you be making jokes?"

"It's called morphine, sweetie." He smiled tiredly at me.

"I think I know who did this to you." At the sight of him, I had that familiar urge to slap Adrienne for associating with someone like Sean and his violent pals.

"One of 'em was Randy's friend," Andrew said. "The guy at the club."

"Randy?"

"Oh, yeah. He was gay, just not okay with it. A freakin' coward too. Had to have one of his friends do it."

"Someone needs to have a discussion with those boys."

"Don't." Andrew took my hand. "It won't do any good. You be careful." He coughed. "Is there any water?" He looked over in the direction of his tray, still with half-eaten food on a plate and a cup of green Jell-O. I scooted over to him and placed a plastic cup with a straw up to his mouth. "You know," he said. "I'm starting to think I should have waited until after college to come out. You should consider it."

My face was redder than a beet. "I don't need to come out…I'm not…"

He coughed again, and I raised the cup to his mouth once more. "It's not for the weak-hearted."

I squeezed his hand. "C'mon, quit talking and get your rest."

* * *

Later that afternoon, I came back to an empty dorm room. Flipping on the light, I went over to my closet and began unbuttoning my shirt. I could hear thunder rumbling outside.

Soon after, Adrienne came in. "Hey," she said, carrying groceries. "How's your friend?"

"He's doing better."

"Good. It's gonna be a big storm." She turned on the TV. A weather bulletin was flashing, but neither of us was paying attention. She absently put soda and beer in the minifridge, while I watched her.

"How did you ever go out with someone like that?" I faced her, letting my shirt hang open. I'd come a long way from the girl who changed clothes under a towel.

Adrienne took out another six-pack. "Not this again."

"I…have to know." I took a deep breath.

"I don't know, okay?"

"I guess you had a few things in common, like the way you call certain people names."

"Huh?"

"That girl down the hall. You had a lot to say about her. And Sean's friends, shouting 'faggot' at my friend Andrew on the beach." I also remembered the gang calling me a dyke outside the club, but I kept that to myself.

"I'm sorry if I made any queer jokes," she said, not looking at me. My political correctness always seemed to annoy her.

"It's kind of ironic."

"Will you quit talking to me like that? I'm trying to apologize." She looked at me, then glanced away sharply, as if she'd heard a gunshot on the other side of the room. The way I stood there with my shirt open, I had this new air of confidence. Adrienne was obviously uncomfortable, maybe even a little intimidated.

"Am I making you nervous?" I asked.

"Don't flatter yourself." She grabbed her backpack. Her discomfort was something I'd never seen before. She seemed anxious to get out of the room.

A bolt of lightning reminded us of the storm raging outside and getting worse. Palm trees bent to their sides, and the afternoon sky was suddenly dark as night.

"You shouldn't go out in this," I said.

"I'm fine."

As soon as Adrienne opened the door, Lydia strode up the hall in her loud swishy pants. "Bad storm brewing. Everyone is advised to stay in."

"We can go anytime we want," Adrienne argued.

"It's not advised!" Lydia's eyes narrowed, daring her to defy her. "If something happens to you, the school is not responsible, because you've been warned."

"What the hell's a matter with you?"

I came out to check on the situation. "Come on, Adrienne. Why not wait it out inside?"

"I don't want to." She turned into a child who wasn't getting her way. Then she looked at Lydia again. "I mean, really? What the fuck is your problem? Why are you so weird? Were you dropped on your head as a kid?"

"Adrienne!" I exclaimed. "She's under a lot of pressure," I explained to Lydia apologetically.

"No, I'm not." Adrienne kept arguing as I yanked her back inside. I gave Lydia an apologetic nod as I closed the door.

"You'd better stay put," Lydia called, "or I'm gonna write you up!"

"You do that!" Adrienne hollered from the other side of the door.

"What's the matter with you?" I was exasperated.

She dropped her backpack and fell onto her bed, staring up at the ceiling. "I don't like people telling me what I can and can't do."

"You know she's kind of nuts. Why do you have to make it worse?"

"Because maybe I don't care, okay?"

There was a long silence. I curled up in my own bed and took out some books to read while flashes of lightning pierced the room, followed by thunder that was getting closer.

The lights went out. In a moment, Adrienne struck a match and lit a nearby peach candle. The wick was nearly buried in wax, barely tall enough to hold the flame, but she was able to connect with it.

"You'll burn your fingers!" I squeaked. Then I saw the lit candle and the glow on Adrienne's anxious face. "What's going on with you?"

"What about you?" She set the candle by her bedside. "You're so mad at me all the time." She seemed sad. "Nothing I do is right. And you're still pissed because I used to see this guy, and you're blaming me for everything he does. That doesn't mean I'd do the same thing, you know. You always talk about stereotypes and how wrong they are. But you stereotyped me from the start. You treat me like I'm stupid if I don't have all the same opinions you do. You're a total snob." There was a lot inside of her, boiling to the surface.

I closed my eyes, taking it all in. I understood that I had to make things right again. "I know it doesn't sound like much, but I'm sorry. I'm sorry I misjudged you. I guess I was never real comfortable around Sean, and I guess I was a little threatened by him."

Her face softened as she moved to my bed. "You don't have to be," she said softly and held my hand. Then she kissed it.

"I know." Without thinking, I wrapped my arms around her and said, "I love you."

There was silence. I didn't notice right away, but Adrienne's body had tensed up at the sound of those words. After another moment or two, she went back to her side of the room.

CHAPTER SIXTY-ONE

Spring in Florida didn't feel like spring, just a slightly less hot version of hell. I knew, though, that with summer around the corner, I didn't have much longer to be with Adrienne. I began to wish summer would pass quickly. I couldn't stand the thought of not seeing her, of being at home where I had to keep my feelings zipped up tightly. So many times I'd thought about calling my brother this semester, but I didn't. I was always afraid that Adrienne would walk in and overhear my phone conversations.

The end of the school year was drawing near. I survived a week of finals, and this afternoon had been the last hurdle. Carol and I walked together under the sprawling oaks of the campus. I breathed in the aroma of nearby flowers, relieved that it was finally over.

I admitted the most embarrassing thing to her: "He gave me a B," I said, talking about our film production teacher. "But he wrote that he wanted to give me a C. Why did he have to write that? You know? It's just hurtful."

"You're lucky. He could've flunked you."

"Thanks." I was troubled. "You think I should have failed?"

Carol gave me her best smart-ass face. "Yeah."

Why did I ask her when I knew I was going to get the unfiltered truth, even if I couldn't handle it? "Fine." My lips tightened, and I walked faster.

"Hey, wait! Are we running a fuckin' marathon?"

"You could keep up if you didn't smoke all those cancer sticks."

"God, you sound like my mother." She coughed, catching up to me. "I would've failed you, yeah. Deal with it."

I stopped and swung around. "Why?"

"'Cause I couldn't tell what the hell your movie was about."

I chewed my lower lip, realizing that Carol, in all her apparent cruelness, was actually right. "I guess I was going more for an artsy style."

"An incoherent mess." Her medication, or her condition, sometimes made her sound more agitated than she intended. And she seemed particularly frustrated with me today. We resumed walking. "You gonna keep in touch over the summer?"

I imagined how my parents would view someone like Carol; they'd judge her immediately for the nose ring, for everything having to do with the way she looked. But what would they say about her mental illness? I hated myself for thinking of everything now through the prism of my parents' narrow viewpoint. It was as if while here, on campus, I'd been living in a bubble of total freedom. Once I climbed out of that bubble, into the outside world again, everything would be different. And not in a good way. I thought of returning home with a sense of dread.

"Hey," Carol shouted. "I asked you a question."

"Yeah. Sure."

"People always say that, but they never mean it."

"I mean it!"

When Carol went her separate way back to her dorm, I was grateful to have some time alone before returning to my own room. I saw some kids in the parking lot already packing up their cars. I was going to stay one more day, especially because Adrienne would be here. I hadn't even begun packing yet. I was sad the year was actually coming to an end.

It was late afternoon. Clouds were clustering together for an afternoon storm. I rushed inside the dormitory just in time to escape the first few raindrops. I got out of the elevator and turned the familiar corner down the hall, to the room. When I opened the door, nothing could prepare me for what I would see.

Two naked bodies were curled up under the white sheet of Adrienne's bed. When I realized that the other body was Sean, I tried, but couldn't, catch my breath. He was resting with one arm possessively hanging over Adrienne's breasts, his hairy forearm secure in its place, and some of his chest hair sprouted over the top line of the sheet. Adrienne's eyes were closed, and her arms were above her head on the pillow.

I gasped loudly, waking Adrienne. "What are you doing!" I cried hoarsely, throwing my backpack so hard it sailed across the room.

Adrienne gathered up the sheet around her as fast as she could, as if it made any difference. "Hang on!" she kept saying.

I couldn't stay and look at the sight any longer. My fists were clenched so tightly I nearly crushed the keys in my hand before tearing out of the room.

CHAPTER SIXTY-TWO

I drove for an hour in the rain. Ironically, "Alone Again" came on the radio, and I turned it up. What a fool, I repeated to myself. *Such a fool.* Of course Adrienne slept with him. She was playing me. She was having it all. And always I would return to the image now engraved in my mind: Sean's arm over her chest. How could she let him touch her? How could she touch him? *After us, how could you go to him?* The whole thing was unfathomable.

Then there was Andrew. I thought of his bruised face and skinny neck popping out of the hospital gown. That's what happened to gay people. Never mind the constant whispering in the halls; they got beaten to a pulp or worse. I came to a fork in the road—literally—and started laughing hysterically at the irony of it. Thankfully I was alone in the car, because my wailing laughter sounded like that of a crazy person. Wet hair stuck to the back of my neck, and I wiped away the strands that were falling and dripping in my eyes from the rain. Not realizing that one of the windows was open a crack, letting more wetness inside, I kept wiping it from my face.

I leaned on the steering wheel, grateful the road was deserted. The part of it that branched off to the left led me back to campus. I knew what was there, what to expect. The other part that veered to the right went to some unknown destination. I didn't know if it led to a good or bad part of town or even whether it led out of town. And the literal symbolism, like Dr. Gentry talked about during both semesters of film theory, it was so obvious it was almost silly. I knew the path to take for the familiar, the one that I knew, although it made me feel humiliated to even be considering it. The other path was unknown darkness, possibly the part of town that was usually on the local news. I always wanted to be strong and brave, someone who would make Bette Davis proud. But as I turned the wheel, heading back toward school, I thought about my English literature class in high school and the poem about the road not taken. The last line: "It has made all the difference." I recalled how that line, which seemed to be a good thing at the time I read it, could also be taken to mean something good *or* bad. A road not taken could be the difference between an easier, comfortable life and an extremely difficult one. As much as I hated to admit it to myself, I'd never be able to look Bette Davis in the eye again.

* * *

"I don't want to hear it." I had begun packing my clothes, a task which I'd been putting off all week.

"Please," Adrienne begged. But she couldn't get me to look at her. "Okay, fine." She sat on her bed and lit a cigarette.

I immediately opened the window to show my disdain for her smoking. "I can't stand that smell!"

"I told you," Adrienne said. "I'm not a queer."

I whipped around. "Is that what you think I am?" My armor immediately came out again for protection. "I'm not...queer either!"

"Okay, well why are you so mad?"

"Because...because... you said he wasn't your boyfriend!"

"He's not. He's just...he's not." She seemed confused and off balance.

My eyes filled. I couldn't look at her without that lump in my throat. I was back to feeling like a fool.

"I hope," she said, "this doesn't change our friendship."

A bitter chuckle. "I don't know." I resumed my packing. *Go. Please go.*

"It shouldn't matter to you," she said.

"Well, I guess it does," I snapped. "I told you something, and you ignored it. But it was true. I do love you." Quickly I added, "But not anymore, so don't worry about it!"

"I want to still be friends." Her voice was thin.

"Please leave." I didn't know how much longer I could last before the tears would come. Finally I heard the door close, and she was gone.

I leaned against my dresser, breathing out, feeling my whole body tremble. What was happening? I couldn't understand my reality anymore. After all that had happened between us, how could she act like this was no big deal?

CHAPTER SIXTY-THREE

I wasted no time packing my car the next morning. I saw that Adrienne's car, parked a few slots away, was only partially filled, with her boxes full of wires in the backseat, stacked up almost, but not quite, to the ceiling.

When I came back into the room for another load, it reminded me of the first day, when everything had looked so barren. Her shrine to heavy metal had been ripped off the walls. I pondered it sadly. Amazingly, we'd added color to the dead cinder blocks with reminders of our favorite things. We'd made a life in that little prison cell. I thought of the two roommates who would share that room next year, and the year after, and the year after that. No one would know what we'd experienced together, and no one would care. To every new student, that dorm room would look as cold and uninviting as it had looked to me. And somehow each student would have to find a way to make a home of it.

Last night, we moved about the space, and each other, with unspoken uneasiness and tension. We went to sleep without a word. Something had been lost—for good, it seemed.

Before I left that morning, Andrew made it over to see me. Even on crutches, he looked good. There was color in his cheeks, and he'd gained a little weight back. I was relieved to see that.

"Are you going to be okay?" I asked.

"Oh, you know me." He grinned at me. "You have fun being a Georgia peach. We'll see each other next year."

"I mean, you have a place to stay?" I remembered that his home wasn't exactly a welcoming environment.

"Yeah, I'm staying with some friends here."

"You could still report it as a hate crime," I said.

He shook his head. "I don't want to make trouble. It's better if I stay under the radar."

"With that laugh?" I smiled at him. "You'll never be under the radar." I meant it as a compliment.

I hugged him gingerly, not sure what part of his body was safe to squeeze. I didn't want to break or dislocate anything. When he left, I said good-bye to him in my mind. He didn't know the plans I'd made last night. No one here did.

After I walked in on Adrienne and Sean last night and drove around in the rain, I went back to campus and called my parents from the library. I told them I wanted to transfer next year. They were all too happy to have me closer to home. Dad said something about "beating the liberal" out of me, pretending it was a joke, but I didn't care.

My plan was to attend Emory and major in political science. Of course Dad was elated at the news. Even though he loved FSU, he worried that it had changed since the fifties and that it was the school's fault for putting "crazy" ideas in my head.

I didn't tell Adrienne. How she could want to live with me again next year "as a friend," I had no idea. But I couldn't. We both filled out the forms for the dormitory again next year. But I was set on my plan. I'd simply call the registrar and residence offices when I returned home, and I'd undo it all, cut any ties to her and this school forever.

I wouldn't tell her about transferring because I didn't want her giving me any grief about giving in to my father or how I really didn't have a rebellious bone in my body—all things Adrienne might say out of hurt or anger. Even if they were true, I didn't want to hear them. I was getting pretty good at ignoring anything I didn't want to hear, even the things my dad was saying over the phone in his elation. He must've said "goddamn liberal" a hundred times, but I refused to hear it.

Most of all, I felt quiet relief to know that the fear—of Adrienne and the feelings she evoked—was almost completely behind me. From this point on, I'd run away from the things I feared most. I'd keep running, feeling sure that the past could never catch up with me.

That morning, I finished packing. Adrienne was outside at her car. I saw her through the window. She had a few more trips left to make, with a couple of her suitcases still waiting on her bare mattress. There was just one more thing left to do. I made sure to leave the heavy metal tape she made for me on the nightstand. I wanted to leave that music—and everything I associated with it—behind forever. I also wanted to send a message, that I was no longer pining for her, even if it wasn't true. It would be true someday, I assured myself. Most of all, I wanted Adrienne to believe that if what we had meant nothing to her, then it meant nothing to me either.

In the parking lot I found Adrienne waiting for me. "I guess this is it." She shrugged. There were a million questions on her face.

"Yeah," I said.

She squinted in the light without her sunglasses. Her dark blue T-shirt seemed to fit the mood of the day. "I'll see you next year," she said, holding out her arms for one last hug.

I hugged her back, knowing it would be the last time. I squeezed her so hard, then finally let go.

"Next year, huh?" she repeated, shielding her eyes from the sun.

"Yeah." My face was ice cold, as I opened my car door. I could tell she wanted to talk more, to somehow wipe away the other day with a wink and a smile as she'd done with other things. Only this time it wouldn't change anything. In an odd way, it was the saddest and the best day of my life. The person who scared me most, who challenged me more than anyone else had, would soon be out of my life forever. It was a comfort, a supreme relief, to know I wouldn't have to deal with her—or *this*—anymore.

As I drove out of the parking lot, I saw Adrienne in the rearview mirror, waving good-bye. I held myself together until I left the campus and turned onto the next street. Then I allowed myself a few tears. They were the last tears I'd shed for her for almost thirty more years. From time to time, though, I'd remember the sight of her, like my fear, getting smaller in the rearview mirror, and how she looked that day, her deep brown eyes squinting and shining in the sun.

CHAPTER SIXTY-FOUR

Robin knocked on Kendrick's door. "Hon? It's Mom."

"Yeah?"

She came in to find her daughter staring at her iPad. That was her closest relationship these days, the one she had with her iPad. She obviously didn't have time to quickly pull out her *Bible* or textbooks, but strangely, Robin didn't seem to care.

Robin said, "Tomorrow I have to go to—"

"Tampa. I know. The big debate."

Robin wanted to talk to her about marriages, how they sometimes don't last, as if she didn't already know that. She imagined some cleverly scripted TV show parent-teen conversation that would end in tears and a hug. Then she realized she didn't have the emotional strength for it.

"How is everything at school?" Robin asked. "With your friend?"

Kendrick looked down and traced the outer line of her iPad. "We're not going to be friends anymore. It's pretty much over."

"I'm sorry to hear that. I really am."

"It's okay. I told you, I still hang around with the others." After a pause, she looked at her mother and said, "I miss her."

"I know you do." Robin patted her leg. "You always will. But it gets better over time. I promise." She looked at Kendrick's iPad and headphones that were lying beside her. "What were you looking at?"

"You don't want to know."

"Yes, I do."

Kendrick seemed very uncomfortable. Her face alternated between embarrassment and anguish.

All kinds of thoughts raced through Robin's head. *Was it porn?*

Kendrick turned the tablet around to face her mother. It was a video of Adrienne's band, Eye of the Storm.

"They're all over YouTube," Kendrick said. "Don't be mad, but I like them."

"I'm not mad." Robin smiled. She wasn't her normal fiery self. She was odd, floating toward the door, as if she'd taken a bottle of sedatives. She turned slightly. "I wish her the best." She patted the doorframe and left.

CHAPTER SIXTY-FIVE

On the plane to Tampa, Robin went over her notes. It would be a town hall-style debate, so any question from the audience was possible. She had to be prepared for anything.

"How are you holding up, Governor?" Peter asked.

She held up her hand. "I'm fine. You know, you really should direct some of your attention to your family once in a while."

"Excuse me?" He was bewildered. "It is the final—"

"I know what it is." She resumed reading, occasionally sipping her Diet Coke, and looking out the window with a calm gaze that unnerved her entire staff. They could almost feel some seismic shift in the atmosphere, although they couldn't be sure what it was exactly.

Though she appeared calm, Robin was unable to relax enough to recline in her seat. In fact, she hadn't even removed her overcoat; she was still wearing it long after takeoff.

"Should be a short flight." She heard the pilot say something like that in the speaker—his voice always so oddly saccharine, reassuring. Even if they were about to slam into a mountain, he'd say there was just a little turbulence ahead.

In times of stress, she couldn't bear calm voices. She remembered Tom's unsettling, pleasant tone as he got dressed for the family holiday photo shoot. Hearing his voice in her head, she leaned against the armrest, her fingers supporting her forehead. As she did so, she heard a crackle sound inside her coat. She realized that Adrienne's gift to her was still in her pocket, a small, wrapped mystery. Robin had forgotten this was the coat she had worn to Adrienne's apartment. She had planned to open it immediately, instead of doing as Adrienne said and waiting until before the debate to open it. But with all the distractions of the last few days and memories of their night together, Robin had forgotten about the gift. She was surprised at herself for forgetting something like this. She tore the wrapping paper and glanced up to make sure her staff wasn't watching. With everyone either reading or arguing with each other, she resumed her unwrapping. She peeled back a big piece of paper to reveal what it was—the heavy metal cassette tape Adrienne had made for her years ago, the tape that Robin had made sure to leave behind before she said good-bye.

Robin held the tape, noting Adrienne's now faded handwriting inside the case. She'd kept it all those years. Robin took a deep breath. This was a treasure worth more to her than all of the money she had.

* * *

The crowd rustled and chattered in the packed Tampa auditorium. There was an excited anticipation and crackling energy in the place.

Preparations reminded Robin of what warming up for a boxing match might be like. Political advisors rubbing candidates' shoulders, coaching them on their talking points.

Peter kept repeating, "Whatever you do, don't say the word 'scandal.' Remember!"

His voice had begun to fade like an annoying bug in her ears or the sounds of traffic noise, especially tractor-trailers, whenever she tried to sleep in a hotel…

"Nothing about scandals," he buzzed incessantly. "Your aunt who slept on a dirt floor…"

She overheard pieces of conversations from other political advisors and their candidates: "Don't tell everyone your plan."

"Which plan?"

"The economic plan. People don't want details. They want a few good phrases they can replay on the news."

Robin felt disgusted, knowing how that was true.

Then Peter grabbed her arm and said, "Don't sound too…you know, *loud*. When you get fired up, you know. Men can be loud, and nobody cares. But, you know, since you're a woman, they'll say you're loud."

"Shut up, Peter." She broke away from him. "Remind me to fire you when this is over."

He stood with gaping mouth as she walked away.

* * *

Graham Goodwin thanked everyone he could, especially God, for the opportunity to have a debate. His hair was more puffy than ever tonight, with a single silver wave that reached to the heavens. As a former preacher, he was always claiming to be the candidate closest to God. He had wasted forty minutes of the last debate, arguing with Jerry Johnson over who went to church more often.

After Graham thanked everyone enough, the other candidates did the same thing, thanking everyone for having the debate, before they could answer a question—all of them except Robin Sanders, who tried to keep her opening remarks brief. Each one received polite applause, but the loudest question hung silently in the air—everyone waited to hear whether or not Robin Sanders would remain as staunchly against gay rights as she was before all of the rumors.

Lara had told her many times before this debate: "It doesn't matter if that chick went on TV and said nothing happened. Something was put out there, and it's hard to close the lid. A question has been put in the people's mind…"

* * *

Miles McGuffy would moderate this debate, not because he was a newsperson with any political knowledge or credentials whatsoever, but because he'd become a popular personality on two reality shows. He was chosen because the networks felt America would be more comfortable with him than a stuffy newsperson who actually knew what was going on in the country.

Governor Robin Sanders smiled at the cameras after she was introduced. She stood tall behind a podium to the right of Graham Goodwin. She wore a deep navy power suit that looked just patriotic enough with a flag lapel pin and a perfectly smooth white shirt with pointed collar, and last but not least, a red scarf to complete the show of patriotism. She'd argued with Lara about this.

"I might as well *wear* a flag!" Robin protested.

"Trust me," Lara said. "With your eyes, it works." She'd learned a long time ago that she could get Robin to do anything simply by adding "with your eyes."

Reluctantly, Robin agreed. Tonight she stood, poised and dignified, with a slightly longer bob hairstyle. Everything about her appearance was, of course, a conscious choice, right down to her small gold earrings that weren't too flashy to be distracting.

Sometimes she fantasized about wearing a baseball cap and a simple white T-shirt and jeans, feeling the softness of cotton for a change. There was such a feeling of freedom in the idea of picking out her own clothes without being controlled. All the silk and fine jewelry in the world didn't matter if it was part of a costume, even one she'd agreed to wear.

They began with a familiar argument. A tired-looking woman stood up and was handed a microphone. "What are your positions on raising the minimum wage?" she asked. "Mr. Goodwin?"

"In the greatest country on earth, there should be no such thing as the working poor!" Graham Goodwin's impassioned plea was met with crickets. He was the only candidate in favor of raising the minimum wage. Outraged, his wife clapped forcefully in the second row.

Robin Sanders countered with her old standby talking point: "Trying to impose such a law will obliterate small business owners." Cheers and applause.

Jerry Johnson wanted a piece of the action. "I wholeheartedly agree with Governor Sanders on this point," he piped up in his high-pitched drawl. "We need our businesses to succeed, not be drownin' in a sea of debt." Jerry's supporters cheered him on.

Myron Welles, the candidate considered the most out of touch with all of America, smirked and straightened his glasses.

Miles McGuffy: "Mr. Welles, you look like you want to weigh in on this issue."

"Yes," Welles began, "I don't exactly share my opponents' sentiments. I believe the minimum wage has gotten far too bloated and frankly needs to be lowered." A stray clap from a wealthy business owner followed.

"Lowered?" Jerry screeched. "You kiddin' me?"

"My grandpa got by on forty cents an hour," Welles chirped.

"During the Depression?" Robin Sanders added to a roar of laughter. "You couldn't be more out of touch." Turning to the audience: "Archaeologists brought him in tonight because he's the oldest fossil in existence." More laughter.

CNN polls lit up with Governor Sanders in the lead.

Welles decided he couldn't do well attacking her, so he went after Jerry Johnson instead. "Do you know anything about running a business, Coach?" Welles liked to call Johnson "Coach" to ridicule his credentials for serving as president. "I didn't think so. How do you know what it takes to run a country?" Unfortunately, Welles' deadpan delivery made him seem like the walking dead, his robotic voice something you'd expect to hear in an airport: "The white zone is for loading and unloading…" Of course this cost him points, and he'd come in last in every debate since the beginning.

Then came the hot-button issue of the night. Forget foreign policy and the economy. This was the thing viewers had really tuned in for: gay marriage and Robin Sanders' affair or nonaffair with another woman.

Miles McGuffy acknowledged a timid-looking woman in the audience who took the mic almost reluctantly. But when she spoke, there was no holding back. She asked Governor Sanders to explain why she'd come out so vehemently against gay marriage, considering that she herself had been rumored to have had a same-sex affair. The auditorium fell silent.

"I think the American people are wondering," she said, "if the rumors are true, and has your position changed regarding gay rights?"

Robin looked out at the crowd. She could see their faces filled with anticipation.

"Do you watch television?" she asked. "Because the woman denied it all." She glanced at her opponents. "Somebody wanted to manufacture a scandal…"

There were roars from the crowd.

She saw Peter cover his eyes. She had said the "S" word! She could tell he was only partly paying attention, though, probably still worried that she was serious about him losing his job.

"I can't imagine who that would be…" Governor Sanders continued, feigning ignorance but glancing at Graham Goodwin. Some in the audience laughed. Lara looked around from behind the curtain and decided to breathe again.

The next one in the audience to take the microphone was Andrew Bennington. His hair was a little thinner, but he had the same happy face and smiling eyes. He wore a gray suit and looked especially dapper as he took the microphone.

"Hi," he said in a familiar voice.

He looked as he had on his wedding day, just like the photos she had found on the Internet. When she returned from visiting Carol, she had gone online and looked up his name. He and his partner had worn matching gray suits.

"What is your position on gay marriage?" he asked in the eerily quiet auditorium. "Governor Sanders?"

Robin imagined the burning metal, the melting tires, and finally the tremendous explosion with flames shooting high into the Mississippi night sky. Torches had been thrown at Andrew's car by a couple of random good ole boys who were provoked by the "Just Married" sign on its bumper. Both Andrew and his husband had burned to death. It had been a last-minute decision, that sign, suggested by a friend when the two were married in New York. Their friend had no idea the tragedy that would follow as they drove back down south and the horror that would await them just outside Biloxi, Mississippi. Robin wouldn't know so many things about that night, only the headline she read online: "Newly Wedded Gay Couple Murdered in Mississippi." It had happened a long time ago, amidst so many antigay hate crimes, that she had never noticed that particular story.

Everything in the auditorium froze as Robin imagined the tragedy unfolding. She heard Andrew's laugh...the most joyful, exuberant expression of what it meant to be alive.

Governor Sanders blinked, returning to the debate. A second or two had passed, an eternity on television. The governor seemed momentarily off balance, but she quickly regained her composure. Of course the young man asking the question wasn't Andrew. He bore a strong resemblance to him, though, standing there, waiting for her response.

McGuffy stepped in. "Could you repeat the question please?"

"What is your position on gay marriage?" The young man repeated.

It's rare for a single moment to define a person's life as in a movie. But for Robin Sanders, everything she was, and everything she was going to be, converged in that moment under the burning spotlight.

"I can't," she said slowly and deliberately, "in good conscience... judge another human being because of whom he loves."

There was a murmur in the audience that grew to a roar. Robin couldn't see or hear anything but what sounded like a pride of angry lions getting louder. She heard the echoing voices of Jerry Johnson: "Well, I'm certainly against it and will not support any legislation that..."

The vultures on stage couldn't wait to start picking over what they assumed was Governor Sanders' carcass, proclaiming their virulent opposition to gay rights.

After the chaos, McGuffy turned back to Governor Sanders. "This is a departure from your former position on gay rights," he said. "Could you elaborate?"

Robin held the podium to maintain her steady, calm demeanor. No one would know what she was feeling inside, how desperately she wanted to escape the stage—and the spotlight—tonight. She knew that her biggest supporters, her staff and her father were all having heart attacks tonight. But she pressed on.

"I believe as human beings, we continue to evolve," she said. "I'd like to think that, since I'm not dead yet, I too can evolve." Her humor awarded her some chuckles in the audience. "As with every issue, I'll have to review everything that comes across my desk carefully. I'm sure the American people don't want some hothead for president." Again she glanced at her opponents.

Backstage, Lara covered her face. As if Robin's bizarre, impromptu press conference hadn't dug a deep enough grave, now she was shoveling piles of manure on top of herself. She wasn't using any of the rehearsed talking points. It was as if she wanted to lose.

"Your speeches," Goodwin snapped, "in which you call gays those who commit 'unnatural acts'...now you're saying you've changed positions?"

She took a sip of water. "I know very few things for certain. I don't know how big the universe truly is, or when the sun will burn out, how we got here...What I do know is that who we love is not a choice. Love chooses you. Try as you might to run away from it...Love is the most precious of all the gifts we're given in this life. Instead of fighting, we should embrace it."

Her opponents were dumbfounded. No one had expected her to change so dramatically. They didn't even have rehearsed retorts. The response was a silent auditorium and more than a few shocked faces.

She smiled at the audience. "I know it's not popular to admit that we may have to revisit an issue," she said. "Or reconsider a viewpoint. There have been presidents who prided themselves on never changing positions, even when they were on a train that was heading toward a brick wall. Personally, I'd like to think I would be a smart president who would see the wall and make a different choice, if necessary."

Goodwin immediately tried to spin that. "So you mean you'd change positions if it was dangerous for *you*?"

"If it was not a smart decision, such as in foreign policy." Her ability to change topics, as well as her charisma, may have been just enough to help her get away with what she said. Certainly no other candidate could have gotten away with it. And only time would tell if the gambit had actually succeeded.

As the debate switched to other subjects, Governor Sanders remained her smart, likeable self. But no one knew whether it would be enough for her to recover after such a bombshell change of positions, especially on a major cornerstone of her campaign.

As Robin left the stage, she carried the cassette tape, so that if Adrienne was watching, she could see it.

CHAPTER SIXTY-SIX

Lara met Robin backstage. She did a fake double air kiss on both of her cheeks, a gesture Robin disliked. She'd get close enough so Robin could hear the dangling earrings clanking next to her ear. "Interesting debate," she said in a voice filled with judgment.

"I don't care," Robin said.

"That's the problem." Peter ran over before news pundits could envelope her. "You don't care about all the blood and sweat we've put into this campaign! You go off-script whenever you damn well please! You don't care about the people who care about you!"

"No, Peter," Robin retorted. "You only care about your own precious neck. By the way, why are you still here?"

He swallowed hard. "It doesn't matter," he replied. "There won't be a job after this debate anyway." He ripped off his lanyard and threw it on the floor. "Good luck," he told Lara as he walked away.

Shortly after, autographs and interviews with news pundits would soon take over. A man whom Robin didn't recognize came over to shake her hand. "I just wanted to say thank you." Then he left as mysteriously as he arrived. He didn't have any press badge or other identification. His soft-spoken way and tear-filled eyes suggested he had some emotional connection not only to the gay rights issue, but possibly to Robin herself. Had he been a friend of Andrew's? Had he been the friend who, caught up in the joyful day of the wedding, had suggested that Andrew and his partner put that sign on the back of their car? Robin would never know.

* * *

It was a long flight back from Tampa. Robin stared out the window, unable to shake the sound of Andrew's wonderfully infectious, high-pitched laugh. She wondered if he had been watching her tonight. For the first time in a long time, she felt proud of herself. It didn't matter that Peter was no longer traveling with her. It didn't matter what silent criticisms Lara had, which she was wisely keeping to herself. It didn't even matter that Robin's father didn't call her as he usually did after her debates. She felt right inside with herself. She felt right about the kind of role model she could be to Kendrick, that it wasn't too late. There was tremendous peace in that.

* * *

"Don't worry, Lara," Robin said. "Everything is going to be fine."

Lara smiled strangely, as though she was suppressing even more venom than Peter had shown.

"Peter was wrong," Robin continued. "I do care very much for everyone who has helped me get this far."

Lara swiveled around to face her. "If I'd known that I was supporting a pilot who thought nothing of ditching in the ocean at any time, I'd have gotten the hell off the plane."

Robin nodded. "I meant what I said out there. New information has caused me to reconsider that issue."

"New information? In the form of a hot rock musician?" Lara smirked. "Oh, I saw her. I might even be able to be swayed by that... information."

Robin turned away, toward the view of the glittering Tampa skyline at night, getting smaller in the window. "You don't have kids, Lara."

"Yeah, thank God."

"I was thinking about my daughter," Robin said. "What am I teaching her? I want her to live a real life, not a rehearsed one."

There was a long silence. She knew Lara couldn't understand much beyond poll numbers. Her press secretary would likely consider this the greatest failure of her career, a blot on her résumé that she'd prefer to erase. Staring into the blackness out the window, Robin saw Adrienne in the afternoon Florida sun, waving good-bye in her rearview mirror all those years ago. She relived it all—the two of them laughing over a plate of doughnuts, throwing wet sand at each other, dancing in a small smoky apartment to heavy metal music. Robin was in a rare place for someone like her—where her reality was actually beginning to make sense. A voice inside told her that if things were falling apart right now, maybe they were supposed to.

CHAPTER SIXTY-SEVEN

One Year Later

Robin dug the tripod in deeper, looking out on a remote stretch of beach in Kauai.

She stared into the lens and wasn't entirely happy with the shot. She wore a T-shirt and shorts, her hair held back with a baseball cap, keeping it out of her eyes. She checked the lens again. There was a light breeze blowing from the west, tousling that long and flowing, sand-streaked hair…

"It's fixed!" Carol called, screwing in a broken light.

"Put that out!" Robin yelled as smoke from Carol's cigarette floated into the shot. She ignored the subsequent cussing from her "crew" and examined the shot again. "I should be doing documentaries like I planned," she muttered to herself.

"Oh, so now you're slumming it?" Adrienne teased, coming out of the water toward her. She wrapped her hair to one side, the ringlets on the ends now wet from the spray of ocean waves.

"No." Robin raised her eyes from the camera lens and smiled up at her. "Your music video is much more important than capturing the voices of minorities in America."

Adrienne reached for her, circling her arms around her waist. They smiled at each other, beaming at the unspoken amazement they both shared that this day had ever come.

"So do it."

"I'm doing you first," Robin said. "I mean your video, you know."

"Are you blushing?" Adrienne laughed.

"It's sunburn."

"Right." Adrienne gave her a brilliantly sarcastic smile before being distracted by a clumsy bandmate who couldn't seem to pull herself out of the shallow water.

"Is this bamboo-ey enough?" Kendrick asked, carrying a regular stick.

"No," Robin replied. "We have a pile over there." She pointed to a stack of real bamboo.

Kendrick had volunteered to spend her summer working with her mother, now that Robin and Tom shared custody. There wasn't much point to them staying married after Robin lost the Republican nomination. By then, she had already disconnected herself from their marriage and her career. Amidst the chaos of all that, she had served out the rest of her term as governor as best she could.

Kendrick handled the news well and actually didn't seem surprised about it. While Robin worried that she was setting a bad example by divorcing, Kenneth assured her that the message she was sending was a positive one—that you should live authentically, staying true to yourself no matter how high the stakes.

Today her daughter was going to learn all of the not-so-glamorous details of filmmaking, as she monitored the consistency of the shots—trying to make sure things that weren't wet from the ocean in a previous scene didn't suddenly appear wet. It was maddening, but Robin kept telling her that at least she was in Hawaii. That probably wasn't as big a selling point to Kendrick as getting to hang out with her favorite band—and her mother.

The greatest sadness for Robin was her father not returning her calls. Though she wasn't completely surprised, she hoped he'd come around someday, before it was too late. She didn't feel isolated from family, though, because after the "stunt she pulled in Tampa," as her brother liked to call it, the two of them were now closer than ever.

When sunset had passed and a crescent moon replaced the raspberry streaks across the sky, Robin told everyone to call it a day. Adrienne and Kendrick helped to pack up equipment. Even though this part of the beach was very secluded, there was a resort not too far away, so occasionally tourists would stroll down the shore. On this particular night, a family taking a sunset walk wandered over. It was a straight couple with two young kids. The husband recognized Robin immediately in spite of her casual attire.

"Governor Sanders?" he called.

She unscrewed the tripod and looked up. "I don't have that title anymore."

"Wow," he marveled. "I can't believe it's really you!"

His wife urged him to keep walking. "She's busy, George. Don't bother her."

"Does it feel weird to still be saying 'President Ellis?'" The man asked. Obviously, he hadn't been one of her supporters.

"Not at all," Robin replied. "Out of all the candidates, I believe he was the best one for the job."

The man was surprised. He guided his group back toward the direction of their hotel. Then with one backward glance: "You think you'll ever run again?"

Robin smiled, looking at Adrienne in the moonlight. "No, I've found another calling."

* * *

After we settled in to the hotel, and Kendrick was ensconced in her nightly PlayStation ritual, Adrienne and I went for a walk along the mostly secluded beach.

As I took her hand in mine, I noticed her silvery profile in the moonlight, reminding me of the first time I'd caught a glimpse of her profile—in the smoky Camaro that first night in Florida.

"I guess we've come full circle," I sighed, noting the granules of sand finding their way inside my bathing suit, in places where they didn't belong.

"I would've never guessed you'd get back into film," Adrienne said. She led me through an area populated by jellyfish, taking my hand and guiding me safely through. I appreciated that, her knowing that I still hadn't made peace with wildlife.

"Me neither," I said. "Making a film was more challenging than anything I've ever done." I kicked at the sand. "It used to be too hard to imagine, the idea of putting myself, *the real me*, out there for the whole world to see."

"What's changed?" she asked.

We stopped walking, and I brushed some of her hair away from her face. "I'm not scared anymore."